THE GREAT WHITE WYRM HAS WAKENED FROM ITS QUARTER CENTURY OF SLEEP, TO TERRORISE KRYNN . . . AS IT HAS DONE FOR CENTURIES.

The only thing standing in its path is
the small band of elves and one
dwarf, a refugee from the Wyrm's attack
on his village, that form the secret
society known as Dragonsbane. And if they
fall, the dragon will ravage Krynn
until there is nothing left.

Ayshe is a dwarf with a purpose that he
does not know, but there is a reason
that Tashara, the blind leader of
Dragonsbane, insisted that he be left
alive and brought along with them on
their quest. There must be a reason,
for if there is not, the perils that he
and the rest of the crew of the
Starfinder face are not worth
the suffering and the risk.

But the reason may be more than the mind
of one dwarf can bear, as his fate
slowly becomes clear.

THE
GREAT WHITE
WYRM

THE
CHAMPIONS

P E T E R
ARCHER

Champions
THE GREAT WHITE WYRM

©2007 Wizards of the Coast, Inc.

Cover art by Duane O. Myers
First Printing: March 2007

9 8 7 6 5 4 3 2 1

ISBN: 978-0-7869-4260-2
620-95926740-001-EN

U.S., CANADA,
ASIA, PACIFIC, & LATIN AMERICA
Wizards of the Coast, Inc.
P.O. Box 707
Renton, WA 98057-0707
+1-800-324-6496

EUROPEAN HEADQUARTERS
Hasbro UK Ltd
Caswell Way
Newport, Gwent NP9 0YH
GREAT BRITAIN
Save this address for your records.

Visit our web site at www.wizards.com

Dedication

Editors are the unsung heroes of publishing. They work long hours and have to deal with deadlines, recalcitrant authors, cover art, cover copy, in-book ads, and a thousand details most people never think about when they pick up a book.

This novel is affectionately dedicated to the group of wonderful editors with whom I've been privileged to work over the years:

Philip Athans
Lizz Baldwin
Nina Hess
J. Robert King
Bill Larson
Jess Lebow

Pat McGilligan
Susan Morris
Mark Sehestedt
Val Vallese
Stacy Whitman

Acknowledgments

My thanks to Margaret Weis and Pat McGilligan for letting me write this book, to Linda Archer for encouraging me, to my cousins Ann and Mark Allison for their hospitality in allowing me to temporarily share their home while struggling to complete a deadline, to Jeff, Wolf, and John for a lot of good advice and support, and to the Schaeffer Pen Company for making the fountain pen with which I wrote this book.

INTRODUCTION

I hope the reader will allow me to insert a small note concerning one of my ancestors.

In 1803, John DeWolf, to whom I'm related on my father's side, left Bristol, Rhode Island, aboard the *Juno*, a 250-ton ship of which he was the owner. His family, the most prominent in Bristol, had made much of their money in the African slave trade, but John wanted no part of such a business. He and his crew sailed around Cape Horn and moved up the west coast of the Americas, acquiring as they went a valuable cargo of furs. When they eventually reached Alaska in 1804, DeWolf made friends with the Russians who occupied the trading post there. He sold them the *Juno* in exchange for a smaller sloop, onto which he loaded his cargo of furs. He then dispatched his crew aboard the sloop to China, with instructions that they were to sell the furs, return to Rhode Island, and deposit the proceeds in his bank account.

DeWolf remained with the Russians throughout the winter of 1804; then together they set off across the Bering Strait. They were blown off course and ended up in Kamchatka, from whence they traveled by dogsled overland to St. Petersburg. The American sea captain remained in the Russian capital for a year or so and finally journeyed across Europe, crossed the Atlantic, and in 1808 returned once more to his native Bristol. There he discovered that his crew had indeed returned from China and had deposited $100,000 in his bank account.

With this windfall he retired from the sea and later married a woman named Mary Melville.

Mary's nephew, Herman, delighted in talking to his uncle about the captain's adventures at sea, and Nor'west John, as he became known, appears in cameo in the novels *White Jacket* and *Moby-Dick*.

This seems an appropriate note on which to begin the story of The White Wyrm.

PART
1

CHAPTER

1

Carried on a current of warm air, the eagle soared and dipped her wings. She circled against the clear, sapphire sky, reveling in the freedom of flight and in the warmth of the sunlight on her feathers. Updrafts bore her on in a great series of swooping arcs, scarcely moving a muscle as she surveyed her domain.

Far below, the land tilted and swayed beneath her. To the east she could see the rugged shapes of mountains framed against the sky. To the west blue water stretched beyond her sight, lined with whitecaps. To the south was more land framed by the endless sea, while to the north the water stretched to the edge of her sight. Far below her lofty heights, shrieking gulls dived for fish.

Directly beneath her, sunlight glinted on the tiled roofs of houses that lined a curving bay and met in an open square. Beyond the square, the buildings thinned and gave way to well-tilled fields fringed with forest. In one such patch of forest, the eagle's nest was filled with chicks waiting for their breakfast.

The eagle spotted movement in one furrow of the fields. With a cry, she folded her wings and dropped, talons outstretched, seeking her prey. She accelerated, a long gray and brown streak, until with a whir and thump, feathered death landed with a crunch of marmot bones. Lifting the limp body of her victim, the eagle gave another cry to announce her triumph and winged her way toward the forest and her waiting children.

Just beyond the last house that marked the boundaries of the village, Ayshe watched the attack, the kill, and the slow flight of the victor, marmot dangling from her claws. He breathed deeply of the morning air, smelling wood smoke, cooking, and a faint whiff of pigsty. Then, with a sigh, he lifted the handles of his firewood-laden barrow and trudged on.

The barrow creaked, and Ayshe's arms bulged. As the only dwarf in a village of humans, he'd had to either construct tools and equipment appropriate to his short stature or force his body to adapt to taller human standards. He'd built the barrow himself some months after coming to work at the smithy. Chaval had informed him his first duty every day was to cut firewood for the forge and bring it to the woodpile behind the smithy. Ayshe had experimented with Chaval's barrow, but its handles were too long and his arms too short for convenience.

This was Ayshe's favorite part of the day—at least at this time of year, early fall, when the harvest time of Reorxmont was fast approaching. The air was cool and crisp in the mornings, warm and golden in the afternoons, and in the chill of early evening, it was good to stand near the blazing fire of the forge where Chaval, bare to the waist, hammered at plowshares and pruning hooks. The fire's ruddy glow drove away the darkness, and it was by no means unusual to find a half dozen of Chaval's cronies crowded into the forge, each with his mug of beer or wine, conversing with the smith as his hammer blows shaped the red-hot metal. Eventually, of course, Chaval's wife, Zininia, would drive away the idlers and bring her husband into the peace of their home, settling their new-born child on his lap to dandle, but even she had to admit this sort of thing kept the smith out of the tavern and out of trouble.

No, Ayshe thought, pushing the barrow along the rutted road, it wasn't a bad life. Three years before when he'd arrived in the village, sick from a voyage from Kharolis, with little money in his pockets and no direction to his future, it had been the blacksmith who'd shown him rough kindness and who had agreed to accept him as his assistant.

"A dwarf assisting a human smith," he growled. "What's Krynn coming to?"

Ayshe had patiently explained that although a dwarf, he knew little of metalworking. His knowledge went to mining, wresting the riches of the earth from its clutches. But the mines of the Kharolis Mountains had been largely abandoned by the dwarves during the War of Souls a few years before, and many of the dwarves had fled after the destruction of Qualinost, Ayshe among them. His last coin had been spent purchasing passage on a ship that sailed north. The sailing master hated dwarves and took the first opportunity to knock Ayshe on the head, steal what few possessions he had, and set him on another ship bound to the west. The dwarf was put ashore on the coast of Northern Ergoth, knowing no one, possessing nothing, and with no idea what the future might hold for him. Under such circumstances, the offer from the smith came like a gift from the gods. Ayshe gladly accepted and showed his gratitude toward Chaval and his wife in many ways.

Most of the townsfolk, whatever they might think behind closed doors of the smith's actions, respected him and his heavily muscled arms enough to accept his choice of Ayshe as his assistant. The blacksmith was a man of standing in the village, and one did not lightly offend his apprentice, whatever one might think in private. They were friendly to the dwarf, and after a few months, children ceased to stare and point when he passed them in the street.

The dwarf skillfully avoided a deep rut between the road's cobblestones. The village's main street, lined with whitewashed cottages, ran parallel to the harbor in which half a dozen fishing boats bobbed under the morning sun. Ayshe saw the boats strung across the gravelly beach where children played in the summer and thought of a planned fishing expedition with his friend Kharast a few days hence. Gulls flew shrieking over the water or called from the chimney pots.

A boy and a taller girl ran across the street. The girl was clutching a bun, the boy pursuing her.

"Give it back! Mum said it was mine!"

The girl was giggling; the boy close to tears. Ayshe set down the cart with a thump.

"Shava! Shava Parbainn! Come here, girl!"

The girl looked doubtfully at the dwarf, then at her brother, then approached, holding the bun out of the boy's reach.

"Good morning, Master Ayshe."

Ayshe made his face as stern as possible. "Are you stealing your brother's breakfast?"

"No!"

"Yes!"

The two answers popped out simultaneously. Ayshe waited, and after a minute the girl said, "Well . . . he took mine yesterday. I'm just getting even."

Ayshe shook his head. "Two wrongs don't make a right, Shava. Give Eliu his bun."

The girl handed the bun to the boy, who took an enormous bite out of it as much to mark his ownership as to eat breakfast. He started to turn away, but the dwarf laid a hand on his shoulder.

"Eliu, is what your sister says true? About yesterday's breakfast?"

The boy seemed to have difficulty swallowing. Red-faced, he nodded.

"Very well," Ayshe told him. "You should apologize."

The boy looked from Ayshe to his sister. Staring at the ground, he mumbled something that might have been taken for "Sorry." The next moment he picked up his heels and ran into the house.

Ayshe lifted the barrow with a grunt. "Next time," he told Shava, "when he takes your bun, sit on him. That'll cure him of bun snatching."

The girl smiled, white teeth gleaming in her dark face.

"Thanks, Master Ayshe." She, too, disappeared into her house, and the dwarf walked on.

At the end of a long row of houses, he let the barrow down to rest again and stretched his arms, smelling a breeze from the sea.

"Dwarf!"

Ayshe groaned inwardly and turned to face Durnant, the baker.

Most of the townspeople of Thargon had been friendly toward Ayshe, especially after Chaval had taken him into the forge. Durnant was one exception. From the day he'd laid eyes on Ayshe, he'd kept up a flow of barbs and sneers. Ayshe had never determined why the baker disliked dwarves, but it was obvious he did. Now Durnant stood on the street, belly hanging over his apron strings, a smear of flour in his dark, curling hair.

Ayshe forced his lips into a smile. "Morning, Master Durnant."

"You've been cutting from my patch again," the baker growled. He pointed to the hewn wood in the barrow. "That's birch. There's no birch save on the eastern end of *my* land. You must have cut from there." His eyes were bright. "That's robbery. Typical, that is. I'll have you up for thieving before Gallipol."

Gallipol, mayor of Thargon, heard all accusations and dispensed justice to the townspeople. Most such affairs concerned animals that had strayed or disputes about grazing rights.

Ayshe sighed and maintained a polite tone. There was no point in provoking a quarrel.

"There are birch trees as well on the western border of Chaval's land where it touches yours. One had fallen, and I cut it this morning."

Durnant's piggy eyes narrowed. "Did it fall onto my land?"

"Yes, a bit of it, but it was growing on Chaval's land."

"If it touched my land when it fell, it belongs to me. That's village law, though you wouldn't know that, being an outsider. So just wheel that barrow over to my kitchen, and I'll forget the matter this time. Otherwise, Gallipol will hear about it, and your master won't be pleased with that."

Ayshe drew a deep breath. "Master Durnant, I'll do no such thing. The tree was on Master Chaval's land, and the wood will go to his forge. As for being an outsider—"

He broke off. The baker's red face was tilted upward, staring at the sky. Ayshe turned to look.

In what had been a clear blue firmament, a small white cloud had appeared to the northeast. It was thick and round, and it was behaving like no cloud the dwarf had ever seen. The center of the cloud appeared to be pushing outward, expanding more rapidly than anything in nature. At the same time, the sky, which moments before had been a bright azure color, was growing gray.

Ayshe sniffed the air. From the water, a heavy damp mist was moving among the houses. Its probing fingers delved into every cranny, bringing a cold wind that thickened rather than dispersed the fog. Ayshe's teeth chattered in the chill.

Durnant's eyes remained fixed on the sky. The strange cloud filled half the horizon. At the center, dark forms stirred, combining and recombining in fantastic shapes. There was a flash of lightning, and a faint *boom!* resounded through the town.

The baker's pale eyes met Ayshe's. "This is no natural storm," he said, voice shaking.

As if confirming his words, there was a second lightning flash, and the rumble of thunder sounded closer. The mist was so thick Ayshe could barely make out the dim shapes of the houses that lined the street. The other side of the square onto which the street emptied was invisible. The cobbles were slick and shining with moisture.

A terrific concussion split the air, and the dwarf found himself sprawled on the street. His ears rang, and his mouth tasted of metal. His knuckles bled where they'd struck the pavement.

Painfully he got to his feet and looked around. His barrow had been hurled twenty feet by the force of the blast, and the wood was scattered and torn to splinters. Where the bakery had stood a moment before, there was only rubble. One wall stood leaning perilously, and even as Ayshe stared at it, it crashed to the ground. He looked for the baker. There was no sign of Durnant, but a long red streak stretched across the cobbles where he'd been standing and ended at the edge of a pile of rubble.

For the first time, Ayshe heard shrieks and crying and realized the bakery was not the only building destroyed. The street resounded with running footsteps as villagers raced toward the scene of the disaster. The dwarf caught a glimpse of Shava and Eliu running behind their mother, clad in an apron.

From the sky came a long, low growl, below the pitch of any human or animal. Ayshe looked up and stood transfixed.

A dragon.

From out of the storm clouds it came, its wings wider than the entire village and trailing lightning. Its head was wreathed in a cloud of frost. Gray like the clouds that birthed it, it was edged in white fire, ridges sweeping back over a long, wicked snout. One webbed wing swept low over the town, smashing the spire of the temple of Zivilyn, the tallest structure on the square.

Stone blocks flew through the air like chaff before a thresher's flail. One smashed into the house from which Eliu and Shava had come running. Another sailed over Ayshe's head and thundered into a dwelling farther along the street. The dwelling of his friend Kharast.

Ayshe ran over toward his friend's house—or what remained of it—then stopped short. The block had smashed through the front door and crushed the parlor beneath its weight, coming to rest against the back wall. From beneath a pile of rubble, mixed with the wreckage of a breakfast table, the dwarf saw an arm protruding, clad in Kharast's characteristic black and orange cloth.

It was the work of a few moments to pull away the stones and only a moment more to realize that Kharast had passed beyond any help.

Shouted orders came from the village square. Gallipol had assembled those townsfolk of Thargon who'd had the wits to pick up weapons.

"Archers! Loose!" came his command.

A hail of arrows were aimed and sped toward the great white dragon. It swept its wing again, batting aside the missiles as if they were toys. Its head darted down and took one of the bowmen, Zahrkeea—Ayshe could see his face clearly—in its massive jaws. There was a crunch, and the two halves of Zahrkeea fell to the ground, spilling blood over the paving stones.

The dragon's growl came again, and with it Ayshe felt a wave of unreasoning, overwhelming, stomach-clenching fear. The street and the figures around him swam before his eyes. He heard Gallipol calling for another volley of arrows, but paid no attention. Instead, he turned and ran. He felt sweat pouring down his forehead as his legs pumped, and his vision became blurred. He scarcely knew where he was running. He had only one thought: to get as far away as he could from that terrifying growl.

He felt the rush of wings above him, and their wind knocked him to his knees. From his prostrate position, he saw the huge white dragon's head sweeping over the town again. It opened its horrific jaws, but no sound emerged. Instead, a shaft of icy cold air struck down in front of the butcher's shop on the town square. The butcher and his wife, who had just exited from their front door, were caught squarely in the middle of it. Ayshe saw their bodies stiffen and their flesh turn white then blue with cold. Frost rimed their hair. They fell forward against the cobblestones and shattered as if their bodies had been made of glass. The butcher's head, eyes wide open, mouth forever shouting in fear, rolled in front of Ayshe. The dwarf sprang to his feet, leaped over the ghastly relic, and ran.

Ahead he saw the smithy. Chaval was standing in the open, staring at the clouds. He half turned as he saw the dwarf. Spurred by fear, Ayshe ignored his master's cry. Beyond the forge was a stout wooden shack in which the smith stored metal ingots as well as odds and ends, broken plows, wheels, shattered tools, and scraps of half-finished metal. Without hesitation, Ayshe headed for it as the mist tore at his beard, and from somewhere behind him he heard a multitude of screams mixed with the dragon's growl.

Never stopping, Ayshe flung himself through the door of the shed. He slammed it shut and dropped across it a bar bound with iron.

The interior of the shed was pitch black, and the dwarf crawled over obstacles, bruising and cutting his hands and knees as he sought the farthest, darkest corner. He crouched there, cradled by the cold earth, and jammed his hands against his ears to shut out the dreadful cries. His face was wet, either with sweat or with tears, and pictures swam before him of Kharast's crushed body, of Zahrkeea falling in a spray of red, of the butcher's silent scream, of the great white dragon's long, low, awful ululation. It seemed to him that he could hear it still, and he wailed to drown out the sound.

As if from far away, he was aware of vibration that made the hut rock and shake. A voice was crying out, a familiar voice, but he blotted it away. For nothing would he open his ears lest he catch the horrid cry of the fearsome wyrm. He buried his head in his knees and knelt in the darkness, praying to all the gods for safety.

Sleep is the body's way of shutting out horror. Ayshe stirred and found himself once more aware and alert in the darkness of the hut. The fear that had immobilized him was gone. All was silent.

Cautiously he rose and stretched his cramped limbs. He stumbled once or twice, moving toward the door. His hands were stiff and sore, and when he brought them to his lips, he could taste dried blood.

Groping in the dark, he found the door and listened, pressing his ear against it. Nothing.

He lifted the heavy bar and pushed. Nothing happened.

He pushed again, and again the door resisted. It felt ice cold.

The dwarf turned away, and his hand came across a long piece of iron—a crowbar, he realized. He lifted it and inserted one end in the crack between the door and its frame. The dwarf bore down on it and, after a few minutes of silent struggle, was rewarded by a groan of tortured wood. A few heartbeats later, with a snapping sound, the door gave way and creaked open a few inches.

Ayshe pushed and shoved and succeeded in opening the gap wide enough for him to squeeze through. For a moment he was so pleased with having escaped the shed that his brain did not register what his eyes saw.

He had escaped death by a miracle. Almost the entire village as far as he could see had been flattened. Piles of stones, half-smashed timbers, a few precariously leaning chimneys—those were all that remained. Crows circled above in the blue sky, their harsh cries mixed with soft moans that arose from a few survivors poking disconsolately among the ruins.

His foot touched something. He turned, then bent double, retching.

Leaning against the shed's door, preventing it from fully opening, was the frost-whitened body of Chaval. His frozen fingers still clutched in vain at the door he had sought to open. The dwarf could see scratches in the wood where his fingernails had scraped.

A few feet behind the smith lay Zininia. She lay on her side, as if sleeping. Only the dead white pallor of her skin and the frost that touched her cheek told the true story. She clutched a bundle to her breast, and Ayshe knew with certitude it was her baby—born only six months earlier.

They had sought shelter, as he had, from the dragon's fury, but they had not found it. Ayshe rocked back and forth in his grief, clutching his brow, bloodied hands tearing at his beard. In his sorrow, he wailed out words in the dwarf tongue, a language he had not spoken in three years or more.

Chaval and his wife had taken the dwarf into their household. They had embraced him, trusted him. In the evenings he'd sat by their fireside, rocking the baby on his lap, listening to her gurgles, humming an old Dwarvish lullaby called up from the dim memories of his soul.

All that destroyed by his cowardice.

"Coward!"

The word tasted bitter on his tongue. He said it again, louder, and struck his hand against the icy door.

His body shook with sobs, but no tears would come, as if his grief were too great for them.

"Master Ayshe!"

Through a cloud of mingled rage, sorrow, and self-loathing, he spotted Gallipol coming toward him. Gallipol's face was streaked with dirt, and he had a nasty cut along his scalp from which blood had trickled down around his eye.

"Right glad I am to see you alive!" He clapped the dwarf on the shoulder. "Have you seen . . . ?"

His voice trailed off as he took in the scene. His body seemed to slump in defeat; then he raised his face and looked down at Ayshe. "So many," he whispered. "So many dead!"

He and the dwarf turned away and walked across what had once been the square. It was strewn with fragments of mortar, timbers, and glass. A few steps brought them to a young man sitting on a boulder that had been hurled from the shore. Ayshe recognized him as Mashalar, son of the town watchman. Before him, lying on her back, was his betrothed, Allanna. Her eyes stared sightlessly at the sky, a pool of blood spread from beneath her head. Mashalar clasped his knees, slowly rocking back and forth, his lips moving soundlessly. At the approach of the dwarf and his companion, he looked up.

"I tried to save her," he muttered. "I tried to save her, but she slipped away from me."

Another wave of guilt and grief washed over Ayshe. As Gallipol bent over the young man, the dwarf turned away, hiding his face. In a gap left by the collapse of a house, he saw another man standing at the edge of the sea. In contrast with the violence of the destruction around them, the waves rippled gently, barely disturbing the sands.

The man kicked at sand and water both, and screamed wordlessly at the sky. He seized stones and hurled them at the indifferent ocean. Still screaming, he rushed forward into the sea.

Ayshe raced after him, ignoring the pain from his bruised legs. He tackled the man—Ulaphon, a fisherman he recognized—and dragged him back from the shallows onto the sand. They clung together for a moment, and Ulaphon twisted out of the dwarf's grip.

"Why?" he shouted. "Why? Why did it attack? Why?" His face was red and contorted.

The dwarf shook his head. "I don't know."

That simple admission loosened something within him. He knelt on the sands, let his tears mingle with the waves that ran against his knees, and let his grief run out to a silent sea.

CHAPTER

2

The smoke from the fires spread like a dark stain across the flawless sky.

Too few villagers had survived to bury the dead. Some made half-hearted attempts to dig graves for friends or relatives slaughtered by the dragon's attack, but they lacked the energy. Indeed, most of the remaining townsfolk felt drained and exhausted, as if their minds and bodies had exceeded the limits of mortal beings.

The stench of decay rose from the ruins, and folk knew it would soon attract the attention of tundra wolves and other scavengers. At last, under Gallipol's direction, they dragged the bodies on improvised sledges to a spot on the pebbled beach left bare by low tide. They piled driftwood around the corpses, and Ayshe struck a spark from flint and tinder. Within minutes the pyre was ablaze, and coils of greasy smoke streamed upward to spread across the heavens.

Later the cleansing sea would wash away what remained.

Gallipol overcame his grief by channeling his energies toward organization and survival. He sent a team through what remained of the village to search for food. Another pair of survivors—noted for being fleet of foot—were sent to the nearest large town to see what help might be obtained. An improvised hostel cared for the injured. Another group collected stones and bricks that had not been shattered in the attack and began construction of a rudimentary shelter. Though the days were warm, at night a chill breeze swept off the water and heralded the coming of winter.

The band that had been sent to the fields to bring in the harvest returned with bad news. The dragon's attack had flattened the wheat fields, and its frosty breath had destroyed the rows of maize, cabbage, and beans. The villagers would have to survive the winter on what they could scrounge from the wreck of the town and on fish from the sea.

The fleet of fishing boats was gone, smashed to matchwood by the beast's fury. Gallipol's face grew longer with each bit of bad news brought to him.

Ayshe picked through the remains of the smithy, salvaging those tools he could find. The shack in which he'd found shelter was one of the few structures that remained standing, and the materials stored within it made it possible for the dwarf to reconstruct a crude forge in a few days.

He threw himself into the work. He spent his days standing by the blazing fire, red-hot metal turning on the anvil before him, muscles bulging as he hammered it into shape. There were times when he was hard at work when he could almost hear Chaval shouting orders and laughing at his own robust jokes.

Nights passed without sleep, and Ayshe found the combination of driving work and insomnia was wearing him thin.

Gallipol spoke to him about it a week after the attack. "You need rest, my friend," he said, leaning heavily on his staff. "You're the only smith we have, and we'll need your skills if we're to survive the winter."

Ayshe ceased his blows on an iron chisel and plunged the metal into a bucket of cold water. There was a rush of steam and a hiss.

"I can't afford rest," he grunted. "Too much to do."

"Not by one man." Gallipol shifted his feet and lowered his voice. "The messengers have returned, my friend. With bad news. The harvest has been bleak elsewhere, and no one can spare much to help us. Nor can they send anyone to help in rebuilding the town. Our only hope, Ayshe, is to conserve our strength. We've barely enough food to ride out the winter. You'll do no favor for us by working yourself to death."

Ayshe let his hands drop to his sides. A great wave of weariness washed over him. "I still hear the beast's roar," he said bitterly.

Gallipol nodded. "As do I. As do we all. Even in our sleep." His glance strayed involuntarily to the sky, as if seeking out a sudden cloud. "It sounded like some feral beast from the depths of the Abyss." He shook himself, as if awakening from a bad dream. "But we cannot dwell forever on its power, Master Ayshe. We must—"

A scream split the air. Dwarf and man spun toward the sound. It rang again, and the pair ran toward it.

As they emerged from the rude shelter in which Ayshe had set up his forge, they saw other villagers sprinting in the direction of the screaming. Its source emerged a moment later when a young girl, perhaps eight or nine, came running from the beach. Her hands were pressed against the sides of her head, her mouth open, and her eyes wide with fear.

Gallipol caught her. "What's wrong, Jalene?"

The girl gestured behind her wordlessly. Ayshe squinted into the bright sea. For a moment the sunlight glinting on the waves blinded him. Then he saw what the girl had seen and cursed.

"Pirates!"

Silhouetted against the horizon, a ship with black sails plunged across the waves. Ayshe's sharp eyes could make out a line of brightly colored shields strung along the deck rail. The sails, filled with wind, bore the ship closer to the village.

Gallipol was shouting orders to the townsfolk who had gathered at the water's edge.

"Hans! Get your bow and take a position in front of the school-house! Majiis, you're with him! Savail, have you got your sword? You're with me. Ayshe . . ."

Ayshe, the moment he spotted the black sail, had dashed back in the direction of the forge. He ran forward as Gallipol called to him, his arms laden with recovered swords, knives, mattocks, and warhammers. A shield was slung across his back. Townsfolk seized weapons from him and scattered to their assigned places. Others, weaponless, picked up rocks and crouched, concealing themselves as best they could. Several gathered up children and led them back to the shelter of some standing walls away from the beach.

The ship hove to in the calm waters of the harbor. Ayshe could see the glint of a spyglass on the poop deck as someone surveyed the town—or what was left of it. As the villagers waited, the crew scurried about the deck like ants at harvest time. They lowered a longboat, and it pulled for shore.

From where he lay behind a partly demolished wall, the dwarf could see the rowers, sun glittering off their sweat-sheened shoulders. A tall, thin man sat in the stern, steering, calling out directions to the oarsmen.

A dozen more strokes beached the craft, and the crew sprang swiftly upon the sands. One threw out a grappling hook to hold the boat secure, while the others fanned out, hands on sword hilts and bows.

"Halt!"

Gallipol rose before them. Over his shoulder, a companion aimed a shaft at the pirate leader. Hans and his fellow archers stood among the ruins of the schoolhouse, bows raised, arrows at the ready.

The pirate leader raised his hands. "Peace, friend. We do not come to do harm."

Hans's arrow didn't waver. Gallipol spoke again, his tone icy as seawater in midwinter. "Hands away from your blades."

None of the seamen moved. The leader kept his hands in the air. "We are merely travelers, friend. Surely you would not have us give up our only protection?"

"I would have you show me why we should not lay out every one of you where you stand," Gallipol growled. "We know how to deal with pirates in these parts."

"I'm sure you do, but we are not pirates."

"What are you, then?"

The man cautiously lowered his hands. His followers stood as still as stones. "Your village seems to have suffered a great calamity recently."

Gallipol grunted. "Yes. What would you know about it?"

"Was it an attack from a dragon?"

The villagers' bows and swords, which had begun to droop, snapped to attention.

"How did you know that?" Gallipol snarled.

The leader looked around. "We seek this dragon. With your permission, we'd like to look around to see if we can find clues that would enable us to better track and destroy it."

There was silence for a few minutes. Ayshe could hear the labored breathing of the townsfolk as they watched their leader.

At last, Gallipol nodded. "Very well."

Ayshe returned to his work in the forge. The rest of the villagers scattered to their various tasks, leaving Gallipol, Hans, and a few others to keep an eye on the strangers.

Rather than men, it was clear they were elves, though of what nation, Gallipol could not say. They were tall and slender, carried swords and bows, and most seemed to have been scarred or injured in some way.

The leader was a human rather than an elf, though he was so

gaunt he might have been taken for one. He did not volunteer a name, and Gallipol did not ask.

The elves walked slowly through the village, examining the damage closely. None spoke, leaving the talking to the human. When they came to the forge, they halted, and Ayshe had a chance to observe them more closely.

He'd had little contact with elves. Like most of his race, he held a prejudice toward the elder-born, a dislike that among most dwarves merged into contempt. Elves, common dwarf wisdom held, felt themselves above the other races of Krynn. They avoided contact with dwarves and men (to say nothing of kender and the like), preferring to isolate themselves.

The War of Souls had changed that isolation. The elf city of Qualinost had been destroyed, and as Ayshe knew from gossip and rumor, the elves had been driven from the Silvanesti kingdom by the minotaurs of the Blood Sea Isles. They were exiles, wandering in search of a kingdom, but misfortune had done nothing to lessen their arrogance.

Ayshe's mistrust of elf folk had never spilled over into active dislike. Nonetheless, the visitors seemed to bear out the promise of haughtiness. It appeared to the dwarf that they looked on him with their noses in the air even as Gallipol explained that Ayshe had escaped death from the dragon's breath by sheltering in the shed.

The human looked interested.

"This shed?" he asked. He and one of his companions—a female, Ayshe noted in some surprise—examined the structure thoroughly, tapping on the walls, studying the barred door. Ayshe watched in stoic silence, fighting down feelings of grief and shame.

His inspection concluded, the human turned to Ayshe. "You're lucky to be alive," he observed. "More than chance saved you. Once the dragon attacks, no structure, from shed to fortress, stands in its way. The gods seem to have preserved you for another fate."

Ayshe said nothing but clenched his hands until his nails dug into his palms and left scarlet half circles in the flesh.

Gallipol, whose irritation had been growing more and more visible, burst into speech. "All right! Fine! You've seen what the beast did. It destroyed our people. Now, what help do you bring?"

The human said nothing. He and the elves began to turn away, but the enraged town master slipped around to stand in front of them, his arms folded.

"No, dammit! Answer me! If you bring no help, at least you seem to know something about the creature. Will it return? Can we expect another attack? Where did it come from? And why attack here? We've nothing—no coin, no arms beyond those you've seen. Dragons covet wealth, so I've been told, but we have none. So why attack us?"

The man was silent for a moment then said, "You are safe from further depredations . . . for the moment." He seemed about to say something more but held his tongue.

Ayshe joined Gallipol, carrying the axe on which he'd been working. Its blade, long and curving, was honed to a razor sharpness.

"Why should we believe you? You seem to know something of this dragon. Why can't you tell us more?"

A faint smile touched the man's lips. He reached out and ran a thumb along the blade of Ayshe's axe. "You have a good weapon," he told the dwarf. "Pray to all the gods that yet remain that you never have to use it against the White Wyrm."

He turned away and shouted something in Elvish. His companions joined him, and the band made their way back to the longboat. Gallipol followed part of the way, hurling questions at their retreating backs, questions to which they made no answers. Silently they shipped their boat and pulled for the dark ship whose sails were outlined against a pale sky.

THE GREAT WHITE WYRM

Dusk came more quickly since the year was waning. Ayshe stood by the forge's fire, but his mind was not on his work.

Clearly the strangers knew what the great white dragon was. They might even know why it had attacked the town. Yet they would not tell the villagers.

A figure emerged from the darkness. Gallipol stepped forward to warm his hands at the forge. After an interval, he looked at the dwarf. "Well, Ayshe, what thought you of the strangers?"

The dwarf shrugged. "They're elves—long of face and high of nose, ragged travelers though this bunch be. We should waste no more time on them."

The mayor nodded. "True. Though they seem to know more of the dragon than they told us. And right now, we need to know as much as we can about the beast, so we can be ready if and when it comes back. I've never heard of a dragon attacking somewhere only once and then never returning. Usually the creatures come back, lay waste to everything they find, and gather what wealth they discover to themselves for their hoards." He looked at the blackness of the sea. "Perhaps these elves would speak more freely between themselves than before us."

The dwarf grunted. "Aye, perhaps." He brought his hammer down on a long piece of hot metal. Under his blows, the metal curled around a jig. Later the smith would file one side of the curved iron to a sharp edge and attach it to a wooden handle. The sickle could be used to harvest crops. Assuming, of course, that the villagers survived the winter to plant crops in the spring.

Gallipol watched Ayshe's actions in silence for some time. Then he said, "That dinghy of Chaval's. Didn't he store it in this shed?"

Ayshe nodded. "Aye. It's there. Not very seaworthy, though, if you were thinking of it for a fishing vessel."

The village leader shook his head. "No. I had in mind another use for it."

"Well, I'd planned to patch it—" Ayshe broke off and stared at the mayor. "You're *not* thinking of rowing out to that ship?"

Gallipol made an inexpressible gesture with his shoulders and head that showed his indecision. "I don't know, Ayshe. We've got to learn more about the dragon, and these elves know more than they're telling. If I can slip aboard and spy for a bit . . ."

Ayshe shook his head. "You'd be caught. And then the village would be without a leader. We don't need that, what with winter coming on and, from what you've said, no help from anyone else. Besides, they'd like as not be speaking Elvish to one another. Do you speak Elvish?"

Gallipol shook his head, his face saying clearly he'd not thought of that difficulty.

Ayshe walked out of the circle of light cast by the forge's fire and gazed into the night's blackness. Far off he could see a spark, a mere glint of light that came from the ghostly ship where it rode at anchor.

He shook his head. "Aye. Well. I suppose I'd better go, then."

"You? Now, wait a minute, Ayshe—"

The dwarf brushed Gallipol aside as he stalked to the shed. "Nay," he said over his shoulder. "I'm the only one in this village that understands Elvish, though I admit I'm a bit rusty at it. And I expect I'm the only one light enough for the boat to carry me without sinking before she gets a hundred feet out to sea. I'll see what I can find out and be back by morning's break. Don't be disappointed, though, if I learn nothing."

Swiftly, lest hesitation make a coward of him, he strapped his axe across his shoulder. With Gallipol's aid, he carried the dinghy and its oars to the beach. The shore was deserted. The surviving townsfolk huddled around fires in the ruins of houses, dining as best they could on scraps of food. The two men launched the boat, though Ayshe looked with concern at the water that swiftly gathered at the bottom of it. He fetched a tin can from the forge for bailing, fitted the oars into the rusted oarlocks, and nodded to Gallipol.

"By my counsel, say nothing of this to anyone until I'm back."

The leader nodded. "Thank you, Ayshe. Be careful."

"Oh, aye. I'll be that. I'm already regretting letting you talk me into this." Ayshe's beard shook and wagged as he seated himself in the boat and pulled on the oars, disappearing rapidly into the darkness.

Though most dwarves dislike water, boats, and swimming, Ayshe had been around the sea long enough to develop some skill in a boat, even one as decrepit as Chaval's dinghy. His arms were short but muscular, well suited for rowing, and his legs braced against the sides of the boat as he stretched and pulled, stretched and pulled. He was aided by the fact that the night was a calm one, and there were no waves to fight. He made rapid progress, even though he had to stop from time to time and bail the water from the bottom of his leaky vessel.

He was relieved when his fingers touched the wooden hull of the elves's ship. Turning, he rowed along the length of the hawser. He reached out and grabbed it, breathing heavily, and hung in the water as the ripples drifted past the silent hulk.

Looking back to shore, he could see several of the villagers' campfires and thought he could even make out a faint glow where the forge should be, its fire still burning. That would serve him well, he thought, as a landmark for his return journey.

No sound came from the ship. Either they kept no watch or no one had seen Ayshe's journey. He tied off the boat and breathed a silent prayer to whatever gods were watching him it would still be there and above water when he was ready to leave. Very cautiously the dwarf began to haul himself, hand over hand, up the anchor rope, clinging to it with his feet and legs as well. He passed the name of the ship painted on the bow—the *Starfinder*—and went on. He saw the figurehead, an elf maid with flowing golden hair pulled back over her shoulders. Somehow he had a feeling he'd seen the image before, perhaps in an old book. He shook his head and bent again to his task. The rope was shiny with seaweed, and his progress was slow.

All at once he heard the sound he dreaded: the soft tread of feet on the deck. He halted, making himself as small as he could against the rope, and waited. He sensed someone at the rail and sent up a prayer to Zivilyn that the elf wouldn't look down.

"Hail, Feystalen!" came a voice. "What cheer?"

There was a pause, then the watcher replied, "I thought I heard splashing a short time past."

The first voice chuckled. "Mayhap you did. Some fish or other, I daresay."

Feystalen sounded unconvinced. "It was big for a fish." He paused again, listening. "Nay, it's gone now."

The two elves turned from the rail, and Ayshe breathed a silent sigh of relief. Fate, it seemed, was with him.

To be on the safe side, he counted very slowly to one hundred, doing his best to ignore the aches in his arms and legs. Then he resumed his climb uninterrupted.

There was a moment of awkwardness in clambering over the rail, but he managed it and crouched on the deck in darkness. Feystalen and his companion had moved to another part of the ship. It crossed Ayshe's mind to wonder why two elves should have been speaking Common rather than Elvish, but he put the thought from him and concentrated on the task of the moment.

Using the rail as a guide, he edged along the deck. Another might have blundered forward, but the dwarf, with a familiarity with dark underground passages, was content to learn the ship's geography before making any decisive move.

Before him, stairs led from the foredeck to the main deck, in the middle of which rose the mainmast. A tangle of rigging surrounded it, stretching up into the sky like a giant spider's web.

To his right Ayshe could dimly see the bars of the capstan. Past the mainmast another stair led to the poop deck, at the top of which he could see the glint of the taffrail in the starlight, as well as the dark outline of the mizzenmast. The deck was piled with coils of rope, casks, boxes bound in iron, and a curious miscellany of tools, weapons, and junk.

The dwarf moved cautiously down the stairs. On his right, below the foremast, the forehatch was a patch of deeper black. Ayshe listened closely, but the only sound was the gentle slap of waves against the ship's side. The moons of Krynn, riding high in a cloudless sky, illuminated the scene in red and white, casting double shadows across everything. Though the moonlight made it easier for the dwarf to navigate, he might have wished for a murkier night when an intruder would be less obvious to any watchers.

He had just started forward again when his ready ear caught the sound of voices coming his way. Without thinking, he ducked back and crept into the forehatch. He almost stumbled over the ladder head but caught himself just in time. Step by step he lowered himself downward until his feet reached solid planking.

Dwarf vision gave him some abilities to see in the dark, something he'd become acutely aware of during his sojourn in a village of humans. He could see the area he'd entered was lined with barrels, and a narrow passage led between them, ending in a stout wooden door.

The voices that had startled him grew louder, and to Ayshe's alarm he saw the head of the ladder glow with the light of a lantern. Swiftly he cast about for a hiding place. At the last minute, as a leg appeared on the top rung of the ladder, he pushed behind the barrels, squeezing his body between them and the wall.

The two who descended into the room were elves and speaking Elvish. Ayshe picked up a few words: *water, storage* and, as he listened, he could make out the general outline of the conversation. It had to do with sufficient supplies of fresh water and what the captain and someone named Harfang would do if the ship ran short. The elves checked the barrels and conferred briefly. Then one went up the ladder. The other, to Ayshe's alarm, leaned against one of the barrels, drew out a long, thin pipe, and began to smoke. He seemed in no hurry to leave, drawing on his pipe and, in between, murmuring softly to himself some fragment of an Elvish song.

Ayshe was beginning to feel his cramped limbs would never be able to straighten again when there was a rumble of feet on deck and a shouted order from above. Instantly the elf knocked out his pipe and leaped up the ladder.

The dwarf emerged from his hiding place and massaged his knotted arms and legs. Clearly there could be no question of returning to the deck, since all was astir there. He wondered if someone had found his boat, in which case, he'd have a long, cold swim back home. He heard voices shouting commands then, to his horror, a sound he dreaded.

With a creaking and groaning, the capstan turned, raising the anchor.

Ayshe could hear the rattle of sails as the canvas was loosened and made fast. The ship shifted beneath him and stirred along her keel. She was moving.

Only by a supreme effort did he prevent himself from running up the ladder onto the deck. He paced back and forth in the confined space. Every moment, the ship was carrying him farther from his home—or what was left of it. If he could just get a moment to leave the ship unseen, he might still be able to swim the distance back to Thargon. Perhaps he could make it unseen back to his own boat, if it had not been discovered.

Or . . .

The door behind him slammed open, and an elf, bare-chested

and carrying a box on one shoulder, emerged. He gave the dwarf a startled look, shouted, dropped the box, and lunged.

Ayshe dodged and leaped for the ladder. Halfway up he felt the elf's hand grip his ankle. He kicked back, struck something that crunched, and heard the elf spit a curse. He clawed his way upward, willing to chance the upper deck.

The doorway of the hatch darkened, and Ayshe, looking up, saw a figure. He had just time to see a handspike descend when darkness overtook him.

CHAPTER

3

A murmur of voices came faintly as if from a long distance. Ayshe stirred and wondered if he ignored the voices whether Chaval would let him sleep another ten minutes. For some reason his pillow seemed unpleasantly hard, and he could use some additional sleep time since his body appeared to be aching.

A bucket of freezing water splashed over him, and he regained consciousness with a painful jerk. All the memories of the past few days came flooding back. He tried to sit up, though an ache in his head told him he wasn't ready for such exercise.

The circle of faces around him drew back. With a great effort, the dwarf raised himself on his elbows and looked about.

The sky was still dark, but a pale glow showed that dawn was not far off. In front of him, a tall elf was holding a torch to illuminate the scene, and it cast its reflections on the wet deck beneath the dwarf. The light flickered and shifted in the breeze. The ship swayed beneath him as she ran before a wind that filled her sails above his head. The noises—the creak of ropes, the groan of wood and iron—brought back to Ayshe his last sea voyage three years earlier, the voyage that had deposited him in Thargon. That voyage and his life before the dragon's attack seemed to belong to another lifetime.

A hand reached down, grasped the front of his shirt, and pulled him to his feet. He found himself staring into the face of the human he'd seen ashore, the man he'd assumed was captain of the ship.

"As I thought!" the man growled. "It's the village smith." He examined Ayshe as if he were some repulsive species of marine life. "What are you doing here, smith?"

Ayshe rubbed his aching head. "I came . . . I came to find answers."

"Answers to what?"

"Why the dragon attacked us. Where it came from. Who you are. You seem to know about the dragon. I think you should have told us what you know." Ayshe was conscious of how thin his speech seemed. Gallipol's plan, which had seemed dubious when he was standing by the forge fire, appeared completely harebrained at the moment. A small voice in his mind said he might have expected something cooked up by the human village mayor would end in disaster.

"How did you get here?"

Ayshe hesitated. Evidently they had not yet found his boat. If he concealed its existence, perhaps he could make use of it again. "I swam," he said sullenly.

The man looked at him with some measure of respect. "A long way to swim on a hope. Why should we give you answers?"

"Because our homes were destroyed!" The dwarf felt rage swell within him—rage directed both at the man before him and at himself for his cowardice. "Because our families were killed!"

" 'Our'?" queried the elf holding the light. "What is a dwarf doing in a village of humans in the first place?"

Ayshe glanced at him. "I came to Thargon three years ago as a stranger, and the people there welcomed me as a friend."

The elf snorted. "More than any humans would do for elves!" he growled.

"Peace, Ridrathannash!" The human continued to examine Ayshe's face. "I told you, dwarf, when I was ashore that the wyrm will not attack again. Why do you ask for more?"

All the dwarf's grief welled up and spilled from his lips. *"Because we have a right to know why!"* he shouted.

"A *right?*" The man put his face within an inch of Ayshe's. "A right? You have no right! Do you imagine you're the first village ever attacked by a dragon? By that particular wyrm? We've seen men, women, and babies slain by that beast and its kin. I've seen men with their guts torn out, women dead with babies plucking at their breasts for milk, children slaughtered at their school desks. A reason? There is no reason, fool! It's a dragon. That's what they do. They kill people." He turned away as if there was no more to be said on the subject.

One of the elves turned to him. "What shall we do with it, Harfang?"

It took Ayshe a moment to realize he was the *it* in the elf's question.

Harfang glanced at him. "He swam out here. Let him swim home."

Ayshe could see through the rail the darkness of Ergoth's shore rapidly receding, and his heart sank into the pit of his stomach. Stealthily boarding his boat and sailing back was not the same as being thrown overboard. Even if he could struggle through the chilled water in his weakened state and somehow reach the shore, he'd be miles from the village. With tundra wolves on the prowl, and who knew what other creatures roaming the empty land, his chances of getting home were small and growing smaller by the moment.

One of the elves grasped him firmly around the middle and carried him toward the rail. Harfang, evidently indifferent to his fate, had turned away to speak to another crew member.

Ayshe struggled, kicking against his captor, but in vain. The elf's wiry strength held him tight. The dwarf gave up hope. Perhaps there was no point in struggling or even in swimming. He would let himself sink beneath the waves and find peace. He could not think what he would say to Chaval and Zininia when he saw them in the halls of the gods, but he would beg forgiveness. Perhaps that would be enough. He saw the dark water beneath him and instinctively drew in his breath in anticipation of the plunge.

"Halt!"

The voice came from behind him, and he felt the arms of his captor stiffen. Silence filled the deck, as if the very sounds of the ship had fallen quiet at the sound of that voice. It was musical, with a crystalline quality, as if it were something unbearably fragile.

Slowly the elf set the dwarf down, and Ayshe turned.

It was another elf. She had emerged from the entrance to the cabin at the stern of the ship and contemplated the scene while the crew stood frozen in their positions. Her hair was pale, almost white, and cut very short—so short that in places Ayshe could see the gleam of her scalp. From one eye to the base of her chin, a horrid scar twisted the flesh, as if a blade of fire had struck her, leaving its mark as shiny tissue.

She was clad in breeches with an old sea cloak wrapped around her. Even so, Ayshe could see that her arm, outstretched toward him, was emaciated, as if time and care had burned away every ounce of superfluous flesh, leaving only muscle and bone. As he saw her more clearly in the rising light of dawn, Ayshe also realized with a shock that she was blind. Her eyes had a white film over them, and she turned her head this way and that, as if hearing sounds beyond the range of mortal beings.

Beside and just behind her was another elf, also thin and pale. His head was shaven save for a single topknot of dark hair that was bound in delicate silver filigree to form a long braid, reaching almost to the ground. His mouth was drawn in a thin line. At his belt, he carried a coiled whip, and he showed great deference to the elf woman.

"Harfang!" she called.

The human presented himself before her, also with deference.

"Who is this"—she sniffed the air—"dwarf?"

"He's a smith, Captain, from the town we just visited. He survived the wyrm's attack and swam out here to spy on us."

"Not so!" The words came unbidden from Ayshe's mouth.

The blind captain turned her sightless eyes to him. "Release him," she ordered. Ayshe shrugged away the elf's hands and walked over to stand before her. She reached out and touched him, running her fingers over his face as if to understand and memorize his features.

"You came for answers," she told him, her musical voice pitched to carry only to he and Harfang. "But there are no answers. Harfang is right—dragons are what they are. Their minds are unfathomable, their souls corrupted, serving the gods of evil. *Des qath e shanfala du qu'esari . . .*" Her voice trailed off into a string of Elvish words the dwarf did not recognize. She seemed to be speaking in a dialect long since fallen into disuse, and suddenly he had a vision of centuries of life, a life beyond comprehension, carrying a burden of unending pain and sorrow born of a great tragedy. Tears sprang into his eyes. He looked up and saw to his surprise that the elf was smiling. She turned to Harfang.

"We have need of a smith, have we not?"

The human glared at Ayshe but answered the captain respectfully. "That's so, ma'am. But I had thought to promote Alyssaran to that position."

The captain shook her head. "We are short of crew with little chance of finding more in these parts save what the fates bring to us. Chance has sent us this dwarf, just as chance sent him to that village three years past." She turned to Ayshe. "Are you skilled at smithing, dwarf?"

Ayshe was still trying to figure out how the strange elf captain knew of his arrival in Thargon, so she had to repeat the question. He reached behind him for his axe and found it missing. Harfang made a gesture, and one of the crew tossed him the axe, which he handed to the captain.

Ayshe cleared his throat. "I forged that . . . from old memories of time with my kindred in the Khalkist Mountains."

The elf captain felt it carefully, running her fingers along the metal, tracing the engraving and decoration, seemingly taking pleasure in their intricacies. She tested the blade with her thumb and smiled again.

"What is your name, dwarf?"

"Ayshe."

"Who was your forebear?"

"Balar," the dwarf replied, somewhat unsettled. He'd not thought of his father in a long time.

"Then Ayshe, son of Balar, you are smith and armorer to the *Starfinder*. What say you?"

In the clear light of morning that was upon them, Ayshe could see the hills of Northern Ergoth marching past. A brisk breeze blew across the deck, stirring his hair and beard. Harfang watched him narrowly, and the dwarf found his mind was already made up.

"Aye, Captain. I accept."

"Good!" The elf clapped him on the shoulder and without another word turned back toward her cabin. At the same time, activity on the deck resumed, and the moment they had stood frozen in time dissipated.

Ayshe looked to the east, where the sun rose over the hills out of the morning mists and spread its joyous rays across the expanse of water. Hope bloomed in his breast. Perhaps the strange elf captain was right. His heart demanded vengeance. He was aboard a ship pursuing the dragon that had destroyed his town and killed his friend. The fates had sent him here. On behalf of the town, he would bear witness and take his revenge.

Malshaunt the mage followed the captain back to her quarters. "With respect, ma'am," he said, his voice cold, "what was the reason for taking aboard a . . . dwarf?" In his mouth, the word sounded like poison.

The captain sat. "My good Malshaunt," she said, staring straight before her, "one must take what the gods send us. The dwarf Ayshe has appeared on the *Starfinder*. No doubt for a reason; it is up to us to determine why he is here."

Malshaunt shrugged. "Doubtless he came here to steal some goods for the aid of his village. One could hardly expect less of a dwarf . . . or of humans."

The blind captain shook her head. "Peace, mage! And have a care. Your hatred of all other races is dangerous."

The mage's mouth tilted in a slight smile, like a cold sun breaking through the clouds on a wintry day. "Yet I've heard you say, Captain Tashara," he observed, "that hatred is a creative power if one has the wit to wield it creatively."

The captain did not match his smile, and a small line appeared on her forehead, but she said nothing for a moment. Then she rose and stepped to a large table on which a chart was pinned. The mage accompanied her.

Tashara ran her hand over the chart. An observer would have seen that unlike most charts, on hers the features were raised slightly: shorelines, names, navigation lines, and notations. Tashara ran her fingers over them then turned to Malshaunt and raised her eyebrows.

The mage stepped before the chart and spread his hand over it, muttering a few words beneath his breath. The lines on the chart rippled and changed. Tashara slowly reached down and placed a single slender finger on a small dot near the west coast of Northern Ergoth. The dot appeared to be moving.

Tashara traced a line with her finger down the coastline and south to the other half of Ergoth. Then she lifted her fingers from the chart and seemed to grope for a moment in the air close above the map, as if feeling the winds that swept above her ship. Malshaunt watched silently. His expression seemed to intensify when he looked at the captain. The captain's face bore an expression of utmost concentration, and small beads of sweat broke out on her brow. Her lips moved but gave no sound. At last she sank back into a seat, exhausted. She rose and staggered slightly. Malshaunt offered a hand, but she pushed it away and made her way to her bunk, where she lay silent. The mage returned to the map, looked at it for a silent moment, then snapped his fingers over it.

He looked once more at the slender figure of his captain and went out.

The dwarf followed Harfang—first mate of the *Starfinder* from the way the rest of the crew addressed him—down the hatch he'd entered on first boarding the ship. They made their way between the barrels and through the door. There was a low-roofed compartment with curving walls, along which and between which were slung the hammocks of the crew before the mast. The mate pointed to one.

"There you'll sleep. When you *do* sleep. There's work enough to keep you occupied night and day." He glanced disdainfully at Ayshe's clothes. "Shamura!"

A tall female elf emerged from the back of the room. "Sir?"

"Get our new smith some clothes." Harfang chuckled without humor. "You'll have to cut down some breeches to fit him. Two sets. Same as everyone else." He waved a hand of dismissal, and the elf disappeared.

They retraced their steps, emerged on deck again, and strode to another hatch near the mainmast. Ayshe knew enough of ship construction to understand that below deck the hull was divided into compartments, made as watertight as possible with tar and caulking, so a breach in the ship's hull might be confined to only one area of the vessel.

Descending into that new area, the mate and smith found themselves amid barrels and boxes of stores. Bags of onions and potatoes hung from the beams that formed the great ribs of the hull, along with smoked hams, sides of bacon, and salt pork. The roof was low, and Harfang was obliged to duck, though Ayshe had no such problem. The dwarf could not shake the feeling he was in the belly of some monstrous sea beast that rode the waves, ignoring the tiny creatures that swarmed over it.

Along one side, partly shielded by a row of crates, was a small smithy. A shuttered port showed where the smoke from the forge could escape, though Harfang informed the dwarf on fair days he would be expected to set up his works on deck. Tools hung neatly along the wall, and Ayshe, inspecting them, was impressed by the care and forethought that had gone into their assemblage. Jigs, files, hammers—their surfaces polished to gleaming silver so no flaw might be transferred from them to the metal they struck—burnishers, and tongs. Some were cruder than he was accustomed to, and others seemed to have come from other parts of Ansalon where practices were different, but on the whole he would want for nothing.

Harfang, who had not suspended his hostility, told him he would be allowed to light the fire for only a few hours at a time. Every precaution had been taken to prevent any of the hot coals from spilling onto the wooden deck. If the dwarf needed assistance, it could be provided, "although we're short-hauled at present," Harfang informed him.

The mate's speech was abrupt. He discouraged questions, and Ayshe did not ask any. Finally the mate said gruffly, "Your mess is at six bells. Someone will show you the way."

Behind him a voice said, "Harfang?"

THE GREAT WHITE WYRM

Harfang turned. "Yes, Feystalen?"

"Begging your pardon, Captain Tashara would be glad of a word, sir."

Harfang nodded. "Aye. Very well. Perhaps you can answer any questions our new crewman has. Any, that is, that *can* be answered." He nodded to Ayshe and went out.

After Malshaunt left the captain's quarters, Tashara remained lying silent in her bunk for a quarter of an hour. At length she rose and crossed with sure feet to the back wall of the cabin. She pressed her hand against a section of the paneling, and an opening was revealed. The captain reached into the dark recess and brought forth a bundle wrapped in cloth. She bore it to the table and drew the cloth from it, revealing a sphere about eighteen inches in diameter. It did not appear hard or fixed but moved and pulsated, as if with a curious life of its own, as if something within it agitated its surface. The captain placed a hand on it and bent her head.

"Tell me!" she muttered. "Tell me! I *must* know!"

For a long time, the only sounds in the cabin were the same whispered words, repeated tens, hundreds, thousands of times.

"I *must* know!"

CHAPTER

4

Feystalen was short for an elf, a relief to Ayshe, who was tired of looking up at Harfang. Also unlike the first mate, he seemed friendlier and less inclined to look on Ayshe as an intruder. He patiently answered the dwarf's questions, showed him about the rest of the ship, and offered advice as to which food to eat and which to avoid in the ship's mess.

At the conclusion of their tour, they returned to the forge, where Ayshe set about acquainting himself with his new tools, reorganizing them so they would be ready to hand as he was accustomed. Feystalen sat silently watching him.

Ayshe made bold enough to ask the question that had been most troubling him. "What's the point of it all?"

Feystalen fumbled in his pockets and came up with a slender pipe, similar to that which the dwarf had seen in the hands of the other elf. He drew out a worn pouch, carefully filled the pipe, lit it with a spark from a tinderbox, and breathed out a long feather of smoke. Ayshe waited patiently.

"What I tell you," the elf said at last, "stays aboard the ship. None but the crew and Captain Tashara know the truth." He looked sternly at the dwarf. "Were you to disclose it to anyone else, your life would be forfeit."

Ayshe said nothing, which the elf took as a sign of assent.

"Have you ever heard of . . . Dragonsbane?"

Ayshe shook his head. "Never. What is it?"

"I'm not surprised. It's one of the best-kept secrets on Krynn, and there are few now alive who remember its history. Its beginnings lie nearly a millennium and a half in the past, during the Third Dragon War. In that war, evil dragons attacked Ansalon. When they bent their attacks toward the Kingdom of Solamnia, the representatives of the Orders of Sorcery—Red Robes, White Robes, and Black Robes—met at the Tower of High Sorcery in Palanthas. There they created five dragon orbs to guard against the onslaught. This also was the age of Huma Dragonsbane, forger of the first dragonlances."

He paused and looked at Ayshe. "You know nothing of this history?"

The dwarf grunted. "A bit. The name Huma has reached my ears, and I suppose I may have learned of the dragon orbs at some time past. What does that have to do with this ship, though? Something to do with Huma? All the events you're speaking of were a long age in the past."

"No, not Huma exactly, though we revere his name. During the war, the elves formed a secret organization to fight the dragons. We put little trust in the deeds of men and of other races; they are short-lived and easily forget the danger to this world. So this organization of elves met in secret and kept their order hidden. The dragons they killed were often slain in such a way as to make their deaths appear as accidents, and no one knew behind these deaths was a band, cold as ice, hard as steel, sworn to one another and to the death of the dragons.

"None knew, I say, but the elves who belonged. The band called itself Dragonsbane—out of admiration for Huma and his sacrifice, perhaps; who, now, can tell?"

Ayshe nodded. "Aye. So what happened to them? If I recall, the Queen of Darkness was defeated by Huma and left Krynn, taking her dragons with her. What did these elf heroes of yours do when there were no more dragons left to fight?"

"When the dragons left," Feystalen continued, drawing on his pipe, "the elves knew they would someday return. Human memory, as I say, is short, but elves bear the wisdom of the long lived, and they know each day, each month, each year is only a fleeting moment in the great cycle of birth and death." He paused for a moment, seeming very sad, then went on.

"Dragonsbane remained. Father passed the knowledge of it to son—and often enough to daughter, for the warriors of Dragonsbane made no distinction in terms of sex.

"And then, more than a thousand years later, when the War of the Lance swept over the land, Dragonsbane once again arose."

Feystalen put down his pipe, his eyes distant. "I was one," he said, speaking no longer to Ayshe. "I answered the call. My father and his father and his father's father had kept the secret. But it was I who was chosen to serve." He turned back to the dwarf, who sat looking at him, open mouthed with awe.

"We tracked many dragons in those days. Some we slew, always careful to preserve our secrecy. Some others we merely tracked and marked down for future death." He fell silent again.

"And when the war ended?" Ayshe prompted.

Feystalen shrugged. "The war ended." He looked at the dwarf with a half smile. "Hard it is when you've done heroic deeds, even in the shadows, to return to an ordinary life. One's hand longs for the sword or bowstring; one's heart aches for the thrill of battle."

Ayshe said nothing. A weight settled in the pit of his stomach as he thought about Feystalen's words.

What does it take to make a hero? Chance and will.

What does it take to make a coward? Chance and fear.

The elf watched his companion's face attentively but said

nothing. Ayshe resumed his reorganization of his tools. "But the dragons came back," he said. "Or rather, different dragons. The overlords came after the Chaos War. What then?"

Feystalen looked sad again. "We fought them," he said slowly. "We did fight them, but they were too big and we were too few. Many elves fell in secret struggle, and none but us marked their resting places." He relit his pipe. "Dragonsbane is now but a shadow of its former self. Our numbers are reduced, our warriors slain or grown old. Many had no children to whom they could pass their legacy. We"—he spread his hands, indicating the *Starfinder* and its crew—"are almost all that is left. The mighty band of Dragonsbane elves."

"Nay," growled Ayshe. "Now with a dwarf. And a man. What about Harfang? Where did *he* come from?"

"Harfang hails from Solamnia," the elf told him. "From Solanthus, I believe. Captain Tashara met him in Palanthas. We'd put ashore there to water and replenish our stores. The captain came aboard with a young lad in tow. He was dirty-faced and foul-mouthed, but the captain insisted we keep him as cabin boy. She said she'd found him starving on the streets and he didn't know who his mother and father were. He'd wandered the roads from Solanthus until he came to Palanthas. There he might have fallen in with some gang of cutthroats if the captain hadn't rescued him.

"We undertook the training of him, and for a year we wrestled with him. He fought every man and woman aboard, save the captain, but when he was beat and knocked down—and he always was, at first—he'd get back up without complaining. He'd sit in silence on the deck, and you could see him thinking out what he'd learned and how he was going to defeat his foe the next time."

"And he did?"

"And he did!" Feystalen acknowledged. "After a while we began to see what the captain had seen in the lad. That was twenty years past. Harfang rose through the ranks. Today he's Captain Tashara's right hand. Nothing happens on this ship without his word. The captain sits in her cabin most of the time, so Harfang's the real master of the *Starfinder*.

"And the mage? Chap with the long hair?"

Feystalen nodded. "If Harfang sits on the captain's right, Malshaunt is ever on her left. He is her oldest servant. He was with her before any of the rest of us knew her, and he knows more of her mind than any aboard the ship."

"Good with magic is he? In a fight?"

Feystalen smiled. "Oh, I think you need have no doubts upon that score, Master Dwarf."

Ayshe, having finished rearranging his tools to his satisfaction, inspected a series of shelves set on the wall of the hull. He turned to Feystalen. "What's all this?"

The elf eased himself up to stand at the dwarf's shoulder.

"In all our time fighting dragons, we've accumulated some specialized equipment."

Ayshe reached onto one shelf and picked up a long spear. The end, sharply pointed, included a barb and was razor sharp. At the other end of the haft, which was made of steel and not of wood, a strong metal ring was fused. In fact, the dwarf saw, the entire spear was made of a single piece of metal, so worked that no part seemed weaker than another.

The dwarf handled it carefully, noting with admiration the intricate designs that had been worked along the shaft where two intertwined serpents mingled their forked tongues. The blade itself was slim but strong. The entire weapon was astonishingly light, unlike the heavy iron-headed spears Chaval and Ayshe had forged for the villagers.

"What is it?" asked the dwarf. "A dragonlance?"

Feystalen shook his head. "Alas, no. There are so few dragon-lances—even less after the War of Souls and the reign of the overlords. We've never obtained one, despite long years of searching. It's said the warriors of Dragonsbane made use of one long years ago in the slaying of a great red, but none of us know now what became of it." He took the spear from Ayshe, spinning it in his hands, handling it with the easy familiarity of one long accustomed to such weapons.

"This is a wyrmbarb. The warrior throws it at his prey and secures a chain fastened to this ring at the end. If several do this, it impedes the dragon's movements, giving others of the band the opportunity for a strike."

Ayshe looked in awe at the spear. "It must be a frightful thing to have a dragon at the end of that."

Feystalen nodded. "Aye, that it is. We have several folk among us, though, who are skilled in the art."

The dwarf nodded. "Very well, but where do you strike a dragon that is vulnerable? I've never seen one—or hadn't until a few days ago—but I understand their scales to be hard as iron."

"You understand rightly," the elf replied, replacing the weapon on the shelf. "But a dragon has its points of weakness." He tapped his neck. *"Here* and"—he motioned beneath his arm—*"here* are where you must strike if you wish to penetrate its flesh. Elsewhere, bladed weapons are useless." He gave the dwarf a keen glance. "Also, you must avoid its breath weapon."

"Its what?"

"Each dragon kind," Feystalen explained, "has a weapon particular to its color. The black spits acid from its jaws, the green, corrosive gas. The blue vomits forth lightning on its foes. The white sends a blast of killing cold. And the red . . . the red breathes fire and destruction." His gaze turned inward. "I saw Malystryx, the great red bitch, once," he murmured, "before she was killed by Mina of hateful memory. I should have liked to have taken her head in trophy."

Ayshe was silent a moment then said, "The dragon that

attacked my village seemed white or gray and breathed freezing cold. But it seemed also as if it could summon electricity from the clouds."

Feystalen nodded. "Yes. Now we come to it. This is no ordinary dragon we seek now. It is a storm dragon. Perhaps it's the only storm dragon in existence—in which case the people of Krynn should thank the gods for their mercy! Born of some great cataclysm of the skies, this wyrm can command the heavens. It moves through clouds and can cause them to appear or vanish. It brings fire and ice in its wake. I've seen it only once, but that was enough. Perhaps that's why the captain took you aboard the *Starfinder*, so you might serve as a guide to us in our battle with the White Wyrm."

"You say you saw it once. What happened then?" Ayshe asked.

Feystalen became occupied with filling his pipe. Ayshe waited for an answer, but none was forthcoming, so he tried another question.

"How long have you been chasing it?"

The elf breathed in the fragrant smoke. "A long time. Aye, a long time indeed." He closed his eyes and pondered.

"It was in the last year of the War of the Lance," he said finally. "We were on foot then, a band of forty companions. We heard a strange tale of a white dragon laying waste up and down the coast of Nordmaar. We traveled there, eager to do battle, but we found nothing but destruction. Wrecked villages and dead bodies were strewn along the coast, but the dragon had vanished.

"Then, when we were prepared to give up the chase, since plainly the dragon was no longer in the area, some among us began to cry out, looking out to sea where the mist rose in the morning. From out of the white fog, a ship came, looking like a vessel of the dead. We could see no one aboard it, and its black sails caught just enough wind to move it within hail of the shore.

"From the foredeck, a voice called to us—the voice of Captain

Tashara. She bade us come aboard. She seemed to know all about us and about Dragonsbane. We took a few boats that survived from the ruins of the village and rowed out to the ship. When we climbed aboard, we found Tashara and the mage Malshaunt were the only crew aboard. None among us could imagine how these two—one blind, the other slight of build—could manage sailing such a ship between them. Tashara told us her name and that her craft was the *Starfinder*, but not a word would she speak of where she came from or how she and Malshaunt had sailed to us. Nor would she tell us how they had found us or how they knew of us. She told us only that they also were Dragonsbane and that they sought the Great White Wyrm, so she called it."

His pipe had gone out, so intent was he on his tale. Listening to him, Ayshe had the sense of a story prepared for telling to children and grandchildren yet to come, almost a song rather than spoken words. The elf relit his pipe and continued.

"What could we do? We were Dragonsbane, pledged to seek out the beasts wherever they might be found. Tashara, too, was Dragonsbane, and she called herself captain of the *Starfinder*. So we gladly became her crew and set sail. A week or two later, we heard of an attack to the south at Sargonath in Kern. We traveled to the land of the ogres, but once again the beast had vanished before we arrived.

"One thing we determined: the dragon appears only near the sea. Most often it seems to come in summer and early fall. It came and went over the years, and we gave chase. Sometimes we nearly caught it. At other times we were half a continent away. But over all that time, we sailed the seas of Krynn, searching, always searching for it.

"Always we found the same tale. Always buildings smashed, temples crushed, people slaughtered. At times, rumor of the wyrm ceased altogether, and for a few years we almost believed it had vanished, but Tashara never doubted there would be a reckoning. And always the White Wyrm reappeared, and the chase resumed."

"So the dragon never strikes inland."

"Never. There is something about water that attracts it. It carries out its depredations along the coasts of Ansalon. Three decades ago, it was, we caught up to it."

The dwarf waited, but Feystalen's pipe was clamped firmly in his lips.

To break the silence before it grew awkward, the dwarf rummaged on another shelf, one containing pieces of armor. Other bits and pieces of plate mail and chain mail hung from hooks on the hull or stood awkwardly against one another, as if they might at any moment be cast over by the motion of the ship. Ayshe's experienced eye roved over them, noting minor spots of rust to be rubbed away, a joint weak and in need of repair, a few links of broken chain. Feystalen watched him, saying nothing.

A clatter sounded from the top of the ladder, and the crew began to descend. From somewhere above, Ayshe heard a bell tapped.

The elves gathered around the newcomer. Ayshe's experience with the race having been limited, he was somewhat surprised to see how different they were from one another, though he would have been insulted had anyone made a similar observation about dwarves.

None were as tall as Harfang. Some were fair-skinned with light brown hair. Others, darker and shorter, had hair of a deeper, richer brown.

Ayshe, average in size for a dwarf, stood about four feet and some inches to spare, and he discovered he was not much shorter—perhaps a foot—than the tallest of the elves.

Most striking among them were two who resembled each other so closely in face and form that Ayshe guessed they were brother and sister. They were barely taller than Ayshe and, while the other elves were clothed in flowing costumes with loose sleeves and pants that allowed the greatest ease in moving about the ship, these two wore close-fitting leather gear, fringed and feathered.

It was their faces and arms, bared to the shoulders, that most attracted the dwarf's attention. Almost every inch of exposed skin was elaborately tattooed with intricate designs. The dwarf detected similarities between the motifs that adorned their skin and those that appeared on the haft of the wyrmbarb he had handled earlier. The elves' tattoos extended to their faces as well, and their bright eyes seemed sunk in a whirling maze of colors and shapes.

The elves examined Ayshe closely, like dogs sniffing a new member of the pack. None spoke for a time. Feystalen faded silently into the background, as if waiting for a sign, while the elves and the dwarf circled round, waiting for someone to speak.

CHAPTER

5

A dwarf!" snarled one of the taller elves, staring at Ayshe. "What next? We might as well take a kender aboard."

One of his companions chuckled and spat. "Perhaps when we sight the wyrm he can walk beneath it and stab its belly. No need for him to crawl."

"Nay," growled the first one. "If we see the wyrm, I know where this one will be. Cowering on *his* belly below deck!"

The male tattooed elf said something in an Elvish dialect Ayshe didn't understand to his sister, who laughed. The second elf looked at them in irritation.

"None of that. Speak so we can all understand. I've no need to hear that Kagonesti noise."

The male Kagonesti—so Ayshe realized the tattooed elves must be—looked at the speaker coolly and said in accented Common, "It's said that dwarves lead their battles from behind."

"Aye, that's so," observed the first speaker. "First to retreat, last to advance."

Ayshe felt anger building in his chest. "And what of the elves, now?" he snarled. "Wandering here and there like a pack of rabid, starving dogs. The mighty Qualinesti! The great Silvanesti!

Where are your towers now?"

"Maybe still standing if not for the cowardice of the dwarves," retorted the elf. "When the last war swept over our homeland, we fought Mina and the Knights of Neraka and died where we fought. We brought down Beryllinthranox!"

"Aye, and pulled down your own city of Qualinost in doing so. A fine victory! Many more such and there'll be no more of you left to tell the tale of your heroism."

The elf snorted. "Where were the dwarves? Cowering underground in your tunnels. When you weren't trying to strike bargains with the knights to save your own hides." He chuckled. "Tunnels like a warren. That's true enough. Scratch a dwarf and find a rabbit."

Something inside Ayshe snapped. Once again he saw the frozen, broken bodies of Chaval, Zininia, and their child. They stared at him, eyes wide with reproach. A red mist rose before him and obscured them. He was dimly aware of shouting and of something pulling his arms and legs, finally became aware that the shouts were his own.

He was astride the elf, hands at his throat. The other elves surrounded him, pulling him back and holding him. Feystalen watched the scene, a faint smile wreathing his lips.

Ayshe ceased to struggle against his captors, and the elf rose, massaging his neck and glaring at the dwarf.

"I cry Meet!" he declared. "This . . . creature . . . has insulted me and laid hands on me. I cry Meet!"

Feystalen rose briskly to his feet. "Samustalen has cried Meet on Ayshe, son of Balar," he announced. "All hands on deck."

One of the Kagonesti twins leaped up the ladder, and Ayshe heard his cry echoing across the ship, commanding the crew's presence on deck. The other elves followed him up the ladder more slowly. Samustalen was the first to mount the ladder, followed by Feystalen. Ayshe was surrounded by the other elves as he followed them, his heart beating faster. Whatever was meant by "calling Meet," he had a feeling it was no good to him.

On deck he found the crew mustered, with the notable absence of Captain Tashara. Feystalen stood by Harfang, speaking quietly to the first mate. The man listened, nodded, and raised his hand for silence.

"Ayshe, son of Balar! Samustalen of Qualinost has called Meet on you. How do you respond?"

One of the elves behind Ayshe muttered, "You accept."

With the barest hesitation, Ayshe replied, "I accept!"

In his cabin in the forecastle of the ship, Malshaunt sat before a table topped with smooth stone. In its center was a shallow indentation. The mage picked up a bottle and poured a silver liquid into the indentation so it formed a pool. He lifted a hand and murmured something, and the ship's motion smoothed to a gentle rocking that in no way disturbed the pool of silver.

The mage stared hard into the pool and passed his hands above it. He chuckled mirthlessly.

Meet already, he thought. The elves waste no time. Now, Ayshe, son of Balar, we'll see whether you have what it takes to fight with the sons and daughters of Dragonsbane. Or more likely your corpse will float in the wake of the *Starfinder* as we pass on our way.

A slight wrinkle creased his forehead. The captain had implied the dwarf had some special role to play in the battle against the wyrm. But what that role was, she had not said, and it was beyond Malshaunt's imagination that a dwarf could be a significant factor in defeating their enemy.

It was a puzzle, and he disliked puzzles.

"So be it." The mate held out his hand, and one of the crew handed him a battered lump of chalk. With it, he traced a crude circle on the deck, roughly ten feet in diameter. Another elf, emerging from below deck, handed Harfang two iron tridents.

The mate beckoned the dwarf and elf to the middle of the circle, while the rest of the crew ranged themselves around the edges of the makeshift arena. It was approaching midday, and though the sun was shining brightly overhead, a chill breeze blew through the rigging, making a soft lament that framed the scene.

Harfang spoke to the opponents, his voice carrying so the rest of the audience could hear as well. "Who marks his opponent three times has won the Meet. Step outside the circle and you forfeit." He handed each of them a trident and retreated. Ayshe and Samustalen stood opposite one another against the edges of the circle.

"Time!" Harfang shouted.

Samustalen darted sideways, scuttling like a crab, twirling the trident in one hand. Ayshe retreated in the other direction, his mind racing. He had little or no experience of this sort of fighting. He'd seen a trident match once or twice in his youth, and he knew enough to keep the edges of the tines slanted up. Beyond that, he was lost.

The elf had the longer reach and the greater height. That much was clear. The circle offered just enough room to maneuver, but the swaying of the deck made it hard for Ayshe to keep his feet, while Samustalen, the experienced sailor, rocked with the motion of the ship, as at home there as he would have been on dry land.

The elf made a sudden leap into the air, coming at Ayshe with the lithe grace of a dancer. As he sprang, he passed the trident from his right hand to his left and slashed.

Ayshe twisted away, trying to keep his face to his opponent, barely keeping his feet beneath him. He felt a burning along his right arm. Looking down, he saw the elf's blow had torn a long gash in his flesh. Blood dripped onto the deck. From far away he heard Harfang's voice.

"One!"

The watchers shouted, and their cries startled a pair of gulls from the mainmast. The birds flew away, shrieking a raucous complaint.

The elf bared his teeth at Ayshe. "Come to me, stinking dwarf!" he taunted. "I could fight you with my eyes closed, your smell is so strong."

Ayshe wasted no breath in answering. His mind was busy turning over possibilities. He remembered a conversation with Chaval the previous year. The smith was mending a sword and used the occasion to give Ayshe an informal lecture on fighting techniques, spiced with anecdotes from his time serving in an army during the War of Souls.

"In any battle," Chaval had said, "each side has advantages and disadvantages. The art of winning is to know your weaknesses and turn them into strengths, while doing the opposite to your enemy. You, for instance"—he looked critically at the dwarf—"are shorter by two heads than me. I have the advantage of height. But you're smaller and more compact. Closer to the ground and your center of balance. That makes you harder to hit, and me easier. That's *your* advantage."

Ayshe studied Samustalen. He's faster than me, the dwarf thought. He's more experienced with a trident. What's my advantage?

The elf leaped again. This time he cartwheeled across the circle. His trident again passed from one hand to the other, and he slashed down at the dwarf.

Without conscious thought, Ayshe dropped to his knees and slid past the elf. He rocked to his feet and spun around. The elf's blades had cut a slit in his shirt front, but the flesh beneath was unmarked.

There was a grudging murmur of admiration from the watching elves. Ayshe and Samustalen resumed their cautious circling.

Ayshe took the initiative on the next pass, darting forward to cut at his opponent's knee. Samustalen twitched away and the stalking resumed.

Ayshe cudgeled his brains. Think! What can you do that an elf can't? What do you know that he doesn't?

You're smaller than him but not by much. You're slower. How is that an advantage? No, better not dwell on it. What else? What else?

Samustalen stopped circling and began to move slowly across the circle, passing the trident from hand to hand. Ayshe had nowhere to retreat. Any move to the side was quickly cut off by the relentless elf.

In desperation Ayshe dived, rolling himself in a ball. He felt the elf's blades scrape along his back and heard Harfang's shout.

"Two!"

Samustalen began the same slow movement back across the circle, the trident poised in his hand. The faces of the elves grew more intent as they watched for the end of the contest. Of the result, they clearly had no doubt.

The elf passed the trident between his hands, and the dwarf's eye was momentarily distracted by the flash of the steel.

No, he corrected himself. Not steel. Iron.

Something stirred in his mind. Something Chaval had told him when he first came to work for the smith.

What do I know? I know about weapons. I know how to make them. I know their strengths.

And their weaknesses.

Samustalen jumped forward. Ayshe kept his eye on the elf's trident. It was in his left hand . . . *there!* The elf switched it to his right hand. Ayshe struck hard. Not with the blade of his trident but with the wooden handle.

His blow caught the trident just below where the prongs extended from the iron shaft. The metal shattered as if it were glass, and the elf pulled his hand back with a cry. Ayshe brought his own weapon up and gave two quick strokes. Blood streamed from the elf's arm where the trident's blades had scored him.

"Two!" Harfang's voice came across the circle.

Samustalen twisted away to the other side of the arena, staring in disbelief at the hilt of his trident. He looked at the advancing dwarf, calmly reversed his weapon, and drew the sharp edge of the iron haft that protruded from the wooden handle across his hand. Then he stepped out of the circle.

Ayshe stopped, uncertain, as Harfang briskly entered the arena.

"Meet has been called, and Meet has been held," he declared. "Ayshe, son of Balar, is the victor."

The crowd dispersed to their tasks, some passing steel coins among themselves, settling bets. Ayshe started toward the stairs when an elf stopped him.

"Come with me," she said.

She led him to a small cabin filled with bottles and jars. She said very little as she expertly bandaged his wounds. The dwarf was content with silence, using the opportunity to absorb what had happened.

He had defeated his opponent, but what would happen next? He was already mistrusted by most of the elves, actively disliked by many. Would someone challenge him again? He could not hope to win a second Meet as he had won his first. Nor would it do him any good among the rest of the crew. For better or worse, he had been taken aboard the *Starfinder* for the long haul, and he would have to find a way to make his peace with Samustalen and the rest of the crew.

She seemed to read his thoughts, and she smiled at him, bright teeth flashing in a darkened face. "You'll be fine, Ayshe," the healer said as she pulled the last wrap of cloth around his arm. "Your wounds will mend in a few days. This"—she lifted a powder she had sprinkled on his wounds before bandaging them—"should ease the pain and make you heal faster." She looked over her work critically, pursing her lips. "Don't worry overmuch. I've seen worse as the result of a first Meet. Now go." She pushed him gently toward the door. "You've duties to perform."

He left the healer and slowly made his way forward to his berth. As he entered, he was startled to hear a loud chorus of greetings. The elves gathered round, slapping him on the back, punching him in the shoulder.

"A fine fight," observed one elf woman, her long hair braided and bound with a leather thong. "You move fast for a dwarf." There was no malice in the remark, merely professional appraisal.

Another elf had retrieved the remains of Samustalen's trident and was examining it. "How did you break it?" he asked the dwarf.

Ayshe took the handle and balanced the remains of the weapon in his calloused palm. "The way this was cast," he explained, "there's a weakness in the metal. Iron doesn't have the same tensile strength as steel or even bronze. It's much more brittle. If the tines strike with the flat or the edge of the blades, they'll be fine. But a blow against here, where the tines are joined with the shaft—that's the weak point in the weapon. A hard strike, precisely delivered, can shatter it."

The elf nodded. "Can you make a weapon without that weakness?"

"Oh, aye."

Chaval and Ayshe had forged many blades, including swords, daggers, and other, more exotic weaponry. The dwarf knew the process well. He took the hilt of the broken trident and examined it carefully. He could forge another weapon from it, stronger and more flexible than the one he'd broken. "The blades will hold an edge better as well," he remarked.

The elf slid off the barrel on which he'd been sitting and offered his hand. "Amanthor."

"Ayshe." The dwarf gripped it.

The others crowded round, introducing themselves and laughing. They were a far different group from the ones who had before been hostile and surly, who had watched and jeered as Ayshe had been marked by Samustalen during the Meet. They were eager to speak with him, almost falling over each other in their efforts to welcome him aboard. Their voices faded as the ladder creaked, the door opened, and Samustalen entered.

Ayshe stood, hoping desperately that their fight would not be resumed in the confined space. To his surprise, the elf walked up to him and placed a firm hand on his shoulder. Samustalen's teeth gleamed in the dim light of the cabin.

"Well done, dwarf. There are few who've bested me in a Meet." He looked about, as if seeking confirmation of his words. There were nods from the assembled elves.

"You used a trick, but one that will serve well in battle."

Ayshe still had his hackles up. "You spoke words about dwarves—" he began.

Samustalen brushed his anger aside. "Pshaw! That was but a way of provoking Meet. We do so with all who come aboard."

"Aye!" Another elf pushed her way forward. She lifted her shirt, and across the smooth brown skin of her belly, Ayshe saw three long scars, the marks of a trident. "We've all had them. A sign of our membership in Dragonsbane."

The others laughed, save for Samustalen. "Some of us," he growled at the elf woman, "have scars from more than dueling in Meet." He turned, pulling up his own shirt to show his back.

Ayshe caught his breath. The lower back and side of the elf were withered and scarred, as if caught in a fiery blast.

Samustalen laughed grimly and dropped his garment. "A present from a red dragon twenty years back."

The other elves gathered round, chattering. Some displayed scars, won either in duels or from dragon attacks. They seemed absurdly proud of their mutilations.

"So now," said Jeannara, the elf woman who'd spoken first, "Ayshe, son of Balar, you have your first scars and are welcome in our fellowship." She pointed to his bandaged arm. "With luck we'll soon find a dragon, and you'll have a chance for more."

The others nodded approval. Ayshe changed the subject.

"What about the captain? Her eyes? That scar? Did she . . . ?"

"Aye." Samustalen nodded. "She lost her eyes to the very wyrm we seek now. But we know not how she lost them. As to the scar . . ." He lowered his voice, as if afraid of being overheard.

"It was a century and more past, well before I came aboard. Harfang, Malshaunt, Feystalen, and a few more have heard the full story, but no others. They say the wyrm dropped from the sky like a bolt of lightning from the clouds. She snapped the bowsprit and sent our crew flying. But the captain defied the beast, even without her sight. She knew just where the beast was because she smelled its foul vapors."

"Nay!" another elf said. "She has sight now, as she did then, but all in her mind. She sees farther than any of us. They say she never sleeps, that she sits alone in her cabin, seeking the White Wyrm in her mind, tracking it, plotting its death."

"True enough!" another chimed in. "She can see the future in a candle and the past in a pool of still water, eyesight or no."

"I've heard," said another elf, younger by his looks, "that she speaks with the dead, that Huma Dragonsbane himself comes to her in the night and tells her how to fight the White Wyrm."

"Captain Tashara has no need of advice about how to fight dragons," said Samustalen. "From the living or the long dead. None can match her skills."

The forecastle filled with the silence of agreement. At last the elves scattered to their hammocks. Ayshe crawled into his berth. He was unused to it, and the breathing of the other elves, as well as the creaks and groans of the ship as it moved through the sea, kept him awake. Despite the promise of the healer, his arm stung beneath the bandage, and his head ached. He felt exhausted from the events of the day. It occurred to him he'd lost an entire night's sleep, something that was probably contributing to his headache.

A week earlier, he'd been content, secure in his daily routine, ready, he thought, for what the world might send his way. He'd foreseen nothing beyond the confines of Thargon until he would gradually sink into old age, surrounded by those he loved. But now he was homeless, friendless, cast upon a strange sea with companions he barely knew, bound on a quest he scarcely understood.

He shook himself, turned over, and let the motion of the *Starfinder* rock him to sleep.

CHAPTER

6

Seven days and nights had passed since Ayshe had boarded the *Starfinder*.

In that time he'd learned to make his way about the ship with tolerable ease. At first, on waking, he felt detached, as if the whole experience were a dream, framed by the dragon's attack and the death of Chaval and his family. Gradually, though, as the days passed, he found himself accepting his new situation as a member of the *Starfinder*'s crew.

All the elves, he noticed, had great pride in their craft, and in truth she was a clever ship. Ayshe knew little of the sea and its ways—even in the village he'd rarely gone on the fishing expeditions that were a daily part of the town's life—but even he could see that the *Starfinder* was everything a sailor could want: small, light, quick to turn and maneuver, and running swift before the wind.

It occurred to Ayshe that those were all highly desirable qualities in a ship of dragon hunters.

Much of the dwarf's time was spent in the smithy, where he was kept busy repairing the numerous fittings and tackle necessary to keep the ship afloat, as well as polishing armor, inspecting steel shields for rust spots, and sharpening swords, pikes, and lances to a razor's edge. He acted as the ship's fletcher as well, making arrows and fitting them with steel heads that had been forged by his predecessor. He found the armor intriguing. In his time he'd seen a fair amount of plate mail and chain mail, but what they had on the ship was of a different design altogether. It was lighter than most to lift, but it was strong and clearly would protect the wearer against many hurts. The goal of the maker seemed to have been to provide the maximum protection with the greatest maneuverability. Ayshe assumed it was of elf crafting, though some of the designs on it seemed to argue a more exotic origin.

The elves who formed his watch proved congenial companions. When their tasks were done, they often sang to one another. Sometimes the songs—mostly in Elvish—seemed raucous and cheerful, the kind of tunes sung in a rough seaside tavern. At other times they were slow and beautiful. Ayshe guessed some of those were love songs or laments.

For the most part, the elves tended to speak in Common. Ayshe realized that was both because they came from different nations—Qualinesti, Silvanesti, and Kagonesti—and because they accepted Harfang and him as equal members of the crew and had no desire to exclude the human and the dwarf from conversation. Ayshe appreciated the gesture.

Oddly enough, the elf to whom he drew closest was Samustalen, his challenger in the Meet. The elf seemed to go out of his way to make friends with the dwarf and often came and sat near the smithy while Ayshe worked, exchanging stories and information with the smith. That, in turn, helped Ayshe to gain acceptance among the rest of the crew since Samustalen was among the older sailors and was held in respect.

Feystalen, Harfang, and the ship's mage, Malshaunt, formed the captain's mess and ate with Tashara each day in the sanctity of her cabin. The other crew members messed together according to the watches they kept.

THE GREAT WHITE WYRM

Malshaunt was gaunt, even for an elf, with somewhat darker skin than normal and large, staring eyes. Ayshe, who had an inborn suspicion of magic-users, found him difficult to speak to, and Malshaunt, for his part, seemed to hold himself apart from the other elves, as if his arcane knowledge had led him to walk paths the others could not understand or appreciate. Ayshe was vaguely aware that becoming a sorcerer meant taking a test in one of the Towers of High Sorcery that lay in various parts of Ansalon, and he further knew all sorcerers were members of one of the three orders: White Robes, adherents of Solinari and good magic; Red Robes, followers of Lunitari, goddess of neutral magic; and the Black Robes, who found their evil magic source in Nuitari, the unseen black moon that ceaselessly circled Krynn.

Ayshe assumed Malshaunt was either a White Robe or a Red Robe, but since the mage wore no robes of any kind but merely the ordinary clothes of a seaman, he was not sure. Nor did he care to ask.

The role the mage's magic played in the ship's daily life became apparent to Ayshe when he realized that even in relatively calm weather, the ship's sails remained full as if by an unfelt wind that drove the *Starfinder* forward. The mage was plainly the origin of the magical wind, but how he created it remained a mystery. Malshaunt spent much of his time in his cabin. When he was on deck, he often walked on the poop deck at the rear of the ship, gazing back over her wake, watching the gulls that circled overhead.

One day, mid-morning, the ship plowed through the waves as usual. Malshaunt was in his spot, staring into the distance. He reached beneath his robes and brought out a small hunk of ship's bread. Breaking it into pieces, he began to toss it to the gulls. They screamed and fought for the novel food, shoving one another aside with their wings.

The mage laid a large crumb of bread directly before him on

the rail. The seabirds eyed it cautiously. A few approached it, only to circle away again in the air. One alighted on the rail and began to sidle forward, keeping one beady eye fixed on the mage. Malshaunt stood motionless.

The bird came within reach of the bread, and its neck darted forward. Just as swiftly, Malshaunt's hand grasped it, clutching it to him. The bird screamed in rage and kicked its feet, but its wings were firmly imprisoned beneath the mage's arm.

Swiftly Malshaunt brought out a glass vial from his robes. Then he drew a small knife. He stared at the bird's eyes, which looked back in terror. Then, in a single motion, he cut the gull's throat. A horrible gurgle came from its beak, and its blood dripped down into the vial. The mage twisted its struggling body as if wringing the blood from it. When the vial was full, he tossed the bird's broken body over the side.

The few elves who witnessed the event moved aside as Malshaunt, after corking the vial and stowing it beneath his clothes, moved past them toward his cabin. One hand was still stained red with the seagull's blood. The mage's lips were curled in a meaningless grimace.

Among the rest of the elves was a rough companionship, as among those who together have looked into the dark valley of death and for whom it holds no terrors. Occasionally, something stronger intruded.

As the moons of Krynn rode their journey through a cloudy sky, gleaming palely on a silent sea, Harfang and Jeannara stood together at the taffrail, gazing at the water.

The elf woman spoke first, gazing over the rail at the star-filled sky that rose above the calm waters. "So beautiful. It reminds me of Qualinesti."

Harfang followed her gaze. "Aye. We never have skies such as this in the north. Even when I was a lad in Palanthas, my heart always longed for the south."

The elf woman turned to look at him and moved closer to him. "Where does your heart draw you now, Harfang?" she asked. Her voice was barely more than a whisper.

The mate shook his head. "Think, Jeannara," he said. "We are travelers on a mighty quest. What place in that is there for anything else?"

She looked away. "None, as far as you are concerned." Her voice was bitter.

"And what of the difference between us? When I am an old man and in my dotage, you will still appear young and beautiful. You will live many lifetimes to my one."

"Others have overcome that obstacle," she said, still turned from him. "But you let it loom forever in the foreground of your thought. It is a sham, though. Don't you think I know the real reason? You cannot turn from *her*."

Her voice cracked, and she disappeared into the darkness. The mate stared after her then turned his face back to the moons and stars. Lunitari, the red moon of Krynn, was swinging low over the horizon, lost behind the clouds, while bright silver Solinari emerged into a clear sky and flooded everything with light.

Unseen by the mate, Malshaunt watched the scene from near the mainmast, his robes blending with the shadows. His face twisted in contempt as he watched the human; then he slipped away after Jeannara.

Malshaunt found her a few minutes later, crouching against the foremast. Her face was wet with tears, and her shoulders were shaking. He watched her silently then bent down beside her.

"He is right, you know." The mage's voice was soft, carrying only to her ears. "There's no future for an elf and a . . . *human*." It would have been difficult to pack more loathing into a single word.

"Be silent!" Jeannara was angry in an instant. "You know nothing of the matter. And who are you to tell me what to feel? What are you doing, mage, spying on me?"

Malshaunt's voice was cold. "It is my task, bo'sun, to guard this ship against any threat. I am the eyes of the captain. You'd do well to remember that."

Jeannara stared at him, her eyes hot and miserable. "Stay . . . away . . . from . . . me," she said, her voice biting off each word. She spun on her heel and vanished down the hatch.

Malshaunt looked after her for a long while.

With most of the crew, Ayshe quickly established terms of familiarity. None—save Malshaunt—seemed to possess the elf prejudice against dwarves that was common throughout Ansalon and that Samustalen had drawn on to provoke the Meet.

Qualinesti and Silvanesti elves worked side by side with no apparent friction. The dwarf was well aware of stories about the tensions between those two nations and the contempt in which each had long held the other. It surprised and impressed him that the shipmates had overcome age-old antagonisms to pursue a common foe.

The exception to that seemed to be the Kagonesti brother and sister, Samath-nyar and Otha-nyar. Their tattoos, Ayshe knew, were well in excess of the custom of their people, who sported oak leaves and other designs on their necks, cheeks, and shoulders. The Kagonesti aboard the *Starfinder*, on the other hand, were covered in colored inks from their necks to their ankles. The designs were beautiful and intricate, lines and shapes interweaving in a tangle of color. For the most part, the art was abstract, but on the rare occasions when he saw the pair unclothed, Ayshe could make out the shape of a dragon weaving over their bodies.

THE GREAT WHITE WYRM

Brother and sister, who were on opposing watches, kept themselves aloof not only from Ayshe, but from the rest of the crew as well. The other elves seemed to regard the wild elves with a touch of awe—something Ayshe found odd since he knew that before the War of the Lance, the Silvanesti had effectively enslaved many of the Kagonesti.

It was on his third day aboard ship that the dwarf came on deck for a breath of fresh, metal-free air only to find a small crowd of elves gathered on the poop deck. On the main deck, a space had been cleared, and two wooden targets had been set up. Each bore in the center a painted image of a white dragon, perhaps a little bigger than Ayshe's hand.

The Kagonesti brother and sister emerged on deck, each carrying a long bundle of cloth bound with leather straps. They undid them and lifted lances, long and slender with broad-bladed heads. To the dwarf's experienced eye, they seemed similar in make to the wyrmbarbs he kept below in his armory, and even from where he stood he could see the intricate engravings in running text on the shafts.

The elves around him began to shout.

"Five steel on the dragon's snout!"

"Ten steel on the dragon's left eye!"

"Done!"

Samath-nyar hefted the lance, ignoring the shouts. He balanced it in his hand for a moment then threw it. It flew like a shaft of sunlight and struck the target with a dull *thunk!*

Ayshe was too far away to see exactly where the blade had imprisoned itself in the painted dragon's head. An elf vaulted over the rail and ran to the target to inspect it.

"Left eye it is!" he shouted, grinning.

Otha-nyar took her brother's place, and again the shouts of the bettors came eagerly. She cast her shaft and struck the dragon's right eye. Samath-nyar said something to her in Kagonesti, half challenging, half playful, and she retorted briskly.

The dwarf noticed that each spear had attached to the haft a fine chain of closely joined links, much as he imagined was used for the wyrmbarbs. His professional eye could not identify the metal, but it was clearly strong, since both elves used it to jerk their spears from the targets and return them to their hands. They coiled the chains beside them so they would not become entangled in the throw.

Each Kagonesti made a dozen more casts, and each struck the intended target except once. Samath-nyar's next to last throw was just shy of the tip of the dragon's tail, and his backers groaned in disappointment.

Over the next few days, Ayshe saw more of these informal contests between the Kagonesti casters. They were, he realized, more than merely practice. They honed the casters' skills while providing much-needed entertainment for the crew.

Alone among the crew of the *Starfinder*, the captain kept herself isolated. Tashara remained for most of the time secluded in her cabin. When she did emerge on rare occasions, it was to pace the deck, looking to the south.

Just atop the bowsprit where it joined the hull was a small rail, with several boards nailed beneath it to provide a perilous perch. The crew referred to it as "Tashara's Nest."

Tashara emerged from her cabin and, with no assistance but her own hands, felt her way across the deck, one ear cocked to catch the smallest sounds made by the vessel as she plunged through the waves. Then, with extraordinary agility, she sprang into her nest and turned her blind face to the fore, standing fixed like some strange figurehead. She remained motionless in that pose for several hours, drenched with spray, blown by the winds.

As abruptly as she had appeared, she dismounted and retreated once more to her cabin.

Feystalen, who with Ayshe had observed her most recent performance, turned to his companion with a smile. "Our captain smells for the White Wyrm," he said.

The ship passed through a strait with land lying some miles to either side and entered Sancrist Crossing, the body of water lying between Cristyne and Sancrist Isle to the west and Northern and Southern Ergoth to the east. Sheltered from the winds, Sancrist Crossing was calm, and the crew could see the great mountains of the northern parts of Sancrist rising from the sea. Somewhere there was Mount Nevermind, home of the gnomes, and home as well to a dragon, the mad Pyrothraxus.

To the east and north were the gentle slopes of Northern Ergoth, green and peaceful. Ayshe remembered enough of his history to know that once, centuries before, Northern and Southern Ergoth had been one and joined to the rest of Ansalon. Then the gods in anger had hurled a mountain down upon the great city of Istar, far to the east, and the resulting Cataclysm had shattered the land, burying Istar forever beneath the waves, swirling the great maelstrom of the Blood Sea into life, and breaking Ergoth into two.

No signs of the violent past appeared on the gentle slopes of the land to their north. But looking south, the dwarf was reminded that dangers were still present. Though the great white overlord, Frost, was no more, the effects of his rule on the southern part of Ergoth could still be seen and felt.

Once a land of temperate breezes and flourishing communities, most of Southern Ergoth was a frozen desert thanks to Frost. The land that had once been green and covered in forest appeared on the horizon as a white frieze. A chill breeze blew from it across the decks of the *Starfinder*, and the elves shivered as they went about their tasks.

In a small, empty bay, the ship put in and sent a boat ashore for watering while others of the crew stayed behind to mend sails, weave ropes, and scrape the hull free of barnacles. Ayshe volunteered for the shore duty, as much as anything for the opportunity to stretch his legs on firm land.

They rowed past patches of ice floating in the water before the boat's keel grated on a stony beach. The elves sprang out, bows at the ready.

"What are we afraid of?" the dwarf asked Feystalen.

"Thanoi. Walrus men." The second mate scanned the frozen horizon with keen eyes. "Look alert!"

Others of the crew opened barrels they had brought and quickly began scooping snow into them, which could be melted for drinking water aboard the ship. Feystalen, his hand on his sword, prowled restlessly at the edge of the activity.

"Ayshe!" he called.

The dwarf joined him. "What is it?"

"See that?"

Fifty or sixty feet away, a dark patch was huddled against the snow.

"Come. And draw your blade." The elf led the way.

As they drew near, the patch resolved itself into the body of an ungainly creature, eight feet or so tall when standing. Dark hair fanned out across the snow, obscuring its face. The hands were horny and calloused, with rough, torn nails. The creature's skin, where Ayshe could see it, was of a yellowish hue. In one hand it grasped the haft of a broken spear.

Feystalen grunted. "Ogre!" He spat on the corpse.

"What's it doing here?" the dwarf asked. Unspoken was the question, are there likely to be any more about?

"The ogres are all over Southern Ergoth," the elf returned. "They did well under Frost's rule, and he gave them the city of Daltigoth for their own." He gestured vaguely to the south. "This might have been some quarrel among a band of ogres. Or—" He looked carefully at the creature's remains. The cause of death was two or three deep gashes in the ogre's back and neck. One had penetrated to the bone. The edges of the wounds were rough and torn.

"I thought as much. Thanoi. Those cuts were made by a tusk."

Ayshe touched the blood that had pooled beneath the corpse. "Frozen."

"Aye," Feystalen agreed, "but there's no point in taking chances." He walked back to the watering party. Ayshe, with a single backward glance, followed him.

Swiftly they rolled the barrels on board and set out for the *Starfinder*. The rowers' strokes came quickly, and the boat and its cargo glided through the waves.

"Hoy!" One of the rowers gave a shout and dropped his oar, pointing to the water. A thick furry head with gleaming ivory tusks rose above the surface, and a claw gripped the side of the longboat, cracking the wood.

"Row, damn you!" roared Feystalen from the stern. At the same time, quick as thought, he snatched up a bow and let an arrow fly. It bit into the creature's neck with a *chunk!* The thanoi gave a gurgling cry and sank below the surface.

"Pull! Put your back into it!" the mate shouted.

The oars stroked as one while the mate's keen eyes scanned the surface of the water. Another arrow was fitted to his string, ready to loose at a moment's notice.

Ayshe, sitting in the gunwale, looked over the side down into the icy waters. For a moment he could have sworn he saw dark shapes flitting beneath him, but then they were gone.

Feystalen drove them to speed even after they reached the ship, hauling the barrels on board and hoisting the longboat to its accustomed position. The thanoi, however, seemed to have drawn off, and nothing more was heard from them.

Ayshe stood watch that night and saw the stars as big as robins' eggs glitter in the velvet sky while thin clouds scudded across the moons.

"Well, dwarf?"

Ayshe started at the voice and turned to find Harfang contemplating him. As usual, when he was near the first mate, Ayshe was aware of the human's great size and his forbidding presence.

"Well, sir?"

"I hear you encountered your first thanoi today."

"Aye, sir."

"Were you frightened?"

Ayshe started. He'd told no one of his cowardice during the dragon attack, though it hung like a millstone round his neck and haunted his dreams. Yet Harfang spoke as if he were aware of the secret the dwarf bore.

"No, sir," he answered, hoping his voice sounded strong and firm.

The mate's mouth curved upward. "You should have been. Thanoi are savage and cruel. Their tusks can rip and tear flesh, and they torture their prisoners, it's said, until they beg for death. Even the ogres, whom they serve, are afraid of them."

Ayshe nodded. "The world is a bigger place than I imagined."

"Aye. Than any of us imagined." He turned to go and said over his shoulder, "Come to my cabin at next watch. There is something I would like to show you."

The dwarf presented himself promptly at Harfang's quarters at the appointed time. They were small and neatly kept.

Harfang sat on his bunk and from beneath it pulled a mass of parchment. "See you this?"

THE GREAT WHITE WYRM

The pages were stained and torn, bound together by a piece of twine strung through their corners. On some pages Ayshe could see drawings interspersed amid the mass of script, which had been composed by many different hands. Some were weak and tremulous while others were firm, graceful, full of strength and power.

"What is it?"

Harfang's hands caressed it. "This is our dragon book. All we've learned of the beasts in the many years we've been hunting them. They're the most cunning, the wisest of all the races of Krynn, for they came from the beginnings of our world, when the gods themselves were young."

He turned several pages, his lips moving as he read the words written on them. " 'The black dragons serve the Dark Queen out of fear rather than loyalty. Horns sweep back from the head. Hating all other beings, the black dragon is a solitary beast.' "

He turned a page. " 'The red dragon is the largest of all dragons, with a long, pointed snout. Skilled and cunning in battle, it desires wealth above all things.' "

He slapped the manuscript shut and handed it to Ayshe. "Study it well, and return it to me. You should know what we're hunting and how to defeat them."

Ayshe nodded. "Is there much about the storm dragon in here? The one we're chasing now?"

Harfang looked sad. "Aye, there is, as much as is known. Captain Tashara, perhaps, could say more if she would. I've written what I could find, which isn't much. Others have written from their observations. The beast breathes cold but can call down lightning from the clouds. It seems to travel between the planes, appearing from a storm. But it can only remain in the planes for a limited time before it must appear in our world. There is no pattern to its attacks; it roams Krynn at will, slaying whom it wishes. Yet always it must appear first over water. That's why we hunt it aboard a ship."

"How can it be defeated?" Ayshe asked. "If it disappears after each attack . . . ? What if it's a ghost dragon?"

The first mate gave him a disgusted look and stood. "It can be killed because it's mortal and no ghost. Don't listen to such non-sense. Study those pages, and learn the ways of dragons. There's no room here for kender tales."

The captain turned her blind face as Malshaunt entered the cabin.

"Ma'am," he acknowledged her.

She waved a greeting. "Mage. Sit."

"Thank you, ma'am." He swept aside his robes, tossed back his braid, and seated himself on the bunk.

Tashara turned back to the chart she had been fingering. "It is time we heard of another sighting," she observed.

"Indeed, ma'am." The mage glanced at the chart. "Do you know where it will be?"

She shook her head. "There is a veil sometimes, Malshaunt. At times the sight comes clearly to me, and at other times, less so." Her blind face strayed toward the cabin wall. Malshaunt followed her gaze but said nothing.

"It is as if . . ."

"As if what, ma'am?"

"As if a thin curtain has been drawn down and everything goes dim. Perhaps when the wyrm is far away in another plane it finds a means to hide itself from me."

The mage shook his head. "It can't hide from you, ma'am. Not forever, at any rate. Sooner or later you'll find its lair, or you'll meet it in battle."

Tashara turned her face to him. "Do you think so, mage? It is good of you to say so."

"I believe you will succeed, ma'am. You've devoted your life to tracking the wyrm. Victory over it is assured. It's simply a matter of time."

She nodded. "Thank you, Malshaunt. You comfort me."

Those familiar with Malshaunt would have been astonished to see his face turned toward his captain. It was full of love and devotion, mixed with the admiration of a young soldier for his captain. The expression was a fleeting one, but it flared with an intensity that rivaled a burning sun.

The mage rose to go.

"Is all well with the rest of the ship?" she asked.

The mage's mouth twisted into a sneer. "Harfang has a new pet, it would seem."

"Do you mean the dwarf?"

"Aye." Malshaunt's eyes glittered with malice, and his fingers drummed on his whip. "He's taken to schooling Master Ayshe in the ways of dragons now. The dwarf reads from the book the crew has compiled. Much good will it do him when he meets one in person."

He seemed about to say more, but the captain raised a hand. "Peace, Malshaunt. It's as well Ayshe learn more of dragons. I've no quarrel with Harfang's action."

The mage shrugged. "Whatever you say, ma'am." He turned toward the cabin door, hesitated, then looked back.

"A question, ma'am."

"Well?"

"Why *did* you take the dwarf aboard? Dragonsbane has always been elves. Never a dwarf. Never since it began, a thousand years past. Why a dwarf now? It's ill enough that we've a human aboard."

Tashara gave a slight smile. "You've never cared for Harfang," she observed.

The mage's silence was assent.

"Master Ayshe has a role to play in our unfolding drama," the captain said calmly. "Neither you nor I can see all the twists and turns ahead, but I believe his part will be an important one. You, above all others, should understand the importance of small things in large schemes."

Malshaunt shrugged. "Your sight is so much farther than mine, ma'am; I've learned not to quarrel with it. But don't expect me to like this dwarf any more than I like the man." He nodded and went out.

Tashara turned swiftly to the wall and withdrew the sphere from its hiding place. She frowned at it.

"There is something . . . something that is in the way. I cannot understand why . . ."

Ayshe spent several days studying Harfang's manuscript. Parts of it were difficult to make out. Plainly the crew of the *Starfinder* had scribbled the notes in odd moments between their duties, and at times they were so cryptic as to defy translation.

Nonetheless, the dwarf learned a great deal. He read of the great dragons of the past: of the silver dragon, Heart, who had befriended Huma and become his love; of Cyan Bloodbane, who had lived disguised among the elves before being slain by Mina during the War of Souls. He learned of the overlords, the great dragons who had come from some place without, who had imposed their reign of terror on Krynn: Malystryx the Red, Onysablet the Black, Beryllinthranox the Green, Khellendros the Blue—who loved the Dragon Highlord Kitiara and was her closest companion. He read about draconians, the horrid result of the corruption of eggs of good dragons, and of dragonspawn, created by the overlords who appeared in Ansalon shortly after the onset of the Age of Mortals.

He read notes about the chromatic dragons, servants of evil, and learned to identify each not only by its color, but also by the shape of its head and body. He studied the lore of the metallic dragons, servants of good.

At the end of a week, he returned the parchments to Harfang. The mate put him through a stern examination, and Ayshe answered most of his questions satisfactorily.

At the end of his interrogation, he emerged again on deck. It was evening, and great purple and golden clouds piled up against the horizon. When he first came aboard, Ayshe would simply have admired the beauty of the scene, but the beginning of a sailor's instinct told him that the clouds meant dirty weather ahead.

Silhouetted against the sky, her face turned south, Captain Tashara rode in her nest. As he drew nearer, Ayshe could hear her singing softly, and he stopped to listen to the words.

> *I rode the North Wind above the clouds.*
> *High on high it bore me*
> *Until the northern lands had passed*
> *In darkened fields below me.*

> *Yet these are not the lands I knew,*
> *Where once I walked unbidden.*
> *Those lands have long since passed away,*
> *And now their fields are hidden.*

> *I sought the homeland of my youth,*
> *The birthplace of my sires,*
> *Where when a child I had found*
> *The heart of my desires.*

> *The groves of trees and grassy knolls,*
> *So green and bright and vast.*
> *Now all are gone without a trace,*
> *For no things ever last.*

> *I shall not ride the wind again*
> *Or seek my youth in sorrow.*
> *My life no longer has a past*
> *But only a tomorrow.*

Her voice faded. The wind blew back the words along the ship, and Ayshe felt his throat choke with emotion. Was that what was in store for him? To cut away the past, to forget people such as Chaval and Zininia had ever existed? Would that, and that alone, bring him peace?

He stepped forward and cleared his throat. "Ma'am—"

With a single jump, Tashara leaped backward out of her nest, landing beside him. One hand rested lightly on his shoulder.

"Ayshe, son of Balar."

"Yes, ma'am?"

"You have done well, Harfang tells me. You have become one of the crew, and you have learned much of our foe."

Since he had just come from Harfang's cabin, the dwarf had cause to wonder how she knew that. "Yes, Captain." He hesitated. "Captain, I was wondering . . ."

He paused, and Tashara's hand tightened on his shoulder. Seen up close, her skin looked paper thin, and he could see the bones and muscles beneath it. "Yes, Ayshe, son of Balar? What were you wondering?"

"Your song . . ." He struggled to find the words. "Do you believe . . . the past . . . is there no going back?"

Tashara was silent for a moment. Then she turned her face to the south. Against the golden sunlight, the fine bones of her face stood out, and her skin seemed translucent. Though she was not beautiful, she had a strange, exotic beauty, the more powerful because she seemed unaware of it.

"Elves know more of the past than other races, Ayshe, because

78

we can recall it. To us, the lives of humans are fleeting, dwarves only a little less so. For our memories can stretch back half a thousand years and recall things long forgotten. So we mourn that which has passed from the world, that which can never be reclaimed.

"Do you see, Ayshe, the waters that flow past the bow of the *Starfinder?* See how our ship cleaves the waves asunder, how we pass through them and behind us they reform, rolling on under the sky as they have rolled for five thousand years and more? So the River of Time flows around us, carrying us in its bosom to some great sea where all our ends shall meet.

"You can no more reclaim the past than you can reclaim a wave or a ripple in the river. It will slip through your fingers and be gone in an instant."

Ayshe bowed his head and felt his grief well up again. That was his fate, then. To be forever burdened with a past he could not change and could not forget. The decision of an instant, taken when death raged overhead, fatefully determined his life.

"And you, Captain?" he asked, emboldened by Tashara's apparent willingness to speak. "Are there moments in your life you would relive differently? To change the past if you could?"

Tashara's fingers traced her cheeks and moved up to stroke her blind eyes. "What is done . . . is . . ." She hesitated. "There *must* be a way," she whispered more to herself than to the dwarf. "Malshaunt says there is. A heart that is true, a soul that is devoted and sacrifices everything without thought . . . surely the gods must answer her prayers." She looked at Ayshe. "The past cannot be changed, but some few souls, ones who bear a higher destiny, can avenge it. But such a thing comes with a terrible price." Again her hands touched her eyes.

"But surely——" Ayshe began. He broke off as the captain's fingers gripped his arm, biting into his flesh. Her face was turned to the wind in an attitude of alertness. She looked like a dog, sniffing the wind at the first sign of danger.

"Dragonsbane!"

The roar from her throat startled the dwarf and sent an errant gull fleeting from the mizzen shrouds.

"Attack!"

There was a clamor of footsteps on the ladders, and Harfang burst through the door of the hatch, blade in hand. Malshaunt, in a whirl of robes, sprang from another hatch onto the deck, followed by a cloud of crewmen. The mage's whip was in his hand. At the same time, Ayshe became aware of a peculiar scraping along the sides of the ship. A moment later a reptilian head, mottled green with horns flaring at the temples and a grinning mouth of razor-sharp teeth, popped above the rail.

CHAPTER

7

Tashara's cry had resounded from one end of the ship to the other. As the crew poured on deck, there were shouted orders, and for a moment Ayshe felt lost amid the clamoring confusion.

He saw, however, that what seemed aimless and anarchic was actually a carefully executed series of maneuvers, carried out with the efficiency that speaks of long, patient drilling.

Much of the crew grouped themselves in threes. Backs to each other, they stood facing outward, blades at the ready. Behind them stood a line of archers strung across the deck, and behind them, Malshaunt struck a pose, ready to hurl spells on command.

Meanwhile, a wave of the creatures slithered over the sides of the ship to group on the foredeck. Roughly humanoid in shape, the creatures stood about six feet and were covered in green and brown scales, with a tail lashing the deck behind each of them, ending in orange flukes. They were armed with barbed tridents, and unlike the tridents the dwarf and Samustalen had fought with in the Meet, their weapons appeared to be fashioned of steel or some harder metal.

The invading party moved slowly down the deck. A foul smell arose from them, like rotten fish.

81

"Loose!"

On Harfang's command, a volley of arrows flew through the air. Some few struck home, but most rebounded from the creatures' scales.

The beasts took that as a sign to attack and charged. From his position aft, Ayshe watched the fighters of Dragonsbane in action. Each triad moved as one, turning and pressing the invaders, blades slashing out, parrying the tridents' thrusts. The archers had drawn daggers as soon as the melee became general and stood ready to battle any of the creatures that broke through the line.

Malshaunt moved his hand in a complicated gesture. Three shafts of light appeared and darted from the mage's hands, slamming into the head and torso of one of the sea creatures. It grunted, gave a high, keening wail, and fell over.

"Again!" Harfang roared. Malshaunt sent him an irritated look and readied another spell. He shouted a command, and a burst of green fire came from his hand, catching one of the creatures. The sea beast's skin dripped with some caustic liquid, and it screamed in agony. It clawed at its flesh, trying to clean itself; failing that, it hurled itself over the side and splashed down into the sea. Meanwhile, the mage sent another flight of magical shafts at the beasts, but the creatures managed to dodge most of them. One hurled his trident at the mage, who flipped a hand. The weapon clanged off an invisible shield that had sprung into being before the mage.

"Forward!"

The triads began to move across the deck, rotating as they did so, each elf protecting the others in his or her group. Ayshe, watching, was reminded of a piece of gnomish machinery he had seen in his youth in which huge cogs and gears moved ceaselessly, grinding anything that was caught in them.

Tashara stood motionless beside Ayshe, her face turned to the battle, her blind eyes seemingly following every move. One of the creatures turned toward her, extended his neck, and breathed out.

Fire shot from his lips. With bare effort, the captain of the *Starfinder* moved to one side, and the cone of flame passed between her and Ayshe to shoot harmlessly out over the sea. A second later, Feystalen's sword came down on the creature's neck, and its head dropped to the deck.

The mage, meanwhile, had forsaken spells for the use of his whip. The leather cracked in the direction of a creature, who dodged to one side. Just as swiftly, the tip of the leather twisted with it and struck it on the cheek. The invader gave a horrid shriek and dropped to the ground, clutching at where the whip had struck it. Its skin began to slough away from its hands and skull. A few seconds later, its skeleton clattered to the deck.

A creature moved toward Ayshe, waving its trident menacingly. The dwarf silently cursed his lack of a weapon. From now on, he thought, I carry my axe at all times.

The creature lunged, and Ayshe barely dodged it. With no alternative and little room to maneuver, he flung himself forward at the creature and grabbed its trident. The two strove for possession of the weapon, rocking back and forth until at last the dwarf lashed out with a foot and hit the creature's knee—or at least where its knee should have been. The beast's leg gave way, and it loosed its hold on the trident.

Ayshe yanked the weapon free and with no hesitation drove it down. The blades plunged into scale-covered flesh, and the beast gave a high-pitched, whining cry. It wriggled horribly for a moment on the end of the trident; then a burst of green blood spat from its mouth and it was still.

The dwarf pulled the weapon free and looked to find another foe. In the few moments his fight had taken, the battle had progressed rapidly.

The archers had divided into two groups and, to the dwarf's

astonishment, disappeared over the sides of the ship. Meanwhile, Malshaunt's whip had destroyed another of the invaders, and others had fallen to elven blades, but most were still on their feet, though some were bleeding.

One of the oddest aspects of the fight, Ayshe thought, was that the combatants moved in silence. The creatures, except for the occasional snarl or guttural command from their leader, concentrated their fury on the elves. The members of Dragonsbane seemed to need little or no encouragement or direction to fight as a disciplined unit.

A shout came from the foredeck, and the archers climbed back over the rails. Ayshe could see what the plan had been now: the archers had scrambled along the hull, even as the ship bore on through the waves, and were poised to take the invasion from the rear. Daggers at the ready, they advanced while the triads pushed back from the opposite direction. Caught between the two forces, the creatures gave way.

The triads, as if at a prearranged signal, split apart and in a smooth, unbroken motion formed a steel-edged line that spanned the width of the ship. Steadily it advanced. Three more of the creatures fell; then another went down. Ayshe, pushing his way into the line, thrust with his trident, catching the weapon of one of the creatures as it was driving the blades down at him. He twisted and pulled, and the barbs on the ends of the blade caught his opponent's tines and jerked the weapon from the creature's claws. Ayshe threw it over his shoulder and drove his trident deep into the foe's body.

The other elves were slashing and thrusting, moving steadily forward along the deck. The attackers realized the battle was lost. One, evidently the leader, gave a wordless shriek. At the signal, his followers dived over the sides. In a moment the ship was clear of them, and Ayshe, looking back in the ship's wake, saw a glinting trident brandish above the waves and disappear. The elves remained in formation a moment longer to ensure it was not some trick of the enemy. Then, at a signal from Harfang, they broke apart, laughing, slapping one another on the back.

Harfang came up to Tashara and saluted. "We're free of 'em, ma'am," he said. "Eight of 'em dead. Not bad."

The captain nodded then, without another word, disappeared into her cabin, followed a few minutes later by Malshaunt.

"What were they?" Ayshe asked the mate.

"Seaspawn." Harfang spat over the rail. "The first ones were created by Brine, the sea dragon overlord, a decade ago. When he was slain, some thought we'd seen an end to them, but Tempest, another sea dragon, seems to know how to create them as well."

"They're not dragons?"

"Nay. They were once men. Some of 'em, at any rate." The mate spat again, and Ayshe sensed an unease about him, previously absent.

"A dragon can take a man, an elf . . . or a dwarf, for that matter. He fuses the humanoid with the shard of a draconian, and we get spawn."

The two walked to where the crew had piled the bodies of the spawn. Harfang drew his sword and with a single blow struck off the head of one of the corpses. He repeated that until a row of eight spawn heads lay before him. At his nod, the elves tossed the headless bodies over the side to splash in the rushing waves.

The heads, much to Ayshe's astonishment, the elves took to the taffrail and spiked there, so their sightless eyes looked back along the path the *Starfinder* cut through the waves.

The dwarf shook his head. He had heard of the savagery of battle, but that action went beyond it. There was something cold blooded—almost barbaric—about the sailors' actions. Blood from the severed heads dripped slowly from them, staining the deck. Ayshe noticed other, older stains beneath.

Harfang saw the dwarf's expression of disgust but said nothing.

He returned to his bunk, and the other elves scattered to their various tasks.

Malshaunt came on deck an hour or so after the battle. He inspected the spiked heads carefully and collected some of the blood that dripped from them in a vial. Harfang watched him in silence.

The mage turned to the mate at last and gave him a mirthless smile. "Do you enjoy this sort of thing?" he asked.

Harfang did not answer.

"I dare say it gratifies some urge humans have," the mage continued. "The need to see other beings bleed. An impulse to kill anything you don't understand."

"I didn't see you hesitate during the fight," the mate growled.

Malshaunt shrugged. "No. I'm perfectly willing to defend myself. But I don't wallow in my opponent's blood afterwards. This"—he gestured at the heads—"this is something I doubt most elves would do if left to themselves."

Harfang came close to the mage. His voice was low and furious. "Are you not willing, Malshaunt, to use the blood of others to further your own ends? Would you prefer to stand back away from the fighting and let others die to protect you?"

The mage did not back away. His voice was pitched equally low. "I'm a faithful servant of the captain, Master Mate. I serve her above all others on this ship. I've served her longer than anyone else, and she trusts and relies on me. You'd do well to remember that ere you speak to me like that again."

He turned on his heel and walked away.

THE GREAT WHITE WYRM

Next morning, as Ayshe was putting the finishing polish on an armored breastplate, he heard a shout from above decks.

"Ship ho!"

Again there was the clatter of feet along passageways and up ladders. Ayshe emerged to find the ship swathed in a thick, cold fog, whose fingers pried beneath his garments. The elves poured onto the deck, staring at the sea, seeking the vessel.

"There!" Samustalen pointed to starboard. The silhouette of a boat was outlined against the fog.

Feystalen snapped orders. Archers concealed themselves behind the blindage—removable screens that lined the sides of the foredeck that would be dropped down when battle with another ship was joined. Other elves picked up long grapples with which to bind the two ships together in the event of a fight. Everyone loosened their swords and waited as the *Starfinder* cautiously approached the ship.

Harfang joined Feystalen at the wheel. "Hail them," he instructed his junior.

"Ahoy!" Feystalen shouted through cupped hands. "Ship ahoy!"

There was no answer. The *Starfinder* was close enough to see that the other boat was much smaller. Nets hanging by her side proclaimed her a fishing vessel. They drew closer still, and Ayshe could see drops of dew glistening on the strange ship's ropes.

"Unship the craft!"

The longboat was swung out over the water and lowered—on the opposite side of the *Starfinder* from the mystery ship to avoid possible arrows.

Feystalen called out names. "Jeannara, Lannlathsar, Ayshe, Omarro, Alyssaran, Samath-nyar. Archers, arrows on string. Let's go."

The crew members named descended the ship's side and took their places. Two took up oars; the rest held weapons alert and ready for battle.

They crossed the space between the ships with a few sure strokes and with no sign from the fishing boat. Ayshe began to breathe more calmly. Possibly the crew had abandoned ship for some reason, leaving her to drift in the fog.

The mist seemed to thicken as they boarded the boat. Ayshe could barely see the forms of his companions as they made their way across the deck, which was covered with salt-crusted fishing tackle. There was an odd smell in the air—tangy, yet sickeningly sweet. The fog was so dense, Feystalen ordered them to light torches to guide their way.

Toward the front of the boat, a small cabin door stood closed. Feystalen halted before it and stared at the planking under his feet. His shout, muffled by the fog, brought the others running. He pointed, wordless.

From beneath the closed door of the cabin, a rivulet of blood curled. It had dried into a thick, viscous pool, and its surface gleamed in the light of Feystalen's torch.

Jeannara and Ayshe put their shoulders to the door. It gave way with little effort. Ayshe looked within and staggered back, retching. He clawed his way to the rail and vomited his breakfast into the indifferent sea.

Several of the elves seemed queasy as well, but they suppressed it. Ayshe was alone at the rail, his stomach cramped, his eyes burning from that first horrific sight.

After a few minutes he felt well enough to rejoin his companions as they stood in the open doorway.

The crew of the ship—a dozen of them, as best could be guessed—were piled inside the cabin. Several had been decapitated. Others had been mutilated in various ways: arms cut off, eyes gouged out, noses removed. One man had been entirely stripped of his skin and was no more than a horrid caricature outlined in bone and muscle. All the expressions that could be deciphered on their faces were of great pain.

THE GREAT WHITE WYRM

The wounds on the body were various, but most seemed inflicted by sharp, pointed blades. Ayshe's eyes went to a man whose naked back showed three deadly piercings, and his mind leaped back to the tridents borne by the seaspawn that had attacked the *Starfinder*.

"Yes," Feystalen said, echoing Ayshe's thought. "This was spawn." He looked around in disgust. "I can smell their foul stink here still. The same band that attacked us, I should guess."

A cry from Jeannara drew them forward. She was kneeling over an elongated body covered with green and brown scales. The spawn lay with the sword that had slain it still thrust through its chest.

Swiftly they completed their investigation. Several barrels and boxes of food lay untouched below deck, and the elves loaded them into the longboat for transport to the *Starfinder*. Samath-nyar took oil from the fishing boat and splashed it over the deck and the bodies in the cabin. He wrapped a rag around a spar, soaked it in oil, and nodded to Feystalen. "Everything ready, sir."

"All hands to the boat! Stay sharp!"

The elves and Ayshe clambered into the longboat and pushed off. Feystalen held the unlit torch's end out to Ayshe. "Smith?"

Ayshe fumbled in his pouch for the tinderbox he always carried. The damp mist made it hard to strike a spark. At last the oil-soaked torch caught and flared.

Standing, Feystalen threw the torch at the fishing boat. Its wavering flame arced up then disappeared in the fog. A few heart-beats later, a greater light sprang up, and the crackle of spreading flames reached their ears.

The mist smelled of burning wood and something else to which Ayshe resolutely closed his mind. The elves pulled steadily for the *Starfinder*, leaving behind a lonely pyre on an empty sea.

PART
2

CHAPTER

8

"It was spawn, ma'am."

Feystalen stood with his feet akimbo, his hands behind his back, looking like an errant schoolboy reporting to his teacher. Before him in the narrow confines of the captain's cabin, Tashara, Malshaunt, and Harfang were arrayed.

"You're sure?" the mate asked.

Feystalen related the discovery of the spawn's body.

Malshaunt stirred. "Why did you not bring it back aboard the *Starfinder?*" he asked.

Feystalen was taken aback. "It was dead and foul. We had no use for it," he replied.

"*I* might have had a use for it, Second Mate. Did that thought never occur to you?" Malshaunt pressed his hands together until the blood left them and they were white as paper. "How many times must I explain this to all of you. I require certain things, things that can often be obtained from dragons and their kind when they are dead—"

"We're warriors and sailors," Feystalen snapped, "not your damned errand boys or carrion crows! Next time, come on the boat yourself and collect your own things. I've no urge to pick over the corpse of a seaspawn because you *think* you *might* use a bit of its ear or a piece of its tongue."

Malshaunt turned away, his mouth still compressed in irritation.

Tashara spoke. "Did you see any signs of more of the spawn nearby?"

"No, ma'am. We kept a sharp eye out, but they were nowhere. I'd expect they were the same ones that attacked us the other day, in which case they're probably lying low somewhere, licking their wounds."

The captain nodded, and Harfang dismissed his subordinate. He turned back to Tashara. "Ma'am, we know that in the past where we've found bands of seaspawn we've sometimes found—"

"Yes, Harfang," the captain interrupted. "I know. I can feel it. The wyrm must be somewhere close." She rose and bent over the chart on the table. The mate and the mage arranged themselves at her sides as she spread a hand over the map, moving slowly and delicately as she probed. At last her finger dropped to the parchment.

"There. Make for that spot."

The day after their discovery of the fishing boat, Harfang stopped Ayshe as the dwarf was taking his evening stroll along the deck. The weather was damp and drizzly. The dwarf had moved to the foredeck to avoid the stench from the rotting seaspawn heads.

"Come!" the mate growled. He led the way across the deck to the taffrail and gestured to the heads. "Look!"

It was not a pretty sight. Seabirds had plucked away the eyes and some of the flesh. On some of the heads, bits of skull gleamed white. The lifeless heads had sagged on their spikes and looked pathetic rather than menacing.

Harfang stared at them. Ayshe followed his lead, trying not to feel sick. Around them the gray mist swirled and eddied.

"Murderers!" Harfang's voice cut through the fog like a knife through warm butter. "Murders of the innocent, that's what they are! Them and all spawn of dragons." He turned to face Ayshe. "There's no room for sentiment when you're fighting such creatures. You saw yesterday what they're capable of. Once"—he stepped forward and brushed one of the heads with his fingertips—"once this was a man. Once this was a baby, cooing in his mother's arms. Once he ran and played with other little boys in the sunlight. Once these lips kissed a girl and made her promises beneath Solinari. No more.

"When he became a spawn, he ceased to be human, and you should harbor no feelings toward this creature save revulsion."

The dwarf shrugged and tried not to think too deeply about the mate's unsettling words. "But why is it necessary to spike these heads here?"

"To remind us of what we're fighting." Harfang bent, his face inches from Ayshe's. "We fight," he whispered, teeth clenched. "We don't fight dragons for adventure. We don't fight them for gold. We don't fight them for revenge. We fight and kill them and their filthy offspring because they're evil. Because they ought to be wiped off the face of Krynn. And as long as dragons remain, we of Dragonsbane will hunt and kill them."

He drew his thumb along the spawn blood that had accumulated on the deck, slightly damp from the rain that was falling. Then he drew a line down his forehead, from the crest of his brow to the middle of his nose. The mark, a dirty greenish brown, gave him, somehow, a slightly feral look. He sent the dwarf a final glare and stalked away.

Jeannara watched the mate as he took his leave. A pace or two behind her, Malshaunt was also watching, his face solemn as usual. But in his eyes was a gleam of malice. Though it was raining, none of the rain seemed to fall on the mage, and his robes, face, hands, and hair were bone-dry.

Malshaunt glanced at Jeannara and said lightly, "It seems Master Harfang's evening sermon is done."

"He cares!" the elf retorted. "At least, Malshaunt, he doesn't stand in the shadows, sneering at everything and everyone. He cares about Dragonsbane and what we stand for. That makes him a worthy companion."

The mage raised an eyebrow. "Forgive me," he said mildly. "I'd no idea companionship was what you were looking for. I'd supposed . . ."

Jeannara faced him, her tone icy. "What *did* you suppose, mage?" she asked.

"I?" Malshaunt held up a slender hand in a deprecating gesture. "No, no. It would be presumptuous of me to suppose anything about companionship between an elf and a . . . man. After all, it could be so much worse."

"What do you mean?"

"You could seek companionship from our *dwarf*." He spoke of Ayshe, still within hearing distance, as one would of a despised mongrel dog.

Jeannara's face reddened, but she made no reply.

Malshaunt said thoughtfully, "You are mistaken, though, if you think I do not care. I care very much." His eyes gazed into the distance at the line between sea and sky, as if they were seeing things hidden from ordinary eyes.

"For what? For what do you care?"

The mage returned his gaze to the bo'sun, his expression cold again. "For that which I think sometimes the rest of you have forgotten. Rest assured, Jeannara, *my* devotion is unwavering." He turned on his heel and disappeared.

Nights turned colder as the ship slipped south over the dirty gray sea. The sun rose lower and set sooner. It was dark by mid-afternoon. The stars swung slowly across the night sky, and Ayshe, looking up at them, wondered what strange happenstance had mingled his destiny with that of the *Starfinder.*

They kept close enough to land to survey the coast of Southern Ergoth as it slid by. Harfang and Feystalen studied it constantly with the aid of a spyglass, and the keenest-eyed of the elves—usually the two Kagonesti—were sent aloft into the shrouds during the hours of darkness. Harfang reported regularly to Tashara as they approached the spot she had indicated. High above the deck in the crow's nest, as the ship pitched uneasily in the waves, the Kagonesti elves stared unblinkingly into the darkness.

It was on one such moonless night, a fortnight after their battle with the spawn, that Ayshe, slumbering uneasily in his hammock, was roused by the distant cry of the Kagonesti lookout.

He hastened on deck, massaging his sleep-dulled eyes. Off to the east, a soft glow lit the horizon.

Samath-nyar, who had the watch, slid nimbly to the deck in front of Harfang and saluted the mate. "A village is burning, sir," he reported.

"It might be pirates."

"It might be, but that's unlikely this late in the year."

Harfang nodded and turned to Feystalen. "Very well. Put in and cast anchor. At first light we'll unship the boat and investigate." He knocked on Tashara's cabin door and, with Malshaunt in his wake, vanished inside.

"Watch reports a burning village, ma'am. Just like the other. It would seem we've found the trail again."

Tashara nodded. Her figure was erect and tall as she paced the narrow confines of the cabin, quivering with excitement.

"Very well. We put in here." She turned to Malshaunt, put a hand on his robed arm, and squeezed gently. "We are close now, mage."

"Aye, ma'am." He stepped back from her touch as if burned. His lips were bloodless. In the long years of their service together, Harfang did not ever remember seeing the mage so agitated, so moved by anything. Once he considered it, he could not remember the captain herself ever touching the mage before.

He did not dwell on the thought. There were too many things to do.

To sleep was impossible. The crew stood on deck, watching as the ship drew inland. Samustalen crouched at the bow, calling off soundings to Otha-nyar, who skillfully guided the vessel closer to shore. Finally the ship was luffed, the capstan bars were unshipped, and the crew lowered the great anchor. Down it came slowly, with a creaking of ropes and a great splash as it entered the water. The longboat, once again, was swung out.

Captain Tashara emerged from her cabin. Ayshe noticed she wore the same clothes in which he'd last seen her and fleetingly wondered if she ever changed them.

"Harfang?"

"Ma'am?"

"Who are you sending ashore to investigate the burning?"

The mate glanced over the assembled crew. "Samath-nyar. Riadon. Jeannara. Samustalen. Feystalen. Me."

She shook her head. "Nay, Harfang. Stay with the ship. I wish to go ashore myself this time."

"But, ma'am—"

"No buts, First Mate. Malshaunt will accompany me." She

started toward the boat and stopped. "And send the smith."

Ayshe felt a sudden lurch in his stomach. If he was going to see sights ashore such as the one he'd seen on the fishing boat, he was content to remain with the ship.

Harfang frowned. "With respect, ma'am, he has plenty of duties aboard the ship. No need to—"

Tashara lifted a hand. "I daresay you are right, Harfang. Nonetheless, I wish him to come ashore with me." She smiled, an expression frosty as snow drops during Aelmont. "Come, old friend. Surely after so many years, you owe me a little indulgence."

The mate looked torn between embarrassment and anger at having his orders contradicted before the crew. "Aye, ma'am," he growled. "Smith! Make ready to go ashore with the party. The rest of you, look lively!"

As the longboat's oars stroked the waters of the bay, the prow pushed through debris floating in the waves. Bits of lumber, splintered as if torn apart by a titanic explosion, bumped the hull of the boat as she approached the shore. Tashara sat in the stern, hand on the tiller, making straight for the village, as easily as if she had sight.

Malshaunt sat tall, dark, and enigmatic. But from time to time, his glance shifted from shore to the figure of the captain. With his left hand, he ceaselessly stroked his right forearm just above the wrist.

The shore was wreathed in smoke and fog. Tashara used the smell of burning to guide the boat to its destination. Through the mist they could see figures running to and fro. It reminded Ayshe of the reception his own village had given the sailors of Dragonsbane, and something caught in his throat.

THE GREAT WHITE WYRM

Tashara grounded the boat expertly and sprang out, followed by the mage. She seemed imbued with a strange energy, and the crew followed her without a word.

"Hail!" she cried in a strong, loud voice. "Hail! I am Tashara of the *Starfinder*. What village is this?"

Silence greeted her.

"I am Tashara of the *Starfinder*. I come in peace. What village is this?"

From somewhere, a stone rattled, and someone coughed softly. Then, from behind a wall, a dark face rose. "This *was* the village of Horend." The man stepped into the open and eyed them. "Elves!" His voice bore all the contempt that could be packed into the single word.

Tashara ignored the implied insult. "Have you seen a dragon? Gray as a storm cloud? Lightning framed? Bending from sky to earth?"

The man stared at her, rage gathering in his eyes. "Do you see *this?*" he roared. "*This* is your dragon's work!" He turned, and from other crannies and cracks in the rubble, ragged scarecrows crawled out. Some were bloodstained, some soot covered; all had wide, dark-rimmed eyes full of horror that stared at the elves.

Tashara turned her blind head from side to side, as if listening to them gather. "From where did this dragon appear?" she asked calmly. "From the sky, aye, but from where? North, south, east, west? Tell me that."

The spokesman shrugged his indifference and pushed out a finger to the north. "There. Out of a clear blue sky. Next minute it filled with clouds, and then it came down on us." His hot eyes searched Tashara's face. "Now, what do you know of this dragon?"

"And when it left?" The elf captain's face was impassive, but her voice bore an underlying urgency. "Which way? In which part of the sky did it vanish?"

"Half our people are gone! Our homes are laid waste!" The headman reached into the crowd and plucked out a dirty-faced little girl with tangled hair and tear-swollen eyes. "Where are her parents? Her brother? Her grandfather? Where have they gone?" He hugged the girl to him fiercely. "The beast shattered our homes. Our hearth fires took flame and joined in the destruction. The fire has burned and smoldered now for two days. We have nothing left. Do you understand? Nothing!"

He pitched his voice to mock Tashara's. "Where did it go? Which way?" Then he practically growled, "Why should we care?"

"Which way?" Tashara's voice gave nothing away.

The headman turned a sullen face south. "That way. It vanished in a thunderclap, drawing fire from the heavens after it." He turned for confirmation to a pathetic figure who served as his deputy.

"Aye." The younger man nodded. "It swept over the village. Its breath blasted our people with cold, but it seemed as if it could also call fire from the sky. It raged for ten minutes, perhaps more. When our last building fell, it hunted those it could find in the open. But it must have tired of the sport. We heard it give a mighty cry but from farther away. A short while later, the sky was clear." His voice still held traces of terror. "What was it? I've heard of the great dragon overlords but never of such a beast as this. It must be a ghost that can vanish into the wind."

A frozen smiled touched Tashara's lips. "No ghost. Oh, no ghost indeed."

"Aye!" snapped the mayor. "A ghost could hardly have done this." He gestured at the destruction around them. "But perhaps it was something brought by you elves. We hear, even here at the edge of the world, what goes on in the rest of Ansalon. We know that you pulled down your houses about you in Qualinost when Beryl, the great green, died. We know you've been driven out of Silvanesti. Now, perhaps, you visit your anger upon the rest of Krynn by summoning up a beast such as this." His eyes were black with suspicion.

Tashara made no answer.

After a moment, Malshaunt stepped forward and faced the mayor. "Your talk is baseless and foolish. We must examine your village," he said calmly. "It may provide clues to the whereabouts of the wyrm we are hunting."

The mayor looked him up and down. "A magic-user, eh. Can your magic fix *this?*" He gestured to the ruin of his village.

Malshaunt looked around idly. "More magic than I have at my command would be required to make this place livable," he said. "My advice is to seek new homes elsewhere."

"Now? With winter coming on? How do you suggest we do that?" demanded the mayor.

Malshaunt ignored the question. "We will examine your village." None of the rest of the company moved.

After a moment, the mayor spat on the ground before the captain and the mage. "Elves!" he snorted. "If I didn't know better, I'd think you still ruled your kingdoms of Qualinesti and Silvanesti the way you talk. But no, now you're just vagabonds, no better than some and worse than many." He threw up his hands. "Fine. Look around. Much good may it do you." He turned his back on the mage and strode off. The other villagers followed him, turning to cast sour glances at Dragonsbane.

The elves walked slowly through the trail of rubble that marked the former site of the village of Horend. Some townsfolk followed them. Others were too busy cleaning away debris or were wrapped in sorrow and ignored the newcomers.

"You're not an elf!"

Ayshe looked around. The little girl, only a few inches shorter than he, was walking by his side, staring at him.

"You're too short. And elves don't grow beards. My pa says that."

Ayshe nodded. "That's right. I'm a dwarf."

"A dwarf?" The girl's eyes grew big. "Really? I've never seen a dwarf. I've seen elves before. Some came here last year to trade with us, but Ma and Pa wouldn't let me talk to them. Where do dwarfs live? Where are you from?"

"From—" Ayshe caught himself, realizing he didn't have a home anymore. "From far away, my girl. What's your name?"

"Lara. What's yours?"

"Ayshe."

"That's a funny name. Like what we sweep out from the hearth in the morning. Ma told me I was named for a very famous person. She was a great general who beat a whole army of evil soldiers and made them crown her queen. And she ruled for a hundred years in peace and goodness and then she went up into the sky and lived there."

Ayshe momentarily wondered at the irony of elf-hating humans who named their daughter after the great elf hero Lauralanthalasa, the Golden General, Companion of the Lance.

Lara looked doubtfully at Ayshe. "Is that where Ma and Pa are now? In the sky? With Jaxal and Grandpa?"

The dwarf blinked. "Yes, I'm sure that's where they are. In fact, they're probably watching you right this instant."

She smiled. "Well, I've been very good. I've hardly cried at all today."

"There's naught wrong with crying when you're sad, Lara. Sometimes crying can make us feel better." Ayshe felt his lips burning as he said those words and knew that for him it was untrue.

"But just now," he told the girl, "I think what your ma and pa would like is for you to tell me what you remember about the dragon attack."

Lara looked grave. "I was in school. Teacher was making us recite, when we heard a big thunder. Teacher went to the window to see what was going on. Then there was another thunder, an even bigger one. Then I don't remember too much. Someone pulled something off me, and I saw the school had fallen down. That's when I saw the . . . the . . ." She hesitated.

"The dragon?"

She nodded. Her brown eyes met his. "I was *scared*. I was really scared. So I ran, but when I got home, it wasn't there anymore. And I called for Ma and Pa, but they didn't answer." Her voice cracked, and she melted into the dwarf's shoulder in a storm of tears.

Tashara and Malshaunt walked through the village together. As usual, the mage walked a step or two behind the captain. The other elves had been detailed to make a complete search of the rubble, looking for anything that might give a further clue to the White Wyrm and its whereabouts.

The captain turned abruptly and faced Malshaunt. "Why is it, do you suppose, mage," she asked, "that in all our time pursuing the wyrm we have never found a scale, never a shred of skin, a piece of claw?"

The mage shrugged. "The beast's insubstantiality is among its greatest challenges, ma'am. Perhaps when it fades into the planes, whatever it leaves behind in its attacks fades as well."

She shook her head. "No. There is something more. But I know that if only I could collect *something* . . ."

"Would that help us track it, ma'am?"

"I am sure of it. A dragon's scales have a power beyond their owner, sometimes. That is why we search these sites so carefully. There must eventually be something."

Ayshe rejoined his companions, having left Lara with a village woman who promised to look after her. The elves were standing by their boat conferring while some of the townspeople looked on.

"It continues south," Malshaunt said.

Tashara nodded. "And so we follow." She turned to Ayshe. "What news?"

The dwarf shrugged. "The little girl said she felt overwhelming fear when the beast attacked. It seems natural enough, this fear, but that's mostly what she remembers."

Tashara kept her face toward him. "And what of you, dwarf?"

Ayshe felt his face redden. "What of me?"

"When the dragon attacked your home, weren't you frightened?"

"What does that have to do with anything?" he almost shouted.

"Dragonfear." The captain's voice was unchanged. "All dragons inspire it. This one more than others, it would seem. It can paralyze the will of even the bravest warrior."

She surprised the dwarf by putting a hand on his shoulder, as though comforting him, then turned to the other elves. "We return to the *Starfinder*."

The crew busied themselves with the longboat, preparing to cast off.

"One moment!" The mayor stepped forward and addressed Tashara. "That ship—no doubt you have supplies? Food?"

The captain's face was expressionless. "Well?"

The mayor gestured around him. "Look at these people—or listen to them, since you can't see them. They've lost everything."

Tashara's voice was cold. "I have been in many dragon-devastated towns," she told the mayor. "Think you not that you are the first."

"Winter is coming on," he replied evenly. "We're midway

through Hiddumont. Soon H'rarmont will be upon us. There will be ice and snow. We've no shelter, no food, no fresh clothing." He paused for a reaction from Tashara and got none. "Stay!" he said, his voice rising. "Help us. If you're chasing this thing, more power to you, but stay and help us through the winter. Take up your quest again in spring."

Tashara ignored him. "Jeannara! Are you ready?"

Ayshe stepped in front of the captain. The picture of Lara's tear-streaked face rose before him. "Captain, perhaps we could do as he asks. At least let's leave some food for these people."

Malshaunt interposed himself between Ayshe and Tashara. "Your captain has given her orders, dwarf!" he snapped. "Now obey them!"

"Jeannara!" Tashara gave no sign she had heard Ayshe's appeal. She stepped around him toward the boat.

The mayor spoke bitterly. "Never mind, dwarf. What do she and her tame mage care if we starve? Like all elves—stiff-necked sons and daughters of darkness! It's just as well a dragon fell on their city. They came crawling for aid, but now they refuse it to us. And why? Because we're humans, not stinking elves!"

The mayor's baiting was having some effect on the *Starfinder*'s crew. Jeannara, Samustalen, and others gave him harsh glances. Tashara, however, continued to ignore his words. The boat had been drawn into the shallows, and she splashed toward it.

The mayor gave a yell of fury. Reaching to his side, he drew a saber and lunged after the elf. Tashara spun at his approach, and Ayshe saw the blade of a knife glittering in her hand as the human's momentum carried him into her.

He stopped, arms outflung. The saber fell from his out-stretched hand into the water. From the watching townsfolk came a soft, horrified moan.

Ayshe jumped to the man's side as he sank to his knees, blood pouring from the stab wound in his chest. Tashara looked straight ahead, motionless, the bloodstained blade still in her hand. Then she bent her head toward her victim.

The mayor coughed into the silence and spat a gob of blood. "I . . . you . . ." He bent almost double, his face paper white.

Tashara shook her head as if unaware of what had happened. The other elves stood frozen.

"I . . . curse you . . . elf!" the man gasped. "In the . . . name of . . . Habbakuk . . . the Blue Phoenix . . . I curse you!" He bent forward again and fell stiffly into the shallow water.

Ayshe stood still, hands stained red.

"Kill them!"

The crowd raced forward. A stone thudded off the boat. Another struck Feystalen's leg, eliciting a cry of pain. Malshaunt brought up his hand, pointing at the stone thrower with fingers twitching in a magical incantation, but Feystalen caught his wrist.

"No!" he shouted. "Enough!"

The mage's face blazed with anger. He pushed the mate from him. His mouth moved to begin a spell.

"Feystalen! Malshaunt! Come!" Tashara's voice cut through the confusion. The mate turned and ran for the boat. Malshaunt followed him.

The company tumbled into the longboat. Jeannara and the Kagonesti grabbed the oars and stroked for dear life. As the crowd continued to hurl rocks, sticks, and anything that came to hand, Tashara sat tall and unmoving. Her knife had disappeared back into her clothing, and her blind eyes were turned toward the *Starfinder*.

Ayshe leaned over the side to wash the blood from his hands. Behind him he could hear faintly the cries, the curses, the moans. He could no longer see the mayor's crumpled body lying in the water at the edge of the sea.

"We should have helped them!" he said disconsolately. "We should have—"

"Silence!" Tashara rapped out the word.

THE GREAT WHITE WYRM

Not another syllable was spoken until just before they had regained the ship. As the bulk of the hull loomed over them, Malshaunt leaned forward to whisper in Feystalen's ear. Ayshe could not hear what the mage said, but from the expression on the mate's face, it was not to his pleasure.

Ayshe's heart pounded uncomfortably in his chest. They regained the deck, and the captain vanished into her cabin. The crew hoisted the sails, and, under a steady wind, the ship drew away from the sad, shattered coast.

CHAPTER

9

"We should have helped them!"

Ayshe gave an extra vigor to his polishing of a sword. As the weather grew colder and damper, the weapons carried by Dragonsbane needed more attention, and Ayshe spent the majority of his days below deck, hard at work in his smithy and armory.

It was four days since the *Starfinder* had left behind the ruins of Horend. When the dwarf closed his eyes at night, he could still see the rush of blood from the mayor's chest, Tashara's knife protruding from his chest. Ayshe could not sleep for thinking of Lara and her probable fate as the long, cold winter of Southern Ergoth closed in. Throughout the day, his eyes burned and his legs and arms felt as if they were fashioned of lead. But each night when he climbed wearily into his hammock and tried to let the motion of the ship rock him to sleep, a pair of bright brown eyes in a dark face rose before him.

Samustalen shifted on his stool, and the bowl of his pipe glowed red. "What could we do?" he asked, his tone reasonable. "We couldn't spare supplies; we've only enough for ourselves to last the next month or two. We couldn't take them with us. There's not enough room aboard the ship. We couldn't stay there. We would have been more mouths to feed."

"We could have stayed long enough to help build them some shelters for the winter," the dwarf retorted.

"And lost track of the White Wyrm? Not likely while Tashara commands the *Starfinder*."

"Your captain's revenge," Ayshe said angrily, "means more to you than the lives of . . ." He paused and stared at Samustalen. "A village of humans."

Samustalen shrugged. "What does it matter if they are humans? They'll survive—most of them."

"Would Tashara have been so quick to leave if they'd been elves?"

Samustalen didn't answer.

Ayshe seated himself behind a grinding wheel and pumped it into action with his foot. "Because they were *humans*. Not *elves*," he repeated, banging the words with his strokes.

Samustalen leaned forward. "Look, Ayshe. You're not an elf, but you're not a human either. Why do you care so much? Humans are short lived and short memoried. Death doesn't mean as much to them as it does to an elf or a dwarf. Besides, for how many years did we elves rule Silvanesti and Qualinesti? We are the lords of Krynn! Not humans!"

Ayshe shook his head. "You don't know what you're talking about. I've lived among these people. They took me in when they could have turned me away."

The elf snorted. "And from what you've told me, you slaved for them day and night. 'Took you in'! Of course they did! And got an unpaid servant!" He knocked out his pipe. "Trust me, my friend. Don't put yourself out for humans. You're better than they are. The elves have helped them before, and where are we today? Our cities destroyed, our treasure scattered, and our people penniless wanderers across the face of Krynn." He leaned forward. "I was in a human city once—Palanthas. And do you know how humans looked at me? As if I were no one . . . less than no one. One boy called me 'dirty elf' and threw stones at me, while other children laughed. Do you want me to care what happens to them?" He gave a short bark of laughter and stood.

"Trust me, Ayshe. A world with a few less humans will only be a better world." He went out, leaving Ayshe brooding over his grinding stone.

◆ ◆ ◆ ◆ ◆

Malshaunt paced his cabin, fingers drumming restlessly. Rain slashed against the panes of the windows that looked out over the turbulent sea.

Before him was a small conch shell, magically enhanced, through which he could listen to any conversation anywhere on the ship. The shell was kept a secret from even Tashara, though the mage was never quite sure how much remained hidden from the captain. As her oldest companion, he knew her best of any of the crew, but even to him there were parts of her that were mysterious.

He had been listening through the shell to Ayshe's conversation with Samustalen. The dwarf's speech had confirmed to the elf mage all his prejudices against dwarfs; despite their reputation as tough, dour fighters, they were, at bottom, weak and foolish. It made it all the more galling that Tashara had taken the dwarf aboard. For some strange reason, she had taken a special interest in the dwarf, even *speaking* to the creature on occasion. He speculated on the possibility of the dwarf having an accident—a fall from the rigging, for instance, artfully arranged—but he dismissed the idea as too dangerous. Malshaunt didn't dare visit any injuries on Ayshe. Somehow the dwarf fit into the captain's plans for the White Wyrm, and it irritated the mage that he did not understand how.

The beating of the rain against the windows slackened and died. The rocking of the ship slowed. Malshaunt had been so long at sea that he scarcely noticed rough weather or calm. He paced without ceasing. The cabin was tiny, with books scattered here and there; several shelves held a collection of oddities magicians would have instantly recognized as spell components. A worn path across the floor showed the mage's accustomed route when pacing.

He turned to brooding on the insult he had received from Feystalen. For the mate to have touched him—*touched him*—was unbearable. Malshaunt was Silvanesti, while Feystalen had come from Qualinost before the city's fall. Though the elves might unite against humans and other lesser breeds, the antagonism between the elf sects remained smoldering not far beneath the surface.

In fact, none of the crew were worthy of their quest, the mage thought. None understood its magnitude. None understood the true heart of Tashara, though even she was capable of occasional weakness, such as her adoption of the insufferable Harfang. Malshaunt had spent many hours wondering at the foolishness of *that* decision.

The sound of the wind faded. The ship's motion slowed. The mage looked up.

Something was different.

Something was wrong.

His conversation with Samustalen made Ayshe even more restless and uninterested in sleep. He climbed to the deck, which was still damp and dripping with the recently fallen rain, and stood on the foredeck, breathing the air which had turned cold, still thick though dry.

Looking at the constellations overhead through the slowly parting clouds, he sought out Reorx of the forge, god of the dwarves, worshiped by all smiths.

Why? he prayed. Why did you send me on this journey? Was it

to teach me the futility of vengeance? To show me how meaningless are the lives of mortals? To show me that no one can understand the ways of the gods? Why?

The stars gazed back through widening gaps in the clouds, cold and silent. Ayshe shivered. An oppressive feeling settled over him that something somewhere was wrong.

Harfang and Feystalen walked across the deck. The first and second mates halted by the rail. Both produced pipes and lit them. A whiff of the fragrant smoke passed over the sea and drifted aimlessly. The elves were silent for a space; then Harfang spoke.

"The night seems to go on forever out there." He gestured toward the invisible horizon.

"Aye." Feystalen nodded. "And still we pursue the dragon."

"Perhaps. We grow closer, though. If Malshaunt is right, we're scarce two days behind the White Wyrm. That's as near as I can recall."

"If the mage is right."

"He's studied these matters deeply. He seems sure."

"He may well be. He's a queer fellow and knows too much. The captain trusts him too deeply."

Harfang shrugged. "She's known him a long time—longer than any of us can imagine. Who else should one trust but the companion of many years?" He cleared his throat. "I heard what happened ashore. You did right, though, to stop him blasting his magic about. It would have made a bad situation worse."

Feystalen shrugged. "It made him no friend of mine, and I don't think he cared for me much before it. Now I'll have to watch my back around him. Sad that I should have to say that of any member of Dragonsbane. Still, there's something wrong in him. The endless years of this chase have twisted him."

Harfang nodded. "Aye. But he is devoted to Tashara, you'll grant that."

"Too much so, perhaps. He's lost the ability to think clearly where she's concerned."

"What do you mean?" the first mate asked.

Feystalen drew on his pipe. "How long, Harfang, have you chased the White Wyrm? Twenty years now, is it? I've pursued it by Tashara's side for thrice that long. Ever we grow near to it, and ever it slips away. I've traversed the length and breadth of Ansalon five times over, and only twice did I catch so much as a glimpse of the beast."

There was a pause; then Harfang said, "But Tashara seems more confident than I've seen her before. This time the signs are strong."

"Tashara!" Feystalen removed the pipe from his mouth to spit into the sea.

"She is our captain," the human said sternly. "We are bound by the oaths of Dragonsbane to follow her."

There was a longer pause.

"D'you ever wonder, Harfang," Feystalen said at last, "if our captain is . . ."

"Is what?"

"Entirely sane?"

A third silence ensued, one that seemed to stretch out to eternity. Then Harfang said, "Sane? Of course she is sane!"

Feystalen's words came in a rush. "Do you remember when you first joined Dragonsbane, Harfang? When you first heard the name? I was a youth when my sire told me, as had his sire before him. My heart swelled with pride. I—I—was to be a dragonslayer, like Huma of old. We would free Krynn from this cursed plague of evil. I left my home in Qualinost and joined the band, battling dragons, slaying them in secret. I felt more alive than I ever have before. And then . . ."

"And then?"

"I met Tashara. She seemed a worthy leader. I learned of the Great White Wyrm—a worthy foe.

"But the years passed. We came no closer to our enemy. Other dragons ravaged the land, and we fought them now and again, but over time we paid them less and less mind. Our sights became set on one and only one.

"Then came Mina. My people were broken, enslaved, driven into exile. The city of my youth was destroyed and lies shattered beneath the Lake of Death. Now the elves wander, homeless, and we, we are homeless as well. Yet still we continue this endless pursuit, year after year, decade after decade. Would you not call that mad?"

"I would call it dedication."

"An admirable trait. But taken too far it becomes something else."

Harfang shifted against the rail and relit his pipe. "It's true," he said after a bit, "that the captain has changed in recent years. Since the fall of Qualinost, she's become more silent. In fact, she will go for weeks now barely uttering a word. I make my report to her each day and she listens but says nothing. She barely eats; she never sleeps. The only person she spends time with is Malshaunt. And yet . . ."

Feystalen finished the sentence for him. "And yet still we drive south—farther south than we've ever gone. How long, Harfang? How long do we keep up this pursuit? Until the elves themselves turn gray with age and fall into dotage? Until the line of Dragonsbane has been broken and there are no more sons and daughters to follow the call?"

"What would you have me do? You know Tashara listens to no one and takes advice from no one—save perhaps Malshaunt, and the mage is as devoted to this quest as she is."

Feystalen glanced about and dropped his voice so that Ayshe

had to strain to hear his next words. "The crew would follow you, Harfang. They wait for someone like you to take her place, to lead them. Someone sane."

The mate drew back in horror. "Are you suggesting . . . ?"

Feystalen said nothing.

"No. No, Tashara is my captain, still, and where she goes, I follow. You would do well to think hard on your own words, and do as I."

"Very well. What about Malshaunt? You know as well as I that the mage stands behind Tashara, ever whispering in her ear, and that he drives her onward. Perhaps he is the real trouble, and if he were not here . . ."

"Malshaunt is a loyal servant of Tashara."

Feystalen shook his head. "He is a servant to only one part of her: the mad part, the part that will not relinquish this quest even if it destroys her, him, and every one of us. But you are a loyal servant to the captain as well, Harfang. A servant to the best part of her. If the mage were not here, you could appeal to her. If she won't relinquish the quest, perhaps she would agree to pause, turn from it for a time, and take it up at a future date."

The first mate stared into the darkness. His pipe, grown cold, rested forgotten in his hand. At length he said, "I like the mage no better than you. And there may be something in what you say. But above all, I'm loyal to Tashara, and she is for the mage. I'll never forget what she did for me, taking me in and giving me something to believe in. But . . ." He had some difficulty proceeding. "But I also have a loyalty to Dragonsbane."

"A higher loyalty," the second mate prompted.

"Aye. And if I decide she or the mage is endangering our noble tradition . . ." The first mate left the sentence unfinished.

Feystalen turned back to gaze into the night. "Well," he observed, "nothing may come of it." He stretched, catlike, and glanced up, and his hand went to Harfang's arm.

"What is it?"

The ship continued to move through the water—elf and man could feel the gentle rocking motion as her prow charged forward—but something had changed.

Harfang cursed. "Bloody magic! I tell you, it's no way to move an honest ship, using magic instead of wind. And right now it isn't working. Call the crew!"

Feystalen stepped to the ship's bell and tolled three strokes. Crewmen ran across the deck, and Malshaunt emerged from his cabin to join them.

Harfang spun around as Malshaunt approached him. "Well, mage? Why are the sails no longer full?"

Malshaunt shook his head. "Something's gone wrong with my spell. I don't know why." The mage's face, usually cold and solemn, was drawn in puzzlement. "I shall try to recast it. Stand back."

He reached under his robe, brought out two small vials and a gull's feather, and laid them on the deck. As the others watched in silence, he produced a piece of charcoal and drew a circle on the boards and another circle within it. The contents of one vial he sprinkled along the outer rim of the first circle, while the second vial was used in the same way on the inner circle. Finally, he laid the gull's feather in the exact center of the double circle. Standing, he held out his hands and repeated a string of words in the ancient language of magic. The last word he shouted, and the gull's feather disappeared in a puff of flame.

The crew looked up at the sails as they lay slack and useless. For a moment, hope sprang into their eyes, but it faded quickly as nothing happened.

Harfang cursed again. "What's the good of your sea magic, mage," he asked savagely, "if it doesn't work?"

"Keep your tongue off matters of which you're ignorant," retorted the mage. "It's not my magic that has failed."

"Then why aren't we moving?"

THE GREAT WHITE WYRM

The mage glanced over the side of the *Starfinder*. "We are moving," he observed.

Feystalen followed his gaze. "But without wind, apparently."

"I know that, you fool!" Malshaunt snarled. "We must be caught in a powerful current of some kind."

Harfang ran a hand through his already tousled hair. "All right. If we can't catch a wind, we'll have to unship the oars and row out of the current." He turned to the assembled elves. "You there!"

"Aye, sir!" Samustalen and several other elves stood at attention, some still rubbing sleep from their eyes.

"Aloft with you," Harfang snapped. "The wind's died to nothing, and our good mage's spell that fills our sails has apparently died as well. Loose every yard of canvas. I want to catch the least breath of breeze."

"But, sir . . ." One of the elves stared about, stupid with sleep. "The spell . . ."

"Did you not hear me just now? The spell's not working. And when magic fails, we must fall back on older, more reliable ways of passage." Harfang raised his voice. "Helmsman!"

"Aye, sir!" The shout came from Samath-nyar, who stood at the wheel, his eyes fixed on the flickering needle of the compass.

"What bearing are we making?"

"South-southwest, sir, fourteen degrees."

"What speed?" Harfang demanded of the second mate.

Feystalen snapped an order. A moment later Samustalen heaved overboard a piece of wood shod with lead at the end of a cord, tied in knots at regular intervals. He let the cord slip through his fingers while Amanthor beside him counted in a monotonous undertone.

"Six knots, sir," Feystalen reported after a whispered colloquy with his two subordinates.

Harfang raised an eyebrow. "A strong current indeed. Helmsman, take a bearing four degrees east."

Samath-nyar struggled with the wheel for a time then shook his head. "Huh! It's no use, sir. The current's too strong all of a sudden. The funny thing is that the bearing never changes. It's straight and true as if the gods were steering us."

Harfang glanced at the compass then at the mage but said not a word.

Meanwhile, other elves had rattled up the lines like monkeys, climbing along the spars, and were busy loosing every other sail the *Starfinder* possessed. Harfang, leaning over the rail, felt a breeze rushing by his face, but he knew it was nothing more than the wind caused by the ship's forward motion. When he drew back his head into the shelter of the deck, he could feel the stillness of the air around them. He looked at the ribbons strung from the ratlines to tell the wind's direction, but they hung motionless.

Malshaunt sat in the middle of his circle, muttering magic words. He tried casting the spell yet again but without results, and in obvious irritation he retired to his cabin.

A few hours passed before Feystalen acknowledged defeat. "It's no good, sir," he reported to Harfang. "We'll have to break out the oars."

"See to it, then." Harfang strode back to his position by the wheel, where, at the shoulder of the Kagonesti steersman, he stared at the compass needle as if he could make it move by sheer force of will.

Gray dawn was beginning to show along the eastern horizon. Ayshe was ordered below with others to unship the great oars that were used to row the ship in calm waters or to maneuver her in case of battle at sea.

Four elves per oar sat side by side, stripped to the waist, arms resting on the shafts of the oars. Their eyes were turned to Feystalen, who stood before them, legs akimbo.

"Stroke!" he roared.

As one, the oars lowered into the water, and the elves and Ayshe pulled back on them, muscles straining and popping, eyes bulging with the effort.

"Stroke!

"Stroke!

"Stroke!"

Each seemed harder than the last. Ayshe could feel the sweat running in rivulets down his forehead and neck, trickling into his beard.

"Stroke!

"Stroke!"

"Enough!"

Harfang's shout came down through the open hatchway.

"Very well. Ship oars and stand to."

The dwarf felt his breath coming in quick, thick gasps. Next to him, Riadon, slender armed, rested lightly against the oar, completely at his ease.

"It's no good. The current's too strong and too wide. We'll have to ride it out." Harfang glanced at the rowers. "Good pull, lads. As you were."

Daylight revealed a barren seascape. The *Starfinder* was beyond sight of land, and as far as the eye could see, peaceful waters stretched lone and far away. Gone were the crying gulls that had marked their progress south.

Harfang stood on the foredeck holding a cross-staff. Beside him, Feystalen and Otha-nyar pored over a mass of charts.

"We continue at the same rate and in the same direction." Harfang lowered his cross-staff and made a note on a piece of parchment tacked to the top of a cask.

Feystalen nodded. "Enstar should be due west"—he gestured vaguely—"but without wind, we're at the mercy of the blasted current. This calm is like nothing in nature. It bodes ill for us."

The little group stared at the charts. To the south of Southern Ergoth were two islands: Enstar and the smaller Nostar. Beyond that, only open sea lay to the south. To the west there was nothing but the Southern Sirrion Sea, unless one believed rumors that far, far to the west lay the land of Taladas.

Feystalen drew near to the first mate and lowered his voice. "Have you informed the captain?"

"Aye."

"And?"

"She says nothing. Sits alone staring at nothing with those eyes. I asked her for orders, and she said nothing. I asked her what to tell the crew, and she said nothing." Harfang brought a hand down on top of the barrel. *"Nothing!"*

"What about Malshaunt?"

Harfang snorted, contempt in his voice. "He's sulking in his cabin. Can't imagine why his spell stopped working. That's what it's come down to—we've become reliant on his magic, and when that fails, we don't know what to do. Well, *I* do!" He looked about. "Muster the crew on deck."

Moments later the ship's bell clanged, and the elf crew poured out onto the planks. Harfang and Feystalen faced them from the foredeck. Just as he began speaking, Malshaunt emerged and stood toward the rear of the crew. The mage's face was once again drawn into a cold stare.

"Dragonsbane!" Harfang declared. "We're becalmed. Until we gain a wind, we can do nothing but wait. We do not know how long we must wait so I'm imposing rationing. Each of you will receive two pints of water a day, with two ounces of dried beef, an ounce of cheese, and a pound of ship's bread. Feystalen, you are responsible for proper allocation of the rations."

There was a faint, disconsolate murmur from the assembled crew.

"Second mate, a barrel of wine. Each of you will receive half a pint to drink success to our long quest and to prepare for what may come."

The murmured response to that was happier and louder, and Ayshe saw Harfang's wisdom in tempering austerity with generosity. Feystalen and another elf rolled forward a small cask. The mate drew a tap from his breeches, and his companion handed him a mallet. Swiftly he placed the tap against the barrel and with a blow drove it through.

A cheer burst from the throats of the watching elves. They might have been hailing a great victory instead of initiating a period of belt-tightening.

"Long live Dragonsbane!" shouted one.

"Long live Captain Tashara!"

"Death to the White Wyrm!"

Someone handed Feystalen a tin cup, and with an exaggerated gesture, he drew a draught. He held it aloft for a moment then lowered the cup to his lips.

The accompanying cheer faltered as he spat wine on the deck in a purple stain.

"Sour!" he gasped into the hush.

"You there," Harfang snarled at Riadon. "Bring up the other wine barrels."

In dreadful silence the crew carried up three more casks of the finest Solanthian vintage. Harfang tapped each one of them and tasted, spitting out each mouthful. Without a word, he hoisted one cask to his shoulder and, staggering slightly, carried it to the rail. He heaved, and there was a splash from below.

At a sign from the second mate, the crew disposed of the other wine barrels in like fashion. They floated by the side of the ship, carried by the current, clinging like offspring to their mother.

Harfang turned to Feystalen. "Check the water," he said in a low voice.

The mate vanished belowdecks and returned shortly, a grim expression on his face. He spoke to Harfang in an undertone. The sailor nodded and gave some further directions.

Harfang approached Ayshe and bent over him. "Smith," he said softly, "can you make a condenser?"

"A what?"

"A condenser! A condenser! For extracting fresh water from salt water. Can you make one?"

Ayshe shook his head. "I don't know how. I've only seen one once before. And if I recall, it used glass or mirrors. Do we have any on board?"

Harfang's silence was answer enough. The mate drummed his fingers against the rail.

"You see," he confided, "most of the water barrels are spoiled as well. We've enough for a few days only, even on short rations."

"If it rains . . ."

"Aye. If."

They stared at the clear blue sky that seemed to mock them in its cloudlessness. The sun burned brightly in it, like an ominous eye that watched their plight.

"Somehow we must get out of this damned current." Harfang struck the rail with the flat of his hand.

"What if we can't?" Ayshe asked.

"If we can't, Master Dwarf," Harfang answered. "If we can't . . ."

His eyes searched the horizon.

"Then the gods have pity on us."

CHAPTER

10

Fourteen days passed. Fourteen days upon a sea as calm as if it were painted and their ship were but a painted vessel. Fourteen days since they had felt a breath of air. Fourteen days since they had seen the welcome sight of land, anything but the endless ocean that stretched to the horizon.

The crew of the *Starfinder* had long since ceased to hope. Listless and haggard, they lay in their bunks or sat on deck, staring at the indifferent sea, awaiting whatever fate had been decreed for them.

Small cups of water, doled out once a day by Harfang, were just enough to keep them alive and make them long for more. Food supplies had steadily dwindled, and the elves, already slender in build, looked like living skeletons.

They made no effort to tend the sails. They knew no wind would come. Each day the horizon was the same and the sun rose blazing over the sea. Each day Harfang brought out the ship's astrolabe and took sightings. Afterward, he disappeared into the captain's cabin, reemerging later, looking grimmer than before.

Malshaunt sat cross-legged on the deck, surrounded by bottles, boxes, and other magical paraphernalia. His lips, dry and cracked from thirst, moved steadily, casting spell after spell. None took effect, even the simplest. It was as if all magic had been drained away from him, leaving him an empty shell. He would not speak to any other member of the crew, even Harfang, and if any came too close to him, he bared his teeth in an animal snarl. The crew soon learned to avoid him and let him be.

Of Tashara herself the crew had seen nothing since their strange journey began, drawn south in the irresistible current. She brooded in her stronghold in silence. Harfang brought her food and water each day in the same portions he gave to the crew. In her absence, the elves began to exchange stories about her. Some said she had spirited herself away from the *Starfinder* by sorcerous powers and even then continued her relentless pursuit of the White Wyrm. Others said she was already dead, and it was to a corpse that Harfang brought food and drink. Still others whispered she was wrapped in a mystical trance from which nothing could waken her until a wind came again to blow them back to the shores they knew.

Tashara sat motionless on a stool. For the past five hours, she had not moved. Her hands rested on her knees, her chin was slightly tilted upward. Her eyes stared sightlessly.

There was a knock on the door, and she stirred.

"Come!"

Harfang entered, bearing his usual portions of bread and water. He placed them on the table without a word and turned to go.

"Harfang!"

"Ma'am?" The mate stopped in surprise.

"Fetch Malshaunt. I wish to speak to you both."

The mate left and returned a few minutes later with the mage. Both stood before the captain, awaiting her orders.

Tashara rose and, from its hiding place, drew forth the cloth-wrapped bundle. "I am about to show you," she said, "a great secret.

I need not say the rest of the crew should know nothing of this."

"Yes, ma'am," Malshaunt said. Harfang grunted an assent.

The captain uncovered the sphere. From both the mate and the mage came sharp intakes of breath.

"Is that what I think it is?" came Harfang's voice, harsh in the stillness.

"A dragon's eye!" Malshaunt's face was sharp and greedy. "May one ask, ma'am, where you obtained this?"

Tashara shook her head. "You may not. I have possessed it for many years. Before even you and I met, Malshaunt. It has been of the greatest assistance to me in tracking dragons—especially in tracking this Great White Wyrm. But now . . . now . . ." Her face was troubled. "Now something is wrong. It will not speak to me. It is as if it has gone blind. That is very unusual and strange. Ominous, I think."

Harfang cleared his throat. "When did this happen, ma'am?"

"Shortly before we came to Horend, the sight began to grow cloudy. Since then, I have seen nothing in it."

Malshaunt, without touching the sphere or the elaborate setting that held it, examined it carefully from every angle. He held a hand above it, eyes closed, face drawn as if concentrating hard, then shook his head. "This is a power beyond anything I know."

Tashara turned her face to Harfang, who stepped back. "No, ma'am. I know nothing of magic. I can sail this ship where you command, but I leave magic to those who understand such things." He shot Malshaunt a glance strongly tinged with dislike. The mage returned it in kind.

Tashara cast a cloth over the eye and rested her chin in her hand. "Very well. We will wait and see."

"Wait for what, ma'am?"

"For something to happen that may restore sight to the eye. For something to return us to our quest for the wyrm. For something, anything, to happen."

Like the elves, Ayshe had ceased to work. Sleep was almost impossible, with the growling pain in his belly and the heat below deck that would not cease, even at night. His eyes felt hot, and his throat sore, so he spoke only if necessary. He noted that his skin was growing thin and papery, as if his body were devouring itself from within.

The sun rose low in the sky, and night fell quickly. Dawn was almost a punishment since it brought a faint hope they might see land or escape the current that bore them inexorably south. That hope grew fainter throughout each day and was dashed as night came. With each dawn, the crew knew their chances grew dimmer, and as hope faded, so, too, did their strength and will.

They told stories of the far south of the world, stories they might have laughed at if they'd heard them in a public house in Palanthas, but out there, beneath the burning southern sun, such tales seemed reasonable and indeed probable.

Ayshe listened as Samustalen and Samath-nyar spoke of what might be beyond the horizon.

"I've heard," said the Kagonesti, "that far south, beyond the lands of ice and snow, is a great forest that stretches out as far as the sky. If we reach it, my sister and I can roam forever free."

"Nay," grunted Samustalen through parched, cracked lips. "Beyond the southern sea, the waters of the world pour forth in a great cataract over the edge of Krynn and plunge endlessly through space. That's our fate: to be flung out among the stars."

Ayshe shut his aching eyes. He did not believe Samustalen, but for a moment he imagined such a thing: a great dark sky, filled with burning lights, a roar of waters beyond anything known in this world. For a moment, the ship was poised on the brink of infinity. Then there came the downward rush, the wind racing through his hair and beard. In his vision he thought he saw, for a moment, a shining figure clad all in white standing at the edge, welcoming arms spread wide. Then the moment passed, and he was back in the world.

He woke with a start, not knowing how long he had been asleep. His arms and legs were burned black by the sun, and though he did not know it, his face, wrinkled and pressed, was surrounded by a halo of hair spattered with gray amid its familiar browns and reds. The elves were gathered on the foredeck, staring over the bowsprit. Ayshe joined them, moving gingerly, wriggling through to gain a clear view of the sea ahead.

The line between sea and sky was thin and white. It was as if distant mountains were arising from the sea itself. They were drawing closer, and the elves gazed at them with fixed eyes, welcoming any change in the monotonous scene.

Harfang joined them, spyglass in hand. He examined the phenomenon closely then passed the glass to Feystalen.

"Icebergs," the second mate observed. "I've seen them once on another southern voyage."

"What are they?" asked Ayshe.

"Mountains of ice. They float in the water; in fact, most of their bulk is under water. They can grind a ship to bits in moments." The mate left that grim picture hanging in the still air for a moment then observed, "I've heard them called Takhisis's Teeth."

Any hope the crew bore that the great ice floes would disrupt the current in which they were caught perished as they grew nearer. The icebergs seemed to open a way for the *Starfinder*. But the meaning of their name was grimly clear.

"Listen!" Shamura called as they came near the first floe.

A horrid grinding, like some giant gnashing his teeth, filled the air. Ayshe saw that the icebergs, though parting to allow the *Starfinder* among them, ceaselessly collided and strove against one another. The noise from their violent conflict filled the air and deafened the crew. Huge sheets and blocks of ice were torn free and crashed into the sea, sending up clouds of spray. For a moment the crew hoped the waves from the violence would move them out of the current that drove them, but they soon realized that for reasons beyond their comprehension, the waves always seemed to be blocked by other floes before they could reach the *Starfinder*, or moved in the wrong direction.

The elves stirred and muttered. Turning, Ayshe saw the noise had drawn Tashara at last from her cabin. The captain of the ship looked like the walking dead. Her face was white, the same color as the surrounding ice, and the bones in her face stood out, casting dark shadows on her flesh. Behind her was the tall figure of Malshaunt, his eyes fixed on the captain. The crew parted for her as she paced to her nest and gazed south with sightless eyes.

The crashing of the bergs intensified, and now and again cascades of finely ground icy spume sprayed across the deck, making it slick and difficult to walk upon. Those of the crew who had the strength staggered below to clothe themselves in warm furs. Others, too weak to stand, lay still while their shipmates covered them in woolen blankets to preserve their lives.

Tashara ignored the snow and ice—her body seemed fashioned of the same substance as their surroundings—as she sought to pierce the icy walls of their prison with her gaze. The ship plowed on, driven forward by the current and by the waves kicked up as parts of the bergs crashed into the sea behind them.

The floes grew larger, towering over the ship. They looked like playthings fashioned by the gods for some titanic game. The sun glittered and shone from their facets. To the elves, it seemed as if the air were shifting and moving about them, distorting sky and sea. All perspective was lost among the cyclopean forms. Sounds echoed and rebounded amid their passage, adding to the tumult and confusion.

Two of the floes in their path struck one another with thunderous force. Shards of ice scattered over the ship, striking the crew, slicing open flesh. Malshaunt screamed magic words to the unheeding air, trying to shield himself and Tashara from the ice storm, but his spells had no effect. Most of the crew clung groaning to the deck, while a few tried to crawl through the hatches to take shelter.

The floes drifted apart, and Harfang raised a feeble shout as he saw ahead a path of clear water. The current pulled them onward, until at last they drifted free. Behind them, the passage through which they had come closed with a snap and crash as two giant icebergs struck together. It was as if a range of mountains had sprung from the sea, barring the way back. The ship drove on under the gleaming sun, whose light turned all their ice cover to a rainbow. The air warmed slightly, but a chill was over the still air. Not a breath of wind stirred the sails, and yet the current drew them farther south.

Three more days and nights passed in like fashion. The ice mountains were far behind them, almost vanished on the northern horizon. The ice that had landed on the boat had not been enough to quench the crew's thirst. The current that held them captive remained the same, both in speed and, as far as they could tell, in width. Tashara had once again retreated to her solitude, and none of the crew save Harfang and Malshaunt saw her.

No one among the crew moved. They lay in painful poses scattered about the deck, never going below. None had any hope. The boards beneath them had shrunk for lack of moisture. Harfang and Feystalen dragged themselves from elf to elf once a day, doling out the pitiful portions of remaining bread and water that alone kept them clinging to life.

The mates dropped heavily to the deck.

"Our supplies grow ever lower," Feystalen said. "There must be some alternative."

Harfang shook his head. "No. The current is too wide and too strong. We cannot row out of it in the *Starfinder*, and we have nothing else to carry the crew." He struck the deck with a fist made feeble by hunger. "We need a cursed wind!"

Feystalen made a ghastly exhalation that sounded like an attempt to laugh. "Exactly! Cursed!"

"What do you mean?"

"I mean this ship is cursed. Didn't you hear what I told you of that man the captain killed in the ruined village. His curse is upon us! It follows us and will drive us to the end of the world."

Harfang snorted. "Curses!"

"Believe in them or not, Harfang, you must admit there's something unnatural about this current. It never wavers, it never slows, and we cannot tell what drives it. What other explanation do you have for it?"

Harfang shrugged and was silent.

After a while, the second mate asked, "What of the captain?"

"What of her?"

"What does she think? What does she command?"

"She sits silent in her cabin," Harfang said after a bit. "She eats almost nothing. She says almost nothing. Malshaunt clings to her like a shadow."

"Then we come to it at last," Feystalen whispered, in an almost inaudible voice. "We've no choice, Harfang. We must rebel. You must lead us. You *must* take the ship!"

The mate shook his head. "Not yet. Not yet."

The night came, and the only relief the crew felt was the sinking of the sun. Ayshe wondered how many more sunsets they would see before hunger and thirst claimed them and the *Starfinder* became a floating grave, a ship crewed only by corpses.

THE GREAT WHITE WYRM

The sun rose red over a scarlet ocean, whose colors dissolved to yellow, blue, and green in the growing morning light. The air was heavy and weighed on the crew. Near where Ayshe lay, Lindholme, a lithe Silvanesti elf, moaned to himself. When Harfang passed among the crew with their daily bread, Lindholme reached up and caught his sleeve.

"I can take no more of this! Release me! Use your knife and release me from this Abyss!"

Harfang jerked away from him. Riadon, lying nearby, cackled with laughter. "No!" he cried. "He can't! And do you know why? Because none of us can die. The ship is cursed! We must starve forever and lie in this accursed current forever, never dying, never finding peace! The ship's cursed!"

A murmur of assent rose from those of the crew whose cracked lips could still form sounds.

Harfang glared at them. "Silence!" he snapped. "Let no one try to spread fright with old wives' tales of curses!"

A footstep sounded nearby, and Malshaunt glided over the deck to stand near Lindholme. His face was filled with contempt and loathing.

"Release you!" he snarled. "You fool, you cannot be released. You are embarked upon the mightiest quest in the history of Krynn, tracking a beast that is without equal. You follow a woman who has more strength and courage in her littlest finger than you have in your entire body. And you beg for *release?* Does your oath mean nothing, then? Will you betray your companions because of a little growling in your stomach? By all the gods, you're not worthy to serve in Dragonsbane. Perhaps you should indeed be 'released' so the rest of us can be free from the stench of your cowardly company!"

Lindholme's eyes scrunched shut as if he were trying to cry but had no moisture in his body for tears. The unsmiling mage stared at him. Lindholme stretched up a skeleton-thin hand as if trying to reach out to Malshaunt, but the mage drew back, pulling his robes with him. He turned his back on Lindholme and stalked toward Tashara's cabin.

A shadow passed over the deck. Harfang turned, and the elves pushed themselves up from their recumbent positions to stare at the sky. Clouds were scudding across it, appearing as if from nowhere, some of them low enough to touch the *Starfinder*'s masts. Lightning flashed between the clouds, and a gray haze spread across the sun. Large drops of rain pelted down, scattering the dust that covered the deck. The elves opened their mouths to drink the water falling from the heavens.

Harfang spun on his heel and shouted to Feystalen, "Sound quarters! Something's wrong! This isn't natural!"

To the north, a great gray sheet swept down from the clouds and brushed the sea. It swept toward them at frightening speed. Spurred by the sight, the elves roused themselves, staring above. The cloud spread and twisted, and from its heart came the sound that haunted Ayshe's dreams: a long, low growl.

The dragon's visage formed, followed by its body, emerging into the sky as if the clouds themselves were creating it. It seemed even larger than the dwarf remembered it from that terrible day so long ago in Thargon. At the time, he'd thought it was gray, but with it before him, he saw it as a blinding white, an unnatural white, the sickly white of a dead fish's belly. The only color about it was its two gleaming emerald eyes.

In length, it seemed to him immense, yet smaller than he remembered it in Thargon. Its wingspan stretched for thirty yards, while its body was a third of that in length from the tip of its snout to the end of its curling tail. Parts of its body were indistinct, as if they hovered between two worlds. Around its neck was a mane that pulsed and swelled. With horror, Ayshe realized it was made up of serpents, each writhing with a life of its own.

The dragon's body was clad in a mail coat of scales, each as big as the dwarf. Its claws were curved like scimitars and razor sharp. It reared back against the sky and plunged, seeming to draw the clouds with it. A blast of its breath narrowly missed the *Starfinder*, and beside the ship a great sheet of ice sprang into being on the surface of the sea. It was torn to pieces a moment later by the waves, and parts of it struck against the hull with hollow booms.

The dragon beat its wings. A gust of wind caught the ship as if it were a toy, and the vessel keeled sideways.

"Steady, all hands!" Harfang roared. "Brace yourselves, lasses and lads!"

The sky had grown completely dark, and icy winds raked the sea, stirring great waves topped with white. The air was filled with the roar of thunder and the crash of the waves as they struck the ship and tossed it to and fro.

Tashara burst from her cabin, her feet steady beneath her as she ran swiftly along the deck and sprang into her nest. "Mage!" she shouted. "Now! Cast a spell!"

Malshaunt thrust out his hands. A ball of fire leaped from them, expanding as it raced for the dragon's chest. It smashed against the cloudy scales and burst like gnome sky rockets, showering down on the turbulent sea. Ayshe could not see clearly through the driving rain, but it looked to him as if the place on the dragon's hide where the fireball had struck was darker. Malshaunt gave a cry of triumph; his magical powers had returned.

The White Wyrm's growl came louder, angrier. Ayshe clapped his hands over his ears. Just as it had that dreadful day in Thargon's streets, a wave of unreasoning fear swept over him. Slowly he forced himself to stand. The images of Chaval and Zininia rose before him. He would *not* give in to fear.

The dragon breathed its icy blast again, barely missing Malshaunt. Ropes and deck boards froze solid, and pieces of rigging shattered and fell overboard. The mage leaped nimbly onto another network of ropes and let loose another fireball. That one struck the beast's wing and dissipated like the other. Beyond Malshaunt, Samath-nyar and his sister circled the deck, wyrmbarbs poised in their hands, waiting to get close enough to the beast to strike. The chains on their spears were linked to iron staples, driven deep into the deck.

The White Wyrm drew back and brought its wings together. The clouds above it thickened, and two eddies extended down from them, fanned by the creature's wings. They touched the water and drew it up into great whirling spouts that roared and shimmered in the twisting lightning that streaked the sky.

"Oars!"

Harfang's voice could barely be heard above the tumult. Ayshe turned and, grasping whatever handholds he could find, began to make his way toward the hatch that led belowdecks. He caught a glimpse of Samath-nyar racing forward, his wyrmbarb in his hand, poised for a strike at his foe, who was hovering overhead.

"Belay that order!" Tashara's cry rang clear, penetrating the storm itself. "Stand fast, every one of you!"

The twin waterspouts bore down on the ship, whipping the sea to foam. The roaring from them drowned all other noises.

"Lash yourselves down!" Tashara's voice came to Ayshe as if from a great distance. He scrambled for a stray rope, flying free in the wind. It whipped across his face, raising a welt of reddened skin. He grabbed for it again, caught it and encircled his waist with it, pulling a knot tight, wrapping his arms and legs about a spar. Around him, he could see through the roiling waters the other elves doing the same. Alone of them, Samath-nyar still stood erect, his wyrmbarb poised to throw.

This is the end, Ayshe thought. No ship can survive this. This is the end. Far above him, he caught a glimpse of the Great White Wyrm's snapping jaws and heard its growl, but amid the chaos, it held no terror for him. The serpents that formed the beast's mane gave their own shrilling cry, venomous as an adder, high-pitched as the sound of iron rubbing against steel. The sound burst through the chaos to strike the crew like a physical blow. Ayshe felt blood burst from his nose and ears and cascade down his beard, which was tangled by the raging wind that sought to tear him from his post.

The waterspouts dipped closer, and the crew could see their glossy sheen and feel the air vibrate with their power. Past the spouts, they saw a great wall of water, three times as tall as the *Starfinder's* mast, bearing down on them. For a moment, some imagined they could see within it titanic faces with swirling hair, mouths open in lament. Ayshe thought he recognized the staring dead faces of Chaval and Zininia, joined with all the White Wyrm's victims in an eternal chorus of sorrow and horror. Their cries overcame his senses.

Waves crashed over him, smashing against the sides of the ship as she heeled first to starboard then to port. There was a great crack and snap as the mainmast broke. A moment later the mizzen crashed onto the deck in a tangle of ropes and shattered wood.

Ayshe opened his eyes against the wash of water to see a wooden beam, caught in a current, bearing down on him. He tried to duck, something struck his temple, and he knew no more.

". . . all right?"

". . . swallowed water . . ."

". . . lucky . . ."

An iron band was wrapped around Ayshe's head. It slowly tightened, then loosened, and he felt blood pounding in his ears. Something was choking him as well. He coughed, spat, and vomited, and the band tightened again.

". . . easy . . ."

". . . don't try . . . get up."

Blurred shapes wandered before his half-open eyes: tall, thin figures. He licked his lips and found to his surprise they were no longer dry, as they had been for the past fortnight. He moved an arm, then a leg, and groaned as pain shot through his chest.

The figure before him resolved into Omanda, the ship's healer. The elf woman smiled at him, dark circles beneath her eyes.

"Master Dwarf, I've always heard dwarves had heads of iron, but I never would have believed it until now." She chuckled. "Anyone else would be dead."

Ayshe reached up and found a bandage bound around his head. He began to rise, groaned again, and sank down.

"Rest easy," Omanda told him. "You'll not be fit to stand for a day or two."

The dwarf realized he was lying in his hammock. For a moment he wondered if the dragon's attack had been only a nightmare.

Omanda moved away to other bunks and hammocks. Turning his head as much as the pain in it would permit, Ayshe saw that half a dozen of his shipmates were also injured. Across from him, Jeannara was lying with her arm bound in a sling, her face dead white in the soft gloom. In another bunk, Samath-nyar lay. One arm was curled behind his head. The other . . .

Ayshe realized with a shock that the elf's other arm was missing, its stump marked with a blood-soaked bandage. He shut his eyes and turned away. Beneath the horror of the attack, one memory rose to comfort him.

He had not run away. He had stood his ground. True, he had not actually fought the dragon, but neither had he fled. That was something. Holding that thought, he fell asleep.

When he awoke, he felt strong enough to rise. To his delight, someone had placed a bowl of water and a bit of bread by his berth. He consumed both with the greed of the long-starved and slowly climbed the ladder to the deck.

A scene of devastation met his eyes. The *Starfinder* had survived the dragon's attack—but barely. Both masts were broken off. Elves labored to clear away the tangle of rigging and spars from the mizzen, which lay fallen on the deck. The other mast had been washed overboard by the fury of the waterspouts.

The bowsprit was gone as well, along with Tashara's nest. Most of the poop deck and part of the ship's stern had been torn away, shattered as if by a giant's hammer. All over the deck, crewmen—some wrapped in bandages and slings, some limping—were pushing, pulling, tying, and hammering.

Of the dragon and the waterspouts, there was no trace.

"Master Dwarf!" Harfang strode up to Ayshe, beaming. "Right glad I am to see you on your feet."

Ayshe nodded his thanks. "I'm glad to see all of us above water."

"Aye. But there is much to be done, and we've need of your skills." Harfang led him across the deck, noting as they went the things that needed to be repaired.

Ayshe lifted his nose and sniffed the air. "A breeze. Wind."

"What's more, from the southwest." Harfang was obviously in a good humor. "Enough, I'd say, to carry us back to land—that is, if we can raise and secure the mast."

The dwarf gave it a quick professional appraisal. "We can rig block and tackles here and here," he told the mate, pointing. "A line here and here to secure it. We can lash it to the stump of the main. It will be good enough to get us to land as long . . . as long as . . ." His voice faltered.

The mate seemed to understand. "Don't worry. The captain thinks the beast is gone for now."

"And why did she appear?" Without waiting for an answer, Ayshe started for the stairs leading to the forge but stopped and looked back at the mate. "Did we lose anyone?"

"All survived save one." Harfang's face was grave. "Feystalen is missing. None saw him fall."

The dwarf closed his eyes. The iron band around his head

tightened. Feystalen, for his part, had befriended the dwarf, had welcomed him aboard the *Starfinder*. He was gone. Ayshe breathed a prayer to Reorx for the soul of the second mate. Shaking his head, he went below.

That the *Starfinder* had survived at all seemed miraculous, let alone with the loss of only a single crewmember. Both masts had been torn down, most of the sails had been washed overboard, along with their rigging, and the hull had been scored and battered from rocks drawn up from the depths of the ocean by the storm's fury as well as by ice floes produced by the wyrm's breath. Fortunately, the rudder had survived intact, and it only remained to jury-rig the surviving mast.

Under Ayshe's direction, the crew raised the mizzen and bound it in place with heavy ropes, bracing it with pieces of broken spars. The rain from the storm clouds that had accompanied the dragon had filled the water barrels sufficiently to allay the worst of the crew's thirst, though food was still in short supply. Among the elves, there were sprains and broken bones, and Omanda went among them, doing what she could, invoking the gods' magic to knit torn flesh and sinew and repair shattered arms and legs.

Samath-nyar appeared above deck a few days after the attack, a thick bandage about the stump where his arm used to be. He would speak to no one save his sister and to her in only monosyllables. He did not take part in any of the crew's work but instead paced silently from one side of the deck to the other, staring at the sea and the sky.

Captain Tashara, much to Ayshe's surprise, was everywhere, leading the repair efforts, taking soundings and sightings, reorganizing the crew's watches to accomplish the work that needed to be done. She announced, on Harfang's recommendation, the promotion of Jeannara, the bo'sun, to second mate. Given the rumors Ayshe had heard from the crew about relations between Harfang and Jeannara, the dwarf wondered if that might lead to some awkwardness, but neither the elf nor the man seemed concerned.

Tashara was in high spirits, and when she stood in her nest, which the crew had rebuilt from broken timbers, she often sang aloud in Elvish, songs that were familiar to the Silvanesti and Qualinesti and spurred them onward in their work. She seemed more like a captain of the ship than at any time since Ayshe had first encountered her, and he wondered at the change.

Malshaunt, too, seemed exultant since his magic had returned. Among his first actions was to make ready the spell that powered the sails of the *Starfinder* even when there was no wind blowing. With other spells, he was able to aid in the repairs, though the ship would still need the attention of trained shipwrights to return her to her former strength.

At last, when all had been made ready, Riadon, Anchallann, and Samustalen climbed the mast and let drop a single broad sail, square and patched together from the remnants of the other sails that had been retrieved.

There was an anticipatory hush. Malshaunt, from the midst of his double circle drawn upon the deck, spoke the word of power. The gull's feather vanished in a puff of flame.

For a moment, the world seemed to stand still. Then a wind from the west caught the canvas and filled it with a crack. The deck shifted under their feet, and the *Starfinder* turned her head east toward land.

"The curse is lifted!" Tashara declared in a ringing voice. More softly, she added, "We have made a blood sacrifice, and the gods are appeased. May they welcome Feystalen among them that he may roam among the stars. Now we must set our eyes on the prize. It lies within our grasp. We have only to reach out and take it."

CHAPTER

11

Running before a brisk wind, the *Starfinder* skimmed across the waves. Spray thrown up by her prow blew back over the deck, and the crew laughed at the fine salt smell even as the moisture soaked them to the bone. The sun shone overhead, but no more was it the harsh blazing eye it had been during their dreadful ordeal. Now it seemed happy and benevolent, sending out its rays to turn the ship's wake every color of the rainbow.

There was no trace of the current that had driven them south. Nor was there any sign of Takhisis's Teeth, which seemed to have drifted farther to the west. Tashara, scanning the horizon with her spyglass, declared nothing but clear sailing ahead to the shores of Ansalon. Malshaunt stood beside her, robes flapping in the breeze, and seemed as happy as it was possible for the mage to appear. He did not even give his customary sneer at the sight of Ayshe.

Leaning over the rail, the dwarf looked on, fascinated, as schools of flying fish flung themselves above the water and landed again in bright splashes. Samustalen watched them by his side.

"Dragonfish," the elf said, chuckling. "A good omen." Seeing the dwarf look puzzled, he explained. "They're so called from the wings that sprout along their shoulders behind their gills. Sailors in these parts take their presence as a sign from the gods that good luck is at hand. Paladine knows, we could use some! And if nothing else, these may bring us dinner tonight."

He gestured toward where three or four elves held a fine net. They cast it back, securing it with two or three ropes to spars. After a few moments, they drew it over the side and dumped a fine catch of the dragonfish, flopping, onto the deck. The elves lit fires on deck, gutted and filleted the fish, and shortly the welcome smell of frying fish spread across the ship. After so many days of privation, the fish, together with their daily allocation of ship's bread, felt like a feast.

Nor was water a problem any longer. Sweet, gentle rain fell every few days, filling the empty barrels and cleaning the ship so that, even in her battered condition, she shone like a pearl. The elves sang to each other, usually songs of happiness about the coming of spring after a long winter. Ayshe began to understand some of the words and phrases of the Silvanesti and Qualinesti tongues and to appreciate the beauty of their languages. Sometimes an elf would lift her voice in a song of lament for her lost homeland, but even these, to Ayshe's ears, had a note of hope running through them, as if a bright counterpoint to melancholy.

Captain Tashara spent much of her time on deck, moving among the warriors of Dragonsbane and encouraging them in their work. Though she rarely smiled and never laughed, her voice and manner were more optimistic and energetic. The crew responded well to their leader's new mood, and the *Starfinder* was as happy a ship as one might find sailing the southern seas.

There were two dissenting notes struck in the chorus. The first was by Harfang, still in mourning for the lost mate, Feystalen. At Tashara's order, they had held a brief memorial for the vanished crewman, but even that ceremony was imbued with more joy than sorrow—for the crew were happy at having survived the curse the dead villager had laid on the ship, and at having caught, at last, a glimpse of their long-sought foe.

Harfang, however, though obviously glad to be under sail once again, continued to brood, and his countenance grew longer with each passing day. Nothing anyone could say or do could stir him from his gloom, and it seemed to Ayshe the mate's mood grew more sour as that of Tashara improved.

A conversation one soft evening showed how far the first mate had sunk. Jeannara had come on deck during the night watch and encountered Harfang by the mast, looking back over the wake thrown up by the *Starfinder*.

"Are you still . . . ?" she asked.

Harfang was silent for a moment. Then he replied, "Look, Jeannara. See how our waves throw up sea creatures." In truth, the ship's wake was illuminated by tiny creatures whose luminous bodies created a shining trail that stretched west under a bright moon.

The mate gestured. "It's a road, Jeannara. A road I can't retrace. It's here for a few moments, and then it sinks back into the sea and vanishes. I cannot find my way back to him . . . or to myself."

Jeannara let his words hang in the air for a moment. "The past is not gone, Harfang," she said at last, "unless we let it die. It lives in our memories."

"Spare me your platitudes!" he snapped.

"It is true. That is why the elves can live in both the past and the present. Unlike you humans, who forget too easily." Her tone was bitter, and the mate turned his eyes to her face.

"It was a mistake—one we never should have made."

"And now neither of us can forget it. I told you, Harfang, the past lives on. If we let it, it drains all life from the present." She turned on her heel and left the mate to his solitary contemplation.

THE GREAT WHITE WYRM

The following day, the crew was reminded that although they had escaped the curse, dangers still beset them. They tacked back and forth, using the real wind, for a change, instead of Malshaunt's spell. The sky was clear, the sun shining. The air was fine and bracing. Armidor sat cross-legged on the deck, nimble fingers mending a net. He yawned, stretched, and rose, sauntering to the rail. He cast the net, watching it intently, looking for more dragonfish.

"Stand by to come about!" Jeannara, who had the watch, called.

Lindholme, manning the helm, nodded in acknowledgment.

"Come about!"

Lindholme spun the wheel. Alyssaran and Riadon hauled on a rope, and the boom swung across the deck as the ship shifted her tack from port to starboard. Armidor straightened at the precise moment the boom swept across. The heavy spar took him in the back of the head and hurled him over the side.

"Man overboard!" Jeannara roared. "Luff! Luff, damn you!"

Lindholme turned the ship into the wind, and the sails flapped idly. Riadon snatched up a rope and ran to the side, staring at the waters with keen eyes.

"There!" He pointed.

Jeannara ignored the rope and, following Riadon's pointing finger, dived headfirst. Her lithe body split the water smoothly. A moment later she was swimming steadily for the spot where Armidor struggled feebly in the water. He was clearly injured but managed to keep his head up.

The second mate's cry had brought others on deck, including Harfang. He watched Jeannara swimming, then picked up the rope and dropped it over the side.

"Lower the boat!" he snapped. Hands sprang to obey, unlashing the longboat. Harfang meanwhile lowered himself hand over hand down the hull, preparing to drop into the longboat as soon as it touched the water.

Jeannara was within ten feet of the struggling Armidor when suddenly he screamed. It was shrill and high, a keening wail of pain. The water around him turned red. His mouth froze open in a cry of agony, and his back arched. Jeannara, taken aback, stopped and trod water.

From beneath the surface, a maze of tentacles burst forth. One gripped the unfortunate Armidor, and the crew of the *Starfinder* could see that both his legs below the knee were gone. The tentacle flourished him, even as his blood stained it red.

"Kraken!" someone cried.

Jeannara had turned and begun to retreat, but her strokes, frantic though they were, seemed to carry her only slowly away from the creature. One tentacle struck at her, falling just short. She redoubled her swimming even as Harfang grasped the oars of the longboat and rowed toward her. At ten feet distant, he snatched a wyrmbarb from the bottom of the longboat. The kraken's tentacles waved as the mate hurled the spear into their center.

The tentacles thrashed, and amid a rumble of waves the creature's bloated body reared to the surface. A single eye rolled wildly. One tentacle thrust the body of Armidor into its beaked mouth while others attempted to pluck the wyrmbarb from where it had struck. The spear had been well-thrown, though, and the creature's efforts were in vain.

Jeannara had reached the longboat and hauled herself aboard, dripping and gasping for breath. Despite her exhaustion, she took one of the oars, while Harfang took the other. The two rowed for the *Starfinder* and safety.

Malshaunt, by then, had appeared on deck and was watching the battle with his usual detachment. As the angered kraken began to pursue the longboat, the mage lifted his hands and chanted.

A sparkling, shimmering wall appeared, extending an unknown depth below the water's surface. The kraken, baffled by the barrier, struck it but could not damage it. Harfang and Jeannara gained the ship's side and clambered up the waiting rope. At a snapped order from the mate, Malshaunt cast his spell of movement, and the ship's sails once again filled with wind. Lindholme put the wheel down hard, and the ship veered away from danger. As they sped off, the crew could see the maddened kraken still trying in vain to pierce Malshaunt's magical barrier.

Harfang turned to his second-in-command. "Are you all right?"

Jeannara, still breathless, nodded. "Aye. But Armidor . . ."

Both of them looked sadly astern.

In her cabin, Tashara sat, hand over the chart on her table. To one side was the dragon's eye covered with its cloth. From time to time, the captain's hand strayed to it, but then she turned back to the chart.

At last she lifted the cloth. The eye, instead of its former milky-white color, was a dark blue, almost black. Deep within glittered sparks that flickered and waned. As before, the surface of the eye was agitated, and it roiled within its setting.

Tashara brought one thin finger down toward it. As the finger neared it, the eye quieted. An observer might have seen in it some strange beast watching the captain's approach. Slowly, carefully, she brought it down until it was within a hairsbreadth of the eye.

With an abrupt motion, she plunged it into the heart of the eye. The sphere quivered as if with pain, and the surface closed around her finger. Tashara sat motionless, staring at the cabin wall.

The dragon's eye began to swirl with white. In a few moments it was opaque.

The captain's eyes were a dark blue-black. She smiled in satisfaction.

Alone among the crew, Samath-nyar, injured in the fight with the White Wyrm, seemed indifferent to the ship's course toward land. Day and night, he seemed never to stop his pacing to and fro, back and forth across the deck. His arm—or rather, the place where his arm used to be—clearly pained him, but he spoke of it to no one and pushed away Omanda when she approached him about changing the bandages or easing his discomfort. In similar terms he repelled advances from the rest of the crew, and they soon learned to leave him alone in his misery.

Samustalen tried to explain to Ayshe. "He's an artist," he told the dwarf. "He can make that wyrmbarb sing like a linnet if he wants to—or could before this. And he's spent his whole life training to fight dragons. Now he has nothing."

"But surely," Ayshe said, "surely he can find another trade. There are plenty of things for a one-armed man to do—"

Samustalen shook his head impatiently. "You're missing the point, my friend. He doesn't *want* to do anything else. This was his whole life and soul, and now he's lost it. He was trained in the ways of Dragonsbane. It is a great honor to be called as one of our band, and now that has been taken away from him. Besides, a *man* might find another trade, but an *elf* in today's world will find nothing."

"What do you mean?"

"Elves are the outcasts of Ansalon today, Ayshe. I've told you that before, but you don't seem to understand. We're hated by everyone—save a few intelligent folk—and we survive at the pleasure of others. On this ship, isolated as we are from the rest of the world, we sometimes forget that, but I never will. I've no time for humans—"

"Even Harfang?" the dwarf interrupted.

"Even Harfang sometimes forgets himself with us, forgets we are his natural superiors. We're elves, longest lived of the races of

Krynn, most favored by the gods. We may have been pushed out of our homelands, but there will come a day when we find our way back, and then our revenge will be sweet."

Ayshe turned away. At times such as those he found the elves difficult to tolerate. The mixture of arrogance and suppressed rage that seemed to brew deep in the heart of all of them disturbed him greatly, the more so as he became closer friends with them.

He slept badly, imagining he heard the ceaseless footsteps of Samath-nyar above him as they grated across the planks.

Dawn was beginning to break, and the ship was silent, save for the creak of ropes and groan of timbers as the waves splashed along her side. Harfang made his way forward to the water barrel and, lifting the dipper, took a long, cool draught.

A cry burst from overhead, shrill and piercing as that of a sea-bird. Harfang looked up to find its source and stood amazed, the iron dipper falling with a clang from his nerveless hand.

Atop the crow's nest of the mast, dark hair flying in the wind like his own sail, stood Samath-nyar. His wyrmbarb rested beside him, and his face was turned to the south. His body seemed to pitch and sway easily with the motion of the ship over the waves.

His wordless cry had aroused the rest of the crew, and they tumbled on deck. Tashara, too, emerged from her cabin and cocked an ear toward the Kagonesti as he stood astride the breaking dawn.

Harfang leaned back to shout. "Samath-nyar, come down! That's an order, damn you!"

The Kagonesti laughed. The mate cast an eye among the assembled elves and saw Otha-nyar gazing at her brother, a rapt expression on her face. He pushed his way through the elves to reach her.

"Tell him to come down! Tell him now!"

Otha-nyar fended him off easily, keeping her eyes on her brother. She cried up to Samath-nyar in the Kagonesti tongue, and he answered her. He lifted the wyrmbarb and brandished it. Then, without warning, he dived.

Clutching the wyrmbarb, its point downward, he fell straight toward the sea. An errant gull that had rested on Tashara's cabin roof screamed and fled. It passed beneath Samath-nyar's plunging body, and his spear pierced it and carried it with him as he cleaved the waters. There was a splash and a flourish of spray and nothing more.

The elves rushed to the side and stared at the spot where the Kagonesti had disappeared, but nothing showed above the waves. The *Starfinder* rushed on, and soon the spot was indistinguishable from the rest of the surrounding sea.

Otha-nyar turned and vanished belowdecks without a word. Harfang stood staring over the side for a long time; then he, too, disappeared, but into Tashara's cabin.

Malshaunt stood by the side of the ship, watching the ripples spread. Then he said to no one in particular, "A happy death."

Samustalen looked at the mage scornfully. "What's happy about it?"

"He could no longer serve Captain Tashara in her quest for the Great White Wyrm. There was nothing left for him, and so he laid himself to rest in the deep. I call that happy." The mage turned on his heel and went below.

The rest of the crew slowly dispersed, leaving no words behind.

The deaths of the Kagonesti and of Armidor shed a bitter gloom over the rest of their voyage toward Ansalon. But after a week's sailing, the lookout raised the cry, "Land ho!" which sent the crew running on deck in jubilation. To the north, a long, low line against the horizon showed the presence at last of a shore. Gulls and terns swooped and dived above the ship, alighting on its ragged sail, filling the air with their raucous cries.

Harfang took a sighting and examined the land carefully through the glass. "Kharolis," he reported to Tashara.

Ayshe, standing nearby, felt his heart beat faster. It had been long since he had glimpsed his native shores, and his mind filled with what he had seen since he'd left the Highguard Mountains more than three years before.

Harfang apparently remembered as well where Ayshe had come from and called, "Master Dwarf!"

Ayshe presented himself to the mate and captain, who stood near the wheel. Malshaunt, as was his habit, stood near and a little behind the captain.

"You know that land?" Tashara asked. Her blind eyes, as always, disconcerted Ayshe.

"A bit. My home was farther to the north, but I journeyed south to the coast on one or two occasions."

"What are the most important coastal cities? Come, look at this chart and tell me."

The dwarf examined the map the captain showed him and fingered his beard. "Than-Khal is the biggest. A road runs north from there, bearing goods from the Highguard range to the coast—at least it did when my people were still mining in the Highguards and farther north."

Tashara nodded. "Very well. Harfang, make for Than-Khal. Master Dwarf, you will help guide us in these waters." She turned her face to the south, from which a cold wind blew. "There lies Icewall, does it not?"

"Aye, ma'am. There and stretching to the east. It's all ice and snow and mountain. I've heard tell that beyond the mountains lie other lands, but I don't know anyone who's ever seen them."

Tashara nodded. "I have seen these mountains," she said, speaking softly, more to herself than to Harfang, Malshaunt, or Ayshe. "In a dream, though never in waking life. Great cliffs and peaks covered with ice and snow. Crevices a mile deep, ridges sharp as blades, mountains like teeth, ready to crush the traveler. Oh, yes, I have seen them." She stopped abruptly and turned away.

Ayshe stood by Harfang and Otha-nyar as the Kagonesti, under the mate's orders, guided the *Starfinder* toward shore. As they neared their destination, they passed and hailed several small fishing vessels manned by humans who regarded the dark-sailed elven ship with a mixture of contempt and alarm.

A swarm of small boats flitted across the waters of the harbor, like gnats disturbing the surface of a pond in summer. The *Starfinder* cast anchor, and Harfang, Jeannara, Samustalen, and a few others entered the longboat and pulled for shore. Ayshe was part of the shore party.

A rough crowd filled the street running along the harbor. Men, dwarves, and the odd group of ogres strolled along the wharves or burst, shouting, from the doors of taverns. The watering holes had distinctly nautical names—The Barnacle, The Spyglass, The Brass and Tackle—while the cobbled street was filled with barrows trundling to and fro bearing nets, coils of rope, and sea trunks. Fishermen hauled their catches up stone ramps from the harbor, and the smell of fish and salt filled the air.

Ayshe was so used to being the only dwarf among humans—and lately, among elves—that it took him a little time to realize that his companions were far more objects of curiosity than he was. Dwarves, though fewer in numbers than humans on the streets of Than-Khal, were common enough members of the population. Disturbances in the mountains and poverty among the clans had driven many southward into the coastal cities. There they found work as smiths and jewelers or embarked for other parts of Ansalon, much as Ayshe himself had done. In truth, the War of Souls and its aftermath had redistributed many of the peoples of Ansalon and had redrawn the political and social lines that had, for centuries, defined the continent. Law and order in towns such as Than-Khal, clinging to the edges of the land, were maintained by those strong enough to wield a sword and decisive enough to use it.

Ayshe looked at the scattering of elves, humans, ogres (and one or two kender, shunned by everyone and hastily turned out of any taverns into which they wandered). Of elves, however, the streets showed not one. Moreover, the men and dwarves gave the crew of the *Starfinder* black looks, and some cried words after them that were by no means complimentary.

In no time a crowd had gathered behind them as they walked along the street, looking for the sign of a shipwright whose services they might engage to mend the ship. Ayshe glanced behind them at the growing number of hostile faces.

"Should we return to the ship?" he asked Harfang. "We can look for some smaller town where folk are friendlier."

The mate ignored his words and strode forward, his brows drawn in a dark bar across his forehead. The elves kept their faces impassive, eyes to the fore.

From an alley, an armed group of men emerged, blocking the way. "Halt!" growled the leader. "In the name of Neraka."

Ayshe's heart sank. He knew from gossip that after Mina had been defeated in the War of Souls and her One God was shown to be none other than Takhisis in another guise, her followers, the Knights of Neraka, had scattered across Krynn. Without a leader, they had formed themselves into roving bands and, in some cases, had seized control of entire cities. It appeared the *Starfinder* had encountered such a place.

The elves, Harfang, and Ayshe stood while the crowd expanded, filling the street behind them while the Knights of Neraka barred the way before them. The leader, a sallow-faced man with a two-day stubble and bleary eyes, looked them over.

"What I can't figure out," he said loudly after a silence, "is what a man and a dwarf are doing, going about with filthy, stinking elves. Pah!" He spat. "Are you elf-lovers? Is that what we got here? A couple o' elf-lovers?"

Harfang's voice was level and expressionless. "Our ship is in need of repair. We're in search of a shipwright to carry out those repairs as speedily as possible. When they're done, we'll be on our way again."

"Oh? Which ship is that? The one that came into the harbor this morning?" The leader's eyes narrowed, and his tone grew cunning. "Did you pay the harborage fee yet?"

"No. We'll pay any fees the law requires. All we need is speed in making the repairs." Harfang's hand, hanging at his side, made a slight gesture. Immediately the elves began sidling so they were ranged in a circle. Backs to one another, they stood regarding the crowd.

The leader of the knights scratched his unshaven chin. "Well, that'd be a problem. Y'see there isn't nobody in town that'd work on an *elf* ship. Can't get the stench outta your clothes afterwards, y'see."

The mate shrugged. "Then we must sail elsewhere."

"Uh-uh." The knight shook his head and dropped his hands to his sword. "You the owner of that ship?"

"No. The ship is the property of Captain Tashara," Harfang answered.

"Elf?"

"Yes."

"Well, then. Law here says that ship is contraband. We have right of seizure."

"What?" Harfang's voice lost the reasonable note it had sustained up to then.

"Stands to reason no *elf* could own a ship. Elves ain't sailors. They ain't got the stomach for it. If there's elves claiming to own that ship, they musta stole it. That makes it contraband. And that means it belongs to us." The knight drew his sword. "Now I'm arresting you in the name of Neraka as partners in thievery. Come along."

Harfang backed a pace and drew his blade. The elves followed suit. Ayshe pulled out a short sword from its sheath and stood, heart in his mouth.

The knight gave a toothless grin. "Hoped you'd try that." He raised his voice. "Take 'em, boys. That's an order."

A circle of flashing steel closed around Dragonsbane, encouraged by shouts from the crowd. Ayshe parried a blow descending from above. By his side, Harfang's sword flashed back and forth. To his left, Samustalen spat an Elvish oath as a knight's blade gashed his leg.

The dwarf cut at his opponent's legs as, under Harfang's shouted directions, the encircled elves moved along the street toward the wharf where they had landed.

One of the knights fell, blood spurting from his side. At the same moment, Ayshe saw Jeannara stagger and trip as a stone, hurled by someone in the crowd, struck her on the side of the head. Harfang half turned to help her and was overwhelmed by his opponent. A wave of bodies swept over the tiny circle and bore the combatants to the ground. Ayshe twisted just in time to see the flat of a knight's sword coming toward his head. Something exploded, and there was only darkness.

His head ached, a dull pain that ran from his jaw to his crown. He tried to reach up and massage his temples and found he could not. His hands and feet were weighted with heavy iron shackles attached to a great staple driven deep into the stone wall. Light in the room was supplied by a single guttering torch.

There was a wooden door with a small barred window set in it opposite Ayshe. The room, as far as the dwarf could tell in the dim light, was empty save for himself. He shouted and was rewarded a few moments later with a face at the window.

"Shut up!" the face growled and vanished.

Ayshe shouted again. That outburst was answered by a rattle of a key chain, and a guard entered. He walked over to the dwarf, kicked him, spat on him, and stalked to the door. "Shut up, I tell you," he snarled. "Next time I'll bring the whip."

Ayshe caught his breath painfully. "Where are my friends?" he asked.

The guard laughed. "You'll see 'em soon enough, friend dwarf. All of you'll be dangling together come tomorrow. They're just trying to find the ship first to get the rest of the stinking elves for a mass hanging."

The dwarf felt a surge of hope. "The ship . . ."

"Don't worry. Someone'll be along about that in a bit." The guard chuckled to himself and disappeared.

Ayshe thought, if the knights had not captured the *Starfinder*, there might still be a chance of rescue. But how the elves on board could come ashore without being set upon and imprisoned was more than he could guess. He wondered where Harfang and the others were being held. He examined his chains, but the locks were strong and looked unbreakable.

A while later there was a tramp of booted feet in the corridor. The door opened, and the leader of the knights who had arrested them entered, followed by two or three other men. The knight pulled Ayshe to his feet.

"All right, dwarf. I ain't got all day. Where's your ship?"

Ayshe shook his head. "I don't—"

The knight struck him across the mouth. "Don't lie! It sailed from the harbor before we could board it, and now it's vanished. Where is it?"

Ayshe was gripped by a feeling of despair. Had Tashara abandoned them? Had she realized something went wrong with the shore party and sailed on to find another port, where the ship's wounds could be healed? Though the dwarf knew of her singlemindedness regarding the White Wyrm, he could not quite believe her so cold-blooded. He glared at the knight and lifted a hand to wipe blood from his mouth. "I don't know. Probably miles away by this time. But if I knew, do you really think I'd tell you?"

"What were you doing in these waters? Are you pirates?"

"No."

"Then why are you here? I ain't never heard of elves crewing a ship, much less in company with a man and a dwarf. What're you looking for that you need a ship?"

Ayshe clamped his lips shut. Whatever Tashara had done, he would remain loyal to her and to the cause that had sent her and her companions halfway around Ansalon.

The knight shrugged and nodded to his two companions. One brought in a wooden stool and, with a kick, bent Ayshe over it. He tore away the dwarf's shirt to expose his back. The other knight hefted a savage-looking whip.

"Last chance," the leader told him.

The dwarf was silent. The blows fell with regularity, and after the first few Ayshe found the pain so intense he slipped into unconsciousness. A bowl of water was thrown over his face, and he reentered a world of agony. At last, after what seemed hours, the knights stopped.

"Nothing from him," he heard the leader say. "Let's try one of the others." They left, locking the door behind them.

Thwack!

Harfang's body curled under the blow, delivered with all the force the big guard could put behind it.

"I ain't gonna ask you so nicely the next time," the leader said. "Now, tell me, what are you doing here?"

"We . . . came for . . . repairs."

"That's what you said before. I didn't believe it then, and I don't believe it now." The leader shook his head. "Stubborn as one of these stiff-necked elves." He nodded toward the corner of the cell where Samustalen lay unconscious, eyes and mouth swollen from repeated beating.

The guard's leader reached down and grasped Harfang's chin, pulling the man's face up to within an inch of his own.

"We're gonna find out what you're doing here, see. And when we do, we're gonna take you out and tie you to some horses and pull you apart. But if you don't tell us what you're doing here, we're gonna do some things first that'll make you look forward to that death."

The mate of the *Starfinder* could find barely enough moisture in his mouth to spit at his tormentor. The guard wiped his face and chuckled.

"Well, boys, let's go try the female elf. That should be more fun."

Harfang gave a roar and staggered to his feet, only to be driven back by a blow. Hands shackled his wrists to the wall, and he could do nothing but lie helplessly, dreading the worst.

Ayshe lay unmoving for a long time then rolled over onto the cold stone floor. He did not so much fall asleep as faint from pain and fear. Hours passed, and he was vaguely aware of the cell door opening and closing again, but he could not summon enough energy to investigate.

THE GREAT WHITE WYRM

When he awoke, he found a rough bandage had been bound around his body. The pain from the whip was still there, but it had abated somewhat. He sat up with a rattle of chains.

Something stirred in the far corner of the cell, and he heard incoherent mumbling.

"Hello," the dwarf whispered cautiously.

The figure stirred again, rolled over, and sat up. Since it was closer to the light, Ayshe could see his fellow inmate was another dwarf. His long black beard was scraggly, and his filthy matted hair fell in tangles over his shoulders. He had wrapped his arms around himself and tucked his hands beneath his armpits. Even at that distance, Ayshe could smell an overwhelming odor of sweat and stale beer.

"Who are you?" he asked. "What is this place?" He kept his voice low.

"Jail." The word came out slightly slurred. The dwarf gave him a lopsided grin. "What . . . whadyou think it wash? Thish . . . thish is the dwarf cell. Whad you do?"

Ayshe pushed himself up to sit against the wall. The rough stone hurt his back, so he leaned forward. "I was with some friends. Elves. And a man. I don't know where they were taken."

"Elvesh!"

"Quiet!" Ayshe looked nervously at the door. As far as he could see, the other dwarf was unshackled. He held out his wrists. "Can you help me get these irons off?"

The other said nothing but stared stupidly at him.

"Come on! Give me a hand!"

White teeth flashed in the stranger's face. "Can't. Don't have one, y'see." He uncoiled his arms, and Ayshe, to his horror, saw both the dwarf's hands had been cut off at the wrists.

"Reorx's beard!" He shrank back. "What happened to you?"

"That's what they do to thieves here. Them they don't hang." The dwarf wriggled his shoulders and back against the wall as if scratching an itch. Then, in a single smooth motion, he stood and strolled over to Ayshe. He winked, showing no signs of his previous drunkenness.

"So why'd they put you in here? Hey?"

Ayshe managed a half-hearted smile. "They don't like elves much in this town, it seems. The Knights of Neraka attacked my companions."

"The knights don't like anyone much if it comes to that." The dwarf squatted and broke wind, and Ayshe almost gagged at his powerful smell. "They just want what they can get by raiding taverns and scaring ordinary folk. At least I'm an honest thief. I never threatened anyone in my life."

"What's your name?" Ayshe asked.

"Barbas. Son of Liffer. Yours? Hey?"

"Ayshe, son of Balar."

"Pleased. I'd shake hands, but . . ." Barbas gave a sharp, explosive chuckle, followed by a fit of coughing. "Damned damp!" he grunted at its conclusion. "It gets down in your lungs, and there's no shifting it." He bent over Ayshe. "What were you doing with elves? Hey?"

Ayshe leaned back. The pain in his back was a bit less, though his neck and shoulders ached.

"We're searching for something."

"All of us are searching for something. I search for unlocked homes. What are you and the elves searching for? Hey?"

Despite himself, Ayshe laughed. It was the first time in many weeks he remembered doing so. Without quite knowing why, he began to tell Barbas of their quest. Words spilled from him, and he found, to his astonishment, he was telling the stranger of his fear during the dragon attack on Thargon and of the deaths of Chaval and Zininia. He told of the search for the Great White Wyrm, of the curse placed on the *Starfinder* and their terrible journey south, of the battle with the dragon, and of the deaths of Feystalen, Armidor, and Samath-nyar.

THE GREAT WHITE WYRM

Barbas heard him out without a word of praise or blame. But Ayshe found that simply telling the story with all its twists made him feel better. It was the first time he had spoken to anyone of some of those things.

The dwarf was silent for a bit when Ayshe finished his narrative. Then he coughed again and spat. "Well, it sounds as if we'd better find your friends. Let's go."

"How?" Ayshe snorted, rattling his chains. "Do you expect me to bite through these?"

Rather than answer, Barbas twisted his head round far to the left so that for a moment it seemed to Ayshe he was looking over his own shoulder. When he brought his head back, he was holding a long piece of metal, flattened at one end, in his teeth. He used his arm stumps to lift Ayshe's right hand and bent his mouth over the shackles, maneuvering the lockpick as easily as if his fingers held it. There was a muffled *click*, and the shackle opened.

Barbas performed the same service for the other shackles while Ayshe sat, open-mouthed. When he finished with the last manacle, he twisted his head about, restoring the lockpick to its hidden pocket in his shirt collar and sat back on his heels, grinning at Ayshe.

The dwarf found his voice. "Where . . . where . . . ?"

"I said I'm a thief, not an idiot. Damned town hasn't built a jail cell yet I can't get out of. Look, d'you mind if we talk it all over later? Hey?" Barbas nodded at the chains. "Think you can do something with them?"

Ayshe picked them up. He stood next to the door while his companion drew a deep breath and shouted. "Hey! Lizard breath! How about something to drink here? Hey?"

There was the sound of rapidly approaching footsteps and the rattle of keys. The guard burst through the door, snarling, "Now see here, you maggot-ridden piece of—"

Ayshe swung the heavy chains around the guard's ankle and

yanked. The man crashed to the ground with a yelp. The smith grasped the manacle and brought it down on his captor's head. The guard collapsed without another word.

"Not bad. C'mon." Barbas led the way out of the cell, looking left and right. Ayshe stopped long enough to collect the key ring the jailer had been holding.

"Which way to the other cells?" he whispered.

"Sure you don't mean, 'Which way to the exit?' Hey?" asked Barbas.

"No! I have to free my friends."

"Even though they're bloody elves, for Reorx's sake? What do you care?"

"They're my friends. I'm not leaving without them."

The other dwarf looked at him in the gloom of the passageway. His eyes gleamed. "Do you mean to say," he whispered, "that you'd risk losing a chance at freedom for the sake of your friends? Hey? We're not playing around here, y'know. If the guards catch you, they'll hang you straight away."

"I don't care what happens to me. I'm not leaving my friends." He felt a burning sensation in his stomach.

Barbas shrugged. "Right. Let's do it quick, then." He turned left, went down the passage, passed through a stone archway, made several more turns with the air of one who knows his way well, and finally halted, a finger to his lips.

Ayshe, peering from behind in the shadows, saw two more guards leaning against the damp brick wall, smoking. They stood next to a wooden door with a barred window like the one that had sealed Ayshe's cell.

"Thass right," one said, voice slurred. "I ssaid to 'im, I ssaid I ain't gonna take anover shif' at night lessen I get double pay. I says to 'im you're a stinkin' Nerakan an' I don' care what you ssay. An' he says—"

He broke off as he glimpsed Barbas, who stood at ease in the passage, arms behind him. "Hey! You, dwarf! C'mere!"

The dwarf strolled forward. The guard stepped toward him, staggering slightly.

"Wha's a matter wi' you? Cat go' yer tongue?" He laughed and turned toward his fellow just as Barbas kicked the back of his knee.

The blow was skillfully placed, and the guard went down with a crash. The other had no more time to say, "Hey!" in an injured tone before Barbas's foot took him in the groin. He doubled up with a *whoosh!* of expelled breath.

The dwarf turned to Ayshe. "Come on!"

Ayshe was stepping over the first guard when a hand gripped his ankle and he tripped. The hulking figure of the first guard, drink knocked out of him by Barbas's kick, rose. His sword glittered in the torchlight.

"Filthy rats!" he snarled. "I'll teach you!"

His arm swung back against the door then halted as a hand and slender wrist shot between the bars and grabbed him. Another reached out, caught his head by the chin, and pulled. The guard's head twisted to the left. There was a sharp, sickening crack of bones, and the guard's body slumped against the door.

Ayshe jumped forward, brandishing the key ring. "Hold fast!" he said in a low voice. "We'll have you out in a moment."

Barbas had disposed of the injured guard with a sharp kick to his temple. He watched the corridor while Ayshe fumbled through a dozen keys before finding the right one.

The elves emerged from the cell. Even in the half-light, Ayshe could see the bloody eyes, broken noses, and bruises that bespoke the brutality of their captors.

"Where's Harfang?" he asked.

"Here!" came a voice farther down the corridor. Ayshe hurried to unlock the cell.

Barbas, using his pick, made short work of the mate's chains, as well as those of Samustalen, and soon the landing party of the *Starfinder* was once more assembled. Except for . . .

"Quick!" Harfang ordered. "We have to find Jeannara! The guards just left to interrogate her. Gods know what they'll do to her."

The group hurled themselves down the corridor, led by Barbas, who seemed to know his way through the dungeons as intimately as if he'd been born there. From a cell at the end of one of the twists and turns, they heard a shrill scream.

"Damn!"

Harfang raced forward. One fist took a guard outside the door under the chin before the man had even opportunity to draw his sword. The man's neck jerked back with a crack, and his head struck against the stone wall. He flopped to the ground and lay still. The mate, ignoring him, leaped over the body and slammed the door open.

The leader of the guards, he who had interrogated Ayshe and Harfang, stood facing them. Jeannara stood behind him, her manacle chain across his throat. To one side, another guard lay on his side, both hands clutched about his groin. His eyes were closed, and he was breathing hard.

As Harfang entered the cell, the guards' leader jerked a knife from his belt. At the same instant, Jeannara twisted the chain and yanked hard. The man's neck snapped and bent to one side as his body sagged. The elf let him fall to the ground. Then she stepped over to the prostrate guard, bent, and whispered something in his ear. Straightening, she kicked him hard on the temple. His eyes rolled up into his skull, and he lay silent.

Harfang looked at her and nodded. "Efficient, as always!" He smiled.

"All right, you lot!" Barbas, to judge from his tone, held something of his race's traditional contempt for elves. He snatched his lockpick with his teeth and made short work of the chains binding

Jeannara. "Follow me, and no wandering about, and we'll get out of here safe and sound. And no killing anybody else!" he snapped, glaring at Riadon, whose handiwork had disposed of the guard. "You're in enough trouble without that."

The elves, dwarves, and human made their way through the labyrinthine passages that made up Than-Khal's prison. Several times the way split in two, but Barbas never hesitated. On two occasions, he halted, the stump of a missing hand to his lips, as guards passed nearby. It seemed their escape had not, however, been discovered.

At last they turned along a passage ending in a blank wall. With every appearance of confidence, Barbas passed his nose along it as if smelling it. Then, stepping back, he struck a sharp blow with the heel of his boot against a spot about a third of the way up. There was a grinding noise, and the wall swung back to reveal another corridor.

"If you're going to have dwarves build your jails," Barbas grumbled more to himself than to the others, "always remember they put in a back door."

He entered the passage, followed by the rest of the party. Ayshe, in the rear, heard and felt the stone door close behind, leaving them in the darkness.

Ayshe could, like all his race, see for some distance in the dark, and he knew the elves could too, although not as far. What worried him was Jeannara, who had a touch of claustrophobia. Indeed, she grumbled a bit as they moved along the passage.

"Isn't there another way out?" she demanded. "This passage is choking me."

"Of course," returned Barbas, half turning. "We'll just go back, missy, and you can ask your friends the guards to please show you out the front gate. That's nice and wide, and I'm sure they've got something built just outside it that'll choke you even more. A nice running noose. Hey?"

Jeannara was silent.

After what seemed an eternity, Barbas reached up and pushed against a stout wooden trapdoor set into the ceiling. It fell back, and the men and women of Dragonsbane emerged into the fresh air under starry skies.

Looking about, they found themselves in a narrow alley, stinking of garbage. At one end they could see the gently bobbing boats moored in the harbor. Harfang turned to Barbas.

"Thank you for your help, Master Dwarf!" he said gruffly. "We'll be all right from here."

The dwarf looked at him unblinkingly. "Will you now? Hey? How are you getting back to that ship of yours? Hey?"

He gestured toward the shore where the moons' light separated the water from the sky in a flood of silver and scarlet. From where the party stood they had a clear view of the harbor.

Of the *Starfinder*, there was no sign.

CHAPTER

12

The disappearance of the *Starfinder* from the harbor at Than-Khal had to Harfang a curious unreality about it. Although he knew, from what Ayshe had managed to whisper to him during their escape from the jail, that the ship had gone, he'd clung to some hope that either the dwarf was mistaken (highly unlikely) or that Tashara had returned under cover of night to find her missing crew members.

It appeared neither of those alternatives was the case. Harfang took no part in the babble of discussion among the rest of Dragonsbane, conducted in undertones to avoid attracting the attention of the night watch. He was struck, though, with the fact that away from their ship and without a notion of where it was moored, the elves appeared to be as lost as an ant separated from its nest, doomed to scurry to and fro with no direction.

He also noticed that Barbas listened carefully to the discussion without saying a word and with a sarcastic smile on his face.

Abruptly Harfang brought the talk to an end. "Tashara would never abandon members of Dragonsbane," he declared decisively. "When she realized there was some problem with the shore party, common sense would have dictated that she secure the ship and sail

165

it elsewhere—near enough that we can find it or she can find us."

Part of his mind wondered if Tashara—with Malshaunt by her side advising her—would be willing to delay the quest by even a day. The dead Feystalen's voice whispered in his ear that common sense was hardly something he would associate with the captain of the *Starfinder*. But Harfang pushed those negative thoughts away.

"But suppose, sir, the ship's been captured?" Samustalen argued.

"In that case it would still be in the harbor and we would have seen or heard our friends in jail," the mate replied. He turned to Barbas. "See here. Were there any other elves in that prison that you know of?"

Barbas shook his head. "No. You're right. The captain has moved the ship. Probably behind one of the little islands in the bay. They're called the Guardians, and no one goes there. Some people round here"—his voice was scornful—"say they're haunted, and they keep off." He gestured to where dark dots rose from the sea. "If you ask *my* opinion . . ."

"We do," the mate grunted wearily.

"You need to get away from the town here before making any move to rejoin your captain. Go along the coast to the east. There's a few fishing villages along there. Steal a boat; sail out to the islands. That's where you'll find your ship. Plenty of places to hide out there if you know what you're doing. Hey? That captain of yours is out there somewhere."

"You seem awfully sure of that." Harfang's eyes narrowed, and he stared at the dwarf.

The other shrugged. "Take my advice—or don't take it. All the same to me. In any case, I doubt you'll find what you're seeking."

Harfang's gaze shifted in an instant from Barbas to Ayshe.

The smith dropped his eyes. "I told him all, sir. When we were in the cell together. It didn't seem to make much difference at that point."

THE GREAT WHITE WYRM

Harfang turned back to Barbas. "And what do you know about the White Wyrm? The storm dragon we seek?"

Barbas glanced about. "No," he said decisively. "This isn't the place for questions. Not here. Do you want your ship back or not? Hey?"

He slipped away in the darkness. After a moment's hesitation, Harfang followed, quickly joined by the elves and Ayshe.

Under Barbas's guidance, the journey out of Than-Khal went smoothly and without incident. Past the last houses of the town, the land rose in a series of low wooded hills that sloped down to sandy beaches.

The dwarf gestured to the sea, glinting in the early morning light. "There's a fishing village along this path another five miles or so. I'd suggest you wait until dark and slip the moorings on one of the boats. Row out to the Guardians. Rejoin your friends out there."

"What about the knights from Than-Khal?" asked one of the elves. "They're sure to come after us as soon as they find we're gone. Especially when they find the dead guard."

Barbas grinned, his white teeth flashing in his grimy face. "Don't you worry your pointy-eared heads about that! They'll not come after you."

"You seem very sure about that," Harfang remarked. Again he looked suspiciously at the dwarf. "How do you know?"

"Because I'm not an idiot! Pah! I told you before—folk here think those islands are haunted. The Knights of Neraka here are as superstitious as the next lot. If the boat was still in the harbor, they'd go after it. But if it's hidden in those islands, even if they think it is there, they'll let it be." The dwarf spat in the path and turned away. "Now, I'll be leaving."

"Not so fast!" The mate shot out a hand and gripped Barbas's shoulder. "You haven't told us what you know about the White Wyrm."

Barbas wriggled out of the big man's grasp without effort. "You've searched for it a long time and not found it. Doesn't that tell you something? Hey? You're not meant to find it! Some things ain't meant to be found. Some mysteries in this world should be let alone, not pried into by a lot of damn fools!"

Harfang glared at him. "If you know something of this beast, spit it out." His hand strayed to his side, forgetting he no longer wore a sword. "Otherwise . . ."

Barbas looked at him then shifted his eyes to the rest of the company. "All right," he said. "There's talk of the White Wyrm up and down the coast. Few have seen it, and fewer still live to tell about it."

"That's nothing we've not heard before, dwarf. What more?"

"Wait for it! Some say it dwells in the lands to the south."

"In Icereach?" Harfang lifted up his eyes, as if they could pierce the miles across the water to the shore on the other side.

"That's right. In Icereach. Ever been there? Hey? Not a place I'd go if I was you. But some say there's three mountains in a circle, all alike, all pointing to the sky. They say one of 'em is black as night and one white with snow. And they say that in the morning's light the other shines red. The Mountains of the Moons they call 'em. And they say that's where the Great White hides."

"The Mountains of the Moons," Harfang repeated. "Where in Icereach can they be found?"

Barbas shook his head. "That I never heard." His voice changed and became softer. "There's an old verse," he said, "among many who live in this land. Maybe it has meaning for you:

> *Where ice and snow*
> *Fall like rain*
> *And fire from the heavens flows,*

THE GREAT WHITE WYRM

Where land and sea
Meet as one
There dwells Death amid the snows.

Harfang snorted. "That's it? That's supposed to mean something to us? We've chased this beast for a century—time enough to learn to ignore common doggerel."

Barbas shrugged. "There's more truth than you know in old folk rhymes. Only fools would lightly dismiss them." He turned his gaze to the south. "In the reaches of the Utter South, folk say, lives a terrible creature of ice and snow, rain and fire. It cannot be slain by mortal hand, and it will destroy, in the end, all who pursue it." He paused. "Destroy them all, body and soul," he added slowly. "All except one. One alone will survive to bring the tale to the living."

He shook himself and broke wind. "No concern of mine. Hey? I just don't like to see folk go off on a quest you've got no hope of surviving."

Harfang smiled faintly. "We're accustomed to danger, Master Barbas."

Barbas sat down on a boulder. He seemed suddenly fatigued. "Turn back," he told them. "Turn back to the north. Hunt dragons if you must. But turn away from this one. It isn't for you. That's my advice. I'm a thief, and the first thing a thief learns is to only do the jobs that are sure things."

The mate said sourly, "You don't know my captain."

Barbas took a deep breath and rose. "Well then, I take my leave of you and won't expect to see any of you again. You know what to do? Hey? Where to go? Hey? Good! Brother"—this to Ayshe—"stay well. We may meet again some day."

He turned and without another word walked back down the road in the direction from which they had come. A hazy mist that had drifted in from the sea obscured his stumpy figure, and he vanished.

Harfang looked after him in silence, as if mulling over his last words.

Jeannara touched his arm. "We'd best be on our way."

The first part of the plan to rejoin the *Starfinder* proved easier than any of them thought. No one was yet stirring in the village when the group crept within sight of the tiny harbor. Three fishing boats floated serenely on the calm waters. Swiftly the party rowed a dinghy to the largest boat and took possession of it, casting nervous looks at the shore. They had raised the sail, hauled anchor, and were negotiating their way out of the harbor when they heard the first shout from land.

A man ran along the quay, shouting. His cries brought forth others from the houses that lined the harbor. In a short while, a dozen men armed with bows and spears were clambering into the other fishing vessels.

Harfang had a brisk wind behind him and superior seamanship, though his boat held more weight than those pursuing him. The commandeered vessel skimmed over the waves toward where the steep hills of the islands rose from the bay. From their vantage point, the elves caught a sight of the shorefront of Than-Khal and had time to wonder if their escape from jail had been detected.

Seeing their quarry gaining speed as the winds picked up, the townsfolk of the fishing village let loose a shower of arrows, but they were too far away for accuracy. One struck the side of the boat between Riadon's fingers; others fell in the water.

"I hope that damned dwarf was right about the ship and what Captain Tashara decided to do," Harfang muttered. "Otherwise we'll have to run farther down the coast in this—thing." He slapped the side of the boat, contemptuous of its clumsy, ungainly lines. Every board of the ship smelled of fish, which only served to remind the party that they couldn't remember the last time they'd eaten.

The pursuit continued, the townsfolk dropping farther astern. The foremost of the isles loomed ahead. Harfang could hear the surf booming against the rocks that lined its coast. He marveled at the sight of the isles, which rose like spikes to guard Than-Khal's harbor, blocking the town from great waves and storms. There were three of them, set in a rough triangle, with about a quarter mile of open water between each pair.

Harfang ordered his crew to turn to starboard and make their way around the isle. The shoreline slid by, and the mate, glancing astern, saw the foremost boat carrying their pursuers was making up lost ground.

"Sir! Look!" Ayshe cried, clutching at the mate's arm.

"I see, I see!" Harfang growled. "Keep a sharp eye peeled for the *Starfinder*."

The isle ended in a rocky promontory, from which seabirds rose, screaming at their approach. The fishing boat rounded it, and the elves gave a shout of relief. There, remarkably, as Barbas had promised, the *Starfinder* rode at anchor. The fishing vessel bumped alongside her, and someone from above threw down a rope ladder. Quickly the elves climbed the hull and with great relief fell onto the familiar deck.

The boats chasing them had halted just out of bowshot. Evidently, the *Starfinder*, though she might be small for a seagoing ship, was more than they had bargained for. That combined with the rumors of ghosts on the islands was enough, and the villagers dropped back and turned around.

Tashara stood on deck, listening as Harfang gave a brief account of their adventures ashore. At his conclusion, she nodded.

"Yes, the knights tried to board the ship. We repelled them but thought it better to retreat and find a way to get word to you of where we had gone."

"Well, the dwarf thief guessed rightly, thank the stars."

Tashara said lightly, "It would seem, Master Ayshe, your race is skilled in many things; fortunately lockpicking without hands is one of them."

Harfang nodded. He had not yet mentioned the information about the White Wyrm supplied by Barbas, and Ayshe did not voice it either.

"Well," Tashara said finally, "we must be grateful for his help, however unlooked for. Now, loose your stolen boat so it can be returned to yon fishermen."

"What about the repairs to the ship?" Harfang asked. "We're still badly in need of them."

Tashara came as close to smiling as Ayshe had ever seen her. "Mayhap, Harfang," she observed, "when we've returned their fishing boat, we can persuade these folk to aid us. At least they can supply us with food and water for the next stage of our journey."

"What stage is that, ma'am?"

"We shall proceed down Ice Mountain Bay. We will make landfall at Donatta."

"In the Plains of Dust?" Ayshe was startled. "Why there, ma'am?"

Tashara looked calmly at him. "From what rumors I have heard, the Knights of Neraka have overrun these lands to the north. Elves are unlikely to find assistance here, but among the Plainsfolk we may find help and perhaps further rumors of our prey."

On Tashara's instructions, the elves cast loose the fishing boat with a small bag of steel pieces and a note explaining their plight and asking for assistance. The fishermen debated it hotly—the elves could see them, though they could not hear the argument—but in the end self-interest won out over anger, and the villagers escorted them back to the hamlet. They were well out of sight of Than-Khal, and the townsfolk informed them the knights never came there because there was little or nothing to steal. For that reason, the crew of the *Starfinder* felt safe in remaining for two or three days while the worst of the ship's hurts were mended and they took on board dried fish, fruit, and fresh water to last them to Donatta.

Harfang questioned the villagers concerning the White Wyrm, but beyond vague rumors of a beast living far to the south, none contributed anything more than was already known to Dragonsbane. Ayshe spent his time helping with the repairs as well as doing some small jobs for the villagers by way of payment for their help. The elves for the most part kept aloof from the villagers, while Tashara and Malshaunt did not show themselves at all.

On the third day, Harfang inspected the repairs and declared the *Starfinder* seaworthy. A new mast had been cut and installed to replace the old one, the sails had been mended, the stern of the ship had been partially rebuilt and resheathed. Even Tashara's nest had been replaced, the villagers doing a better job with fresh wood than the crew had done with the remnants they'd had. Though the *Starfinder* still showed signs of her brutal encounter with the White Wyrm, she was far from the battered hulk that had limped into Than-Khal.

At last they moved into open waters and sailed east.

As the sun sank behind the western horizon and Solinari and Lunitari rose in the star-dappled sky, Harfang sought out Ayshe.

"Come!" the mate said. He led the way to Tashara's cabin, where they found Malshaunt waiting. Harfang rapped on the door, and the captain's voice bade them enter.

Ayshe had never before been in Tashara's quarters, and he looked around with curiosity. He was struck by the sparse furnishings. A wooden bunk, neatly made, was built into the wall. A large chest, bound in iron, presumably contained the captain's personal effects, which were nowhere else in evidence. A small table and chair were the cabin's only other embellishments. A chart was pinned to the table, and other charts, rolled in great cylinders, rested on a shelf. A porthole looked back over the ship's wake, glowing white and red in the moonlight.

The captain, seated at the table, received them without rising. The three visitors grouped before her in the cramped space, and Harfang cleared his throat.

"While we were ashore at Than-Khal, ma'am, we heard some things relevant to our quest for the White Wyrm."

Tashara's face did not change. "Go on."

Briefly, and with impressive thoroughness of recall, Harfang reported their conversation with Barbas, not omitting the dwarf's strange verse.

Tashara listened to it all in silence. When Harfang had finished, she sat motionless for a time then turned to Ayshe. "So, Master Dwarf—what think you of your fellow?"

Ayshe found his voice trembling slightly as he replied, "I think he was trustworthy—*is* trustworthy. He had no reason to help me escape. It's odd he seemed to know so much about us—knew where you'd taken the ship, but I suppose he guessed well. Or he might have heard rumors among the guards—"

Tashara interrupted. "And concerning the White Wyrm? How did he know of that? And how should we take his advice?"

"I myself told him something of our search, ma'am, when we were imprisoned. But as to what he told us afterwards . . . well, ma'am . . ." Ayshe hesitated then blurted out, "Perhaps you should heed his advice. A century is a long time to chase something. We lost Feystalen in the fight with the beast, and you said that was a blood sacrifice. How many more of those will we be obliged to make?"

The captain turned back to Harfang. "And you? What is your advice?"

Harfang seemed to have some difficulty speaking. When at last he did, his words, like Ayshe's, came in a rush. "How long, Captain? How long? How many miles must we sail; how many seas must we cross? And for what? For a wyrm that appears and disappears like a phantom. In all our years of chasing this phantom wyrm, most of the crew have seen it only once—this last fight. How many of us must die running after a shadow in the sky?"

He paused, and Ayshe could feel the silence in the cabin grow heavier, as if an invisible hand were pressing down upon them.

The mate continued, "We're nearing the ends of the world, Captain. The wyrm is running south, probably to Icewall. Let it stay there. Give up the chase. Let us return Dragonsbane to what has been our purpose all these long years."

Tashara's voice came in a dull monotone. "No, we must hunt the White Wyrm," she said. "We must hunt it until we kill it. That is our fate. Those are my orders."

"With respect, Captain," Harfang said, "Dragonsbane is an ancient, honorable sect, which was founded centuries ago to protect the people of Krynn."

"Well?" Tashara's query was cold as ice.

"It was—is—dedicated to ridding the land of the scourge of dragons. That is for the good, and I accept its mission. But Dragonsbane was never intended as," he hesitated, fumbling for words, "as an instrument of personal vengeance."

Before Tashara could reply, Malshaunt spoke for the first time. "And do you think that is what the captain has made it?" he muttered softly.

Harfang swallowed once or twice. When he spoke, he spoke to Tashara, answering the mage's question as if she had asked it. "Yes, ma'am, I do."

Malshaunt stepped from behind Tashara's seat. His hand moved quickly. Harfang fell back against the door, blood trickling from the corner of his mouth. He recovered in an instant, and his dirk was in his hand when Ayshe stepped in front of him. Malshaunt's hands were poised, his lips ready to spit out the words to a spell.

The tableau remained for a moment of tense silence. Then Tashara's voice came, low and furious. "Dismissed. All of you."

Slowly Harfang and Ayshe turned. Malshaunt remained standing next to Tashara. She said, without a trace of emotion in her voice, "*All* of you."

The mage's face drained of blood. He opened his mouth once or twice as if to speak then bowed and followed the mate and the dwarf.

Outside Harfang wiped his mouth with a rag. Malshaunt whirled away in a rush of robes. The mate stared after him, his face working. Then he turned to Ayshe and slammed a hand against the rail.

"So it goes on!" He gazed south, where a thin white line showed at the edge of sight.

Ayshe shrugged. "Maybe she'll change her mind."

The mate gave a short, harsh bark of laughter.

The dwarf knew, in his heart, Harfang was right. As Tashara had spoken, so they would go on.

The captain's table that evening was completely silent during the sparse meal. Malshaunt and Harfang sat at either end of the table, looking daggers at one another. Tashara, in the middle of the two warring crewmates, said nothing but ate her food with the disinterest she always reserved for food. At the end of the meal, she pushed back her chair from the table and turned her face to her lieutenants. Her expression was grim.

"We are on the last stage of our long journey," she said, her voice flat and expressionless. "I feel it. I see it in my mind. The

White Wyrm has set out for its lair, and now we have a clue as to the location. This is the moment for which I have sought my entire life."

She paused then continued. "I have no intention of letting victory slip from my grasp because you do not see eye to eye. Rather than imperil my victory, one or both of you will leave my ship if necessary."

Harfang did not speak, but his hand closed tight on the table until his fingers were white. Malshaunt, too, was silent, his mouth drawn in a thin line, his lips bloodless.

"Everything I do," Tashara said, "I do for a reason. Those reasons are best known to me and to me alone. I alone among you have been touched by the gods themselves to destroy this bane. You will *not* interfere with that charge." She turned her blind eyes from one to the other. "Do I make myself clear?"

"Aye, ma'am." Harfang's voice was rough. His breath came in fast, thick pants, and his face was red.

Malshaunt bent his head and said, in a voice so cold it might have been fashioned of an ice floe, "Aye, ma'am."

"Very good. Let nothing more be said concerning my decisions. They are what they are. You will accept them and know there are good reasons for them." She stood abruptly, and the two—elf and man—filed out of the cabin. Neither spoke again, nor did they break their silence before another day and night had passed.

CHAPTER

13

In fact, Tashara did change her mind but only regarding the *Starfinder*'s next port of call. Rather than proceeding directly to Donatta, they stopped first at Rigitt, on the northern edge of the Plains of Dust, a brief voyage they made without incident. Though the repairs made by the villagers to the *Starfinder* seemed strong and lasting, Harfang preferred to cling to the shore rather than sail into open water, and Tashara accepted his concerns as valid. Three days after the mate had confronted Tashara and Malshaunt, the shores of the Plains opened before them.

It was an area with which much of the crew of the *Starfinder* was entirely unfamiliar. The Plains were a vast dust bowl that stretched for nearly four hundred miles across the southern borders of Ansalon, separating the lush woodlands of Tarsis and Qualinesti in the west from Silvanesti in the east. There were only a few settlements, mostly along the edges of the Plains, and very few roads. Some years after the fall of Qualinesti and the destruction of Qualinost by Beryl, the Green overlord, the Qualinesti elves had undertaken a long journey on foot across the Plains, only to find that the Silvanesti forests were occupied by the Knights of Neraka. Afterward the elves were a broken nation, scattered over the face of Krynn. Many of the elves aboard the *Starfinder* had kin who had participated in the epic trek across the Plains only to find disappointment and death at the other end. A few had even participated in the battle of Qualinost and seen their city destroyed by the last throes of Beryl and the sacrifice of Laurana.

Since her confrontation with Harfang and his companions, Tashara remained isolated in her cabin and, more significantly, had taken her meals alone rather than in the company of Harfang and Malshaunt. The mate's face grew longer, and he rarely spoke save to give an order. Malshaunt moved about the ship like a specter, eating little, saying less, collecting materials for his spells and brooding like a dark shadow over the crew.

Rigitt proved to be a bustling port town, free from any presence of the Knights of Neraka. The streets were filled with humans and the odd centaur trotting calmly among them. There were even a few elves, though they kept to themselves and were none too kindly regarded by the town's inhabitants. Still, the townsfolk looked easily at steel, and, for the price Harfang offered, they readily agreed to overhaul the *Starfinder* and refit her.

As well, among the inhabitants of the town were Plainsfolk. The townspeople here were not much different from those Ayshe had met in Than-Khal or even in his own village. Their skin was a bit darker than among folk of the north, and blond hair was comparatively rare among them. They were tall and spare, but they drank, laughed, shouted, and sang much like the men of the north.

Among the Plainsfolk were others—physically resembling their brethren but standing apart from them by reason of their silence and solitude. They were the nomads of the Plains. Clad in animal skins, often with feathers and beads in their long hair, they preferred to camp outside the town and enter it only to trade. They bore great knives with intricately decorated handles, and from them their hands rarely strayed, for they trusted no one outside their tribe, folk to whom they were bound by ties of blood.

Even fewer in number were some wearing heavier clothes—bear furs or seal skins made into cloaks and capes. Their faces were paler and stood in sharp contrast to their reddish hair and green-gray eyes. They were Ice Folk, who dwelled amid the snows of Icereach to the south. Even their brethren of the Plains thought them strange and did not mingle with them. The Ice Folk ebbed and flowed through the town depending on the seasons, coming in the summer to trade and leaving in the winter months to scour the barren wastes for furs and ivory. With winter fast approaching, there were few enough of them in Rigitt, and those were preparing to depart.

Tashara went ashore with the crew and, like them, mingled in the narrow, winding streets of Rigitt. The town's buildings were of a kind of brick made of baked clay, and their roofs, for the most part, were thatched with heather. Smoke from countless fireplaces coated the walls in soot before escaping into the crisp, clean air above. To the west, Ice Mountain Bay gleamed and sparkled in the sunlight, but to the east, the lands stretched away, bare and hard. A single road led north to the once-great city of Tarsis, which in ancient times had been a thriving port. But the Cataclysm had stranded it in the midst of dry land.

While the elves of Dragonsbane frequented the taverns, seeking out fellow elves for news of their people, Tashara looked for Plainsmen, especially the nomads who had ranged to the eastern edge of the Plains or to the south. Them she questioned intently regarding the Great White Wyrm. Occasionally Harfang and Malshaunt accompanied her on her expeditions, though she made it clear to them they were not to speak.

Ayshe found Rigitt a lonely place. There were no dwarves in the town, and he found that the human blacksmiths did not welcome his presence. Once again he was oppressed by the feeling of being an outsider, cut off from his own race and regarded as an alien by those surrounding him. After exploring the town, he withdrew to the ship and spent his time polishing weapons and armor. Only once or twice did he venture into the town.

The captain seemed oblivious to the strange glances she drew in town. An elf of any kind attracted attention, but her blind eyes and close-cropped hair warranted more than the usual number of sidelong glances. Still, she carried with her such an air of powerful reserve that none dared interfere with her, and what catcalls and jeers might have followed another elf died on the lips of those who saw her. Harfang and Malshaunt, plodding in her wake, listened as she patiently trolled for stories of her prey.

Some of the nomads had heard of the White Wyrm. Others claimed to know people who had seen it, though none themselves had been witness to its devastating attacks. Among the Ice Folk, from what Harfang could tell, rumors and stories of the beast were more prevalent. Several repeated versions of the verse Barbas had related to them. In each of those cases, Tashara questioned the tribesmen intently, but she gained no fresh information.

Whomever she spoke to, Tashara asked repeatedly about the Mountains of the Moons. Though a few claimed to have heard of great mountains far to the south, the name Barbas had given touched no chords of memory or legend. Harfang wondered if the strange dwarf thief had made up the name or if indeed they were chasing nothing more than a myth.

Once only did the captain learn something new. On a day when rains and mist floated in off the bay, mixing with the dust from the Plains to cover the streets of Rigitt in mud, Harfang accompanied Tashara to a down-and-out tavern on the edge of town. Malshaunt had chosen to remain in his cabin, studying one of the leather-bound tomes he carried with him, tracing with a slender finger the strange characters and runes that filled its pages.

To call the building a tavern was to be overly complimentary. It consisted of a clay-and-wattle hut with a single room. Rough stools lined the walls, and Plainsfolk lined the room, sipping from mugs, partaking in the powerful liquor that was doled out by a one-eyed barman through a tiny window in the wall of an inner room.

Tashara entered with the mate, ordering drinks for both of them. Harfang put his aside after a single sip; the beer tasted as if it had been brewed in a horse's trough. They looked about slowly. A tall young man sat down next to them and emptied half his mug in a single draught. Next to him was a thin woman, covered in dust, her hair and skin much the same color as the brick interior of the tavern. There were circles under her eyes, and her hair was the consistency of straw. She turned her tired eyes on Tashara.

"You are the one? The one who wants to learn of the *shamath'la'hassan?*"

Tashara's reply was cautious. "I wish to learn of the White Wyrm—a great white dragon that appears amid storms. Is this the beast you speak of?"

The woman said something to the man, who laughed and spat forth an explosion of syllables in a tongue that sounded familiar to Harfang but which he could not identify.

"My brother says if you look for the—White Wyrm, you call it?—you should arrange for your burial here and now. But you are blind, sister, so perhaps you do not care about death if you cannot see it."

She and her brother laughed.

Tashara ignored the sally. "Yes, the White Wyrm," she repeated. "What have you heard of it?"

The woman looked cunning. "What will you give?"

At a signal from Tashara, Harfang pulled out his purse and counted out five steel coins. He laid them on the bench. The woman looked at them and spat.

"What are those to me? I cannot eat them. I cannot burn them for warmth. Do you imagine we are fools?" She pulled a lump of dark, crushed leaves from a leather pouch and stuffed them into her mouth. She chewed, and a dribble of dark juice ran down her chin. She handed the pouch to her brother, who followed suit. Others in the tavern, the mate noticed, were chewing portions of the same leaf, stopping now and then to spit. The floor was slippery with spittle.

Not at all disconcerted, Tashara replied, "No insult was intended, sister. What will you prefer for information?"

The woman looked them over searchingly. Her hand shot out and plucked Harfang's dirk from his side. He gave an exclamation, and his hand flashed out to retrieve it, but Tashara stopped him.

The woman examined the dirk and tested the blade against her hand. She passed it to her brother, who also examined it and nodded his satisfaction.

"We will take this."

"Very well," the captain answered. "And now tell me, please, sister, what you and your brother know of the wyrm."

The young man spoke again, and the young woman translated. "The *shamath'la'hassan* has no permanent home. It lives between the . . ." She hesitated. "The *echphinam*, the places without. But it cannot remain there for long. It must reappear in our own world, where it attacks with terrible fury."

"You have seen it?" Tashara's voice was very gentle.

"Yes, I have seen it." The woman translated, but it was clear she was also telling her own story. "It was years ago, in Donatta, when there was a Plainsfolk settlement there. We roamed over the Plains, but in the winter we returned to Donatta and lived by the edge of the sea. There, on a clear winter's day, it came from the skies. It brought storms with it, and it was wreathed in fire and in serpents. Its breath was frozen death. It killed our people and destroyed our homes. Few were left to bury the dead and pay tribute to the gods so their souls might find their way into the next world.

"When the beast had done attacking us, instead of vanishing

again into the clouds, it soared away to the south. That was the last we saw of it. But the Plainsfolk did not return to Donatta. The place is accursed because of those who died there. Their spirits wander the ruins and do not suffer those who disturb their peace."

"Where to the south?" Tashara's voice was intense. "Where did it go?"

"Across the *Mallsenshiva*." The girl hesitated, and the man repeated the word. "The . . . Snow Sea, they call it here."

"What is it? This Snow Sea?"

"A plain of snow, where it is always winter." The woman and man laughed without humor. "If you go there, blind one, you will lose your bones in the sea. It is vast, and there is no shelter for those who try to cross it. There the wind blows ever from the south and freezes the blood."

Tashara ignored the comment. "How do you know that the White Wyrm lives between the planes?"

The woman translated, and the man shrugged his shoulders and replied. "So it was said by the wise ones of our tribe," his sister translated. "That was passed down from father to son to son. So it must be true." She coughed, doubling over and spitting a stream of black and brown phlegm onto the floor. The other patrons ignored them; plainly that was common custom. The woman spat out the plug of leaves and took a new dose of the drug from her pouch. Harfang, nauseated by the smell, turned away, but Tashara seemed unaffected.

The woman lifted the steel coins Harfang had first offered and turned back to her brother, whispering. She stowed them away on her person and turned from the elf and human. Together the brother and sister rose and staggered to the tiny window where drinks were dispensed and demanded ale. Tashara and Harfang rose and made their way out into the street. Even the dusty air of Rigitt seemed sweet and fresh after the tavern.

Tashara strode along the street and plunged into the door of a more respectable drinking house. Harfang followed her as she sat down at a rough-hewn table, unaware of the startled glances she received from the other drinkers. She ordered an ale for the mate and water for herself and sat until Harfang found the silence uncomfortable.

"Ma'am?"

"Yes, Harfang?"

"You have been hunting this White Wyrm for a century."

Tashara said nothing.

"I've been at your side for twenty years now. Back and forth we've sailed, along every coast of Ansalon, around every bay, up every backwater. We've visited cities, towns, hamlets—places like this. Again and again. Sometimes the same places, sometimes new. But I've seen more of land and sea than I ever thought existed."

"Well?" The captain's voice had the same icy quality Harfang remembered from the argument in her cabin. Nonetheless, he pressed on.

"Ma'am, every man and woman aboard the *Starfinder* is loyal to you. Every one would die for you." He hesitated. "Myself included."

Silence.

"But what if we never find this elusive, mythical creature?"

The silence after that question was almost unbearably long. Then, abruptly, the captain turned to him. Her blind eyes stared at his. She placed both hands on his shoulders, and for the first time in their long companionship, he could feel himself trembling.

"Faith!" she whispered so softly he could barely hear her. "All the other voices of the tavern faded, leaving only hers. "Faith, Harfang! You *must* have faith. You must believe in me and in my visions. They hold us to this course, which was set for all of us before we were born. Believe me, my friend, they will carry you to everlasting glory. But you *must* believe! When all else fails, we have that left to us."

She rose and left the tavern. Harfang sighed. After the confrontation in the cabin and after his many years aboard the *Starfinder*, he should have expected such an answer. He rose and was about to follow her when someone tapped his arm.

"Master?"

An old man stood by the table. His hair was white and thinning, his face lined with age. He was short and wore a cloak of rough cloth stained and stiffened with the salt of many harbors. Despite his age, he stood straight and tall. His voice was low.

"May I sit, master?"

Harfang gave assent with a nod. "Why not?"

"You are from the elven ship, are you not?"

"I am," the human agreed.

"What, if I may ask, is a human like yourself doing in the company of elves?"

Harfang looked at the old man through narrowed eyes. "Why should I confide in you?" he growled.

The old man said nothing but sat rocking back and forth in his seat. His hands twitched at his robe.

Harfang's sense of duty finally overcame his reticence. "Hunting dragons," he growled.

The old man chuckled. "Aye. So I hear. I wanted to hear it from your lips. And not just any dragon. You seek the White Wyrm, the great storm dragon."

Harfang felt his heart beat faster but kept his voice casual. "So? What have you heard of it?"

"You have been warned, I believe," his companion whispered. "Oh, yes. I think you have been warned. Yet you go on. Why?"

The mate shrugged. "We follow our captain's orders."

"But *you*." The old man's eyes glittered. "Why *you*? Surely you know your quest is in vain? You have questioned it. You have sought to turn your captain from her purpose, yet she will not be turned. Why do you not leave now, I wonder. Why not be done with this madness and return to the world of the living rather than the walking dead?"

Harfang stared, and the old man laughed again. "Oh, yes," he said in answer to the unspoken question. "Every one of you who follows the captain on her quest for the White Wyrm is doomed. Your bodies do not know it yet, but you are the dead. You walk as if among the living, but you are the dead."

Harfang drew back, but some part of him recognized his interlocutor was asking the very question he'd been asking himself. Why not leave? Ashore it would be an easy matter to slip away and hide until the *Starfinder* had raised anchor. Surely the quest that drove Tashara had turned into madness. Harfang could hide until the ship was gone. Malshaunt would be happy to see him gone. The mage and the captain would drive one another forward in their search for the White Wyrm, a search that, as the peculiar dwarf and the old man warned, could only end in death. Why should the mate, who prided himself in his down-to-earth practicality, hold to that fatal course?

His thoughts turned to Feystalen and to his last conversations with the second mate. "The crew is loyal to you," Feystalen had said. "They will follow you."

But would they? No, Harfang knew that their first loyalty was, above all, to Tashara. The blind captain had bound them to her with hoops of steel, bonds nothing would break. Feystalen had been wrong. If Harfang was to break from Tashara, he must forget loyalty and forget leading. He must leave the *Starfinder*.

For just a moment, he had a vision of himself tramping the road to Tarsis, the *Starfinder* and Tashara behind him and fading into memory. He saw himself wandering the streets of Tarsis, making his way across Ansalon to a port, finding berth aboard a ship, sailing the seas with no lingering fears of death or insanity surrounding him. Free of the malignant presence of Malshaunt, who for twenty years had been a black shadow lingering on the edge of his life.

He saw himself in old age, retired from the sea, happy and at peace, surrounded by children and grandchildren, sinking slowly into the quiet contemplation that comes before death, looking back on a life well spent.

If he remained in Rigitt, he could travel northwest and make his way back to the Kharolis Mountains. From there it would be an easy journey by foot to one of the centers of civilization. There would be no difficulty in finding a ship to take him on. He could invent some explanation for his past and leave the two decades spent with Tashara behind him.

Yet he wouldn't travel in peace. That road was closed to him, and he answered the old man. "I have a debt to pay."

"Have you not paid it already?"

The mate shook his head. "No. I begin to see my way, but I still owe. And so I'll go on." He could not tell the old man his long history with Tashara, of the bonds and memories that bound him to her, of what she had done for him in taking him from the streets of Palanthas and, at last, giving him something to live for. To leave her in Rigitt was out of the question.

His questioner sat back in his chair, and for a moment his face seemed to grow even older. Then he reached into a leather pouch he wore at his side. "Has anyone ever read *charon* cards for you?"

Harfang shook his head. He'd heard of that method of fortune telling, popular among humans in the west of Ansalon. *Charon* was derived from the Ergothian word for *fate*. The cards were laid out on the table in a certain order, from which the fortuneteller purported to read the future.

"I pay no attention to such nonsense."

The old man's hands shuffled his worn deck, his motions precise and economical. Harfang realized he was watching a ritual, practiced for years, that had been brought to perfection. The cards combined, divided, and recombined as the pale fingers manipulated them.

"Nonsense," the old man said calmly, "is sometimes in the eye of the beholder, master. If you open your mind, you may find the cards are a useful guide to you. You need not pay any attention to them if you wish, but they can occasionally foretell and perhaps point you between two courses of action."

The old man dealt five cards: four in a square and one in the middle. Across the top of the square, he laid a further three. Then he placed the deck facedown to the left of the assembled cards.

He looked at the mate. "The cards—despite what you may have heard—do not always tell what *will* happen. Rather, they show what *may* happen. All beings have free will and can change their fate, though few will do so.

"Now, let us see what the gods have in store for you." He turned over the middle card of the square.

Despite his cynicism about such things, the mate found himself interested.

"This is you."

The card showed a man, sword in hand, staring into the distance. Despite himself, Harfang was impressed. He'd watched the old man closely and had seen no evidence of trickery. Yet somehow the dealer had made his first card mirror the mate.

The old man indicated the four cards that formed the square. "These are the fates that circle round you. Like the sun, they travel from east to west, so that which appears here is ascendant"—he touched the upper left-hand card—"while the others appear in ascending order. The three cards above stand for the three moons: Solinari, Lunitari, and the dark moon, Nuitari. There are nine cards in all, nine for the moons, the fates, and the elements."

"But there are only eight cards," Harfang protested.

The old man's finger hovered over the deck. "The top card is turned last of all. All the rest must be read in its light."

Swiftly he turned over the four cards that made up the square. The top card was an elf. It was followed by a man, a forge, and a ship.

"These are the things that surround you now," the old man explained. "The elf is dominant, but the first of the moon cards will suggest if that dominance is for good or for ill." He turned over the top left card of the three that lay above the top of the square.

A scarlet phoenix burst from a goblet of flames.

The old man's brow creased. "Lunitari!" he exclaimed. "The color of neutrality. The potential of this card"—he pointed to the elf—"has not yet been revealed."

He turned over the second card, in which a black knight stood, arms crossed over his sword, a shield blocking his legs. The third card depicted a silver dove in flight against a rising sun.

The old man looked closely at Harfang. "It would seem your fate has not yet been decided by the gods," he said. "The phoenix signals life renewed from fire, perhaps death or hope regained from tragedy. Sometimes it can show one saved from sure death. The knight is violence, while the dove is peace and tranquility, so these cards balance one another. Now for the last."

His hand reached for the deck. Harfang knew, with a sudden shrinking in his stomach, what the image would be on the final card.

A dragon.

A white dragon.

Silence seemed to have fallen over the tavern's boisterous patrons, as if a shadow had crossed the midday sun. Harfang gazed fixedly at the cards spread out before him.

The old man's voice came as from a great distance. "Remember, Harfang, the cards show only what *may* be."

The noise resumed. The mate shook his head to clear it and looked suspiciously at his ale. Then he raised his head to ask a question.

The old man had gone.

The cards lay spread out across the table. Next to them was the leather case in which their owner had stored them. But of the old man, there was no trace.

Harfang waited a bit then slowly packed the cards in their case. He pulled the strap over his head and approached the master of the house.

"Who was that old man I was speaking to just now?" he asked.

The master looked blank. Harfang repeated the question, and the man shook his head. "Don't know what you're talking about, master. Don't remember seeing an old man in here today." He bustled off to visit other tables, leaving behind a puzzled Harfang.

The mate stepped into the sun-dappled street. The newly acquired *charon* deck rested against his hip with a comforting weight. He began to make his way back to the *Starfinder*, but one question more than any other revolved in his brain.

When had he told the old man his name?

Repairs and fittings to the *Starfinder* were swiftly completed. The day after the workmen finished, Tashara mustered the crew on deck. The sun shone in a cloudless sky, and the air was full of seabirds' cries.

The blind elf spoke without preamble, her voice clear and ringing, reaching every point of the ship.

"Dragonsbane!" she cried. "For centuries we have battled our foe. Many are the wyrms fallen by our hand. Many are our brave ancestors who gave their lives in this fight. We remember B'ynn al'Tor, the greatest warrior of all, who created Dragonsbane during the Third Dragon War.

"Now you face your greatest challenge!"

She drew breath, and her sightless eyes seemed to move slowly over the assembled crew.

"The White Wyrm! A dragon beyond all others. Beyond the dragon overlords. Beyond Malystryx, the great Red Bitch-Queen. Beyond Khellendros the Blue, companion of the Highlord Kitiara. Beyond Beryllinthranox the Green, who destroyed the city of Qualinost. Beyond Cyan Bloodbane, who betrayed and destroyed the Silvanesti people.

"All these monsters are no more. Yet the Great White Wyrm remains. It is the last great foe of the dragon hunters. All others are dead, but this one, sent by the gods to challenge me, this one remains."

She gestured south. "We have learned now the location of the lair of this beast. There, across the Snow Sea, lies the last great foe of mortals on Krynn. It is my dream to slay it. It is my destiny to slay it. Did not the gods proclaim this the Age of Mortals? Should not all living things be subordinate to us?"

Again she paused. Again there was silence.

"This is the last road," she said finally. "Tomorrow we take the path to the south—to the last battle.

"If some of you fear this fight, turn back. If you fear the White Wyrm, turn back! If you fear everlasting glory, turn back!

"But those of you who have no fear, those in whose breast hearts beat as strong as that of Huma Dragonsbane, I say to you that you are welcome. And that we band of dragonslayers, we who will live through the ages in songs of our descendants, we shall go south knowing that our quest can only end in victory!"

A cheer came from the elves, full and hearty. Ayshe found his mouth open, his voice roaring acclamation. The elves pounded staves and handspikes on the deck and stamped their feet. Alone among them, Harfang and Malshaunt remained silent. Malshaunt stood slightly behind the captain, his dark face turned toward her in admiration, his eyes gleaming. He swept up a hand, and a cloud of sparks flashed across the sky, turning different colors and bursting in a rainbow that showered down upon the upturned faces of

the elves. On the other side of the captain, Harfang stood, tall and
silent, but with worry lines creasing the flesh around his eyes.

The crew was in a good mood that night, fortified by an extra
barrel of wine the captain had ordered served out. Some sang; some
told stories of past exploits of Dragonsbane. All seemed happy, save
the mate, who sat on deck and brooded over a small fire that burned
in a brazier to keep off the evening chill. Ayshe saw Harfang sitting
but forbore to approach him. Later Jeannara joined Harfang at the
fire, and they seemed to be taking some comfort from each other's
presence, or so the dwarf imagined.

Unseen by anyone, when Harfang at last went belowdecks, in the
solitude of his workshop, he took out the *charon* cards. His calloused
hands had difficulty shuffling them, but at last he dealt them as he
had seen the old man do. One by one he turned them over. One by
one they appeared the same as they had in the tavern.

And the last was the dragon.

At the rising of the sun, the *Starfinder* moved out of her slip and
turned her head south. Despite the early hour, many from the town
had turned out to see her departure. Word of the strange elves and
their ship had spread throughout Rigitt, and in that remote place,
folk were eager for anything out of the ordinary.

The elves swarmed up the rigging and along the masts to
release the repaired mainsail and mizzen. The topsails were loosed
to catch the wind, while the jib flapped in the wind and grew taut.
That near land, Harfang did not care to use Malshaunt's spell for
filling the sails with wind. There was enough suspicion among the
townsfolk of Rigitt of the strange elf vessel with its black sails and

blind captain without adding to their concerns. Later, when they were well at sea, the mage could cast his enchantment; for now, they would rely on nature.

Ropes creaked and Otha-nyar, standing at the wheel, spun it in response to a command and stood upon a spar to hold to their course. Harfang, standing next to her and calling orders, had one eye on the compass and with the other surveyed the crowd that lined the dock. Some shouted words of encouragement, others less friendly advice.

Harfang stiffened. There, hidden behind a man and a small boy, stood a thin, white-haired figure. The old man's hand lifted in ironic farewell as the *Starfinder*'s sails filled with the morning breeze.

CHAPTER

14

As the ship made its way south along the coast of the Plains of Dust, the crew had plenty of time to watch as the landscape changed. From the heather and low-growing bushes of the north around Rigitt, the land gave way to barren rock sloping down to the sea. The air grew still colder, and an icy wind blew from the frozen peaks that framed the southern sky. Tashara had the lookout, constantly studying those peaks through the glass, and the elves knew she was searching for three that matched the description of the Mountains of the Moons.

A few ice floes drifted in the water, though none so spectacular as those the crew had seen to the west in the Sirrion Sea when they passed through Takhisis's Teeth. Harfang ordered a sharp watch kept for thanoi, since the walrus men were known to inhabit those waters.

The mate did not speak to anyone of his mysterious old man and the *charon* cards, least of all Tashara. Daily, between the dozens of decisions, orders, and duties that were part of the ship's voyage, he practiced shuffling and dealing the cards. He tried to guess at the meaning of some of the combinations and was even tempted to ask Malshaunt if he knew, but he suspected the mage would tell the captain, and she would want to know more of the mysterious old man. Something held the mate back from revealing the story—perhaps memory of his own temptation to desert, though he had rejected that course. In any case, he told himself, every piece of information he knew that the mage did not was a small bit of power he possessed to counter Malshaunt's pernicious influence over Tashara.

Sometimes the pattern the old man had shown Harfang repeated itself. At other times there were variations. But of one thing the mate could be sure: no matter how many times he dealt the cards, and no matter how thoroughly he shuffled them, the last card on top of the inverted deck was invariably the white dragon.

After two days' sailing, the *Starfinder* bore east and entered a broad bay lined by rocky shores. On those rocks were dozens of giant tortoises—larger than any the crew had ever seen—sunning themselves, and they moved slowly over the rocks, slipping into the shallows then climbing back into the sunlight.

Though the sun burned brightly there, the air was cold, and the crew—except for Tashara and Malshaunt—wrapped themselves in furs. The *Starfinder* dropped anchor, and on Tashara's orders the entire crew put ashore. Over the following few days, they ferried supplies to their camp, established near the shore. The tortoises proved an excellent source of food, supplemented by birds' eggs, which they found in abundance in nests along the shore.

Half a mile inland, there rose from the sands the ruins of great buildings, worn down by the restless wind and desert. Ayshe, inspecting them, wondered if the camp of the Plainsmen the brother and sister in Rigitt had referred to had been established among the older ruins, village built upon village, town built upon town, until time itself forgot the origins of the settlement. The story the Plainsfolk had told to Tashara and Harfang had spread among the crew, adorned with such details as the imagination of the elves could supply.

Gray stones protruded at crazy angles like rotten teeth sticking up from the dusty ground. Many of them were cracked and shattered, and some still bore the marks of burning, as if a great fire had swept over them. Some had writing carved deep into the stone, but Ayshe could not read it. Jeannara, who examined the runes with him, could not understand it either.

"It's the script of a people now long gone," she told him. "They left only the ruins of Donatta. They are forgotten, and even the elves don't remember them."

Ayshe recalled Tashara's song from many weeks previous. "Do you have regrets, Jeannara?" he asked. "Do you worry that when you're gone, you'll be forgotten, like the people of these ruins?"

The elf woman smiled. "The deeds of Dragonsbane, Master Ayshe, have been carried down through the centuries. Our feats will outlive us, even the longest-lived among the elves." Her expression turned sad. "No, I have no regrets. I can have no regrets lest I try to turn back the River of Time. It is a mighty river, Ayshe, and it sweeps us all before it, whether we would or no."

Together the elf and dwarf contemplated the ruins. The wind passing through them made a high whistling sound that sounded like weeping. Ayshe shuddered, remembering the stories of unquiet spirits. He clutched at Jeannara's arm. "D'you see?"

"What? Where?"

Ayshe did not say more for a moment. His eyes studied the gray stones intently. Surely . . . Yes! "There!"

Jeannara followed his gaze and gasped.

The stone surface of one pillar seemed to be rippling, moving. Bulges formed in it and resolved themselves into a human face, its mouth gaping in agony. On either side of the mouth were the outlines of hands, as if the figure were pressing to free itself from the stone. Then it faded away. A moment later, another face came to the surface of the rock. Its features, as well, were distorted in pain, its mouth crying out.

Ayshe realized with a shock the sound he had thought was the wind was, in fact, the noise of dozens, hundreds, thousands of voices wailing in a never-ending lament.

"Reorx's Beard!" he muttered. "Is this what happens to those slain by the wyrm?"

"Nay!" Jeannara's voice was unsteady. "But for these poor souls there has been, for some reason, no release. They have remained here, frozen and burned into the very stone." She shook her head. "Either that, or the stones themselves remember the pain of those who died here."

"How can stones remember?" grunted the dwarf. He held his axe uneasily and flinched as another face surfaced and gave a prolonged shriek before vanishing.

Jeannara's voice sank to a whisper. "Some say that if a soul dies in enough pain, the land itself remembers and can never be free of its pain until the last great Cataclysm comes to wash Krynn clean of all who dwell on her." She backed away from the stones. "Let's go. Let's get away from this place."

"We should tell the captain," Ayshe said, shouldering his axe.

"Nay. Keep silent." Seeing his face, she added, "It's best. Best that the rest of the crew not see this. Trust me. Be still."

The dwarf nodded, and they turned their backs on the unquiet ruins. The wails pursued them as they returned to camp.

In three days the supplies had been off-loaded from the *Starfinder*. On the morning of the fourth day, the crew assembled, bearing heavy packs. In addition to their supplies, on Tashara's orders Otha-nyar and Lindholme carried, on a framework of sticks and canvas dragging behind them, several bundles wrapped in tattered rags, which they were reluctant to allow the others near. Tashara addressed the crew.

"We make for Zeriak." She pointed east across the low foothills that rolled up from the south. "There we'll purchase any more supplies we need and strike out across the Snow Sea. Then on to the Mountains of the Moons. On to our final victory over the White Wyrm!"

The elves raised a brief cheer and began their trek. As they walked forward, Ayshe cast a glance backward to the ship that had been his home for so many months. She looked forlorn, standing at the edge of the sea, the sun shining on her sides, her sails down, her rigging drooping. He shook his head sadly and turned his back on her.

The party soon found that their time aboard the *Starfinder* had not accustomed them to walking long distances. Even Ayshe, who as a dwarf had a hardier constitution than either the elves or Harfang, was hard put, and they found they could manage only about fifteen miles a day.

The hills, which from a distance had seemed barren, were covered in a thick, low scrub that clung to their ankles as if to hold them back. Gullies and crevices cut across their way and had to be clambered over. Some of them were filled with sluggish streams coursing from the mountains to the south. In spring, they would be full, and the party counted themselves lucky they were making the traverse in late fall. Still, they were rarely dry and never warm. Even the evening campfires did little to keep out the icy wind that blew steadily from the south. The wind kicked up the dust, swirling it in eddies, driving it in clouds. After the first day, the elves had no doubt what had given the Plains their name. They were covered with copper-colored dust; it filled their mouths, parched their tongues, covered their food, and burnished their skin raw and red.

Tashara kept them angled slightly north so they would strike the road that led to Zeriak before the town itself. Her plan was to conceal the nature of their quest and to pretend they were simply one of the wandering band of elves who traversed the Plains after the fall of Qualinost.

Ayshe was not sure how she planned to explain the presence in such a band of a dwarf and a man, but he kept his mouth shut.

The road, when they encountered it on the fourth day of their journey, proved to be little more than a dusty trail worn by the passage of wagons and many feet. They moved along the road, grateful that at least some of the obstacles to their passage had been removed.

Another day's journey at last brought them to the mud walls of Zeriak. The sun there seemed to shine even brighter, and the shadows were sharper, the air drier, as they approached the town in the late afternoon.

A great cloud of red-brown dust had been kicked up outside the gates by a troop of mules led by a bad-tempered driver who was shouting at the gate guards.

"D'y'think I brought them here for me bloody health? Of course I want t'sell them! Now, open the gods-blasted gates and let me through, ye pack o' snaggle-toothed lazy pieces o' dragon spit!"

Through the braying of the mules and the angry shouts of the driver, Ayshe could hear a grumbling voice saying something about tax.

"'S bloody highway robbery, tha's what it is! I paid a bloody tax in bloody Hopeful! I paid a bloody tax in Tarsis! And now here! By Chemosh's breath, it'll cost me more to bring these damned animals to market than I'll make selling 'em!"

The low voice grumbled again; then came the chink of steel coin passing from hand to hand. The wooden doors swung open, and the driver and his noisy pack passed through them. The gates shut swiftly, and a small door at eye level popped open.

"What business hast thou in Zeriak?"

Harfang, who was standing near Tashara at the front of the company, saw a handsome face with rippling brown hair pushed back from a pale forehead. Though he could not see the gatekeeper's body, the formality of his speech stirred a chord in his memory.

"A centaur!" he hissed to Tashara. "He's a centaur."

The elf captain gave no sign she had heard Harfang and addressed the gatekeeper pleasantly. "Good afternoon, friend. We seek permission to enter Zeriak."

" 'Friend'! Be careful to whom thou addresseth that word, elf." The centaur's voice held nothing but contempt. "There are no friends of elves within these walls—save, perhaps, other elves."

"Very well," Tashara returned. "We seek permission to enter Zeriak. Sir."

"Why? Hast thou goods to sell?"

"Nay, master. We wish to buy goods. We are on a long journey to the fabled Pillar of Flame and are in need of food, lodging, and equipment for the trip."

The centaur's eyes flickered over them. "What is a dwarf doing with such as thou?" he demanded.

Tashara turned her blind eyes to Ayshe. "A chance companion met on the road," she lied easily. "He, too, is traveling east."

"Master Dwarf, where art thou bound?" the centaur demanded.

Ayshe's mind raced. He'd had only a glimpse of the maps of the Plains that Tashara and Harfang had pored over. One name had struck in his memory. "The Missing City," he growled.

The centaur seemed taken aback. "Thou hast a long road ahead of thee," he said at last. "And the man by thy side, elf. What of him? Another chance companion?"

Tashara smiled slightly. "He is my servant," she said. "I keep him near me to amuse myself. He is feeble minded and makes no complaint."

Harfang could hear a soft snigger from just behind him where

Malshaunt was standing. His hands clenched, but he made no movement.

The centaur looked over Harfang then stared at Tashara with an expression of contempt. "Thou hast a fool for a servant, elf. Maybe that means thou art thyself a fool."

"Perhaps," admitted the elf calmly. "Perhaps."

There was another long silence behind the gate. Then the centaur's voice came again. "For thy companions and thyself, Zeriak demands an entry tax of twelve steel."

Tashara snapped her fingers, and Harfang handed her a leather pouch. She counted out coins and passed them to the centaur.

"Enter!" he said sternly. "But look for no easy welcome, elf. The Bone and Bristle at the far end of town may serve thee. No other taverns will let elves through their doors."

The gates swung back, and Dragonsbane passed into Zeriak.

The town was certainly not much to look at—or to smell.

Low, mud-brick buildings crowded along narrow streets. A few rose to two stories, but most were squat and ugly, like fat old men crouched in the dust. Heaps of refuse choked the alleys and lay rotting in the streets. Many of the inhabitants lounged in doorways, smoking, spitting, and gossiping. They gave the elves unfriendly looks as they passed, and a few shouted insults and advice to return whence they came and leave honest folk alone.

Behind them in the street they heard the sounds of a fight breaking out, with the clash of steel and a cry of pain. If there was a watch in Zeriak, it kept a low profile, for no one came to break up the dispute. The elves hurried along lest they be caught up in the scuffle. After Than-Khal, they had had enough of local jails.

The Bone and Bristle proved to be a ramshackle building crowded against the town's eastern wall. The party entered the common room and found a few men in the last stages of drunkenness sprawled on benches.

The landlord grudgingly gave them three rooms, under the prodding of Tashara's coin and Harfang's glare. He charged them an excessive amount, but the elf leader paid it without question. Dragonsbane crowded into the largest of the rooms, while the captain addressed them in a low voice.

"Harfang, Samustalen, Riadon, you take steel and purchase food and supplies for our journey. Try to make the purchases from several merchants so as not to excite suspicion of our real goal."

"Aye," interjected Malshaunt. "And remember, Harfang, that you are feeble minded." He gave a snort of laughter. Harfang's face turned pale, but with an effort he shrugged off the insult. Tashara gave no sign she had heard the mage.

"Ayshe," she said, "go about town. Ask about rumors of the White Wyrm, but be discreet and avoid being too widely noticed. The rest of us will remain here. It seems elves are none too popular in Zeriak."

Ayshe wasn't any too sure how popular dwarves were going to be either, but he nodded and slipped out of the inn.

The town was not large, and after wandering for a half hour, his feet led him to the sight and sound of Zeriak's smithy. A large, bare-chested man stood before a glowing forge holding a pair of iron tongs. With the tongs he turned the blade of a reaper as he shaped it on the anvil with blows of his hammer. Around him were arrayed the familiar tools of the trade: bickerns, stakes, swages, hammers, punches, tongs, chisels, fullers, and more.

"Holla, Master Dwarf! What can I do for you today?"

"Nothing, thank you." Ayshe returned. "I was merely enjoying watching a craft well performed by a master hand."

The smith chuckled. "I never heard dwarves rated for the sweetness of their tongues. A compliment like that makes me think you must want something."

The dwarf sauntered over to the anvil as the smith plunged the reaper blade into a bucket of cold water, sending up a cloud of steam. "I wouldn't think there'd be much use for that," he said, gesturing at the tool. "Where are the fields around here?"

"South, between here and the glacier, the land is good enough that some can grow a few crops. But for the most part, we get what we need in trade." The smith laid the blade aside to cool further and picked up a harness.

Ayshe's sharp eyes saw the broken buckle. "Would you care for a hand in this?" he asked. "It's been too long since I've done aught but sharpen blades and polish steel."

The smith laughed again and tossed the harness to him. "There's plenty of that to do here as well," he said, "but if it suits you to work, please yourself."

For the next few hours, Ayshe found himself more content than at almost any time since he'd left home to join the crew of the *Starfinder*. The smith—whose name was Saleh—was jovial and talkative, and Ayshe was content to let him talk, the flow of speech punctuated by the rattle of tools, the clang of the hammer, and the hiss of hot metal cooling.

From Saleh, the dwarf learned that life in a frontier town such as Zeriak was not for the faint of heart. Comforts were scarce, and foes were many. Saleh spoke of attacks on the town by the thanoi and, during the War of Souls, by the Knights of Neraka.

"We fought them off, though," he said proudly. "And they left us alone after that."

Not that it was easy, living in Zeriak. The road north to Tarsis was long and lonely, and occasionally travelers on it were attacked by raiding bands of thanoi, ogres, and sometimes by less easily identified creatures. It was the only road north by which goods and supplies could reach Zeriak. Ayshe began to understand why the centaur at the gate had been so suspicious. Along the borders, men barred their doors after the sun went down. None would venture beyond the town walls after dark.

The smith knew about the elves from the *Starfinder*; news in Zeriak evidently traveled fast. He expressed no opinion of elves and did not seem to think any less of Ayshe for traveling with them. The dwarf gathered that wandering bands of elves roved to and fro over the Plains but were not especially welcome in towns and villages. For the most part they camped in the open and kept themselves aloof from humans.

At last Ayshe found a chance to introduce the topic he'd been sent to inquire about. "D'you see anything of the white dragon Cryonis here?"

Cryonis, the dwarf knew from the book aboard the *Starfinder*, was a white dragon who lived in or around the Icereach glacier but occasionally left the area to raid and plunder.

Saleh shook his head. "His reach is to the west by two hundred miles or so. We've enough problems without that, thank the gods!"

"So there've never been dragons here?" Ayshe hazarded.

The smith gave him a sharp glance. "I didn't say that."

The dwarf waited for him to go on.

"'Twas a long time ago—twenty years or so. I was barely out of my teens and first apprenticed to Holmann, who was then the smith here. The town was attacked by a mighty white dragon."

Ayshe concentrated on the saddle he was mending. "A white dragon? But not Cryonis?"

"No. This was before Cryonis came to the southern reaches. And this was no ordinary dragon."

"How so?" Ayshe asked.

"It came out of a cloud in the sky." The smith's voice sank to a near whisper. "It swept over Zeriak, crumbling buildings like a storm. Its mane was serpents, and its claws were sharp as those of a tiger. Folk ran, but they couldn't escape. It slaughtered with lightning blasts, though that's said to be the power of blues, not whites. And it breathed a killing cold. Those it caught, it tore to pieces. Holmann and I ran for cover while houses were lifted up and tossed about like leaves in a storm. So much dust was in the air from the beating of the beast's wings, you couldn't see your hand in front of your face, and the sky was dark as night, though it was noon. And then, just like *that*"—he snapped his fingers—"it was gone."

"Where? Where did it go?"

The smith shrugged his big shoulders and picked up his hammer. "Who knows? Somewhere out there, I suppose." His arm swept south. "Folk here say it lairs beyond the Snow Sea, but who knows, really? As long as it never comes back here, I don't care."

"I've heard tell of the Snow Sea," the dwarf said. "Big, is it?"

"Big as a real sea, from all accounts. Not that anyone here has traversed it, mind you, but one or two of the younger, hardier men have been as far as its borders. They say it stretches out endlessly and that the wind is so fierce there that it whips the snow into waves. There's foam and storms, just as there are on the water." He shook his head. "Sounds like a terrible place to me. Whatever lies beyond it can keep its secrets for all of me."

Ayshe put down the saddle and gave the leather a final polish. "I must rejoin my companions," he said, standing. He held out a hand to Saleh. "Thank you for letting me forget my troubles for a few hours."

The smith took his hand. "Thank you, Master Dwarf. You're a fine craftsman, like many of your race. If you pass this way again and want to settle down, there's a spot here waiting for you." He lifted his hammer in farewell as Ayshe walked down the street.

THE GREAT WHITE WYRM

Harfang and his elf companions had returned by the time Ayshe reached the Bone and Bristle. Tashara was nowhere to be found, so the dwarf reported his findings to the mate, with the mage Malshaunt standing nearby. After the dwarf had finished and gone to get meat and drink, Harfang nodded thoughtfully.

"That fits with what we've learned," he said. "The White Wyrm lairs in the south somewhere. It can move between the planes, but it must come back into our reality every few weeks, just as a whale rises to the surface to breathe. It seems to emerge from its lair about every twenty to twenty-five years. We hear of it for a time, and then it disappears again. Perhaps it needs to rest. Perhaps there is something in its lair that gives it strength or that allows it to pass between the planes."

Malshaunt, passing his whip from hand to hand, grunted grudging assent. "And now we know where the lair is," he added with grim satisfaction. "The quest is within our reach."

Harfang shook his head and looked worried. "No, we know the general direction—that way"—he flung out a hand to the south—"but not the particular place. And finding three mountains in that mass is like looking for a white bear in a snowstorm. Not only that, but what you tell me of this Snow Sea doesn't make me feel better. If we—" He broke off, drumming his fingers nervously on the table. "We're not ready for this," he muttered. "The captain is like one possessed. She won't listen to reason, and she's determined to pursue the White Wyrm, even if it kills her and no matter the rest of us. And we still know nothing more about the precise location of the lair."

"What more would you have us know?" snapped the mage. "We know now, after all these years of searching, of these 'Mountains of the Moons.' We know they lie to the south, across the Snow Sea. Captain Tashara knows more of these matters than either you or I. *I* at least have confidence that she will guide us aright!"

Harfang stared south, where the mountains of Icereach reared up against the sky. "No, it's madness," he said. "Somewhere in that wilderness is the lair, but we've almost less than nothing to go on. Yet she proposes to drag us on this wild chase into *that* . . ." He gestured south.

Malshaunt stood before the mate, his eyes spitting fire. "You have never believed in this quest," he told Harfang. "From the time Tashara dragged you aboard the ship as a ragged urchin, you resisted her. She pulled you from the gutter, and you could not even show proper gratitude."

"And you would have been happy to throw me back, eh?"

"I accepted her decision because I believe in her. I accept her visions. Such things should not be argued with; they must be fed and nurtured. Yet, apparently, I am alone in Dragonsbane in understanding such a simple thing as accepting the captain's decisions."

Harfang looked at the mage. "Tell me, Malshaunt," he said at last, "where do your loyalties really lie? With Dragonsbane? Or with Tashara? And what would you do if you thought the captain had turned from her true path?"

The mage shook his head. "Weak, Harfang. Weak and weeping, like your pet dwarf. My loyalties lie with the person to whom I owe my life. To the person who is more to me than a captain, more than a leader, more than a companion of centuries. As a *man*"—he packed every ounce of scorn possible into the word—"I would not expect you to understand that." He turned on his heel and went out.

◆ ◆ ◉ ◆ ◆

That evening, Dragonsbane gathered once again. Tashara had isolated herself in a room all day, eating and drinking nothing. She emerged only long enough for Harfang to tell her of Ayshe's conversation with the Zeriak smith and the news of the wyrm. She stood next to the three mysterious bundles taken from the *Starfinder* and carried by the elves on their journey to Zeriak. Her pale skin seemed white and paper-thin, showing the blue veins beneath and slipping over bone and muscle. Ayshe thought she appeared thinner as well, as if the chase were devouring her from the inside. Although circles under her opaque eyes spoke of lack of sleep, her voice was clear and strong.

"Friends," she said, "so I may call you after our long leagues together. We stand on the edge of glory. The Great White Wyrm has retreated to its lair. We have, at long last, a clue as to the location of that lair. Now we shall track it and finally destroy it."

She lifted a bag that jingled as it moved. "Here are two hundred steel. They go to the first among you who sights the wyrm's lair and can direct us to it." She bent and pulled from the first bundle a shield. It was bright red with an argent border. In the center, also argent, was a rampant dragon, so realistic Ayshe could almost hear its low, sinister growl.

"This shield," she said, "belonged to B'ynn al'Tor, greatest of all Dragonsbane. For fifteen hundred years, it has guarded the leaders of our band and served us in our battle against the dragons. I swear before all of you that this is the shield I will carry into the last battle with the White Wyrm!"

From the elves there came a low murmur of admiration.

Tashara lifted the second bundle, a long shape wrapped in cloth and bound with leather thongs. "In these wrappings is the sword of Tess Kuthendra, borne by her for Dragonsbane when Istar thrived and the Swordsheath Scroll was young. After the Cataclysm, it was carried away from the north to Silvanesti, where it rested in secret for many centuries in the vaults of Silvanost before coming at last to me.

"This is the sword I pledge to bear in the last battle against the White Wyrm!"

Finally, she lifted the third bundle. Casting aside the rags that surrounded it, she revealed a box of black wood bound in steel.

She flung back the lid and brought forth the dragon's eye.

The elves gasped. The eye, straining against its bonds of gold and silver, surged this way and that, as if seeking to burst free. Within it, a pupil blinked malevolently and turned, surveying its watchers. Some of the elves turned aside or put their hands before their faces as if to shield themselves from its gaze.

Tashara looked at it for a moment in silence then spoke. "This dragon's eye I have borne for many a long year. None of you knew I carried it. It gave me sight with which to follow our enemy. It has served its purpose well."

She lifted the sword. The eye swung up, and for the first time it showed terror amid its hatred. The blind elf brought the sword down with a crash, slicing through the center of the eye, slashing the box that held it, driving through the table and onto the stone floor. Sparks sprang up from where the sword struck the stones, and they cracked and broke. There was a blinding flash of light and a hideous stench that set the elves of Dragonsbane, as well as Ayshe and Harfang, to gagging.

When they looked, the eye's halves lay still upon the floor, blood and ooze seeping from them. Tashara's voice swept away their astonishment and horror.

"I no longer have need of this foul remnant of wyrms. My sight is clear within me, and I know now where our foe is lodged. There is no turning back!

"My friends, we are here gathered, we hearty band of companions forged in fire and ice. We are the last heroes of Krynn. All others have perished in the wars and gone to wander among the stars. But we are here; we are the last. And our deed in slaying the White Wyrm will shine down through the centuries to come. We shall be worthy to sit at the side of Huma, of Magius, and of Lauralanthalasa, the Golden General.

"Who will join me in this quest?"

"I!"

THE GREAT WHITE WYRM

Every elf in the room sprang to his feet. Ayshe, too, was on his feet, his hand raised in salute. Malshaunt, his grim face alight, stamped his foot. The other elves took it up until the blows resounded through the inn, shaking the walls, accompanied by a chant:

"Tashara! Tashara! Tashara!"

The captain raised her hand for silence. "So be it. We leave in two days." She turned to Harfang, whose voice Ayshe did not recall hearing in the chorus of approbation.

"Check our supplies. Purchase anything additional we need. And patrol the town again. I want no crowds following us when we leave."

"Aye, Captain." The mate, expressionless, took a bag of steel from his commander. "Ayshe, you're with me. The rest of you," he said, turning to the elves, "stay here. There's no point in stirring up trouble."

Two days later, before dawn's first light had broken, the crew of the *Starfinder* stood assembled before the door of the Bone and Bristle. The air was crisp and cold, and their breath came in white clouds, mingling and hanging in the air. Each bore a heavy pack. They were clad in clothing as warm as they were able to find. The dwarf thought of their rations stowed in their supplies and wondered gloomily how long they would last when faced with the endless Snow Sea.

Beneath their garments, the elves wore leather armor, light enough to wear comfortably but heavy enough to give some protection. Each elf bore a shield and sword except for Otha-nyar, who carried her wyrmbarb, and Riadon and Lindholme, who bore bows and quivers of arrows. Tashara was unarmed, but behind her Ridrathannash carried the bundles that concealed the sword of Tess Kuthendra and the shield of B'ynn al'Tor. Malshaunt, as usual, bore his whip. Harfang carried a long sword as well as a short sword. The dwarf carried his axe and wore a suit of studded leather armor that he had fashioned for himself on board the ship.

Tashara turned her blind face to the south, where the mountains were dark shapes against a paling sky. Without a word, she set out, stepping briskly along the cobbles.

Silently, Dragonsbane followed her.

PART
3

CHAPTER

15

Outside Zeriak, the foothills that rose in the south were covered with the same low-growing scrub the party had encountered on their trek east from Ice Mountain Bay. In a few places, it had been cleared away to leave the fields Saleh had described to Ayshe, but they looked cold and barren under the winter sun, with only stubble showing above ground. Ayshe, laboring along behind Riadon and Samustalen, was at least partially shielded from the cold wind that blew against their faces over the bare earth.

At first Tashara ordered a careful watch to be sure none of the townsfolk were following them, but it soon became clear no one from Zeriak had any interest in venturing into the icy wastes to the south.

The party tramped along mostly in silence. The exuberance they had felt at Tashara's speech in the Bone and Bristle began to fade in the face of the terrain's harsh and indifferent cold. Harfang, pacing at Tashara's side, rarely spoke, save to give an order to halt or to resume the march. The captain herself spoke not a single word though she walked steadily, her back straight, her head held high. Not for the first time, Ayshe marveled at the ability of the blind elf woman to move without aid or hesitation.

Malshaunt walked close behind her, his black cloak flapping in the breeze. He looked, to the dwarf, like a black crow, its feathers stirred by the wind, its beak thrust forward. The mage's right hand, lean and clawlike, rested perpetually on his whip.

Because of the rough character of the landscape, their progress was slow—not more than six or seven miles a day. The dwarf wondered how that would affect their stock of provisions but thought it best not to raise the subject with either of Dragonsbane's commanders.

At night their fires were small and smoked heavily with little warmth. They wrapped themselves in blankets, keeping out the cold as best they might and sleeping fitfully. Ayshe remembered with longing his comfortable hammock swinging belowdecks aboard the *Starfinder*, and the warmth of the forge fire as it sent sparks from the deck into the night sky scattered with stars. On the Plains the moons rose each night in a cloudless sky, glaring down in silver and red until sometimes they seemed like great eyes watching Dragonsbane's progress. Most of the party avoided looking at them.

On their fifth day out from Zeriak, the hill they were climbing ended in a rocky ridge, as if it were the spine of some great animal buried beneath the earth. Riadon—whose slight build and miraculous ability to blend with the landscape made him an admirable scout—and Jeannara went forward, keeping low to the ground, and crawled up the rocks to peer over the top.

They returned shortly, faces grim. Jeannara reported to Tashara. "There's a valley," she said. "It's covered in boulders, some large as houses. Beyond, there's smoke."

"Ogres?" queried the elf.

"Thanoi."

Riadon added, "We watched through the glass. It's a village, lying on a river running from the mountains. I'd guess there are sixty or seventy of the walrus folk there."

Tashara nodded. "Are there boulders between us and the settlement where we could find concealment?" she asked.

"Aye," the second mate returned. "Two to the west, three or four to the east, about fifty yards from the nearest huts."

Ayshe, listening, had expected the captain to order them to pass around the settlement and continue. Instead, to his surprise, she prepared her followers for an attack.

"Harfang, you take five bowmen and conceal yourselves behind the boulders to the south. On my signal, commence volleying your arrows. The remainder of us will attack from the north and draw them into the open. Again on my signal, charge."

The elves divided, and Harfang's party slipped south about a furlong then cautiously mounted the rocky ridge and disappeared over it. Tashara, aided by Jeannara and Malshaunt, led the remainder of Dragonsbane north and over the ridge.

Having seen the elves prepare for battle only on board the *Starfinder*, Ayshe was impressed at how expertly and easily they moved on land. At the top of the ridge, they wriggled like snakes through the scant cover, each intent on reaching a preassigned battle station. The dwarf did his best to imitate their stealth, but from the irritated glances Jeannara flashed at him, he knew he was clumsy.

The boulders were enormous—great rocks that might have been hurled by giants in some gargantuan contest of strength or skill. They concealed the elves completely from the cluster of huts that marked the thanoi settlement. Beyond, Ayshe could just make out a glint of water where the river meandered aimlessly through the valley.

Jeannara surveyed everything carefully through her glass then tugged Tashara's sleeve. "All in place and ready, ma'am."

"Malshaunt!" the captain whispered.

The dour elf mage crawled forward.

Tashara jerked her head in the direction of the huts. "On my mark!"

The mage muttered softly to himself, his hands cupped in front of him. Ayshe, his axe in his hands, could see a glow through Malshaunt's fingers.

"Now!"

Malshaunt spat a harsh, guttural word and lifted his hands. From them a spark flew toward the thanoi village, expanding as it became a ball of fire. It burst in the center of the huts with a boom that rocked the valley floor.

The burst was so brilliant, Ayshe turned his face away lest he be blinded. When he looked back, the huts at the center of the village had been flattened, while many of the others were burning brightly.

Malshaunt lifted his hands again and spoke another word. His hands sent forth a group of bolts, like arrows of light. They wove through the air just in time to meet walrus men rushing toward the source of the fireball. The missiles crashed into their chests and exploded. The thanoi fell backward and lay in the snow, their bodies still twitching.

Cries came from the huts, and other dark figures ran toward the boulder where Tashara, Malshaunt, and the others lay concealed. The figures drew closer, covering the distance with surprising speed. Tashara, her whole body as finely drawn as a bowstring, raised her arm and brought it down.

"Now!"

Malshaunt hurled another set of bolts, not at the charging thanoi, but into the sky. In answer, a flight of arrows came from the south, taking the leading thanoi in the side and dropping them in their tracks.

The archers with Tashara loosed as well, and Malshaunt sent forth another flight of magical bolts as the walrus men turned and swayed, unsure which way to charge.

"*Now!*" Tashara roared again in a voice that sounded over the thanoi's cries.

The elves and Ayshe burst from their hiding place and bore down on the walrus folk, just as Harfang and his companions did the same. Only Malshaunt hung back from the melee, sending another fireball crashing into the remains of the village.

To his surprise, Ayshe felt a wild joy seize him, as a red mist lowered before his eyes. He ran forward and met a thanoi lifting a crude wooden spear, its haft bound in leather.

It was the first time the dwarf had seen one of the walrus folk close up and out of water. As if suspended in time, he noted the bristling mustache and hair, the claw-tipped flippers, and especially the long, razor-sharp tusks that protruded on either side of its tooth-filled mouth.

He slashed down with his axe and the creature parried with its spear, blocking the blow with a force that made the dwarf's teeth rattle. It thrust at Ayshe, and he managed to twist away, swinging his blade at the huge foot that clawed at him. His axe gashed the creature, which snarled and lunged again. The dwarf brought his blade down on the wooden spear and sliced cleanly through it. His backstroke slashed away one of the thanoi's tusks and most of its check to an accompanying spurt of blood.

The creature howled in pain and staggered. Ayshe saw his opportunity and brought his axe around in a wide arc. The thanoi's head leaped from its shoulders, and its body toppled into the suddenly reddened snow.

Another walrus man rushed at the dwarf, and Ayshe brought up the flat of his blade to catch it a ringing blow on the front of its skull. The creature stopped dead and fell forward. With a shriek, Jeannara leaped on its unconscious body and slashed her dirk across its throat.

Two more of the creatures hurled themselves forward. Jeannara came up with a twist and knifed one of them in the leg as she rolled

THE GREAT WHITE WYRM

past it. Ayshe, bracing himself, his legs spread wide, met a blow
from the other's spear with his axe. The two weapons rang together,
and the dwarf dodged to one side, bringing his axe around again.
Dim memories came to him of his old training master beneath the
Khalkist Mountains shouting angrily at a group of young dwarves,
practicing with wooden axes.

"Fast on your feet! *Fast*, you slugworms! *Fast*, or die where you
stand!"

Ayshe's thanoi spun with a speed surprising for its bulk, and
struck high. The dwarf parried, trying to catch the spear's haft
in his axe blade, but the walrus man was too crafty for that and
drew the weapon back. The dwarf noticed that the creature had a
necklace of teeth and bones strung about its neck, bearing, at the
center, a carven pendant, and he wondered if it were some sort of
chief or shaman among the thanoi.

He had little time to think. The walrus man struck again, with
a clawed flipper instead of the spear. Ayshe did not dodge in time,
and its claws raked his arm. He felt red-hot pains shoot up into
his chest, but he did not dare let himself become distracted. One
part of his mind worked, as if distanced from the battle, reviewing
tactics, seeking an opening.

There! He found it. The thanoi's back step was just a bit too
short. Ayshe slashed down and felt, with satisfaction, his blade bite
into flesh. The creature howled and sprayed red across the snow.
The dwarf followed up with a thrust with the top of his axe that
caught the thanoi in the chest, propelling it backward. It sprawled,
and the dwarf cut its head from its shoulders in a single stroke.

Jeannara had dispatched her thanoi with a deep stab to the
heart. Her face was streaked with blood, but none of it appeared
to be her own.

Ayshe looked around the battleground. The thanoi were
scrambling back to the ruins of their village, except for the many
dead, who lay in untidy heaps in the snow. Tashara, a red blade in

her hand, stood over several bodies. The dwarf could not help but notice the sword she carried was not the one in her bundle, the one she had said would be used in the final battle with the wyrm. The captain cocked an ear toward the retreating thanoi, then, dropping the sword, snatched a bow from the elf standing next to her and sent an arrow into the back of a walrus man. He dropped with a groan.

Following her lead, the elves of Dragonsbane loosed their shafts with such skill that not one of the thanoi reached the burning huts. Tashara lifted her sword again.

"Sweep the settlement!" she called. The band marched forward, slashing at any bodies that moved. One or two thanoi concealed among the remains of the settlement fled for the river and were ruthlessly cut down. Within minutes, no living walrus folk were on the plain.

Ayshe watched the slaughter without participating, his stomach churning. Killing in the heat of battle was one thing, but that brutal cleansing was something else. Not for the first time, he felt there was something cold-blooded about Tashara and her followers.

"Well fought, Master Dwarf!" Harfang, coming up from behind him, put a hand on his shoulder. He had a streak of blood across his forehead but seemed unharmed. The mate looked happier than he had for days, as if the battle had been cathartic.

Ayshe turned away. "Did we have to kill them all?" he demanded. "Come to that, why did we attack them in the first place? They were doing no harm. We could easily have gone around them, and they would have been none the wiser."

The mate snorted. "Not very familiar with thanoi, are you? I thought you'd learned your lesson from that fishing boat we encountered—the one attacked by spawn." He led the way past the huts, burning down to smoldering cinders. Malshaunt, oblivious to the destruction, was sitting on the ground in the middle of it all, his eyes closed, his body rigid. The dwarf had seen the mage do that before and knew that after such an expenditure of magic, immediate rest was essential for Malshaunt.

The huts were—or had been—grouped in a crude circle around an open area where there had recently been a fire. Along one side of the fire stood two poles, about five feet apart, with a rope strung between them. Dangling from the rope were a collection of objects that it took Ayshe a moment to identify. Then he gasped.

They were human heads. The thanoi had strung them through the ears so they gazed with the blank stares of the dead. Most were men, but there were several female heads as well. One or two had been hacked or gored in a savage manner.

Harfang looked at them and said without expression, "The thanoi make regular raids on caravans of travelers, either on the edge of Icewall or, occasionally, farther south. So they told me in Zeriak. These are probably Ice Folk." He glanced at the dwarf. "Do you still regret attacking them?"

Ayshe was silent. There seemed nothing to say.

The settlement yielded a small cache of dried fish but little else Dragonsbane found useful. They spent the night among the ruins—having buried the heads Ayshe and Harfang had found— and early the next morning continued on their way.

The tundra had given way to snow, and the land sloped gently up to meet the edges of a swelling range of hills. Wind from the distant mountains whistled around the rocks and seemed to sing a never-ending lament for something lost beyond recall. When the sun shone on the snow, the light was blinding, and the party learned to wrap rags around their eyes to protect them from the glare. All were clad in their warmest clothes, purchased in Zeriak, which they wore over their padded armor. Fur-lined cloaks and pants kept out the worst of the cold.

At night they huddled together for warmth. Malshaunt managed to keep a small magical fire burning but only for a little time. The mage seemed more withdrawn than usual and stayed close to Tashara, his eyes rarely leaving the captain. Harfang had sunk back into his gloom, and nothing the other elves could say or do seemed to stir him from it. The low feeling communicated itself to the rest of the company, and fewer and fewer words passed among them as they made their way south. Still, they took comfort from the mountain peaks drawing steadily closer, and so far, the way had not been burdensome. Some, in fact, wondered aloud if the stories of the Snow Sea they had heard in Zeriak had been exaggerated, perhaps because so few in the town traveled into the frozen reaches of the south.

On the third day after the battle with the thanoi, they reached another ridge crowned with the windswept rocks that seemed to abound in that country. The snow blew against the stone, and, looking to the south, it was clear their eyes had deceived them. The mountains, among whose majestic peaks were somewhere concealed the Mountains of the Moons and the lair of their quarry, were much farther off than imagined. Before them the hills fell to a great plain, white and featureless. The whiteness was blinding, and they looked away from it to avoid harming their sight even behind the rags they wore.

"The Snow Sea," observed Jeannara, coming up behind Harfang. Tashara stood a little way away, her face turned, as always, to the south, as if her blind eyes, proof against the whiteness, could somehow envision the end of their journey.

Harfang sighed. "I know. How long to cross it, d'you think?"

Jeannara pursed her lips. "Well, there doesn't seem to be any obstacles, and we'll be traveling on flat ground. Still . . . a week at least."

"How are supplies?"

"We'll last," the elf said grimly, "provided we don't have far to go beyond that. That's not what worries me, though."

The mate turned his gaze to her face without saying anything.

She shrugged. "We may get there. If we're on the right track, if these Mountains of the Moons stand out clearly from the other mountains, if our captain's visions or voices or seeings or whatever's driving her forward are leading us in the right direction."

"Well?"

"So we get there. But I wonder if we'll ever get back."

Harfang made no answer and returned to his study of the Snow Sea. Since he'd cast his fortune with Dragonsbane—or had it cast, more accurately, by Tashara's relentless call—he had refused to think about the future more than a week or two ahead. In part, that was a habit born of his years on the streets of Palanthas, when daily survival was the most important thing. What would happen? What role would he play? Where he would go after they caught up with the Great White Wyrm? He had no idea of the answers to those questions. For the first time in his life, he confronted the idea that, beyond the quest on which he'd embarked twenty years ago, he might not have a future.

Otha-nyar came up and saluted. "Something to the east, sir."

Harfang swung around, brought the spyglass to his eye, and stared for several minutes.

"Thanoi," he said at last.

"Aye, sir. Only three of them. If we move fast, we can catch them."

"Do it."

Otha-nyar sped away and vanished east, taking three other elves with her. Harfang could see them gradually overtaking the tiny dark figures whom he had identified as walrus folk. The thanoi were fleeing, but their large bodies made them clumsier than the fleet-footed elves. At last they turned and stood at bay. As the rest of Dragonsbane made their way toward the confrontation, two of the thanoi fell to elven arrows. The third stood motionless, surrounded.

When the rest of the band caught up, Tashara stalked to the front and began questioning the creature, speaking in the Common tongue. The thanoi answered, its voice rasping and heavily accented, as if its vocal chords had some difficulty forming the syllables of Common speech.

"What is your name?"

The thanoi responded with a string of unpronounceable syllables.

"Where are you going?"

The creature flung out a clawed flipper. "Brackenrock."

"Why?"

"Ogres send out scouts. Report back. Use thanoi."

"Know you of the Mountains of the Moons?"

The creature was silent. Harfang struck it with the flat of his sword, leaving a trickle of blood along its bloated face.

"Yes," the thanoi moaned.

"Where are they?"

"There—somewhere." Again the flipper gestured, this time to the south and west.

"How can we find them?"

"Cannot!" The creature's voice grated on their nerves, coming as harsh as the sound of ice breaking. "Across Snow Sea it is! You find white death there if you go. Bad place."

Tashara's voice remained calm, and her tone was unchanged. "Where? How can we find this place, the Mountains of the Moons?"

The creature shook its head, and Harfang struck it again. His blow cracked one of its tusks, and the creature shrieked in pain. "Death there!" it wailed. "Death on white wings!"

Tashara pushed her face next to the wounded walrus man. Though she was smaller by a head and a half, the creature recoiled from her as if terrified of her blind visage.

"I am fated to find those mountains," she told the thanoi. "Help me, and you shall live."

The creature stopped its wailing and stared at her. Its face went blank, as if the walrus man and the elf were communicating in some way the watchers could not understand.

"Look for place of joining moons," it said at last, its tone sullen. "Where moons and mountain meet, there is Mountains of Moons."

Tashara turned to Harfang. "There." There was a note of triumph in her voice.

An odd sound came from the walrus man. After a moment, Ayshe realized the creature was laughing.

"Yes! Go!" he chuckled. "Go and die, foolish elf! Is written in prophecy that elves seek wyrm and die."

Tashara turned back, her face very still. "What did you say?"

"Elves seek wyrm and die. So is told!"

"What prophecy is this?"

"Old prophecy. Very old." The thanoi closed one eye, partly swollen from Harfang's blows, in an attempt to look cunning. "You go, you die. That what prophecy tell thanoi. We watch. We watch White Wyrm many, many years. But it not kill us. Because we watch."

Tashara listened, head tilted slightly to one side. When the thanoi's voice stopped, she lifted the bound bundle that she carried, the sword of Kuthendra. She cast it on the ground before the thanoi.

"Open it!"

The walrus man did not move. Jeannara bent and loosened the straps. She pulled the sword free of its swaddling and handed it to the captain.

The thanoi gaped at the sword. Its handle was bound in black leather, studded in gems that shone with an inner fire. Its well-polished blade, etched with Elvish runes, gleamed in the low evening sun, casting a golden reflection.

Tashara lifted it, turning it this way and that. "With this

sword," she told the thanoi, "I shall slay the White Wyrm."

The creature stared at her. Then suddenly it snarled and lunged, claws outstretched. Harfang started forward, but Tashara, spinning like a dancer, whirled the blade over her head and brought it across, slashing the thanoi's head from its shoulders. A spray of blood fanned across the snow.

Tashara plunged the blade into the snow and drew it out, wiping it clean. "Kuthendra's sword has been baptized," she said. She handed the blade to Jeannara and without hesitation turned toward the southwest, setting off across the vast, empty expanse of the Snow Sea.

The snow that covered the Snow Sea looked smooth, but it was deep, in some cases rising to the thighs of the elves who plowed their way through it. It slowed their pace and wearied their limbs until all their existence seemed to have been spent struggling through that unending field of white. Although near the edges of the sea, the snow was smooth and featureless, it soon rose in waves, the crests of which sometimes reared high over the party's heads. Sometimes they were able to break through those waves and beat a path across them. Other times they struggled, pushing aside the snow and forging a way over the tops of the swells before plunging down again. It was painful, wearying work, and the snow soon covered them, dampening their clothing and freezing them.

When night came—and it came very early—they hollowed out caves in the snow in which to sleep. The caves kept out the worst of the wind, but even wrapped in every blanket and cloak they could find, the party felt the bitter cold acutely.

Ayshe found that what he had thought was cold before had been the merest chill compared to what he felt at that moment. Every bone in his body was stiff with frost. His fingers and toes felt numb, and he had to massage them constantly before sleeping for fear of frostbite. In the mornings when he awoke, usually after only a few hours of restless sleep, his blanket was stiff and cold, and he had to struggle to get up. He realized his great enemy in that environment was his own sweat, which froze almost instantly and covered his clothing in ice. His hair and beard were brittle, and after a few days, his beard actually shortened as parts froze and broke off. The party slept close to one another, huddling for warmth.

Malshaunt's magical fires melted enough snow to fill their water bottles but gave little real heat and could not be sustained for long. After each fire, the mage sat, eyes closed, resting and renewing his magical energies. Each time it was more of a struggle for him, and yet his dark eyes shone as brightly as ever, following Tashara as she rose each morning and set out toward the mountains that rimmed the southern edge of the sea.

The party's spirits, which had risen after the battle with the thanoi, fell again. Riadon, who plodded next to Ayshe in the line, seemed to the dwarf to be growing more morose and withdrawn with each step. He spoke little and ate less, and his strength ebbed from his emaciated body.

Two nights after they had begun the crossing of the Snow Sea, Ayshe lay awake and listened to the labored breathing of the elf. The two lay with their backs to one another, but the dwarf could draw little or no warmth from his companion. When at last light crept across the sky and Ayshe rose, Riadon lay wrapped in his blanket. The dwarf shook him and, looking more closely, called for Harfang.

The mate, Jeannara, and Ayshe stood in a little circle around the frozen body of their companion. Riadon's face was pale, his lips blue. The mate reached over him and loosened his blanket with a jerk. He spread the woolen shroud over the elf and turned away.

"Aren't we going to bury him?" the dwarf asked.

Harfang looked up at the leaden sky. Snowflakes were drifting down in a lazy pattern, brushing their faces with a gentle caress. "He'll be buried soon enough," he grunted. "We have no fuel to give him a proper funeral." He turned his back.

Ayshe and Jeannara shouldered their packs and followed the rest of Dragonsbane on what seemed a never-ending journey south.

CHAPTER

16

The flakes whirled faster in a growing wind that scoured the Snow Sea. The wind, instead of the whistles and cries it had emitted amid the rocky hills leading to the vast plain, resolved itself into a long, continuous moaning, like a woman in pain. Several times Ayshe imagined he could hear words in its lament, but he knew he must be mistaken.

The figures of his companions became gray shadows ahead of him, toiling onward, bent against the blast, like old trees clinging to the soil amid a winter storm. The dwarf's short legs struggled through the drifts to keep up with them.

The snow grew thicker. Several times the dwarf lost sight of Jeannara, the elf closest to him, but then her bent back and legs came into view again.

A gust of wind roared over the Snow Sea, catching Ayshe by surprise and upending him into a drift. He struggled to free himself and at last stood up, soaked to the skin, shivering violently. Of the elves, there was no sign.

He rushed forward to catch up. His eyes were glued to the landscape in front of him, searching for signs of his companions' passage, but the swift-falling snow blotted out all tracks. He shouted, but the wind swallowed his words.

He looked about. Was he right? Was that the direction in which they had been traveling? He searched his senses but couldn't be sure. Again and again he cried out, but there was no answer but snow and wind.

He had stood in one place so long the snow had drifted against him, piling around his legs as high as his thighs. He had to move forward, or he would be covered. He was dizzy, aching from his fall, and soaked to the skin. He could feel the dampness hardening into a sheet of thin ice covering his flesh. The impenetrable whiteness blotted out everything. He blinked in an attempt to clear his eyes, and still everything swam before him. He rubbed his eyes and, choosing a direction at random, set out, bending his head against the storm. He staggered on until, his feet like lead, he sank to his knees.

A feeling of futility came over the dwarf. Was there any point? He was lost and alone in that great expanse of snow with nothing to shield him from the elements. Who knew how long the storm would blow? Who knew how long before his companions would miss him? And even when they discovered him gone, would they imperil the quest to turn back and look for a dwarf, one who had, in a way, forced himself on their company?

It would be easier, so much easier to remain there.

He felt drowsy, and for the first time he could remember, his legs and feet were growing warm. He was not even aware of sinking deeper into the snow. Visions flashed before him: of Chaval and Zininia sitting before the fire in their home, Zininia cuddling her new baby; of afternoons boating with Kharast, both of them pretending to fish but really floating idly and enjoying the comfort of companionship and warm sunshine. His memory stretched further back to his first wanderings away from the Khalkist Mountains, and before that time, to the great caverns where he and his fellow dwarves had mined for riches.

THE GREAT WHITE WYRM

A gray veil fell over his sight, and he reached up to push it away. Beyond it, dark shapes were moving.

Dark figures.

They had found him! Ayshe lifted up a shout with every ounce of strength left in his aching chest. The veil parted, and a hand grasped his cloak and pulled him out of the bed of snow.

No, a clawed hand!

Ayshe followed the arm, clad in heavy black armor. It was attached to a muscular shoulder, from behind which protruded a pair of slender wings. The nightmare vision was topped by a narrow, reptilian face with a pair of bright red eyes.

The clawed hand reached for the dwarf's face, and blackness mercifully blotted out his consciousness.

He was bound tightly, hand and foot. That was the first thing he was aware of. The second was that he was warm, more or less. His face and limbs tingled, but he was awake and alert, free of the paralyzing drowsiness that had overtaken him in the storm.

Ayshe looked around and realized that although he was warm, the storm had not abated. He could hear the howling of the wind, and his nose smelled snow in the air. Yet he was sheltered from the worst of it. He lay on the floor of a tent made of animal skins crudely stitched together. A fire was burning in the middle of the tent—a magical fire, Ayshe surmised, since it appeared not to consume any fuel and did not give off smoke. But it filled the tent with heat, and that was all that mattered to him.

Around the fire, sitting cross-legged, were four or five of the creatures who had captured him. Their wings, Ayshe saw, were too small to give support to their ungainly bodies. They were eating—tearing at meat still on the bone. What sort of meat it was, the dwarf did not care to imagine.

Ayshe had never seen them in the flesh before, but from others' descriptions, he knew they were draconians. Formed from a corruption of the eggs of good dragons toward the beginning of the War of the Lance, they were, by all accounts, savage and uninclined to kindness. A part of the dwarf's brain wondered why he was still alive, why they had not hacked him to death on the spot.

One of the dragon men noticed him stirring. The creature rose, took one of the meat bones, and held it out to him with a gesture indicating that he should eat it. Ayshe shook his head, and the draconian shrugged and returned to the fire. Shortly afterward, he offered Ayshe some water, and that the dwarf drank greedily.

The draconians' language seemed to be made up of hisses and snarls, and Ayshe could make no sense of it. In a while, though, another draconian came through the tent flap, shaking snow from his armor. The others rose hastily and saluted. The officer returned their salutes and came to crouch near Ayshe.

He was bigger than his comrades, with flaring horns on either side of his head. His eyes glinted with intelligence and malice.

"Well, my little friend," he growled in heavily accented Common, "what brings a dwarf so far out into the Snow Sea?"

Ayshe, his blurred mind racing, made no reply. The draconian casually slapped him. His claws left deep scratches across the dwarf's face. They burned, and Ayshe wondered momentarily if the draconians' claws carried poison of some sort.

"I . . . I was lost," the dwarf managed to gasp through cracked and swollen lips.

"Lost?" The creature gave a short, harsh bark of laughter. "One doesn't lose oneself in the Snow Sea. Where were you going?"

The few moments had given Ayshe time to focus. Whatever the cost, he decided, he must keep the draconians from learning of the presence of Dragonsbane in the Snow Sea. The dragon men were strong, well fed, warm, and well equipped—more than a match for the elves. To what end the draconians were traveling there and what plans they had in mind for him he could not fathom, but he was sure he would not survive his capture. Let that be his sacrifice, then, his final atonement for Chaval, Zininia, and their child. The thought filled him with a great peace.

The draconian leader repeated, "Where were you going?"

Ayshe clamped his mouth shut.

The leader shrugged and nodded to a pair of the smaller dragon men. They dragged him out of the tent and back into the howling wind and driving snow. Dimly he could see the shapes of other tents, set in orderly rows radiating out from a central space. To that space he was pulled by the draconians. One produced a short knife with a jagged blade stained with something dark. Ayshe tried to keep his thoughts on his friends, on the smith and his wife, but he could not keep his knees from trembling.

The draconian made a quick slash. Ayshe, to his surprise, felt no pain. His cloak fell to the snow, cut from his shoulders. The draconian tore away his shirt, and the dwarf felt the sting of cold wind and snow against his bare flesh. Only then did he notice the officer was wielding a short, savage-looking whip. A moment later, the first blow fell across his back.

The draconian was far more skilled in torture than the jailer in Than-Khal. The dwarf thought he had never known what pain was until that instant. The cold wind blew against the welts raised by the whip, and Ayshe's mind wandered along dark roads to far-off places.

He must have fainted. He felt himself borne along, slung roughly over the shoulder of a draconian. A blanket—or the remains of his cloak, he was not sure—had been thrown over him and secured with a rope. It rubbed against the raw, bleeding flesh of his back with each step the draconian took. His mouth was dry, his face numb from the cold. He could no longer feel his hands and feet and gave them up to frostbite. He coughed.

The draconian carrying him looked around, his face inches from that of the dwarf. He gave a raucous screech of laughter. "Waking up? Had a good sleep? Well, sleep while you can, you maggoty slime. You won't get much when we get to Brackenrock."

Ayshe managed to gasp a single word. "Brackenrock?"

"Yes. That's where we're taking you, my beauty. To Brackenrock." The draconian gave a high-pitched giggle that ended in a squeal. "You're lucky, little maggot. It's almost time for—" His voice veered into a torrent of guttural syllables. "Dragondream. That's right. Maybe you'll get to witness part of it before they cut you into pieces and feed you to the yeti."

Despite himself, Ayshe felt better. Concentrating on the draconian's speech, which was slurred and difficult to understand at times, seemed to help. It made him feel less cold and made his back hurt less.

"What's Dragondream?"

The act of talking fluently while running did not seem to bother the creature at all. He bore the dwarf as if the latter were made of feathers.

"Every twenty years, the Great Wyrm of the South sleeps. And in its sleeping, it sends out dreams to us. At Brackenrock, the great festival of Dragondream celebrates five years of such dreams as you can't imagine. They are *rr'spathgh chal'achrragh . . .*" His voice spun away into the noises of his own speech, as if he'd forgotten he was speaking to the dwarf. Finally he caught himself and laughed again. "Perhaps you'll have a part to play in the festival, you stinking dwarf maggot. Perhaps we'll eat your flesh and drink your blood in honor of the Great Wyrm."

Ayshe fought down a wave of nausea. "Where . . . does the wyrm sleep?"

THE GREAT WHITE WYRM

A cry from the leader cut short whatever reply the dwarf's bearer might have given to the question. The draconians halted, and Ayshe was flung down in the snow. Flakes still filled the air, stirred by a restless wind, but the draconians had marched or run without hesitation, as if their noses could detect the scent of home in that wilderness. Still, their progress had been slow, hampered as they were by the drifts. The dwarf guessed the party might be ten miles from where he'd been captured but no more.

On the orders of the captain, the dragon men set about their assigned tasks with military precision. Swiftly they cleared the snow from a large area and erected their tents, following the same wheel-spoke pattern Ayshe had noted earlier. Some of the dragon men skilled in magic kindled fires in the tents and one large fire in the center of the encampment. It gave off a generous heat and melted the snow beneath their feet. One dragged Ayshe near the fire, as much to guard him in comfort as for the dwarf's benefit.

When all was done to ready the camp, the draconians assembled in their ranks and faced southwest, their faces toward the driving snow. Led by their captain, they began a slow, sonorous chant in the draconian language. The wind whipped away the words from their narrow lips. Ayshe could make nothing of it, but several times he was sure the dragon men had chanted the same words used by his captor when speaking of Dragondream.

Perhaps it was only his imagination. A great weariness stole over him. So that was to be his fate: Torn apart by draconians as part of a ceremony worshiping a mysterious white dragon in the frozen south. If he'd heard the tale years before, he would have laughed at it.

The ceremony over, his captor returned and carried him to a tent. There, the draconian soldiers sat, eating and drinking, shouting every now and then with laughter at some jest in their snarling language. Ayshe, tightly tied, listened, hoping for a clue, though he knew any more information he gained about the White Wyrm was pointless. He drank water and ate a bit of bread that was offered him.

Finally, when the conversation had died down, he asked, "What dreams does the wyrm send you?"

The draconians were silent, and Ayshe wondered if they were surprised or offended by his effrontery. Then the draconian who had carried the dwarf during the day squawked with laughter and turned to Ayshe. He seemed to enjoy talking.

"Why do you want to know, maggot? Want some of the dreams? The wyrm doesn't give her gifts to maggoty dwarves."

"She?" Ayshe asked. In the time he'd been with Dragonsbane, he could not remember that the wyrm had been assigned a gender.

The draconian ignored the question and went on. "She sends us dreams of the world ruled by dragons. A world where dragons fill the skies and the thunder of their wings makes all over creatures flee in terror. *Tasshaff'shch marellcha gach massstichent . . .*" He shook his head and glared at Ayshe, as if he'd been trapped into revealing too much. "Such things are not for the maggoty likes of you."

Ayshe nodded humbly. "Does the wyrm visit Brackenrock?" he asked.

"Nay. Such things are kept hidden in secret places. She lairs beneath the Mountains of the Moons, and from her Dreamchamber she sends forth her thoughts over the frozen lands."

One of the draconian's companions put out a claw, attempting to restrain the other from speaking, but the speaker shook it off angrily and hissed a reply, with a jerk of his head toward Ayshe. Without understanding their language, Ayshe could read the meaning plainly: he would be dead soon, and whatever knowledge he gained would die with him.

With nothing to lose, he asked, "Where are these Mountains of the Moons?"

The draconian stretched out his hand. "Beyond the Snow Sea. Through the Pass of Tarmock's Fangs lies the Valley of White

Death, surrounded by the Mountains of the Moons. There lies the Great Wyrm's Dreamchamber.

Ayshe shut his eyes. It was the supreme irony, he thought. He had it. He had the knowledge for which Dragonsbane had been seeking all those long decades. And he was going to die.

Presently the draconians in the tent rolled themselves in blankets and lay down. They kept no watch over the prisoner, since as well as his bonds, there was nowhere for the dwarf to go should he escape from the tent. Ayshe, well aware of that, lay on his side, thinking. A draconian had thrown a blanket over him as well, and the magical fire continued to burn. The dwarf found it odd that under the circumstances he was more physically comfortable than he had been while in the company of his friends.

The snoring of the draconians made his head ache, and his heart was oppressed with the knowledge that there was no way out for him. Even if he could slip free, it was impossible for him to traverse the long miles over the Snow Sea back to Zeriak with no direction and no supplies. Only death awaited him, in some hideous form at Brackenrock.

Draconian voices swelled in a hideous cacophony that not even the tent and the still-falling snow could mask. They drove against the dwarf's mind like the strokes of the whip he'd endured earlier. There seemed something odd about their guttural voices, however. They contained not ecstasy, but a note of terror.

With a great effort, the dwarf rolled over and raised his head. The draconians in the tent were on their feet, swords drawn. Several rushed out, while the one who had earlier spoken with Ayshe grabbed the captive and hauled him outside into the whirling snow and cold.

The snowflakes parted like a curtain, and a lithe, leaping, dark figure burst through them, a sword in one hand, a long dagger in the other. The attacker swept the sword across the throat of the draconian, pirouetted, and plunged the dagger into the neck of another. The dragon man went down, kicking and clutching at the blade. He pulled it out, and a shower of blood from a severed artery turned the snow around him to crimson. He thrashed a few more times and was still.

Another dark figure sprang forward and thrust a blade into the torso of a draconian standing near Ayshe. The attacker—she, the dwarf saw her long hair flying out behind her—pulled the blade up and gutted the creature, who fell backward, knocking Ayshe to the ground.

Shrieks and groans came from other parts of the camp, accompanied by the clash of steel and the soft hiss of arrows. Ayshe, face pressed against the snow by the weight of the body across him, could see nothing. Then the pressure was relieved and a pair of hands raised him to a sitting position. Someone slit his bonds, and he was able to stretch his hands in front of him. He looked up and saw Samustalen's eyes dark in a face swathed with cloth to keep out the cold and wind. Without saying a word, the elf clapped him on the shoulder.

Around them, the sounds of battle diminished as the snow grew less and stopped altogether. Bodies lay sprawled on the ground, shrouded in white. Samustalen led Ayshe around them, at the same time wrapping a fresh cloak around the dwarf's shivering shoulders.

A short distance away, they found Harfang cleaning his sword. The draconian leader lay in the snow, arms outstretched, claws digging into the frozen ground. The first mate looked at Ayshe with satisfaction. "Master Dwarf! Still with us!"

Ayshe nodded and managed a smile. "Aye, sir." He wanted to say something more in gratitude but couldn't find the words.

Jeannara appeared, nodded to Ayshe, and said something softly to Harfang. The lines in the man's face deepened, and he cursed. Spinning on his heel, he walked away. Jeannara followed, and Ayshe and Samustalen joined her.

They found the mate and several other companions of Dragonsbane staring at a body sprawled in the snow. It was Omanda, the elf healer. Her bag, containing herbs and potions, lay beside her, its contents spilling onto the snow. Her face was peaceful despite the horrid wound that gaped at her neck.

From somewhere Tashara appeared. She stood next to the body for a moment, sniffing the air. "Omanda?" she asked.

"Aye!" Harfang's answer was spat out.

The captain nodded. "Give her the best burial we're able." She turned away. "Take the stores of these creatures and make an inventory. The tents will be a welcome addition. Burn the draconian bodies."

Harfang looked after her, his expression unreadable.

Ayshe touched his arm. "Sir?"

"What?"

"I'm . . . I'm sorry about Omanda, sir. It's my fault. If I hadn't gotten lost in the snow storm, you wouldn't have had to come after me, and she'd still be alive."

Harfang shook his head. "In Dragonsbane, we leave no one behind. Did you not know that by now, Master Ayshe? Omanda was a good warrior and a good companion, but she took the same chances we all took when we joined Dragonsbane. She's no different than Feystalen, Armidor, or Riadon in that regard." He rubbed his head. "But without a healer . . ."

Samustalen finished the thought. ". . . what chance do we stand against the White Wyrm?" He turned and left the mate and dwarf standing in the snow beside the body.

"Was she that important to your battle plans?" Ayshe asked miserably.

"Not so much to the battle itself. But out here where the

slightest injury can mean the risk of death . . ." He shrugged. "I could advise the captain to turn back, but it's no use. She'll not listen. We're plunging deeper and deeper into that"—he gestured toward the Snow Sea—"with no idea where we're going or how to get there, let alone what awaits us if we should find it—"

He stopped and looked closer at Ayshe, who was chewing his lip. "You know something. What is it?"

Ayshe nodded. "When I was captive, the draconians spoke of the White Wyrm. They said something about Dragondream and the Dreamchamber. They seemed to know where the lair is." He was so excited he forgot Omanda and his cold and aches and pains from the beating he'd received. "Sir, they said the wyrm is returning to sleep, sending out dreams to the draconians. It's returning to its Dreamchamber."

"Which is where? Did they say that?"

"Yes. We should look for the Pass of Tarmock's Fangs and the Valley of the White Death. That's where we'll find the Mountains of the Moons and the lair." Ayshe pointed to the southwest, as nearly as he could remember the direction the draconians had been facing. "The draconians worship the wyrm. They were going to sacrifice me to it, I think, at Brackenrock, in some sort of ceremony."

Harfang listened in silence. Ayshe felt pride at his information and the vigor returning to his frozen limbs.

"This is our chance, sir!" he said. "If the wyrm is sleeping and dreaming—"

Harfang turned his face to the dwarf.

"Ever woke up a sleeping dragon, Master Dwarf?"

Ayshe faltered.

"It's an ugly business, hunting dragons, even if they're asleep. They're far bigger than us, far stronger. I should have thought you'd have learned that by now. Even with a strong band, well rested and fully equipped, it's a dangerous business." He gestured around. "Do you see such a band? Tired, cold, and now without a healer." He shook his head. "Only our swords and ourselves. Not very good odds, Ayshe. Not very good odds at all."

The elves gathered in the center of the camp. To one side, they had gathered the draconians' bodies, and a word and gesture from Malshaunt had set them flaming, sending spirals of greasy smoke into the still-snow-filled sky. The elves stood in a line next to a pyre made of wood scrounged from the camp. On it rested the figure of Omanda, her hands crossed over her breast, her dagger clasped between her hands.

Tashara stood to one side, her sightless face watching the scene. Next to her, Malshaunt lifted his hand.

"Now!" the captain ordered.

Flames sprang up around the pyre. At the same time, the elves began to sing, voices rising and fading against the hiss of snow and the whine of wind. The language was not any Elvish that was spoken in Krynn, but one that would have been recognized by elves four thousand years before—a tongue both rich and strange, words twisting in complex syllables that seemed to wend their way about the fire as it rose higher, obscuring the figure of the healer. Unlike the fire that had consumed the draconian corpses, the fire around Omanda sent out no smoke and little heat but burned bright and cold against a slowly clearing sky.

To Harfang, watching without joining in the elves' song, the scene seemed to mark the end of one life and the beginning of another for him. The years of standing faithfully by Tashara's side, of battling dragons, sailing the seas around Krynn aboard the *Starfinder*, those faded as if consumed by the flames. But the future still remained hidden to the mate.

That night, after he retired to his tent, grateful for the shelter from the elements, he once again laid out the *charon* cards. And once again, he sat staring at the last card as his mind turned over and over what to do.

Malshaunt stood by the pyre until the last of it was consumed by his magical flames. The nearby snow had melted and ran in puddles that froze in glittering mirrors, reflecting the starlight above. Of Omanda's body there remained not a trace. The mage looked at the spot for a long time. Then he turned, bowed low in the direction of Tashara's tent, and disappeared into his own shelter.

CHAPTER

17

The draconians' supplies were extensive. The company separated out food and drink they could take with them on the
last stage of their journey. They took two of the tents, all they could
comfortably carry. The dwarf watched Harfang closely to see if the
mate would pass along Ayshe's information to Tashara, but the man
showed no signs of doing so.

The dwarf wondered if he himself should speak to the captain,
but he knew that, in some way, that would be a betrayal of Harfang,
and so he remained silent, watching and waiting.

They stayed encamped at the site one more night after the
funeral of the healer, resting their weary bodies in far more comfort
than they had previously known. Malshaunt's magic sustained a
magical fire in the middle of the camp, melting the snow around
it and spreading its warmth seemingly further than it had before,
across their welcoming faces and hands. The company gathered
round as overhead night stretched its long fingers across the sky
and stars studded the heavens.

Whether because of their success against the draconians or
the warmth of the fire and the prospect of more food and drink,
everyone—almost everyone—seemed in better spirits. The feeling of

fear and oppression that had hung over them since leaving Zeriak had lifted, and even Omanda's death did not dampen their mood. Seated around the fire, Samustalen and the other elves explained to Ayshe how they had found him. They had missed him almost immediately and searched for him, but the storm made it impossible for them to spot his tracks. Then someone had heard a shout in the draconians' hissing language, and they realized they were not the only travelers on the Snow Sea. They tracked the draconians and from signs realized the missing dwarf was a captive of their foe.

Dragonsbane, on Tashara's orders, had followed, waiting for a chance to strike. The raging storm had delayed their opportunities, until they began to fear Ayshe would be dead before they could reach him. At last they saw their chance when the dragon men had made their camp. The storm still blanketed everything, but Tashara and Harfang were determined to use it as cover for their attack. The draconians were completely taken by surprise.

"They never knew what hit them," said Samustalen, chuckling. "Half of them were dead before they even realized they were under assault. I'd always heard draconians were a hard bunch, but this was far easier than I expected." He drew on his pipe. "Next time, Master Ayshe, work those legs a bit harder to keep up."

The elves laughed, and Ayshe felt the warmth and companionship flow around the fire like a draught of good wine. His conscience gave a sharp twinge. They had turned back to rescue him. Would he have risked all and done the same for one of them, a straggler? He thought so, but he was not so sure.

"Where were the draconians taking you anyway?" asked Otha-nyar. As was her habit, she was holding her wyrmbarb, sharpening the head with a whetstone. She did that so often, Ayshe was surprised the steel head of the spear was not entirely worn away with sharpening.

"Brackenrock," he replied.

There was a collective intake of breath around the fire.

"Good job we found you, then," Samustalen observed. "Those who go into Brackenrock, it's said, don't come out again. I've heard said it's the worst place in this whole damned wasteland." His hand spread out to encompass all the southlands. "Why didn't they kill you at once, I wonder."

Ayshe shot a glance at Harfang. "I think . . . I think . . ." He hesitated.

From the far side of the circle came Tashara's calm voice. "What do you think, Ayshe, son of Balar?"

"They were going to sacrifice me, I think. In a festival or ceremony of some sort."

Tashara's voice was still without expression. "What festival is that?"

"I think it was . . . they called it Dragondream. I think it was dedicated to the White Wyrm."

There was utter silence for a moment, save for the whistle of the wind and the hiss of snow blowing across the frozen ground. At last Tashara smiled.

"I believe I have heard of this festival," she said, "though I never paid much credence to it. It was long rumored the draconians of Icereach worshiped a dragon, but I believed it must be Cryonis. I never knew until now it is the one we seek."

Harfang cleared his throat loudly. "We still don't know that, ma'am. The dwarf might be mistaken. He was cold and in bad pain. He might not have heard right."

Malshaunt's chill voice came from beyond the circle, where he stood behind Tashara. "Possibly, Master Harfang. But what I find curious is that he did not say anything about it until now." His grim eyes bored through the dwarf. "Why did you keep silent, Master Dwarf? Is there anything else you are concealing from Captain Tashara?"

Ayshe's body stiffened as he groped for words.

Tashara ignored the mage's question. "When is this festival? Did they say?"

"No, ma'am. But I don't think more than a few days hence." Ayshe glanced at Harfang once again, and his obligation became clear to him. He squared his shoulders. "There is more to tell, ma'am. When the draconians stopped to camp for the night, they conducted a ceremony connected with the dragon. And one of them told me more. He said the beast was preparing to sleep in its lair and to send out dreams to draconians. He called it the Dreamchamber." Ayshe related what he'd heard about the location of the lair, while Tashara rose and paced back and forth, her hands working. She questioned him intently about every aspect of his conversation with the draconian, making him repeat over and over again the details about the Pass of Tarmock's Fangs and the Valley of White Death.

"You're sure it was in that direction?" She pointed.

Ayshe nodded. "Dwarves have a strong sense of direction, ma'am. We have to since most of us live underground."

"It did you no good in the snowstorm, Master Dwarf," growled Harfang. "Ma'am, we should treat this intelligence with caution."

"Why?" snapped Malshaunt. "Assuming this dwarf is not lying"—he ignored Ayshe's snort of fury—"this is vital information for which we've been searching many years. And now that we've obtained what we have coveted, why you would have us ignore it?"

A babble of voices rose around the fire.

Jeannara slammed a hand onto the ground. "Sleep! If the wyrm's asleep—"

"Then we've got him!" Samustalen finished with a bark of laughter. "All we have to do is find the lair, and thanks to Ayshe, now we know almost exactly where it is."

All the elves were astir. They laughed and joked, happier than Ayshe could remember in a long time. Tashara stood with an odd expression. Ayshe realized it was a half smile. After a short time, she clapped her hands for silence. "Enough! We have a long way to go, and even if we catch the wyrm asleep, it may be stirred by our approach."

She turned to Ayshe. "I'll not forget this, Master Dwarf."

THE GREAT WHITE WYRM

She moved away toward her tent, and Harfang took her place in the circle around the fire. His mouth was drawn in a thin line, his face red. "Nor will I," he told Ayshe through clenched teeth.

Malshaunt followed Tashara, favoring both the mate and the dwarf with a sour smile.

The next morning, they set out. The storm had passed, and the sky was cloudless, a deep blue. Around them stretched the seemingly endless expanse of white, except to the south, where a ridge of mountains reared against the horizon.

Ayshe looked back. A few dark shapes marked the remains of the draconian camp. He breathed a prayer to Reorx for the soul of Omanda, wherever it might be.

The news that they were headed in the right direction and knew where the dragon was laired, in addition to the renewed supplies and a warm night's rest, cheered the elves of Dragonsbane. They laughed and sang songs in Elvish—no laments, but stirring battle marches and chants. Some of them, Samustalen told Ayshe, dated back to the ancient days of the Dragon Wars.

They made swift progress, though in places the snow was deep and they had to plow their way through huge drifts. Toward evening, they came to a place where the drifts lessened, then fell away altogether, revealing bare, stony ground, bound with a film of ice. The mountains seemed to have drawn dramatically closer, and Ayshe again realized how deceptive distances could be in a setting such as theirs. He estimated they were no more than one or two days' march from the beginnings of the mountains.

That night they again made a fire in the midst of their camp, a real wood fire with fuel taken from the draconian camp, and they sat in its ruddy light, smoking their pipes, sending circles and streams of smoke into the star-filled sky.

Tashara was largely silent. Once or twice she actually laughed aloud, almost as though at some private joke, the first time the dwarf remembered hearing her do so, and the many lines in her face seemed erased. The dwarf, looking at her in the leaping light of the fire, thought he had an idea of what she must have looked like when she was young.

The elves' voices took up stories of the grand wyrms slain by Dragonsbane over the centuries. Listening to them Ayshe thought, as he had before, how strange it was to hear beings whose lives were measured in hundreds rather than tens of years. The elves' memories stretched back before the War of Souls, before the Chaos War, before the War of the Lance when Flint Fireforge and his companions walked the roads of Ansalon.

He was lost in thought when he realized the captain was standing, flickering flames illuminating her tall, spare shape. The fire waxed and waned, red and yellow against the white of the surrounding snow. The elves fell silent as Tashara began to speak. Her blind eyes turned to the stars that glowed like orbs of fire in the sky. The cadences of her speech seemed to echo some ancient story of which her tale was only a small part.

"I was but newly made in Dragonsbane. Before me my mother had borne the burden of the secret, and before her my grandfather. We lived on the banks of the great southern ocean, where every day the gulls called to me, and I smelled the salt in the air. Every day I awoke and ran down to the rippling water, letting the tides carry away my childish sorrows into the never-ending rills and waves.

"It was many years past. Two centuries ago. My mother raised me alone. I never knew my father, and she never spoke of him. The males I knew were of our house among the Silvanesti, and they never spoke of my father either.

"I was happy as only one without care or sorrow can be. Since I never knew my father, I did not miss him. All I needed was my mother—the warmth of her embrace, the gleam of her smile, the sound of her voice calling me as dusk settled over the ocean.

"It was on a summer day, and I was playing on the beach when the air grew chill, and the sky was suddenly overlaid with clouds. I ran from the water without knowing why. I felt the clouds behind me swell and give birth to an awful thing I dared not look upon. I tripped and fell on the path to our house. From the doorway my mother came running to gather me to safety. She wore a sword girt at her hip, a thing I had never seen her wear before. Even as she reached for me, she drew it and cried out defiance.

"A great blast of thunder came from behind me, and I turned back to look . . ."

The captain's voice faded for a moment. All was deathly still. Into the silence she whispered, "I saw *white!*"

No one moved. No one breathed. In a moment Tashara's voice resumed. "When I woke, the voices of the village men told me my mother was close to death. I could not see them. I could not see anything.

"They took me to my mother's side, and I felt her face and hands. She told me, her voice breaking with the pain, of Dragonsbane and of my legacy. She placed in my hands the destiny of the Great White Wyrm that killed her.

"Ever since then I have hunted it. We have slain many other dragons, but this one I have hunted in vain. And now, at last, this one I shall kill."

She stopped then began to hum softly. The other elves took up the rhythm, slapping hands against the ground to keep time, beating it out on their packs, and stamping their feet. To Ayshe's surprise, he saw Malshaunt joining in the song, his face transformed, his eyes shining.

The music was strange to Ayshe, as were the words, but somehow he recognized their power to move men and women, elves and dwarves, to great deeds, to draw from them that which they did not know they possessed. He found his own feet beating out the song as Tashara's voice filled the air and went sailing over the Snow Sea toward the edge of night.

That night, Harfang once again took out the *charon* cards from his pack. He laid them out on the floor of the tent after everyone else was asleep. They felt different to him, rougher, and he felt an odd resistance as he laid them on the canvas, as if they were in some way reluctant to do their job and show him anything.

Eight cards: four in a square, one in the middle, three above. The ninth card on top of the rest of the pack.

He turned over the first card, the card in the middle. Rather than the Man, as it had been every other time he laid out the cards, it was the Cup. Harfang stared at it, wondering what the change meant. A cup was meant to be filled . . . but after it was drunk from . . . it was empty. He shook his head, and turned over the first card in the surrounding square.

It was the Dwarf. That was puzzling. Yet, perhaps not. If the four outside cards represented the four fates, surely that must be Reorx, god of the dwarves. It would be a comforting thought to know that some god, even the god of the dwarves, was watching over Dragonsbane.

Or perhaps the dwarf was Ayshe. Harfang knit his brow. The dwarf . . . indeed there was something strange about the dwarf.

No, there was nothing strange about him, but about Tashara's interest in him. Why had she insisted he be brought aboard the *Starfinder?* Not even Malshaunt understood why, and Harfang suspected her decision grated on the mage. It was clear, though, the dwarf had some key role to play in their quest, a role known to or suspected by Tashara, and by her alone.

He turned the next card. It bore a Red Rose.

The sign of Majere. That was favorable. Majere favored Good.

His followers, if Harfang remembered correctly, were schooled in disciplines both martial and mental. He couldn't remember too many details, but Majere was Good—he was sure of that.

The third card. The Feather. That, he remembered, was the sign of Chislev, god of nature. It was ironic, the mate mused, that he had drawn that card in the midst of such a vast exercise of nature's power over mortals. Perhaps that was the point. And Chislev was Neutral, as was Reorx. So. A god of Good and two gods of Neutral.

He turned over the final card in the square.

The Skull.

Chemosh.

The god of death.

A shudder passed over Harfang, and he drew his cloak and his blanket more firmly about his shoulders. On the other side of the tent, Jeannara stirred uneasily in her sleep and cried out some broken words in Elvish.

The mate shook his head firmly. He was being ridiculous. The cards could not predict the future. In any case, the old man had told him that they showed only possible futures, not what *must* happen. Besides, there were the three cards of the moons.

The first, in the position of Solinari, showed a Knight, his sword drawn, his face stern and noble. The second, for Lunitari, showed a red-robed wizard, one hand lifted while casting a spell. For one odd moment, Harfang seemed to see the face of the wizard as that of Malshaunt.

The third, for the dark moon, Nuitari, showed a Skeleton—another omen of death. The moons seemed to be balanced between the differing tendencies of Good, Evil, and Neutrality.

Harfang turned over the last card. As always, he knew before seeing it what it would be.

The White Dragon.

He gathered up the cards and returned them to their case. He rolled himself in his blanket. But it was a long time before he sank into slumber.

The following morning the sun rose in a clear sky. A light wind from the north blew against their backs, sending fine clouds of snow along the surface. The sunlight caught the spume and spun it into gossamer threads and clouds that misted the party's feet as they trudged south.

They were quiet, heads bent, brows furrowed with effort as they walked. Each one's eyes were on the back of the figure ahead—all save Tashara, who with her blind gaze confidently led them. Behind her walked Harfang, his face grim. Jeannara stepped close behind, and every now and again her eyes strayed to the man whose footsteps she was following.

Ayshe walked near the rear of the party. Despite the drama of Tashara's story and the excitement of her song the previous night, his heart was burdened with misgivings. It felt too much like walking into a trap, and he was oppressed with the thought that if disaster befell the party, it might be said to have been of his making, since he'd set them on their course.

He raised his head and gazed at the mountains that soared into the blue sky. They were larger by far than the Khalkists under which he had labored. They were white with snow and ice and looked like jagged teeth, ready to devour any who chanced their slopes. Above the tallest, far away, a mist had gathered like a cloudy crown. He watched as it stretched and embraced the mountaintop. Something about it looked unnatural. He caught his breath then shouted. The others halted and followed his pointing finger.

There was no doubt of it. Far ahead and above, the clouds were heralding another breach of the White Wyrm.

CHAPTER

18

Tashara alone of Dragonsbane made no comment as the elves, Harfang, and Ayshe watched the swiftly expanding clouds they knew signaled the presence of their destined foe. They spoke in whispers, though they knew the White Wyrm could not possibly hear them at that distance. All of them were visited with a passing wish that they might bury themselves in the surrounding snowdrifts and, thus, elude detection.

The clouds were thick about the mountaintop, and a light mist blocked the sun's rays. The wind picked up. Ayshe shivered and wrapped his cloak tight about his shoulders. Curiously, he was almost getting used to the cold. A wind such as that in his first day or two on the Snow Sea would have been unbearable rather than merely uncomfortable. He had some idea now of how the Ice Folk survived in the frozen waste.

At a gesture from Harfang, the company moved on. The snow grew shallower, scarcely deep enough to cover their feet. Ahead of them, the ground rose in a series of low hills, ascending in uneven steps until they met the steep slopes of the mountains, some ten miles distant. To the west, a few miles beyond that, Ayshe could see the beginnings of what looked like a pass between the mountains.

He fancied he could even see the rudiments of a road or path leading up into it, but perhaps his eyes, aching from the snow glare, were seeing things. They reached the summit of the first of the hills, halted, and looked back the way they had come.

Before them stretched the Snow Sea, vast and featureless. Its drifts appeared as waves and ripples, and Ayshe imagined he could almost hear the surf booming against the rocks scattered across the lower slopes of the hill on which they stood.

To the south, the mountains marched onward, east and west, until they were lost to sight. Harfang and Jeannara consulted with Tashara.

"If yonder is the Pass of Tarmock's Fangs," the mate observed, we should make for it along the top of this ridge. We can reach it in another two days' march."

Tashara nodded assent. She sniffed the air, much as a hound might do if it had caught an elusive scent. "Yes. We can camp in the valley to be out of the way of the wind," she observed. "How is our fuel?"

"Running low. After tonight we'll not have any more." The mate rubbed a hand across his face, almost hidden behind wrappings of cloth. "Fortunately, we seem to be coming close to our goal."

They set out again, and the feeling of oppression and dread was strong on all of them. Somewhere ahead, hidden in the jagged peaks, were the Mountains of the Moons and the lair of the White Wyrm. And somewhere there, some of them suspected, were their own deaths.

Ignoring the cold clouds that covered the sky, the captain led the way with confidence along the slope. She climbed along assertively, needing no guidance of her eyes. The others struggled to keep up with her.

She halted at the top of the next hill. A kind of path had appeared, worn and marked every twenty or thirty feet by a stone. Many of the stones were cracked; some were missing. The path wandered off to the west in the direction they were going. Dwarf work, Ayshe guessed. He walked forward to the nearest stone and knelt by it. Sure enough, a shaky Dwarvish rune was graven in it, worn almost flat by the passage of time and weather. It was the rune signifying *mine*.

Ayshe communicated that to the others.

"Do you think, Master Dwarf, that any of your kin dwell in these mountains?" Tashara asked.

Privately, Ayshe thought no dwarf was likely to be foolish enough to live anywhere near that godsforsaken place, but he answered evenly. "I never heard tell of any, ma'am, but the dwarves have wandered far, and it's possible, I suppose, that some might be found here. But these marks are so old they may have been placed here centuries ago.

Tashara nodded. "It seems well placed for our purposes," she remarked and strode off along the path. Harfang hoisted his pack with a grunt and followed after.

The party traveled along the path, down one hill, up another, and down again. More rocks appeared about them. The wind was sharper, shaped by the defiles and crannies of the mountains. As evening fell they stepped off the path and went down onto the southern slopes of the hill to find a place to camp. They were silent as they moved about their tasks, each one afraid, each one fearing to say so.

The following day they resumed the westward journey. The pathway bent down and climbed several more hills before turning south and heading for what was plainly the pass. The mountains rose in steep cliffs on either side, their stones crumbling. The path itself was strewn with rocks, some big, some smaller, but it made for slow going as the company picked their way cautiously between them. Ayshe, used to such conditions, stumbled less than the elves, but even he knew his hands and legs would be bruised the following day. Now and again they heard a dull rumble as a boulder crashed down the slopes from a height.

Harfang looked again and again at the slopes, his brow drawn in a dark line. He spoke to Jeannara now and then, always in a low tone.

A sharp cry came from one side. Lindholme had tripped and caught his ankle between two of the stones. He cursed, trying to pull it free.

"Go help him," Harfang ordered Thasalana as he strode on.

The tall elf stepped to Lindholme's side and bent, tugging at the imprisoning rock. The company passed the two elves and continued along the path. Thasalana joked good-naturedly with her friend. "Clumsy idiot! Can't take you for a walk!"

Another rumble sounded from above, louder than any they had heard before.

"Look out!" The cry came from Samustalen. He stood stock still in the pathway, his face turned upward, an expression of horror filling his visage. Ayshe followed his gaze.

A cloud of white was racing down the mountain, faster than the fastest horses could run. It was headed straight for them.

"Avalanche!" Harfang shouted. "Run!"

The companions raced along the trail. They leaped over rocks, smashing knees and fingers, their cries drowned by the roar of the approaching avalanche. Ayshe, sprinting ahead of them despite his short legs, turned and looked back. Framed against the white snow were the figures of Thasalana and Lindholme. The elf woman was still struggling to free the male. For a single heartbeat, they were outlined; then the snow cloud overwhelmed them.

The avalanche roared past, filling the place with snow. Slowly Dragonsbane rose, nursing bruised and aching bodies, and looked behind. Samustalen began to run back to where Thasalana and

THE GREAT WHITE WYRM

Lindholme had been buried, but Harfang called him back.

"It's no good," he said. "We could never find them in time, and we'd waste time and energy looking. The mountain has taken them. Let them rest in peace."

"We can't just leave them there!" Samustalen shouted angrily. He sank to the ground, white with surrounding snow. He stared up at Harfang, Jeannara, and the gaunt, remote figure of Tashara. Slamming his palms against a rock, he bent, weeping.

Harfang walked over to stand beside him and placed a hand on his shoulder. Man and elf stood in silent communion as the wind and snow hissed around them. From above came the sound of more falling rocks.

"Come," said Harfang. "We must go on."

They marched until the sky darkened—early afternoon by Ayshe's reckoning. He knew that as far south as they were and at that time of year there would be few daylight hours during which they might journey. Several times rocks rolled down the slopes near them, dislodged by the violent gusts of wind that swept through the mountains. Fortunately, none came near the party. They had no fire, and they were cold and depressed by more death.

The wind itself proved their greatest obstacle the following day. Its force was so great that sometimes they could walk only bent over double, their hands groping before them as if to shield a blow. The wind would ease for a few minutes, then return with renewed force, bringing with it clouds of fine snow and slivers of ice that ground against exposed skin. Ayshe suffered less than the elves because he stood closer to the ground, but even he felt the violent rage of nature against those who dared penetrate the sanctum.

As daylight dimmed once again, they emerged from the area of sharp rocks and jagged cliffs to find themselves at the bottom of the pass. To their relief, the march ahead appeared far easier. The path slanted smoothly upward along a gentle slope, while the mountains on either side fell away. Their spirits rose slightly.

Harfang gave a shout and moved to one side. At the bottom of the pass, next to one of the cliffs they had just left, a dark opening loomed. A large boulder stood just to one side, as if it were a door welcoming them. Grateful, the party staggered inside the cavern and collapsed.

Harfang alone remained standing, squinting into the darkness. He called to Ayshe, and the dwarf reluctantly roused himself.

"Here."

From his backpack, Harfang pulled a torch—a piece of wood with a rag wrapped about the end. He poured oil from a flask over the rag and handed it to the dwarf. Ayshe took out his tinderbox and succeeded in striking a spark. The oil-soaked rag lit and illuminated their surroundings.

The cave was large but not very deep. Toward the back it slanted down until not even the dwarf could stand upright. The floor was firm dirt and rock. Fortunately for them, the entrance seemed to be slanted away from the direction of the wind, so little snow drifted in.

Most curiously, branches lay in the back, piled in an untidy heap. Some were sticks, some sizable logs. Mixed in the woodpile were the bones of small animals; some still had fur clinging to them.

Harfang examined all of that with a worried look. Ayshe watched impatiently. "Come, sir," he remarked finally. "This'll make a lovely fire. Bring some color back into our cheeks."

Harfang grunted. "Aye," he said after a silence. "Aye, fire will be no bad thing. See to it."

Ayshe and several of the elves swiftly gathered wood and started a merry blaze near the front of the cavern. The rest of the elves except Tashara busied themselves in laying out blankets and cloaks near the fire and eating from their meager supplies.

THE GREAT WHITE WYRM

Harfang, after completing his examination of the cave, sat down near the flames and pulled out his whetstone. Ignoring the others, he drew his sword and passed the stone along the blade again and again.

Tashara, as usual isolated from her crew, drew up her knees beneath her cloak and sat against the rocky wall, blind eyes turned to the fire's light.

The blaze threw leaping shadows on the cave walls, and the elves and dwarf of Dragonsbane felt better than on the previous fireless night. Some elves brought out their pipes, while others conversed in low voices. Samustalen sat silently staring into the fire, his eyes sad. Ayshe knew he was thinking of Lindholme and Thasalana.

Harfang's raised voice drew their attention. "Jeannara, you and Noortheleen have first watch. Shamura and Omarro the second. Stay sharp. The rest of you, get some sleep. You'll need it on the morrow."

Ayshe wrapped himself in his blanket. The fire was bigger than any that they'd made with the draconians' fuel, and the walls of the cave kept the warmth in. He was almost comfortable. How long, he wondered drowsily, since he had slept a night of unbroken slumber? Zeriak, perhaps. Or before that, in his hammock aboard the *Starfinder?* His thoughts turned to the gentle sway of the ship's decks beneath his feet, to the mewling cries of the gulls, and the hum of the sea breeze through the rigging.

Suddenly the gulls' cries grew louder and more insistent. They seemed to be shouting words. There was motion all around them, shadows in the air.

He rolled over and came to his feet, reaching for his axe. The fire had burned down, but beyond it against the blackness of the cave mouth, he saw a great dark shape and two small, pale figures.

The scene resolved itself in his sleep-befuddled eyes. At the cave entrance was a huge, fur-covered beast, at least eight feet tall.

Long, savage incisors hung down over its jaws, and wickedly sharp claws gleamed at the ends of its paws. Its mouth was open in fury, revealing a row of gleaming teeth.

Elves surrounded it, slashing at it with swords and daggers, leaping nimbly to avoid the sweep of its huge claws. Stains of red on the beast's white fur showed where its opponents' blades had penetrated, but its wounds did not seem to diminish its energy.

The creature swung a paw, missing an elf and slamming into the wall. It slashed again. Jeannara came down in front of it, blade in either hand, and struck quickly. The beast roared, shaking the entire cave, and Jeannara went flying backward to crash on the ground. Ayshe could see the results of her blows: two long cuts across the yeti's chest. Blood poured from them.

Malshaunt's hands were busy with a spell, but before he could release his magic, the creature turned toward him with a growl and backhanded him. The mage smashed against the wall of the cave, blood gushing from his forehead.

Ayshe had his axe in hand, creeping around the outside of the fight, looking for an opening. The yeti roared again and struck at Amanthor, who barely evaded the blow.

The dwarf swung his axe, putting every ounce of his strength behind it. The yeti's roar turned to a shriek of rage and pain as one of its clawed paws fell to the ground. It waved the bloody stump at the dwarf as if it couldn't understand how the paw came to be missing.

Amanthor struck from the side, thrusting his sword into the creature's flank. The yeti turned, tearing the weapon from his hand. Its other paw raised for a blow and stopped in mid-attack. Six inches of steel protruded from its breast.

The yeti stared at the blade for a moment in puzzlement. A low rumbling came from its throat. Its legs collapsed, and it fell forward.

Otha-nyar stepped on top of the body and, with a powerful jerk of her arm, tore her wyrmbarb free of its back. The weapon brought a chunk of flesh, fur, and blood with it. The cavern seemed very quiet; then there was the sound of elves—and a dwarf—breathing heavily. The Kagonesti bent and ran a hand over the yeti's fur as if satisfying herself that it was, indeed, dead. Then she wiped her blade on it and sat down again by the edge of the fire.

Shamura and Samustalen bent over the mage, who pushed their hands away from his bloodied forehead impatiently. He rose, tore a strip from the bottom of his robe, and bound it about his head. Then he came forward to examine the yeti.

Harfang knelt at Jeannara's side. Her chest and stomach were covered in blood, and the mate could see at a glance that both her arms were broken. Harfang tore away her shirt and caught his breath. The yeti's claws had torn enormous gashes, their edges ragged. Swiftly the mate tore her shirt into strips.

"Get some hot water," he snapped at the others.

The elves boiled water from melted snow. As Harfang watched, Alyssaran soaked the makeshift bandages in it and bound them around the injured elf woman. Despite the heat of the bandages, she shivered violently.

Alyssaran set Jeannara's arms in splints fashioned from some of the branches they had found in the yeti's cave. Harfang covered her with his cloak and sat by her side, his hand resting on her hair. Alyssaran, meanwhile, drew dried herbs from Omanda's pack and brewed a drink by the fire.

"Give her this," she told the mate. "I saw Omanda make this once before. I'm not quite sure of the proportions, but it may do her good."

Gently, Harfang managed to get some of the healing brew between Jeannara's lips. She soon stopped shivering, and some of the color returned to her face, but her eyes stayed closed, and her injuries remained. Harfang nodded his satisfaction for her help to Alyssaran.

"Is there more you can do for her?" he asked her.

The elf shook her head sadly. "If Omanda were still alive," she said, "she would know what to do—she could even call upon the gods' magic. I can ease her pain somewhat, but only time and care will make her well." She shook her head. "But the yeti's claws, like many such beasts, are often infected. She'll be lucky if she doesn't worsen."

The others watched, but no one spoke the obvious: With her injuries, it would be impossible for the elf woman to continue on their journey. Even if she could walk, the strain of the cold and the ardors of the extreme landscape would make her survival unlikely. And with both arms disabled, she would be useless in the final battle.

Harfang turned to Malshaunt. "Mage!"

He had to call twice more before Malshaunt slowly turned from the yeti and approached.

"Can you do anything?"

Malshaunt examined Jeannara perfunctorily and stood. "No. Her injuries are too severe. And I have no healing magic, as you know." He turned away.

"Damn you, I'm not asking you to heal her!" Harfang snarled. "But isn't there anything you can do to at least help us take her with us?"

Malshaunt's face was hidden in shadow. He looked at Harfang in silence for some times then walked to the front of the cave. He spoke to Tashara in a low voice then turned his back on the others, sitting against the cave wall, wrapping himself in his cloak.

The elves gloomily settled themselves down again near the fire. Alyssaran remained with Harfang and Jeannara for a time, then rose and joined the rest of the company. They were too exhausted to move the yeti's body, so they let it lie where it had fallen. Harfang sat with the second mate for a while, stroking her head and speaking to her in a low voice. At last he, too, came to the fire and lay down.

◆ ◆ ◆ ◆ ◆

THE GREAT WHITE WYRM

The dim glow of daylight filtered into the cave, waking them. Shamura and Omarro, the two sentries, stirred and woke with a start, rubbing sleep from their eyes, looking at one another sheepishly. The body of the yeti lay where it had fallen.

Harfang rose, massaged the stiffness from his limbs, and turned toward the back of the cave. Malshaunt stood by Jeannara.

"How is—?" the mate started to ask.

"Dead," the mage said shortly.

"What?"

Harfang sprang to the second mate's side. He knelt for a moment, staring at her still body and face, peaceful in repose. Then he glared up at Malshaunt.

"You! What have you done?"

He was on his feet in a moment, sword out and stepping forward for a blow. Malshaunt raised his hands in a gesture of magic. His eyes glittered, his lips beginning to form a spell.

Samustalen thrust himself between the two. "No!" he shouted.

From the front of the cave, Tashara walked back and stood before her two followers. "Enough!" she said harshly. She bent and touched Jeannara's cold face with her fingers and rose. "Enough. What is done is done."

Harfang's voice shook. "No! This man murdered one of our comrades!"

Malshaunt's voice was full of scorn. "I am not a *man!* I am an elf. I know what needs to be done. I do what needs to be done." He turned to Tashara. "She could not have accompanied us. Nothing remained for her but to die in pain and sickness. If we had taken her, she would have held us back." He turned his face back to Harfang. "Do you understand? *I did what needed to be done!*"

Tashara was silent for a long time. Finally she turned her face to Harfang. "The mage speaks the truth. It's a mercy so. We could not take her with us, and she would have lingered in this cave, cold and alone, until death claimed her. It's better for her this way." She leaned forward, said something else in a low voice, then turned away. Malshaunt followed her, casting a backward look of malevolence at the mate.

Harfang's eyes were hard and dry. He stared after the captain and her mage, his mouth working. At last, with an angry ring, he resheathed his sword and turned to the others, who stood, watching.

"Come!" he said. "We need to travel lighter from here. We'll leave some of our supplies and lighten our packs."

Under his command, the party began to sort through what they had brought, separating the essential from the unnecessary. They could not keep from looking at the still body of Jeannara. Harfang cast a blanket over her but did not linger near the elf woman's body again. Hour after hour, he worked in silence, but many noticed he did not come near either Malshaunt or the captain and did not speak to either of them.

They decided to remain one more day in the yeti's cave to husband their strength for the last push in their mission. As well, it was still snowing heavily outside, and they hoped the weather might ease with the passage of another day.

They carried Jeannara's body to the back of the cave and built a cairn of stones over it to keep wild animals—if any existed in the mountains—from disturbing her eternal rest. When Harfang returned to the fire, Ayshe joined him.

"A word, sir?"

"Well?"

The human had taken out his pipe and sat on the floor by the cairn, spreading his cloak around him. In the mate's face, Ayshe saw only dead eyes, an expression devoid of all human feeling. He cleared his throat and spoke.

THE GREAT WHITE WYRM

"I've been looking over our supplies, sir. Even if we retrieve what we're caching here, I'm afraid we'll be short-run on the return journey. There'll be little hunting until we reach the other side of the Snow Sea, and—"

Harfang held up a hand. "I shouldn't worry about it, Master Dwarf."

Cold, weary, and heartsick, Ayshe felt bolder than usual. "Why not?"

Harfang twisted around to glare at him. "Because, Master Ayshe, I doubt that any of us will be making that return journey. Think of what awaits us within these mountains. You have glimpsed the White Wyrm. You've experienced its power. Do you think we will survive? And in a condition to make the return journey?"

Ayshe made no answer, but some part of him knew the mate was right. Even if they survived the fight with the wyrm, his spirit quailed at the thought of the trek back through that endless sea of white.

"If I may ask," he said, "if you believe this to be a hopeless battle, why have you come this far? Why?"

Harfang drew deeply on his pipe, and the interior of the bowl glowed cherry red in the darkness. He expelled a mouthful of smoke and, keeping his voice low, said, "Because of a debt."

The dwarf waited in silence.

"I daresay you've heard that Tashara found me on the streets of Palanthas. That was thirty years ago, just after the Chaos War ended." Harfang laughed bitterly. "Chaos War. Apt name, for it brought chaos in its wake. Even on the streets, we heard many mighty rulers were gone—killed or vanished. The gods had deserted us. We heard that too. But to me, it felt as if the gods had abandoned me from birth.

"I never knew my parents. My earliest memory is of an old woman, wrinkled and hideous. She told me to call her Aunt, but whether she was, in fact, my true aunt, I never knew or cared.

"When I was old enough to walk, Aunt taught me to steal. I was an accomplished pickpocket and thief before I was five. Gangs love to recruit small children, of course, because they can enter houses in ways older men and women can't. And they can gain the trust of a mark more easily. Aunt had other boys who stole for her, though I was the only one who lived in her household.

"I walked every street, every square, every alley in Palanthas. Have you ever been there?"

Ayshe shook his head.

"Aye, well, it's a great city—but in the high towers and the marbled homes they never see the filth that runs in the gutters. The street rats that claw each other to survive.

"I was about ten, sharp as a whistle. I knew the city like I know the back of my hand. I was king of the streets, and if things had gone differently, I probably would have gathered my own band of thieves—if I wasn't caught and hanged by the City Watch first.

"One day I spied an elf walking. She was near the Great Library, and I realized at once she was blind."

"Tashara!" Ayshe exclaimed.

"None other. Oho, I thought. Here's an easy one. I followed her for a street or two, then made my move. I ran behind her and pushed a stick between her legs. With her on the ground, I could pick her clean and be half a street away before she was back on her feet."

Harfang paused to relight his pipe, which had gone out. His tone was distant and held a note of amusement at his own folly.

"She fell, just as I expected, then rolled and was standing with a hand on my collar before I could blink. I twisted and turned, kicked and bit, but she held on to me and kept walking as if nothing had happened.

"Then something queer happened. Queerer, I mean, than the fact a blind elf had been able to best the quickest thief in Palanthas. She said to me, 'Harfang, come with me and leave off struggling. It will be easier for both of us if you do.' "

"Wait a minute," Ayshe said. "How did she know your name?"

There was a pause, and Harfang shrugged. "How does she know anything? I never found out. Whatever the case, she took me along with her to the wharves and hauled me aboard the *Starfinder*.

"I don't mind telling you it was a revelation. Here I'd been running on the streets, covered with muck, only seeing the sky framed by bricks and mortar. Now I was aboard a ship where the air was clean and fresh, and where the blue waters sparkled in the Bay of Branchala. It didn't take much persuasion for me to agree to sail along on the ship. Besides, I imagined that if I didn't like life at sea, I could jump ship at the next port."

He chuckled mirthlessly. "I was a rare little brat. Fought with everyone, refused to take orders. But Tashara stuck by me. And when we'd been at sea for a time, she opened the door to Dragonsbane for me.

"I'd heard of dragons, of course—how they'd been gone for centuries then returned during the War of the Lance. But I'd never seen one, even in the aftermath of the Chaos War. Tashara taught me their lore, told me all Dragonsbane had learned in centuries of stalking and fighting the beasts. She taught me to handle a weapon and to fight with others in my party, and not by myself.

"The first one I helped track was a small green. It was in the time of the overlords, in the first years of the Dragonpurge, when the overlords were killing smaller dragons and adding their skulls to their totems. Dragonsbane found the green on the coast of Southlund. We trapped it and killed it, taking its head. I dare say Beryllinthranox herself paid no attention to its death. Then there were others, great as well as trivial."

Ayshe had listened quietly to the tale before he ventured another question. "When did you first hear of the White Wyrm?"

The mate's voice grew heavier, as if he were reluctant to discuss the subject, but he responded. "Tashara told me herself, when she initially told me the story of Dragonsbane. She told me our great task was to chase a white dragon that was like no other, that could come from the clouds on a bright summer's day. She told me it was her destiny to find and kill this dragon." He paused. "And she told me it was my destiny as well."

He paused again. Ayshe sat watching him. He saw in his eyes the mate's love for his leader, for the woman who had drawn him from a life of poverty and squalor and had given him a cause to live and die for. He saw as well the mate's anguish as he watched Tashara's pursuit of the White Wyrm slowly turn to zealotry and madness. And he understood the mate could do no more than what he had promised: follow her to the end.

CHAPTER

19

The company awoke the next morning feeling rested and as cheerful as was possible under the circumstances. Nothing had disturbed their sleep, and the fire had kept them warm. They dragged the yeti's corpse from the cave and left it under a gathering snowdrift. Already some of the elves were beginning to speak of their return journey and to make plans for traveling overland from Zeriak to once again board the *Starfinder*. Harfang listened to their talk without comment.

Emerging from the yeti's cave, they were greeted by a blue sky across which wisps of cloud gusted, alternating with plumes of snow blown from the surrounding peaks. Ahead was the pass over which their road lay. Beyond it, if the draconians had spoken truly, were the Mountains of the Moons and the White Wyrm's lair.

With lightened packs, the elves looked at the climb to the pass without trepidation. Each obstacle on their long road had been met and overcome. At last they were almost within sight of their goal, and they looked on the rest of the quest as practically accomplished.

They shouldered their packs and moved on. Harfang brought up the rear and stopped outside the cave's mouth, faced it, and bowed solemnly in final tribute to Jeannara's body, resting beneath its cairn of stones. He turned and followed the company, led by Tashara. Closely behind her, as usual, was the gaunt dark figure of Malshaunt, his robes flapping around him. At times he seemed like a dark cloud following a pale moon across a night sky.

The snow had blown away from the gravel-strewn slope, and they could see their way clearly toward the pass. Tashara led the way, head raised, sniffing the wind for elusive scents that evaded the noses of her sighted followers.

The air seemed to grow thinner, and some of the elves once or twice had to stop and catch their breath. Harfang's heart pounded in his chest, and he could feel the veins in his temples throbbing. He looked back and was surprised to see how far the party had already climbed. The sun was fully overhead, and the day felt very warm. His face was red with exertion.

"Company halt!" he called.

The elves stopped, and Tashara turned.

"Harfang!"

The mate walked forward.

"Why are we stopping? We are near. I can feel it." Tashara's face, as always, was pale, but Harfang could hear her voice break in quick, sharp pants. Beside her, Malshaunt leaned against a rock. His pale face twisted in pain.

"We should go slowly, ma'am," the mate replied. "Air is scarce here, and we must preserve our strength to fight. Better to exercise some prudence."

Tashara was unhappy with the delay but agreed to a short rest. While the others sat on the path and concentrated on their breathing, she paced to and fro.

From their height, they could see the valley spread out below them. A distant smudge marked the entrance to the yeti's cave. Beyond, the rock-strewn way extended back into the distance. A patch of whiteness showed where the avalanche had fallen, snuffing out the lives of Thasalana and Lindholme.

THE GREAT WHITE WYRM

At the very edge of sight was a thin line of brilliant white that marked the beginning of the great Snow Sea. The mate looked in awe, marveling at how far they had come.

Harfang's thoughts turned farther, north and west. What of his old home, of Palanthas? To his surprise he even found himself giving a thought to Aunt and wondering at her fate.

He turned and saw the dwarf watching him. For the first time since Ayshe had come aboard the *Starfinder*, it was he who spoke words of comfort and advice to the mate. He gestured toward the horizon.

"You can't go back, you know," he said in a low voice so the others couldn't hear. "I have learned that now. Palanthas is too far back and too far away. As it is for me, so it is for you. There's no road back."

Harfang was startled to find the dwarf had read his thoughts. "What about you, Master Dwarf?" he asked. "Is there any road back to the lands of the living for you?"

Ayshe shook his head. "I don't know. Perhaps not. And yet . . . and yet . . ." He hesitated. "One part of me will not give up hope."

The mate nodded. "This journey is different for each us," he said, "but for each of us, as well, there is something in common. You made this labor to atone for your sins. Oh, yes," he said, lifting a hand to still Ayshe's startled exclamation. "I know why you came. That was clear from the start. What you did in the past I neither know nor care, but when you came aboard the *Starfinder*, I could see the guilt writ plain on your face. I should know. I read the face of every male and female who comes aboard the ship.

"Every member of this band, Master Dwarf, is seeking to blot out some part of the past. Many of us have sinned and are trying to forget that sin, to pay back fate. We're a ship of the damned, and now we've landed on a strange shore. But I can tell you, my friend, even if you expiate your deed, the past is gone. What's done is done."

Ayshe smiled and jerked his head in the direction of the pacing Tashara. "Does *she* believe that?" he asked.

The mate shook his head. "No. I don't believe she does. Therein lies the tragedy, Master Ayshe, one we're now heading toward, with our eyes wide open."

He rose and called the company to order. Once again they set off.

Distances in that land continued to deceive. Harfang, looking toward the head of the pass, had thought it seemed no more than a mile or two away, but they labored through the morning without cresting it. Several more times they were forced to halt for rest. They'd been steadily climbing ever since leaving the Snow Sea, days before.

The slope was broken and scored in a way that had not been obvious from below. Some of the crevices they could go around or even leap across, but some were too wide even for that, and they could traverse them only by means of ropes and tackle. It was a slow, cautious business, and Tashara openly chafed at each delay.

The sun had crossed the zenith when they mounted the last part of the summit. Tashara halted at the top of the slope, staring with her blind eyes. The others gathered around her, looking at the scene beyond in wonderment.

The road dipped down there, for a distance of perhaps a half mile, into a long valley that ran north and south as far as they could see. Its floor was filled with dense-growing evergreens of great height. The path led directly beneath their boughs. On the other side of the valley, two or three miles distant, at about an equal height to where they stood, was a gap between two mountains.

"Look!" Otha-nyar cried.

They gazed upward. The peak of one of the mountains was white with snow, but through it the companions could see dark streaks, as if the drifts had blown apart enough to reveal a dark sheen of rock. To the right, the facing mountain slope showed a glow of red beneath the snow, while beyond the two mountains was a third, somewhat taller than the other two, of pure, gleaming white.

"The Mountains of the Moons!" Malshaunt exclaimed. His face was rapt, his expression mirroring that on the visage of Tashara. Indeed, it seemed for a moment to the others that they were two halves of the same being, one sighted, the other blind, but both gazing on something that filled them with awe and joy. The others also stared in silence.

"What about the wood?" Samustalen finally said.

"What about it?" Harfang growled. "We go through it. We'll rest here the night and tackle this first thing in the morning."

"No!" Tashara's voice rang out, and the company looked at her, surprised. It was rare for the captain to contradict the mate's orders, and usually only in dire circumstances.

"No," she repeated. "We cannot afford the delay. We go on now. The wood is not wide—I can smell the snow on the other side of the trees. It will not take us long to cross it."

Harfang stepped to her side. "There's no need for hurry," he said in a low voice. "The crew is tired. By morning they'll be rested and ready for battle."

Tashara shook her head. "You don't know what you're speaking of, Harfang. I know the signs. I know the time. We must hurry." She strode away along the path, which wound downward toward the trees' edge.

Harfang stared after her a moment, then turned to the others. "You heard the captain. Forward!"

Like many dwarves, Ayshe had no great love of forests. The land around Thargon had included patches of woods, but they were mostly low trees, widely spaced—stands of poplars, elms, and birch. The trees around him, on the other hand, were tall, hundreds of feet high, and they grew so close together, their tops blocked out the light. The path wound around the trunks and vanished into the forest. The elves walked along it without hesitation. Ayshe paused a moment and looked back at the snow, almost ruefully. He turned, gritted his teeth, and plunged into another color, the darkness of the trees.

The first thing he noticed was there was no wind. Out on the Snow Sea, the wind had been constant; after the party had left and entered the pass, it had whistled and hummed incessantly. Apart from the awful time when the *Starfinder* had drifted helplessly south, the wind had been a steady companion throughout his journey. With it gone, absent, vanished, it was as though someone had clapped a hand over its mouth.

Minus the wind, the silence was deafening. In the forests around Thargon, there were always sounds of the creaking and scraping of tree branches, the scuttle of squirrels as they ran from twig to twig, the chatter of birds, and a hundred other sounds that brought the forest alive. But there was nothing around them . . . only grim silence.

He turned to Samustalen, who walked next to him. "It's so quiet," he said in a whisper, as if some part of him were reluctant to break the spell.

The elf made no reply, and Ayshe looked at him. Perhaps it was the pale light that filtered through from far above, where the needles of the evergreens met the sky, but he thought the elf looked strangely white. When Samustalen spoke at last, his voice seemed drained, as though it were coming from far away down some tunnel or corridor.

"This forest is dead," he said. "The trees are here, they're green, but they have no life. Nothing here is alive except for us. Can't you feel it? All around us is death, cloaked in the appearance of life."

Ayshe noticed the other elves were similarly affected by the forest. When they'd first seen it, they'd been eager to once more walk among trees, their natural habitat. But once they were on the path, they spoke in whispers or not at all, their hands resting on their swords and bows. Harfang had drawn his blade and walked just behind Tashara. Malshaunt walked stiffly next to them, his entire body bespeaking alertness. The captain alone seemed unaffected by the weird forest and stepped along the path as usual, her head erect.

The air was very cold, but there was no snow there. Evidently the tree branches prevented any from reaching the floor of the forest. The ground was covered in gray lichens except for the path, which curiously stayed free of them. To each side, Ayshe could see nothing but endlessly receding trunks until they were lost in the darkness.

The silence was so intense, he became aware of his companions' breathing, and each step they took seemed to echo. He began to long for the forest's end, when he could emerge into the familiar white snow and feel the wind on his face. The darkness was suffocating, intolerable.

He could keep no clear track of time, but after a while, began to feel something was wrong. He could see his companions felt the same, for the members of Dragonsbane began to glance warily at one another and around them. The wood had only appeared to be about three miles thick when they saw it from the top of the pass, and it should have taken them only about an hour to move through it. Yet much more time than that had elapsed, and they were still walking with no sign of emerging.

At last, up ahead, they spied a stronger light and hurried toward it, eager to escape. However, they found themselves not at the edge of the wood, but in a great clearing. The trees there had not been cut, but instead simply stopped growing as abruptly as they had started at the edge of the wood. The clearing was roughly circular, and above they could spot clear blue sky darkening with evening. It lifted their spirits a bit to see something beyond the dark-banded trees, but at the same time it appeared they had another great distance to go.

In the very center of the clearing was an obelisk of white stone. Its four sides were smooth and polished, and it rose some fifty feet into the air, where it ended in a sharp point. It rested upon a large black stone, which bore many carvings. The edges of the incisions were sharp and distinct, yet the obelisk and its base had an indefinable air of antiquity.

The carvings were in a language none of the party recognized, though Ayshe thought they bore some resemblance to dwarf runes. They walked around it, puzzling over what it was doing there and how it had escaped the ravages of time.

Alone among them, Samustalen hung back. His face, sorrowful since the death of Thasalana and Lindholme in the pass, was even more unhappily wrought.

"Let's go on!" he urged Harfang. "Why do we wait here? There's nothing here."

The mate looked about. "No," he said finally. "Not by my advice. Already the light is beginning to fade, and though I'd rather not be caught here after darkness falls, better to be here where there's some room and some light than among the trees. I don't know how long it's going to take us to get out of this damned wood, but I won't chance having to make camp on the dark path ahead." He gestured to the far side of the clearing, where the path they had been traveling on continued among the thick tree trunks.

Samustalen shuddered. Ayshe approached him.

"Are you cold?" he asked the elf. "Here, I've an extra blanket in my pack."

The elf shook his head. His teeth were chattering, and he wrapped his arms around himself. "No. It's just . . . I don't like this place. There's something wrong about it." He moved away to stare at the obelisk. Something about it appeared to both fascinate and repel him, and he could scarcely take his eyes off it.

Harfang, meanwhile, was speaking to Tashara. The captain appeared to take the news they were stopping for the night in bad grace, but she admitted it made more sense to camp near the obelisk than along the path. The elves set up their tents and started a small fire. The flames twinkled and glowed beneath the great gloom of the strange forest, making them feel even smaller and more isolated than before. Malshaunt bent in meditation, concentrating on his spells, but after a time he rose and joined the others by the fire.

"I cannot rest," he said. His face was troubled. "Something here drives the words of my spells from my mind." He sat silent, apparently brooding on his failure.

Samustalen sat a little apart from the others, his head turned toward the obelisk. He took no part in the general talk, which was brief and whispered. All of them were puzzled by the wood and the strange stone monument, and it was with some relief that they scattered to the tents to sleep until morning.

Late that night, Ayshe awoke. The silence was oppressive, and the soft breathing of his companions sounded unnaturally loud. He sat up and realized one space in the tent was empty. Samustalen was missing.

Ayshe crawled to the tent entrance and looked out. The elf was sitting by the coals of the fire. His back was hunched, and he was staring again at the obelisk. The dwarf debated whether to approach him but decided against it. Whatever was bothering Samustalen, he did not seem willing to communicate his thoughts to the others. Perhaps it was still the memories of his dead friends; perhaps it was the silence and foreboding of the forest. The dwarf sighed and returned to his blanket.

The morning's light came as a relief to all of them. They emerged from their tents, yawning; then Shamura gave a cry.

Samustalen was sitting upright where Ayshe had seen him the previous night. His eyes were open, staring blindly before him. A trickle of red ran down his cheek from beneath his right eye. His face was white as paper, his body stiff and cold.

Ayshe stared at him in horror. The elf's expression was one of utmost terror and loathing. His dead gaze was still fixed on the obelisk. Ayshe peered closely at the obelisk, running his eyes over it from the base to the apex. It might be some trick of the light, but he could swear that the sharpened tip of the stone glowed red.

Harfang hurried up and stared at the body. He looked at the others, who stood in groups, fear writ plain on their faces.

"Shamura, Ridrathannash, dig a hole. The rest of you pack. Ready to leave in ten minutes. Move!"

Spurred by fear, the party fell on their chores with hasty fingers. Once the camp was packed, the elves took the body of Samustalen and gently lowered it into the grave. The two elves had dug a hole as far as possible from the obelisk, beneath the boughs of the trees that bordered the clearing. They covered the grave and faced it for a few minutes, heads uncovered. No other ritual, such as that they had given others who had died, was possible. All of them were anxious to leave that grove of horror.

Ayshe could not help but reflect on the shrinking party. It seemed very far from the proud band he'd first encountered aboard the *Starfinder*. Even if they came safely to the lair of the White Wyrm, he wondered, would they have the force to conquer it?

Led by Tashara, Dragonsbane passed out of the clearing and back into the forest.

Either their luck was improving or the forest, having received its blood debt, decided to let the travelers go without further incident. After a march of two hours or so, to their great joy, they saw the trees fall away and they tumbled into the familiar winter landscape. Sounds also resumed as soon as they stepped from the forest, and Ayshe never thought the noise of the wind whistling over snow could sound as sweet. Looking back, they saw the forest, dark and forbidding, and they realized they had passed the last barrier. Before them lay the Mountains of the Moons and the pass to the Valley of the White Death.

A low call went up from one of the elves toward the front. Ahead of them, near the top of the pass, were arrayed a group of small figures.

"Dwarves!" observed Harfang. "Come, Master Ayshe. Let's find out what your kinsmen are doing in this godsforsaken place."

The two, accompanied by Tashara and Malshaunt, hurried forward. The dwarves approached, walking down the slope in a disciplined band. All bore axes, and most carried large packs. They were wrapped in furs and seemed well accustomed to the harshness of their surroundings.

Harfang lifted a hand. "Halt! Greetings!"

One of the dwarves stepped forward, his face a picture of astonishment. "Hail, strangers! We did not look to meet anyone here on the edge of forever."

"Nor did we," replied the mate, his face grim. "Are you miners?"

"Yes. We're leaving a site within these mountains." The dwarf looked on them with open curiosity. "What brings elves and a human into the frozen wastes?"

"And a dwarf," said Ayshe, stepping from behind Tashara. "Hello, Brother," he said, speaking Dwarvish.

"Hail, Brother! I'm Callach, son of Oriolle." The dwarf's accent marked him as Daewar, a well-respected clan of dwarves that included branches dwelling near Thoradin and Blöde to the north. "In the name of Reorx, what are you doing here?"

"Let everyone understand," Ayshe answered, switching to Common. "This is Callach."

Harfang nodded. "Aye. No need for missed speech or misunderstandings."

Callach shrugged, his dark eyes flicking over the party. "Very well. What business have you in these mountains?"

Tashara spoke for the first time. "We hunt the White Wyrm, Master Dwarf."

Callach's face beneath his beard turned almost as white as the snow, but his voice remained steady. "Then you are fools, mistress."

There was silence so deep Ayshe could hear the hiss of the wind. Malshaunt's body tightened, and he glared at the dwarf, his face pale save for two spots of red in his cheeks.

Tashara's face betrayed no emotion. "We have held to this quest for a long time, Callach, son of Oriolle."

Ayshe frowned. He was sure he had not mentioned Callach's patronymic. Did the captain understand Dwarvish? Or did she know of the dwarf leader in some other fashion? He was constantly surprised by her. He realized she was still speaking.

"Tell us what you know of the Great White Wyrm and where it lairs. If we are fools, that is our own affair."

Callach shrugged. "The White Wyrm, mistress, is no ordinary white dragon. It bursts from the sky even on a clear day with no warning to its victims. It carries ice and fire in its breath. Those who hunt it do not survive."

Tashara gestured impatiently. "Yes, yes. All this we know. Where is its lair? Beyond this pass? That is what we have been told."

"Yes." The word came reluctantly, as if dragged from Callach's throat. "You'll find a valley, the Valley of the White Death. On the far side of that valley is a deep cave, called by some the Dreamchamber. When the wyrm sleeps, it lairs there."

"When? When does it sleep?" Malshaunt broke in, his face sharp with impatience.

"Soon," Callach answered. "The sun and the stars have come round to their appointed places. They're only waiting for the three moons to join them, and then it'll be time for the wyrm to sleep until she issues forth again to bring death to Krynn." He took a step closer, and his voice grew softer, as if he feared being overheard. "Take this warning kindly, mistress. Go back! There is nothing here but white death."

Tashara smiled slightly. "In that case, Master Callach, what are you doing here?"

Callach glanced back over his band. "Seeking a way out of here, truth be told. We've been mining near here. Fear of the wyrm keeps most far away from here, and there are rich pickings in these mountains for those bold enough to seek them when the wyrm is roving the rest of Krynn. But enough's enough! I know the signs. The wyrm's due back, and the three moons will converge. We'll not be here when the beast comes. Neither will you, if you've any sense."

"On the contrary," the elf woman told him, "we shall wait for it. We shall wait and conquer it. And someday, in some tavern, you may hear the Tale of Tashara and how she slew the Great White Wyrm, the legendary Death That Comes From the Sky."

Callach stared at her, shaking his head. "Well," he observed, "if you're bound and determined to die, I won't stop you. But remember what I said. That's no natural dragon. It's a scourge sent down by the gods!"

Tashara burst out laughing. In that cold, high place it seemed to Ayshe that the surrounding peaks of the Mountains of the Moons bent closer, as if to stifle the unaccustomed sound.

"The gods!" she cried. "The gods on whom every fool blames woes that fall upon him! The gods who hurled a mountain upon Istar because they so loved the people of Krynn! The gods who visit war and ruin upon Ansalon in the name of divine justice! The gods who deserted us for centuries and returned upon a whim! I have never seen these gods! Why should we even believe they exist?"

Callach's face was very grave. "Careful, mistress," he said. "It never does to blaspheme something, even something you've never witnessed. I've never seen Reorx, but damned if I'll say aught against him."

"The more fool you, then!" retorted the captain. "I say the Great White Wyrm, if indeed it was sent by the gods, is a sign that once again they have abandoned us. I say I shall slay it and free all Krynn from its terror. I say that in this wasteland there is no god but me!"

Harfang gave Tashara a long, astonished stare, and Ayshe saw his fingers work, but he remained silent. Malshaunt was quiet as well, but his face was turned to his leader in adoration.

The dwarf leader shrugged again. "Well, mistress, as I say, it's all one to me." He turned to Ayshe. "Are you part of this foolishness, Brother?" he asked in Dwarvish.

Ayshe hesitated then nodded. "Yes. These are my friends and companions. I will not abandon them." As he spoke the words, he stood straighter and knew he had made his final, irrevocable choice. There would be no turning back, even if it meant his life.

The dwarves insisted that Dragonsbane share a meal with them, and the two parties broke bread, sitting on the lap of the nearest peak, the one whose rocks shone red in the sunlight. Callach said little more beyond some general directions to the Dreamchamber in the valley beyond. The valley itself, he told them, was only a mile or two broad. Though the sky above them was clear, he warned several times of what they already knew: the White Wyrm could materialize without warning from a cloudless firmament. In exchange, Tashara told him about their fight with the yeti and the stores they had left in the beast's cave.

Harfang was silent through much of the meal. Toward its conclusion he asked, "What do you know of yonder forest, Master Callach?"

Callach looked at him. "It's a place best traveled quickly, master. The Glen of Darkness some call it. It stretches twenty miles in that direction"—he waved north—"and farther there," he said, gesturing to the south. "We've passed through it once, but I would not make that journey again unless I had magical means to defend myself."

"Do you know of the great stone pillar in its midst," Harfang asked.

"Aye." Callach's face paled again.

"What do you know of it?"

Callach shook his head. "I'll not speak of it. It's evil and should be avoided. We're going north around the edge of the glen. It will add some days to our journey, but I'd rather have a whole skin at the end of the road." He would say no more concerning the obelisk.

Finally Callach stood, and his followers joined him, assembled in their marching order.

"Well, mistress, all I can say is good luck. You're fools, I think, but brave fools. There's no denying that." He turned to Ayshe. "Farewell, Brother," he said in Dwarvish. "May your axe always be sharp."

"Farewell," Ayshe returned.

Dragonsbane stood as the dwarves filed past. The elves, Ayshe, and Harfang watched as they turned north at the border of the forest and moved along its edge, leaving a wide margin between themselves and the perilous wood.

Harfang, Tashara, and the mage turned. Ahead, their road rose to a crest, covered with snow and flanked by the jutting peaks.

The rest of Dragonsbane turned as well. Silently they shouldered their packs and lifted their weapons. They moved off up the slope, still with no word spoken among them.

CHAPTER

20

The mate was surprised, not for the first time, at how well his lungs had adjusted to the change in altitude. Breathing, though strenuous, was not nearly as difficult as it had been the previous day, though he still walked more slowly than he might have on lower ground.

Much of the rest of the company appeared similarly affected. Only Tashara walked with the same steady gait as she had maintained from the beginning of their journey.

They approached the pass's summit cautiously. Twenty yards from the top, at a signal from Harfang, they drew weapons. They crouched slightly as if expecting a blow. The mate felt his heart pounding in his chest. This was it, perhaps. The culmination of twenty years of hunting. The thing that had driven him since that long-ago day when Tashara plucked him from the streets of Palanthas.

Spreading out in as wide a line as the pathway would permit, they formed two ranks, with the archers in the rear. Harfang and Tashara stood in the center, the captain a little before the others.

They came to the top of the pass and halted. Tashara turned to Harfang. "Tell me what you see."

THE GREAT WHITE WYRM

The mate kept his voice low. "There is a valley, just as the dwarf said. On the other side rises the white mountain, while the red and the black are on this side. Their ridges extend to one another, encircling the valley and cutting it off. The floor is flat and snow covered. There's a stony slope that leads down from where we're standing. The sides of the mountains are covered with snow. On the far side of the valley, I can see—"

"A dark hole, the mouth of a cave," Tashara interrupted him. "Above it is a shelf of gray rock, and to one side stands a single pillar of black stone."

The mate looked at her with astonishment.

"I have seen this place in my dreams," she said. "For decades I have dreamed of the lair of my foe, and now I stand at its doorstep." A tear trickled from one blind eye and froze on her cheek, leaving a trail like a pale scar. Her voice was sharp and decisive. "We will circle to the north and approach the cave that way. Keep a single file, weapons readied."

The party turned and trekked north. To his surprise, Harfang found the path they had been walking along had turned into a paved road, its worn stones partly hidden beneath the snow. He wondered who in what ancient time had inhabited that remote, frightening place. If it had, in fact, been dwarves, as Ayshe had mentioned to him, they must have been of a hardy race that died out in some unforeseen catastrophe. If it was not made by dwarves, the road must have been fashioned by a people just as skilled in engineering, for its stones were still close-set and even.

The road wound along the sides of the surrounding mountains, dipping and rising. In a few places, it overlooked a steep descent to the floor of the valley, some hundred feet below, and Harfang was careful of his footing lest he slip and tumble. The silence and fear that hung like a mist over the valley oppressed them all, and they tried to avoid making noise for fear that it would arouse their foe.

The mate brooded on the coming fight. No battle plan had

been discussed, but Dragonsbane had had enough experience fighting dragons to know what was expected of each of them. Yet they were short-handed and facing an opponent the like of which none had ever defeated. Tashara seemed, more than ever, to be trusting to her luck. One part of Harfang's mind wished he had the leisure to again lay out the *charon* cards and see what they might tell him about the coming confrontation.

It was early afternoon when they came to the pillar Tashara had described from across the valley. It was perhaps twenty feet high, and clearly no work of nature. The pillar was of the same polished black stone that had been used for the base of the obelisk in the glen. Runes in the same unknown tongue encircled it, rising in a spiral to the top.

Harfang brushed away a light coating of snow, staring at the letters. "I can't read them. What about you, Master Ayshe?"

The dwarf shook his head. "No. They aren't in any Dwarvish dialect I recognize." He hesitated a moment. "I think they might be similar to the carvings I saw at Donatta. Possibly they are in the language of whoever built this road."

Harfang nodded. "There are a good many people who lived in this land long before humans and dwarves," he observed. "It would seem they left this for us to wonder over."

"Sir!" Anchallann called in a low voice. "Come look at this."

A few yards farther was the entrance to the cavern, penetrating the slope of the white mountain. The doorway was huge, dwarfing the yeti's cave. It rose at least seventy feet at its highest point, forming an archway easily spanning a hundred feet, that had been carved and shaped with considerable skill. Above it, beneath the shelf of gray stone, was cut a bas-relief of a dragon rampant.

Harfang looked at it curiously. "You said," he muttered to Ayshe, speaking so that the others could not hear, "there was some sort of cult of the wyrm among the draconians who captured you?"

The dwarf nodded.

"Well, I wonder if that cult is not rooted in something much older. Whoever carved this dragon and built this archway, it would seem, held dragons in reverence."

The thought did not make him feel better.

They left some supplies just inside the entrance to the cave. In a fight, they wanted to be as unencumbered as possible. Most wore leather armor, which would provide little protection against the dragon but might save them from scrapes and bruises if they fell or were knocked down. Their weapons, cared for by Ayshe over the long months of their journey, were razor sharp and gleaming. Otha-nyar carried her wyrmbarb. Malshaunt bore his whip in one hand, but his eyes gleamed, and he seemed to have found a strength beyond any of the others. His body was drawn taut as a bowstring and quivered as he walked.

Tashara joined them last of all. While the others had made ready, she stood by the pillar, ceaselessly running her hands over the graven characters as if by mere touch she might translate them. At last she stopped and, unwrapping one of the bundles she had borne from the *Starfinder*, she donned the breastplate of B'ynn al'Tor. It glittered on her as though newly polished, despite the many days she had carried it wrapped in its cloth. From the other bundle, she drew Kuthendra's sword and swung it hissing through the air.

The small band entered the cavern, moving quietly, in battle-ready formation. Harfang carried a torch. The elves and Ayshe relied on their ability to see in the dark. The cave plunged straight ahead and down, but fifty feet into the tunnel it was sealed by a smooth wall of the same black stone as the pillar with runes. The elves searched it, looking for some lever or device that would open it, but they could find nothing.

"Can we tunnel through this?" Harfang inquired of Ayshe.

The dwarf studied the stone, tapping it and listening to it. Then he turned to the mate. "No. Not without better tools than we have here. And even then, I doubt it would do us much good." Ayshe ran a hand over the surface. "There's something odd about this. Something magical."

"Aye," added Alyssaran. The elf woman had looked increasingly unhappy as they went into the cave. She stood near the wall, looking at the smooth black wall with distaste. "Can't you feel it? There's some sort of magic emanating from it. It makes me feel . . . dirty. Ugh!" She twitched her shoulders in disgust.

The elves sank down before the wall, discouragement in every face. Since entering the Valley of the White Death, they had so anticipated the long-awaited battle that their nerves were keyed up to the snapping point. Frustration came hard.

Malshaunt stepped up to the wall. He passed his hands lightly over it, muttering to the air. Nothing happened. He made several more passes.

"Well, mage?" Harfang's voice sounded loud and harsh in the stillness.

"Well?" Malshaunt did not deign to look at the man. His fingers were everywhere, probing, pushing, stroking the blank surface that confronted them.

"Can't you find a way past the magic?"

"With time, yes. And if you are silent, possibly. This is a refined magic, unlike any I've seen before." The mage's face twisted in annoyance at Harfang's sigh. "If you think you can do better by battering on it with your sword, be my guest!"

A shadow fell on the wall. Tashara had stood passively while her crew examined the barrier. Saying nothing, she ran her hands over the wall. She placed her cheek against its surface, her hands spread wide touching it. She rested there as if she were listening to the stone. Then she bent and, with her fingers twisted in an odd configuration, placed her hands together on a spot at the center of the wall.

She spoke a single word. Magical power flared from beneath her hands in a glow of blue and white light. The glow spread in thin lines across the wall. With a harsh grinding sound, the wall swung back, revealed as two doors, so closely aligned that when they were shut, no line or crack could be discerned between them.

Every member of the party sprang to his or her feet in astonishment. Malshaunt, for the first time since Ayshe had known him, was stunned into incoherence.

"How . . . how . . . ?" he stuttered.

Darkness flowed from the cave like a vapor. Tashara started forward, but the mate blocked her way.

"How did you do that?" Harfang demanded.

Ayshe noticed he had dropped the professional politeness with which he usually addressed his captain. His expression was angry.

"You can do magic! You kept that from me! All these years, you kept it from me! And from Dragonsbane. What else can you do, Captain Tashara? Could you have saved Jeannara? Could you have healed her? Could you have saved the others who've died on this mad escapade?"

Tashara looked at him with something very like scorn in her face, but her voice was neutral. "Power, Harfang, comes to those willing to take it. I claim such power as I need to destroy my enemy. I have power you have not seen, because unlike you, I am willing to accept it as my fate. It is my destiny to enter this cave. Therefore, the wall could not stand in my way, and I was fated to find the magic with which to open it. Nothing can stand in my way."

Harfang stood his ground. "That's nonsense, and you know it! Those who claim power in their own name desire it for their own ends. They may begin by wishing to do good, but they end as tyrants."

Tashara stared at him with her blind eyes. "Is that what you think I have become, Harfang? A tyrant?" She gestured to the crew, who stood stock still, watching the confrontation. "Ask these good elves. Is there any one of them who did not willingly come with me? Are there any here whose hearts did not soar at the thought of destroying the White Wyrm? Their destiny is bound to mine, human! As is yours!"

Harfang shook his head. "Nay! I'm my own man."

The captain snorted. "No one is his own, Harfang. I thought in our long years together you had at least learned that. Our fate is shaped for us from the day we are born. Each choice we make, each step we take, moves us farther along the road whose course is already set. Even these words you speak to me now have been foretold in the stars. Is it not true that when you lay out the *charon* cards, each time the last card is the White Wyrm?"

Harfang's mouth opened. He had not mentioned the *charon* cards to anyone, least of all Tashara. How had she known?

"Yes, ma'am. But . . ."

The captain overrode him. "You see, Harfang. I am bound by fate to the wyrm, and you—all of you—through me. You have no choice but to walk this road with me."

Harfang glared at her, and Ayshe waited for him to draw his sword. His hand hovered above the pommel, and the veins in his neck stood out. The air was heavy between them, and the elves stared at them in silence.

Malshaunt stepped forward, placing himself between the mate and the captain. "You have said enough!" he snapped. "You speak mutiny by questioning your captain. Do it again and you answer to me!"

The mate's fingers closed on his sword, and the rest of Dragonsbane stood, awaiting the stroke. Then his hand eased from his hilt, and there was a faint sigh of relief from the onlookers. Defeat was in Harfang's face, but he remained defiant.

THE GREAT WHITE WYRM

"If I'm to walk behind you, ma'am," he snarled to the captain, "I prefer not to do it blind!"

Malshaunt coiled in fury, but Tashara gave no sign of resenting the remark. "We shall go on," she said and stepped around Harfang into the blackness of the tunnel.

The way forward was broad and the floor smooth, sloping downward at a gentle grade. The elves maintained their double line with Harfang and Ayshe—the dwarf seeing farther in the dark than any of the others—in the lead just behind Tashara.

The walls of the cave were worn smooth as if by the passage of some great beast. The way was straight and true. Ayshe listened intently but could hear nothing but the breathing of the elves and the gentler exhalations of the man by his side.

How long they continued that way was hard to say, since time in that place seemed suspended. All at once, the walls to either side fell away, and they found themselves in a vast space, the dimensions of which could not be guessed.

Harfang motioned to the others to wait while he, the mage, and Tashara slowly advanced across the floor. They stopped, and by the twinkling light of the mate's torch, Ayshe could see they were sixty or seventy yards distant. They seemed to have encountered some object, but what it was he could not tell. Of one thing he was sure: the White Wyrm was not in the cavern. He felt none of the dragonfear he'd experienced the past two times he'd encountered the beast.

Without warning, a great light glowed in the center of the cave. It rose in a vast pillar to the ceiling of the room, which the company could see loomed at least three hundred feet above them. The walls of the cavern were, like those of the tunnel, smooth, but it was impossible to say if they were worked by mortal hands or not. They looked strange.

The light that illuminated the area was golden but without warmth. It came, they could see, from a pillar by which Tashara and Harfang stood, a pillar made of translucent stone. From within the rock shone the light that revealed every facet of the room.

The sheer size of the space made Ayshe's spine tingle. From end to end, the diameter was no less than a thousand feet. There were other widely spaced pillars in the hall that also gave out glows, though none so intense as the one by the mate and the captain. There seemed no egress from the cave other than by the way they had traveled, and Ayshe wondered what the original purpose of so huge a space could have been. If it had been constructed, he marveled at the skill of the hands that had built it. Such a feat, he knew, was well beyond the skills of any race of dwarves living in Ansalon during his time.

Many of the elves seemed similarly awed by the space. Othanyar stared upward, her face drained of blood, her wyrmbarb slack in her hand. Omarro staggered as if dizzy. Ayshe had been in many strange places beneath the earth but never had any given him such a feeling of disorientation.

Harfang returned to the party, who still stood at the entrance.

"The Dreamchamber," he said grimly, "but our target isn't home. Did the draconians say anything else about this place, Master Ayshe?"

The dwarf shook his head. "Nothing beyond what I told you before. Only that it's here the beast sleeps and sends out her dreams." He shivered.

Harfang alone seemed unaffected by the strange, vast room. "Scatter," he ordered, "and examine this place. I want to know if there's any other way in or out. Report in half an hour. Go!"

The elves moved out along the walls, tapping, listening, searching. Ayshe remained with Harfang.

"What did you do to turn on the light?" he asked.

"I? Nothing," returned the mate. "When the captain touched

the pillar, it began to glow." His voice sank, though they were far from any of the others. "I tell you, Ayshe, it's as if this damned place *recognizes* her. I don't understand what's going on. I've been by her side for years, and I've never seen her like this. That scene in the tunnel, now—that never would have happened before. But since we entered this damned land, she's like a woman possessed!" He shook his head and turned away. Together he and the dwarf walked from pillar to pillar. All glowed, but the farther they went from the central pillar, the softer the glow became. As a result, the far reaches of the cavern were still shrouded in shadow.

All of a sudden, they heard a long, low moan. To Ayshe, in that dark, strange place, it was the most sorrowful sound he had ever heard, like a soul trapped forever in the Abyss.

"What's that?" he whispered to Harfang, instinctively dropping his voice.

The moan came again, louder and more prolonged. Without answering Ayshe, Harfang lifted his torch and walked forward, skirting the stone wall.

The moan turned into a wail, ending in a shriek of maniacal laughter. By that time the elves were running toward the sound, swords drawn, faces grim. Ayshe and Harfang hurried forward.

A dark form huddled next to the wall, far from the nearest light, wailed again and turned its face to Harfang's torch.

"It's Omarro!" gasped Shamura.

The elf, dark hair scattered around his face, was breathing heavily. His eyes were shut, his brow was damp with sweat. Tears poured from beneath his closed lids and made dark tracks down his face.

"Oh, gods!" Shamura whispered. "He's weeping *blood!*"

The elf lifted his face again and gave a wordless cry that echoed throughout the chamber. He turned and smashed his face against the rock wall. Hands grasped his shoulders to restrain him. He fought furiously, screaming and shouting in a language no one recognized. The words seemed twisted and poisonous and boomed through the air like shafts seeking their targets. Meanwhile the bloody tears continued to pour in streams down his face and pool on the cave's floor.

"He'll give us away," snapped Harfang. "Gag him!"

One of the other elves tore a strip of cloth from Omarro's shirt and bound it over his mouth. The elf continued to groan for a few minutes, then fell silent, though he still struggled with his captors. They finally had to tie his hands and feet and carry him back, writhing silently, to lay him on the floor near the central pillar where Tashara and Malshaunt stood, impassively observing the scene.

Alyssaran bent by him, trying to stanch the flow of blood from his eyes. After a short while, she stood and shook her head. "I don't know what's causing this," she said. "What was there that he saw or heard or met that did this to him?"

Several of the other elves were looking unwell. Alyssaran herself was paler than usual and brushed a hand over her forehead.

Harfang looked about. "This is a Dreamchamber," he said. "Perhaps the wyrm's dreams are still about." He glanced at Tashara then away. "Let's go. There's nothing more for us here. If we're going to fight the wyrm, I'd rather do it in an open valley than in this cave."

The captain did not resist, and the party left, carrying Omarro with them.

It had been late afternoon when they entered the tunnel that descended to the Dreamchamber, and Ayshe expected when they emerged to see stars. Instead he was startled to see the sun's rays still glowing golden upon the surrounding mountains. It seemed as if no time at all had passed since they went below. Or perhaps, the dwarf wondered, an entire day had gone by without their noticing it.

They set up their camp a little distance from the black stone, speaking few words and those only in whispers. Omarro they laid on the ground near the fire, tended by Alyssaran. She tried again and again to stop the flow of blood, but he never opened his eyes, never ceased to struggle against his bonds, and never stopped weeping. Alyssaran resigned herself to wrapping him in blankets, several of which quickly became blood-soaked. As the stars brightened in the sky, the stricken elf uttered a long sigh and was at last silent. Alyssaran undid the bandage around his mouth, untied him, and arranged his limbs beneath the blanket before she pulled it over his face.

One more, Ayshe thought. One more of the company gone. Crushed by an avalanche, slain by draconians, destroyed in the woods, driven mad by the Dreamchamber . . . and Jeannara. He looked at Malshaunt's dark robes, gathered closely around the mage, then turned away. He did not want to think about how Jeannara had died.

The air about them was fresh and clean, and the night seemed to embrace them like dark velvet. Most of the elves seemed disheartened, both by the death of their companion and because, having sought their prize so long, they were unsure what to do. They spoke in low tones and cast uneasy glances into the dark valley that spread below them.

Harfang set watches, but no one slept. The mate stood through all the watches, tall and unmoving save for the ruffling of his hair by the unceasing wind. Tashara did not sleep either, but sat alert by the fire.

Ayshe closed his eyes several times, but cold and a growing feeling of dread kept him awake. At last he rose, lifted his axe, and went to stand beside the silent human.

Pale light shone in the eastern part of the sky. As the night drew to an end, Ayshe wandered about, stretching his legs but avoiding the body of Omarro beneath its shroud. He found himself standing next to the black stone. The glow of the red moon and the silver were reflected in its surface as they rode high in the sky, slowly paling with the coming of the morning. He looked up.

High above, the disks of Solinari and Lunitari met and joined. For a few moments, it seemed to Ayshe, as he gazed on the spectacle of the two moons, that beyond them he could glimpse a third moon, a dark moon staring at Krynn like some unfathomable eye. He recalled the words of Callach.

The sun and the stars have come round to their appointed places. They're only waiting for the three moons to join them, and then it'll be time for the wyrm to sleep until she issues forth again to bring death to Krynn.

"Sir!" he called.

Harfang turned. Ayshe gestured toward the moons.

The tips of the Mountains of the Moons glowed pink in the coming dawn. No, the dwarf realized, it was more than that. They shone with their own power, as if they glowed from within, mimicking the light from the three moons—red, white, and black.

Lightning leaped into the sky. Not, Ayshe realized, from a cloud, but from one of the peaks itself. Another bolt burst from the red mountaintop and struck the black summit. There was a deep, resounding boom, and the valley shuddered. There came another flash and another, faster, so the vale seemed crowned with a ring of blue-white fire.

Above the roar of the thunderous detonations, Harfang shouted commands. The elves spread out in a line, sprinting to put distance between themselves so each had room to fight. Nearest him, Ayshe saw Otha-nyar testing the edge of her wyrmbarb with her thumb. A look of exultation was in her eyes. Malshaunt stood at attention, hands uplifted, either in prayer or in rapture.

Above the noise, Tashara's voice rose and echoed through the valley. "Hold, Dragonsbane!" she cried. "Not until I give you leave! This is *my* fight!"

Harfang turned toward her in consternation. "No!" he roared. "We fight as one! Captain, we are one!"

Malshaunt turned toward him. Behind the mage, Tashara drew her great sword, the sword of Kuthendra. In the blazing light of the peaks, the blade sparkled and hissed.

"Stand back, human!" the mage screamed. "This is *her* command! Obey your captain!"

The pass on the other side of the valley seemed dim and distant to Ayshe. He realized a gray mist was creeping up from the valley floor. It obscured the faces of his companions then drew itself into the center of the valley. The lightning among the peaks seemed to have lessened, but the air was charged with electricity. The black stone near which the dwarf stood was warm to the touch. Snow around it melted and ran in rivulets about Ayshe's feet.

The mists and clouds that had gathered in the midst of the valley solidified and assumed a terrible form: a head, a long snout, row upon row of gleaming teeth. From it, two emerald eyes regarded its foes with unspeakable malice.

The White Wyrm had come home.

CHAPTER

21

The dragonfear that swept over Ayshe struck him like a physical blow and knocked him from his feet. His head struck
the black stone, and, for a few moments, he lost consciousness.
When he found his footing again, the scene before him seemed
unchanged. The Great White Wyrm was crouched in the middle of
the valley. It was less than a quarter mile away, and at that distance,
the force of its aura was hideously powerful.

The elves seemed less affected by it than Ayshe. Harfang, too,
stood straight and proud, showing no signs of any fear caused by
the creature.

The tableau held for a moment. Then with a great cry, Tashara
launched herself, running down the slope toward the wyrm.

The beast turned its head and stared at her but made no move.
To the dwarf, it looked almost as if the dragon were waiting for
her.

The creature's mane swept back from her head, the serpents in
it writhing, hissing, and spitting in fury. There in the valley of its
lair, its outline and features were terribly clear. Its claws were long,
cruel, and curved. The points glistened in the rising sun. Its tail
swept back and forth, stirring the snow on the valley floor to a froth

and sending clouds of spume into the air, clouds that glistened and sparkled, twisting the light in a thousand different ways.

Tashara held her sword high and the rising sun, shining through a break in the clouds, made it gleam silver. The rays caught her shield and breastplate, and she seemed, for a moment, a figure of white fire.

The creature lifted its great bat wings. They spread across the valley. It beat them, and the force of the wind hurled the fighters of Dragonsbane like chaff before a thresher's flail. Tashara alone remained on her feet.

The White Wyrm rose above the valley floor, its reptilian visage twisting in hatred at the mortal who was hunting it. The wind of its wings stirred snow into a mist, drawing it up into whirling eddies that obscured Tashara for a moment. Then the wyrm dropped, claws outstretched.

The elf woman leaped back, high and nimble. Her sword swept down, aimed at the wyrm's claws, which were outstretched to rend her. The sound of the blow raced across the valley as Tashara's blade struck. The wyrm gave a horrid shriek, and one of its claws fell.

The watching elves gave a shout of approval. Tashara did not stop, but leaped and spun, slashing at the wyrm. Her body, honed as a perfect fighting machine, bent and swayed with each movement of the dragon. The beast struck at her again and again, and each time she dodged. The wyrm's claws made great rents in the snow. Tashara swung her blade again, and another claw fell, lying in the snow like a glittering jewel. The wyrm screamed and backed across the valley, and the captain of the *Starfinder* pursued her.

But the retreat was only a feint. As Tashara came on, the wyrm struck again, with her breath instead of her claws. A cone of freezing cold surged toward the captain of the *Starfinder*. She sprang aside only just in time, almost dropping her shield. Mired in snow, she slipped.

"Tashara!" Malshaunt cried, leaping down the slope toward the combat. The other elves of Dragonsbane joined him in a mad race toward their captain. Harfang, cannier than the rest, brought up the rear, circling round, trying to get behind the wyrm. The others, impelled by loyalty to their captain and their cause, gave no thought to such strategy. All their long training seemed to fall away from them as they charged straight at the wyrm that had so long eluded them.

Ayshe, too, lifted his axe and ran down the steep slope, struggling to keep his footing. He found, somewhat to his surprise, his fear had abated. His entire soul was consumed with a passion to kill the storm dragon. The faces of Chaval and Zininia rose before him as they had so often done, but the mouths of his old friends were open in cries of encouragement, their eyes gleaming with pride as they hailed him as their avenger.

The wyrm's head snapped up, and Tashara took the opportunity to regain her feet. She slashed again at the creature but missed. The wyrm swung her head about and stared balefully at the charging elves. It reared its head, gave a cry, and took to the air. The wind from its wings beat hard against the elves, but they managed, for the most part, to keep their feet.

Tashara turned and sensed the approaching elves. Her expression changed to fury. "Stay back!" she shouted. "Did I not say this is my fight alone?"

The elves hesitated—all but Malshaunt. The mage's hands were already contorted in a spell. A fireball leaped from his fingers, striking toward the wyrm.

The wyrm lifted its head. A bolt of lightning leaped from the peak of the red mountain and plunged onto the floor of the valley. It met Malshaunt's fireball and divided it, shattering it into a thousand pieces that fell to the valley floor and hissed into the snow. The sides of the surrounding mountains turned red from the blast.

THE GREAT WHITE WYRM

Without hesitation, Malshaunt hurled another missile. The White Wyrm dodged, and the fireball arced beyond it, crashing into the side of the mountain. A cloud of snow and boulders plunged toward the valley floor.

The Great White Wyrm lifted its head and screamed again. Another lightning bolt from the red mountain crashed through the air. It struck Shamura, and the elf was outlined for a second in bright fire. She collapsed, smoke rising from her clothing. Even at a distance, Ayshe could see her hands and face were black and charred.

Otha-nyar circled swiftly around, finding the wyrm's left side. As the mighty wings continued to beat, she hurled her wyrmbarb. "For my brother!" she shrieked.

The chain attached to the end of the barb snaked upward. The spear struck the wyrm beneath its wing, its point vanishing into the mighty muscle. The wyrm cried again.

But Ayshe saw the weakness of the Kagonesti's attack. Under ordinary circumstances—if fighting a dragon could be called ordinary under any circumstances—he knew Otha-nyar and her brother would have attacked from opposite sides. Once both wyrmbarbs had found their target, they would have secured the chains to something. The dragon would be slowed by the attack long enough for the other elves of Dragonsbane to strike, wounding and killing it.

But with Samath-nyar dead and lying beneath the sea, Otha-nyar was alone. Moreover, on the valley floor there was no way to bind the chain from her barb. The wyrm's wings flapped again, and it rose higher. Otha-nyar, clutching the chain, was lifted from her feet.

The three elf archers loosed a hail of arrows, but they bounced off the wyrm's armored body as Otha-nyar's struggling figure rose in the air.

"Let go, damn you!" roared Harfang.

It was too late. The wyrm had gained height too rapidly, and

Otha-nyar was some hundreds of feet in the air, clinging desperately to the chain. The wyrm turned in midair and slashed at her with its claw. She gave a cry, a shower of red gushing from her as her arm was severed from her torso, and she fell. Her body smashed into the snow and lay still. Ayshe reached her first, but he did not need to examine her to know that the Kagonesti was dead. No one could topple from that height and live.

The remaining fighters of Dragonsbane ran toward the center of the valley. "Scatter!" Harfang shouted furiously. "To your posts! Dragonsbane! Heed me!"

The elves paid no attention. The closeness of the White Wyrm seemed to have plunged them into a fog through which their minds and bodies struggled to continue their planned attack. They milled about in the middle of the valley, while above them the wyrm circled on great wings. Malshaunt alone had retained his awareness, and he watched the wyrm with eager eyes, hands poised to launch another magical blast at it.

Tashara, after her outburst of rage, seemed withdrawn. She turned her face this way and that, listening for her foe. Her sword and shield gleamed bright in her hands.

Another bolt of lightning struck the floor of the valley, barely missing Anchallann. He drew back on his bow and sent a shaft darting toward the wyrm's eye, but the beast jerked aside at the last moment and evaded it. The wyrm opened its mouth and sent out a long blast of cold. Anchallann tried to move aside, but hampered by the snow, he struggled, and the freezing breath struck both his legs. The wyrm descended upon him, and its long jaws snapped and met. It caught up the elf in its jaws, shaking him as a dog might shake a rat. His body was tossed to the ground, mangled and torn. The legs shattered into pieces.

Harfang shouted to Tashara. "Higher ground!" he roared. For a moment she stood still then nodded. The other elves began scrambling back toward the slope leading to the Dreamchamber entrance. Ayshe, with his shorter legs, tried to keep up. He glanced over his shoulder. The dragon seemed to be hovering. Surely its eye was fixed on him. He felt another surge of dragonfear and desperately tried to shrug it off.

The wyrm swept around, cutting off the party, blocking their path. It crashed to the ground before the Dreamchamber, and the mountains around it shook. The elves staggered to a halt, some falling back into the snow.

Tashara, in the lead, never hesitated. With a cry of hatred, she charged straight at the wyrm, her blade held out in front of her. She struck one of the mighty wings, and her sword tore a long gash in it. At the same time, three bolts of light from Malshaunt's fingers smashed into its neck. Serpents in its mane twisted but were caught by the missiles. For a heartbeat they were outlined in magical fire, then lay limp.

The cry of the White Wyrm was so loud that rocks from the peaks above boomed to the ground and shattered. Ayshe fell as well, his ears ringing with the awful sound. Just in front of him, he saw Harfang stagger to his knees, blood running from his nose.

The wyrm leaped into the air again. It rose higher than before then dropped. Straight down it fell, legs splayed out. It struck the floor of the valley with a crash that echoed beyond the peaks and sent bolts of lightning leaping. The valley rocked and shuddered.

Ayshe suddenly realized what accounted for the land's unnatural shape. It was no valley. Rather, it was a lake.

The Great White Wyrm's fall shattered the ice that covered the lake. Pieces flew through the air. Out of the corner of his eye, Ayshe saw one smash Noortheleen, crushing her body, leaving a bloody smear in its wake. A wave of freezing water swept toward him. He felt a hand on his collar and realized Harfang was pulling him to safety.

He lay panting for a moment, tasting blood and snow. His body was shaking uncontrollably, and the air was filled with icy spray. He saw the mate had a long gash across one cheek from which blood was dripping on the snow. He sat up and looked around.

The lake was revealed. An enormous hole in the center showed where the dragon had gone. Plates of ice six feet thick reared up against one another in disarray. The fiery display of lightning from the surrounding peaks that had accompanied the wyrm had ceased. Ayshe looked around in vain for the other members of Dragonsbane.

Harfang followed his gaze and shook his head. For a long time, neither spoke.

"Dead," Harfang said. "All dead." His voice held a note of horror and defeat that Ayshe had never heard there before.

The dwarf rose. On the ice below them, Ayshe could see the broken bodies of the elves. Otha-nyar's corpse floated in the water. Nearby was another body that, from the bow clutched in its stiffened hand, Ayshe recognized as Lannlathsar, one of the elf archers. Huddled bundles showed where others had fallen, destroyed by the White Wyrm's fall.

Harfang stood beside him. "It's the end," he said quietly. "It's the end of it all. They are all dead, and we have survived. We alone survive."

Ayshe gazed at the scene of devastation, as so many months and a lifetime before he had looked on his ruined village. Harfang placed a hand on his shoulder. Man and dwarf stood and wept together for their lost friends.

But they were not alone. Tashara stood erect nearby. Her sword dripped blood from its stroke against the Great White Wyrm. Her face was suffused with triumph. She lifted the blade and gave a shout that made the mountains ring. It was long and ululating, and within it were words in an ancient Elvish tongue. A single ray of the morning sun broke through the clouds and surrounded her figure in a nimbus of light.

Next to her, Malshaunt's dark robes hung over the mage's gaunt body. He stared at the hole into which the wyrm's body had vanished, and his face was transformed, its harsh features softened. For a moment, he looked young, as he might have looked when he first met Tashara and heard the tale of the White Wyrm.

Harfang stared at the pair, captain and mage. "So you have triumphed," he said softly. "And what of the cost?" He shook his head and bent to pick up his sword.

The water of the lake began to bubble. Pieces of ice flew high into the air and smashed against the mountainsides. The shore shook, knocking man and dwarf to their knees. From the center of the lake, the wyrm rose. Water streamed from its body, and its green eyes looked death at the elf who had wounded it. It staggered in the air, suffering from the dreadful gash in its wing torn by Tashara's sword.

It lashed its tail, striking the ground, smashing a portion of the old road to pieces. It opened its mouth and issued a roar—not the mere growl from its previous attacks, but a terrible, booming cry that bounded from mountaintop to mountaintop.

Tashara held her blade ready. Her voice lifted in challenge. "Come to me! Come to me, spawn of darkness! I have been long waiting for you.

"I am she whose coming was foretold to you when you were a hatchling! I am she who fills your dreams as you have filled mine. I am the Wyrmslayer!

The Great White Wyrm beat its wings again and settled on that ice that still covered parts of the lake. Its blood, falling on the snow, steamed as if boiling hot. From its side, Otha-nyar's wyrmbarb still protruded. The beast's edges were misty, and clouds boiled around it.

"It's fading," Harfang cried. "It's fleeing from us into the other plane!"

Clouds swept over the valley, and the mist became thicker. Then, without warning, it began to disperse. The figure of the wyrm remained, though, its eyes blazing.

Tashara laughed wildly. "You cannot flee from me, wyrm!" she cried. "Though you took my sight, I can see you. I can see into your innermost being! I can see your fear of me, for I am fated to destroy you."

As if in a dream, Ayshe listened to her words, and as if in a dream, he understood, at last, the strange link between elf and dragon, the destiny, decreed centuries before, that had bound them together. It seemed to him as if one could not exist without the other, that they were, in some strange way, each a part of a single being. Each saw into the heart of the other and understood. And there, at the world's end, they were joined at last.

The moment passed, and Tashara appeared but a slight elf woman holding her small sword defiantly against the white death.

The wyrm rose, and a blast of blue fire leaped from the clouds above to strike Tashara. She jumped aside just in time but was hurled from her feet to smash to the ground away from the entrance to the Dreamchamber. With a cry, the wyrm sprang forward on its wings and disappeared through the entrance.

Tashara was on her feet in a moment and, without hesitation, raced after the beast, passing through the great doorway to vanish into the blackness. Malshaunt followed her, robes flapping behind him.

"Gods!" cried Harfang. "Come!" He rose and ran like a madman after his captain. Ayshe sprang to his feet and followed suit. Without thought, he pounded down the tunnel, struggling to catch up with the mate and captain. From ahead of him, he heard Malshaunt's voice cry, "Tashara!"

At the very entrance to the Dreamchamber, he saw the elf

woman. Her figure was limned by the light that flowed from the chamber once its mistress, the wyrm, occupied it.

The mate sprang forward with a shout. "No! Stop! This is suicide!"

From one side, Malshaunt stepped, a knife gleaming in his hand.

Harfang stopped dead, his back still to the dwarf. He faced Malshaunt, and for a moment the two, elf and man, seemed to cling together before the captain they both served.

The mage stepped back. For a moment, absolute silence surrounded them. Harfang half turned toward the dwarf. His face bore a puzzled expression, as if he were trying desperately to understand something. A trickle of blood came from the corner of his mouth, and he collapsed.

Ayshe was paralyzed with horror. Tashara seemed momentarily confused by what had happened. She put a hand forward, as if groping in the dark. "Harfang?" she said. "Harfang?" For a second, she sounded like an elf child searching for a lost parent.

From behind her in the chamber came a snarl. She turned and sprang forward, her sword raised for battle. Malshaunt turned away from the mate and followed his captain.

Ayshe jumped to the side of the mate. Harfang's eyes were closed, his breathing labored.

A roar and a shout drew the dwarf's attention back to the battle unfolding before him. The Great White Wyrm filled almost half the chamber. Unable to fly, it darted its head and struck with its tail at the elf who circled near it, looking for a chance to strike. The pair wound among the pillars, feinting at one another, each seeking an opening.

Tashara swung her sword and scored a long gash on the wyrm's foreleg. It snarled again in pain and extended its head with the speed of a striking snake. Its teeth clashed, just short of the elf captain's head. She struck again at its face, but the beast was too fast for her and sprang back from her blow. It struck against one of the pillars of light, which trembled and broke. The walls of the chamber shook, and a shower of rocks fell from the vaulted ceiling far above their heads.

Tashara followed forward, striking again and again. The wyrm evaded some of her blows. Others struck against its scales and failed to wound it. The two foes circled round the pillars. One of the wyrm's claws shot out, and Tashara did not evade it entirely. It opened a long cut along her side, but she ignored the wound and fought on.

Ayshe, bereft of his axe and sick at Malshaunt's attack on Harfang, could only watch helplessly.

The White Wyrm struck against another pillar, smashing it. More rocks fell.

Ayshe looked up. He could see above him a dark gap in the roof, which was widening. He raised his voice. "Captain! The ceiling!"

Tashara did not so much as glance in his direction. Round and round she circled, striking at her opponent, evading its slashes at her.

A creaking groan came from above, the sound of buckling stone taxed beyond its limits. The walls of the tunnel seemed to lean inward. A great stone rumbled from above. Malshaunt, intent on the fight before him, seeking to hurl a spell at the wyrm, did not see the danger in time. The stone crashed downward. Ayshe had a brief glimpse of an upturned white face, mouth open in horror and rage; then Malshaunt was gone.

The dwarf stood, indecisive. He glanced down at Harfang, and all at once he knew what he must do. He must survive. He seized the mate's body, straining his muscular arms. Though Harfang was a large man, the dwarf felt as if somehow he had been imbued with extraordinary strength. He pulled the man's body roughly over his shoulder. Staggering with the weight, he gave a last glance at the battle then turned and fled up the tunnel.

THE GREAT WHITE WYRM

A crash came from behind. He half turned as he ran and saw the passage roof crumbling behind him. Clouds of dust obscured any sight of the Dreamchamber where Tashara and the wyrm still fought one another. A dark cloud filled the air and rushed toward him. He ran fast, faster than he thought possible. The weight of Harfang's body was almost too much for him to bear. Sweat poured down his face in rivers. The tunnel seemed to stretch before him endlessly, and his legs felt as if they'd turned to lead. At last he saw the light and raced toward it. He leaped from the entrance, half pushed by the expulsion of air behind him as the tunnel completed its collapse. The shelf of rock above the great doorway cracked and fell. Splinters of rock cut the dwarf's face as he staggered forward, pushing the mate's body before him into the open air. He felt the wind on his face. He was alive.

Ayshe stared at the blocked entrance to the Dreamchamber. He imagined he could feel the ground trembling, shaken by the titanic combat beneath his feet. But it was just an illusion. Above him, the clouds parted, and the sun lit the Valley of White Death, turning the snow to silver. He could see no sign of the bodies of his brave companions. They had vanished beneath the still waters of the lake.

"Master Dwarf!"

Ayshe turned. Harfang's eyes were open. The bloody trickle at the corner of his mouth had become stronger, dripping red into the white snow. His hand struggled to rise then fell back.

"You . . . are alive!"

Ayshe nodded. "So are you."

Harfang's mouth quivered. "Not . . . long. But you . . ." His head fell back for a moment; then he resumed. "That was why you . . . were fated to come . . . with us."

"Why?" Ayshe shook his head. Tears nearly blinded him. "Why? What was the point? They're all dead. All of them." He gestured at the valley.

"But . . . you survive! You alone . . . are left . . . to tell the tale." The mate's voice was growing weaker. "Tell the tale . . . of the White Wyrm."

His eyes closed.

Ayshe looked at him for a long time. He crossed the mate's hands upon his chest. Then he rose. Slowly he turned his back to the tomb of Tashara, Malshaunt, and the White Wyrm and began to walk, limping and halting, back along the road toward the pass.

EPILOGUE

At the head of the pass, Ayshe saw below him a group of small figures. The dwarves, he realized. Callach and his band, who had turned back from their journey away from the valley. He made his way down to them. Callach greeted him with a shout.

"Brother! We feared you were dead."

Ayshe smiled wearily. "Perhaps I am and don't know it yet."

"And the elf woman?"

Ayshe shook his head. "Everyone is dead, Callach. They are all dead, save me."

"What of the Great White Wyrm?"

Above them, the vault of the sky was cloudless. The dwarf stared at it. "I cannot say, Master Callach. Perhaps later. But I can't speak of what happened now. Give me time."

The dwarf leader nodded and did not press the issue. "Come!" he said. "Let's get away from this place. There's a curse upon it."

Ayshe nodded. Together they set out on their long, weary march.

PETER ARCHER

The White Wyrm has never again been seen upon Krynn. Some say the *Starfinder* disappeared from her mooring at the edge of the Plains of Dust and sailed the seas with a ghostly crew of elves, seeking something they could never find. Some even say it was captained by a blind elf, who stood forever watching the seas and strove ever to sail the ship south. But these are stories that are bandied about in seaside taverns when the patrons have drunk too much, so perhaps little credence should be placed in them.

Many legends of the Great White Wyrm grew up, especially in the lands to the south. In Zeriak and among the Plainsfolk and the Ice Folk, these legends were strongest.

There men look to the icy lands to their south. They gaze on the distant mountains, and some wonder what lies beyond their peaks.

And when, in the depths of winter, they see a mist gather round the mountains far across the wastes of the Snow Sea and hear the rumble of distant thunder and the flash of lightning, they say then that, in the depths of the world, the elf and the wyrm continue their battle, linked forever, as they will do—*must* do—for as long as the three moons rise and the stars turn over Krynn.

A World of Adventure Awaits

The FORGOTTEN REALMS world is the biggest, most detailed, most vibrant, and most beloved of the DUNGEONS & DRAGONS® campaign settings. Created by best-selling fantasy author Ed Greenwood the FORGOTTEN REALMS setting has grown in almost unimaginable ways since the first line was drawn on the now infamous "Ed's Original Maps."

Still the home of many a group of DUNGEONS & DRAGONS players, the FORGOTTEN REALMS world is brought to life in dozens of novels, including hugely popular best sellers by some of the fantasy genre's most exciting authors. FORGOTTEN REALMS novels are fast, furious, action-packed adventure stories in the grand tradition of sword and sorcery fantasy, but that doesn't mean they're all flash and no substance. There's always something to learn and explore in this richly textured world.

To find out more about the Realms go to www.wizards.com and follow the links from Books to FORGOTTEN REALMS. There you'll find a detailed reader's guide that will tell you where to start if you've never read a FORGOTTEN REALMS novel before, or where to go next if you're a long-time fan!

WELCOME TO THE

WORLD

Created by Keith Baker and developed by Bill Slavicsek and James Wyatt, EBERRON® is the latest setting designed for the DUNGEONS & DRAGONS® Roleplaying game, novels, comic books, and electronic games.

ANCIENT, WIDESPREAD MAGIC

Magic pervades the EBERRON world. Artificers create wonders of engineering and architecture. Wizards and sorcerers use their spells in war and peace. Magic also leaves its mark—the coveted dragonmark—on members of a gifted aristocracy. Some use their gifts to rule wisely and well, but too many rule with ruthless greed, seeking only to expand their own dominance.

INTRIGUE AND MYSTERY

A land ravaged by generations of war. Enemy nations that fought each other to a standstill over countless, bloody battlefields now turn to subtler methods of conflict. While nations scheme and merchants bicker, priceless secrets from the past lie buried and lost in the devastation, waiting to be tracked down by intrepid scholars and rediscovered by audacious adventurers.

SWASHBUCKLING ADVENTURE

The EBERRON setting is no place for the timid. Courage, strength, and quick thinking are needed to survive and prosper in this land of peril and high adventure.